THE GATES OF HELL

MORE TALES FROM THE LYON'S DEN

Edited by
Chris Kennedy and Mark Wandrey

Seventh Seal Press
Virginia Beach, VA

Chris Kennedy/Seventh Seal Press
2052 Bierce Dr., Virginia Beach, VA 23454
http://chriskennedypublishing.com/

The Gates of Hell/Chris Kennedy and Mark Wandrey -- 1st ed.
ISBN 978-1648550188

For those who went to the gates of hell to protect the ones they loved…and never returned.

Contents

* * * * *

Bayonets by Kacey Ezell

Renzo blinked the sweat out of his eyes for the millionth time and toggled open a communication channel.

"Almost there, Alces," he said, static crackling through his voice as he broadcast on the company's local network. "It's been a hell of a fight, but we're nearly at the end. Five more klicks to Phase Line Green and friendly lines, and then that's all she wrote on this damned contract. We get to sit back and wait our turn to evac this rock."

"Praise all the gods in all the pantheons," said Tom Chamberlain, his deputy commanding officer and best friend, causing Renzo to grin. Tom was an equal-opportunity worshiper, but his faith ran deep. Renzo didn't consider himself able to judge one way or the other. If Tom's faiths gave him strength, more power to the man. All the gods in all the pantheons knew they'd needed it lately.

It felt as if they'd been on blasted Laupapalaiti for decades. In reality, it had been just under two years since Alcey's Alces, an Earth-based mercenary company under the command of Colonel Jackson Alcey, had accepted the contract to protect a small Caroon settlement in the hilly uplands of the planet. As a first contract for the hundred-CASPer-strong company, it had seemed a good choice.

But that was before they'd realized the hyper-ionized atmosphere prevented any possibility of air support on the planet. Before the Zuparti mining concern that also had a stake in Laupapalaiti decided they wanted possession of the natural caverns the Caroons had claimed for their colony. Before the negotiations broke down, and the fighting started. Before the fighting got ugly in a way rarely seen in mercenary combat; prisoners were killed, and whole companies were slaughtered. And somehow Alcey's Alces' happy little garrison contract had become a bitter slog in a grinding war of attrition.

Renzo had taken command four and a half months ago, when Colonel Alcey had taken a MAC round to the chestplate at the end of a long day of firefights. His CASPer had imploded, and he'd been unable to get out while it burned. Sometimes, in his dreams, Renzo could still hear Jack screaming as they tried to tear open the CASPer while the stench of over-roasted meat filled the air. He hadn't been able to sleep downwind of the cookfires ever since.

"Colonel Stewardson!"

Renzo turned his CASPer just in time to see a trooper in a scout rig come bounding up their current path, broadcasting audibly using his loudspeaker. The scout CASPer didn't carry the moose-head insignia of the Alces. Rather, Renzo recognized the mottled grey paint scheme as belonging to the headquarters element of The Strong Company, led by Colonel Rangith Vincent. Technically the Alces were subcontracted to The Strong, but Renzo respected and appreciated Col. Vincent's leadership and expertise, and saw him more as a higher commander and a mentor.

"Here, man, what is it?" Renzo asked, toggling his own speaker on.

"Message from Colonel Vincent, sir. The atmospheric ionization has taken the command net down again."

"I thought they reinforced the signal and hardened the repeaters?"

"They did, sir. It wasn't enough. The weather algorithm is predicting a dry electrical storm for the next two days because of the increase in ionization. Only our local line of sight network is working, and that just barely. Anything outside of five hundred meters is useless."

"Fantastic," Renzo grumbled, toggling his mic off so he was his only audience. He took a deep breath and switched the mic back on.

"Very good," he continued once he had his reactions under control. "Please relay my thanks to the colonel for the update and advise him of our approach. ETA to the Settlement, approximately two hours for food and resupply."

"Negative, sir. That's the second part of my message." The trooper had the grace to sound apologetic, but it didn't change the ringing sense of doom Renzo heard in the man's every word. "Colonel Vincent requests you alter your course to attend him immediately, thirty-five klicks to the south and west of here, on the extreme southern edge of Settlement Ridge. He'll meet you there with further orders."

Renzo's CASPer chimed with an incoming data burst, and a topographical satellite map appeared in his heads-up display, with a small hill highlighted in blinking white and orange.

"Trooper," he said, "my men and women are on the brink."

"Colonel Vincent knows, sir."

Renzo pursed his lips, and then nodded, though the man couldn't see the expression. Rangith knew the losses Alcey's Alces had taken at Fred's Highway and earlier on this contract. He was asking anyway. Shit.

"Very well," he said. "Return my compliments to the colonel and tell him I'll see him in approximately two hours at the coordinates he specified."

"Renzo," Tom said on a private channel as the scout CASPer lifted its hand and turned to head back up the path. "The troopers..."

"I know, Tom," Renzo replied, "but you know Rangith as well as I do. He really *wouldn't* ask unless there was a need. That hill is key terrain for the rearguard action. Without it, the civvies aren't getting out of here, and neither are we."

"Fantastic," Tom said morosely, his voice crackling with static. "And now we've got an electrical storm to deal with, too?"

"Looks like," Renzo said, reaching out to clap Tom's CASPer on the shoulder with his own metal hand. "I'm bursting the coordinates over to you now, before we lose our line of sight comms. Let's move."

* * *

The "small hill" turned out to be a hill only in the most understated of terms. Laupapalaiti had some of nastiest, most vertical terrain Renzo had ever seen. On Earth, the steep edifice stretching up at least seven hundred meters from the valley below would easily have been classed a mountain...or a cliff, for the slope wasn't far from vertical. As if that wasn't enough, the western and southern faces of the "hill" were littered with tumbled, broken boulders, some twice as tall as a CASPer. The whole thing was heavily forested besides, with the thick-trunked, iron-hard, barkless trees native to the planet creating tangled, impassable thickets here and there.

"I'm sure glad we don't have to attack this position," he muttered softly as he turned slowly in place, watching as his officers and NCOs directed his troopers to begin improving their defensive positions. They set to work gathering boulders and fallen trees to create a makeshift breastwork. Several of those thickets were coming in quite handy, he could see.

"Renzo!"

The colonel turned at the sound of his name ringing through the trees and smiled. Another CASPer painted in The Strong's livery bounded forward, but unlike the earlier scout, this version was configured for full-on heavy assault. It also carried the subdued eagle insignia of the unit commander, and Renzo raised his hand to greet his friend and mentor.

"Colonel Vincent," he said, utilizing his external speaker. "We're here, sir, as ordered."

"And I'm damned glad of it, too," Rangith Vincent said as he caught his jump at the last second and settled neatly beside Renzo. "How are your comms?"

"Degrading fast," Renzo admitted, "but usable line of sight, for now."

"Come up on a secure channel for a moment," Col. Vincent said. "We must talk."

That didn't sound good. Renzo obediently opened up a secure channel and burst the encryption information over to his senior commander, wincing inwardly at the loud, crackly static that resulted.

"The ionization is getting worse, so I'll make this quick," Colonel Vincent said, his voice tinny and slightly garbled by the transmission.

"We're in a hell of a bind here, Renzo. The damned Besquith of the Blood Sickle clan took the early termination penalty and have left the battlefield entirely. Seems their alpha didn't like the terrain she was assigned and decided to move forward without orders…hell, in *defiance* of her orders. When General Meedo called her on it, she up and quit. But that's Meedo's problem at this point. Our problem is this left flank. The Zuparti have hired two Human CASPer companies, and our intel suggests they're planning to use them to attack this position. They're already on their way. Your orders are to hold this hill at all costs, do you understand? You're the key to the entire line right here. I don't have to tell you what happens if this flank collapses."

"CASPer companies? But how? Who would—" Renzo cut himself off and forced his mind to focus on the problem at hand. "The Zuparti mercs will roll up the line of the whole army, cutting us off from the Settlement and preventing the evacuation," he filled in, his voice grim as the cold reality set in.

"Precisely. We're asking the same questions. But for now, I've got you, The Strong, and two other North American CASPer companies here. I know your men and women are tired and you need resupply. I give you my word you'll get it as soon as I can make it happen. But you have to hold. Understand, Renzo? At all costs. You must hold!"

"I understand, sir," Renzo said. Col. Vincent reached out and clapped him on the shoulder with a *clang*. "What about arty?"

"Good man," Col. Vincent said. "We're working on getting an artillery battery set up on the crest of this hill. I wish I had better news on that front, but we're all scrambling since that Besquith bitch threw her tantrum and left. I'll leave you to it. I'll send that resupply as soon as I can!" The commander of The Strong Company cut the connection and turned his CASPer away to begin vaulting carefully through the trees back up toward the summit of the hill.

"Orders, sir?"

Renzo turned back and looked downslope to see his senior NCO, Sergeant Major Carl Spoljoric.

"Are we dug in?"

"As well as we can be, sir," Spoljoric replied.

"Divvy up our remaining jumpjuice, power cells, and MAC rounds. Tell the men to choose their shots and make them count. We're going to hold this line against the enemy's advance."

"When, sir?"

"Very soon, Sergeant Major. Very soon."

* * *

He wasn't wrong.

Renzo had just turned from his conversation with Sgt Maj Spoljoric and begun to make his way to the center of his lines. Static crackled in his ear as dry lightning exploded overhead, arcing from tree to tree.

He bit back a torrent of cursing and cut the command net dead, shutting down all electronic communications between the suits, then dialed his volume up and bellowed out a message.

"Voice comms only! Stay grounded as best you can! Captain McCoy!" he called out, naming one of his promising junior officers.

"Sir," Jim McCoy said, materializing out of the thicket to stand in front of him.

"Jim, take Bravo Squad and work east, past our extreme left flank. We're married up with the rest of The Strong Company on the right, but I'm worried about that left. Take your troopers and form a skirmish line out there. See if you can get eyes on the enemy and ID who they are. Col. Vincent said the Zups have hired a couple CAS-Per companies of their own. I don't know how that came about, so don't ask. But I need intel, and I need to ensure they can't work around that left flank and catch us in an envelopment, understand?"

"Yes, sir," Jim said, his voice cool and unemotional as ever.

"Good. Move."

Renzo turned away to the sound of Jim relaying his orders. As he worked back toward the center of his line, Renzo could hear his officers calling out voice commands to dig in and be ready. Overhead, more dry lightning cracked through the air with a blinding flash and deafening report. A high-pitched ringing reverberated through his skull, and Renzo shook his head to try to clear it.

"Stay grounded!" he shouted again. "Squad leaders, call your fire!" He blinked rapidly to clear his vision from the temporary flash blindness. The shapes around him began to resolve into McCoy and his men, crouched low and moving off east across the slope, when another sound caught his attention: the *crack-boom* of MAC rounds, and the crashing of CASPers vaulting toward them up the slope to the right.

"Here they come!" Spoljoric shouted. "Be ready!"

The first few CASPers appeared through the trees, and Renzo's troopers opened fire. Renzo sent Jim a silent wish for good luck and turned his attention to the slope in front of him. More lightning crackled through the trees, arcing from branch to boulder. A deafening burst of static rocked through his comm set, despite the fact that he'd killed all the network comms. "Stay low!" he shouted. "Don't let the lightning fry your suits!"

His troopers knew that, he didn't need to tell them, but shouting it out made Renzo feel as if he weren't entirely helpless as the sky exploded in electrical fire overhead, and the shouts and MAC rounds ricocheted up the slope from the attacking enemy.

Crack-Boom!

The ground shook beneath his CASPer, threatening to topple him as a physical shockwave of sound rippled out from an explosion somewhere on the left. Dirt and rock flew up into the air to pelt down on the lines of his troopers and the charging enemy alike. The smaller, buzzing *crack* of a MAC round whizzed by his suit, and it seemed almost inconsequential by comparison. What had happened?

It was a risk, but Renzo had to know. With his heart threatening to climb up into his throat, he toggled open a channel and attempted to reach Jim McCoy on the command net.

Instantaneous, deafening static resulted. It nearly drove him to his knees in pain. He snapped the channel shut while a pit of loss opened up in his stomach.

"Sir?" Sgt Maj Spoljoric asked, firing his shoulder-mounted MAC over the boulder in front of them.

"Bravo squad is gone," Renzo said, careful to keep his voice emotionless. "We've got nothing on our left."

"Terrain's pretty nasty there," Spoljoric said, "and they're not touching the left at all right now. Nor do they seem to have any more artillery than we do. Be thankful for small mercies, sir, and drive on. Our troopers are putting up a hell of a fight."

And so they were. As the opposing force's CASPers came into view, Renzo could see his troopers firing in a disciplined mass on the orders of his junior officers. A rolling wave of molten destruction resulted, pouring forth in a wall of heat that seemed to cause the oncoming ranks of CASPers to melt in the face of withering destruction. Renzo stepped back and began to walk slowly along the line, feeling more than seeing Sergeant Major Spoljoric falling into step with him. Desperate pride in his company swelled inside his chest, causing his eyes to prickle with unshed tears as he watched them repeating their actions over and over again. Hold. Stand. Fire. Drop. Hold. Stand. Fire…

Downslope, through the trees and the smoke and the near-continuous dry lightning flashes, Renzo could see CASPers lying in heaps, most still moving as they fought to get back to their own lines, but some terribly still. During one particularly brilliant discharge, he could make out the crest of a crimson wave painted on the chestplate of one of the downed CASPers. It lay crumpled over a comrade, bearing a single white star on a circular blue field, outlined in red and white.

"The Lone Star Company," Renzo said, "and the Red Tide, unless I miss my guess. Looks like that's who we're facing today, Sergeant Major. Not who I would have expected to take a contract against other Humans."

"Tough companies, sir," Spoljoric replied, "but so are we." As he spoke, the squad in front of them stood and fired again, their MAC reports reverberating through the trees and echoing off the boulders. Overhead, another lightning flash boomed through the air. Renzo felt the noise in his chest and dragged in a breath in response.

Down the slope, the tone of the attackers' shouts changed, and they began to hop-jump their way back down the slope. The Alces kept up their withering fire, but to the enemy's credit, both companies continued to retreat in good order. All along Renzo's lines, officers shouted orders to reload and remain ready.

"Get me a medic and mechanic's report," Renzo said.

"Yes, sir," Spoljoric replied, and moved out to check in with the docs and CASPer repair techs already circulating through the ranks. In the meantime, Renzo risked trying the comms one more time. He waited until the lightning discharged over his head, and then opened a command channel.

"McCoy!"

Nothing but static. He toggled over to a different channel. Maybe he could get an update on the artillery situation? "Colonel Vincent?"

Crack! Lightning arced overhead, flashing fire into existence and striking his CASPer hard enough to pick him up and throw him several meters into a nearby boulder. His internal controls blinked and stuttered, but recovered. The ringing in his ears jacked up to a deafening squeal. Inside his skull, a hammering started in counterpoint to the noise.

"Right," he muttered, burning a little bit of jumpjuice to stagger back to his feet. "Voice comms only. Got it."

"Sir!" Spoljoric's voice cut through the tinnitus and brought Renzo's attention back to the real world. "Report is in, mostly head and shoulder wounds. None fatal yet, though the medics are running through their nanite supply right quick. A couple of the CASPers are operating in the yellow, with only two at less than 50% capacity. The mechanics are working on them as best they can with this damned lightning."

"Yeah," Renzo said, "I just got hit. Tell the mechanics to take every precaution, to include knocking off repairs for a time if necessary. I've got thirty CASPers. I've only got five mechanics."

"Yes, sir."

"How are we fixed otherwise?"

"MAC rounds are running low. We'll be needing resupply before nightfall at this rate."

"Colonel Vincent is aware," Renzo said, trying his best to sound reassuring. "He's promised me more ammo and fuel cells as soon as possible."

"Well, our troopers are doing a hell of a job. We'll be just fine, sir. Just fine."

"Here they come!"

Renzo never saw who shouted the warning, but it echoed down the line, mingling with the crackling of the lightning and the oncoming sounds of more CASPers charging up the slope toward them. Another fusillade of MAC rounds zinged through the air all around, and Renzo ducked behind a boulder and resumed moving down the line of his troops. Once again fire rolled forth from the ranks of the Alces as Renzo's troops met the oncoming Lone Star and Red Tide attackers as they bounded up the hill. They, too, had eschewed radio comms, for Renzo could hear the enemy officers shouting orders and encouragement to their subordinates while the lightning cracked all around them.

The disciplined wave of fire began to spread out as the enemy CASPers drew nearer. Renzo's officers shouted for their troopers to fire at will, and the whole hillside exploded in noise and destruction. Renzo toggled his own shoulder-mounted cannon down and took a deep breath as he scanned for targets.

There, a Lone Star trooper charged up the hill, letting out an undulating cry of rage as her jumpjets powered her leap. Renzo stilled, focused, and fired. His suit rocked back on its heels as the shot left his barrel. Three rounds ripped into the center fuselage of her CASPer, right through the pristine white star. She faltered, jets stuttering and flaming out. The CASPer crashed to the ground, gouging a deep trench in the rocky soil of the slope before coming to rest at the base of one of the tangled tree thickets. No further movement.

Some emotion he couldn't name threatened to rise up and overwhelm him, but he pushed it back with a savagery he didn't know he had. Later. He'd deal with all of this later. For now, he had to stay alive and fight to keep his troopers alive. He pictured himself shoving his emotional being into a box and slamming the lid closed, and willed a frozen calm to flow through his being.

There, another charging CASPer, this one bearing the crimson crest of the Red Tide. Another deep breath, another burst fired. Another CASPer slammed to the ground, unable to reach out and hurt his company anymore.

Renzo continued to fire methodically, clinging to the icy calm that wrapped around his mind and allowed him to continue to function. He lost his sense of time in the mechanics of firing and finding targets, and it wasn't until his deputy called his name that he realized, with a start, that the enemy was retreating once again.

The Alces had withstood another charge. How many more would they be required to endure?

* * *

"Tom," Renzo said, gasping slightly as his focus fell away, and he once again became aware of more than just the oncoming enemy. Sudden thirst assailed him, and he realized his haptic suit and face were wet with sweat. He toggled his drink tube forward and sipped, then dismissed the flashing red warning that his in-suit water supply was running low. "Got a report for me?"

"We've held them off, sir," Tom said, his voice pitched to reassure, "but I don't know how much longer we can do this without more MAC rounds."

"Casualties?"

"Still counting," Tom said as SGM Spoljoric bounded up. Like everyone else, he used a particular type of stutter-jump designed to conserve as much juice as possible. Ammo wasn't the only thing in short supply. "The troops are holding well, but they did more damage this time and got a lot closer. The mechanics are doing their best to get everyone back up as quickly as possible. Medics, too, though I hear we just used our last nanite dose."

"Have the men gather ammo from the wounded, and from any CASPers at less than 40% functionality," Renzo said. "Jumpjuice, too, get one of the mechanics to siphon it off and cannibalize whatever they can from the most badly disabled suits. Grab the power cells, hydrogen, batteries…anything usable. I can't get a message out to Col. Vincent in this electrical storm, but he knows we're strapped for ammo and supplies. Help is coming, we just have to hold until it gets here."

Renzo hated the tiny note of desperation he heard in his voice, and he hoped neither of the other two men picked up on it.

"Yes, sir," Tom said. "We got this. Just like that night next to Fred's Highway." Renzo pictured his deputy's confident grin as he turned away to relay the orders to the mechanics and medics.

"Yeah," Renzo said, pushing away the memory of spending the night sheltering behind the lifeless CASPer of a dead trooper. It had been miserable, but they'd lived…barely. "Just like that."

"Sir," SGM Spoljoric said then, pointing. Renzo turned to look in the direction indicated, and dialed up the magnification on his suit's visual sensors. It was hard to see through the trees, and the picture wavered with static from the electrical storm that still raged overhead, but Renzo could just make out the movement of several ranks of CASPers bounding eastward, parallel to the slope of the hill.

"Looks like they've brought in their reserve," Spoljoric said. "I'm not seeing any other company insignia, though. Just the Red Tide."

"They're trying to find our left flank," Renzo said, scaling back the magnification and looking around at the lines of his troopers. Just then, another cry went up from the right, and yet more volleys of fire and MAC rounds sang out through the trees as the enemy attacked the right once again. Renzo stepped up to the line and fired a few shots, and then looked around to take stock of the situation.

"Have the troopers switch to energy weapons as their rounds run low," he said to Spoljoric, shouting so as to be heard over the report from the sergeant major's MAC. "It'll burn through our power cells faster, but we've got to balance our resources. I don't want to be forced to rely on one or the other."

"Yes, sir," Spoljoric shouted, still firing. He relayed this order to a nearby NCO, who immediately opened fire with his laser cannon and blistered a smoking hole in the line advancing up the slope. The enemy, too, was stutter-hopping, Renzo noted with interest. They must be conserving their resources as well.

Pressure on Renzo's immediate position eased, allowing him to step back and think as the latest assault faltered. Another magnified glance below and to the left showed him more CASPers, still in motion.

"Tom!" Renzo called out as a plan began to take shape in his head. "Rally the officers here."

"Yes, sir!" Tom called out, and one by one, the various squad leaders and SGM Spoljoric converged on his position. Once they were all in place, Renzo turned his back away from the line and addressed them en masse.

"The enemy has called up their reserves and is moving left to flank us," he said. "Here's what we're going to do. We'll keep up a barrage of fire from the extreme right, where our lines meet The Strong's. Stay nice and tight on them, all right? There can be zero break in the line. Captain Hooper, that's you. No breaks, understand?" Renzo pointed at the CASPer of the barrel-chested young officer commanding the extreme right of his company's position. John Hooper gave him a "thumbs up" in acknowledgment.

"Right. Now. The rest of the company will sidestep to the left, thinning out the line until we're single file, with no more than two regular arms-length distance between each of us. You see Lieutenant Mata here? She's going to end up at the extreme left end. When you reach that point, we're going to refuse the line, understand? We'll form a new line perpendicular to this one. Stay in single depth to pull up as much of our reserve as possible, so we can counterattack whenever there's a hole. Is that clear? Any questions?"

Renzo scanned the CASPers in his group, wishing he could see the faces of the men and women inside. But with the storm preventing radio communications, all he could see were inscrutable CASPer fuselages.

"No, sir," Lieutenant Nicholas Fauls said, from his place next to John Hooper. Renzo took a deep breath and sent a prayer out to whichever of Tom's gods might be listening that he was doing the right thing. A tiny stab of bitter regret bearing Jim McCoy's name ran him through, but he pushed it away and forced his mind to remain focused.

"Fine," Renzo said then, swiping his hand to the side and pointing east. "Move."

The officers swung their CASPers around and headed back to their various squads within the company. Renzo turned and found Lieutenant Aeryn Mata close at his shoulder.

"Lieutenant, you're with me," he said. "Double-time."

"Yes, sir," she replied, her voice hard and almost eager. They began to stutter-hop forward, pouring on as much speed as they dared while keeping their trajectories low. They hoped to stay mostly below the line of boulders and thickets for two reasons. One, it was easier to dodge lightning strikes if you stayed closer to the ground; and two, it kept them out of the direct line of fire from the Red Tide and Lone Star troopers who lurked downslope somewhere.

They pushed out to a miniature curve in the cliff-like contour of the hill before Renzo held up a hand, indicating she should stop there.

"Roger," Aeryn said and pushed forward to stand in front of him, planting her heels in the rocky clay of the soil and pointing her shoulder-mounted MAC down the hill. Behind her, the Alces streamed in a stutter-hopping wave, stringing out to the distance Renzo had ordered, and reformed the line stretching northward up the slope of the hill. Lieutenant Fauls bounded past, shouting encouragement and exhortations to the troopers who followed him as he took up his post at the extreme end of the line.

Renzo had time to see Fauls plant his CASPer and take aim with his laser weapon before the air came alive again with the *crack* of MAC fire and the flash of laser shots through the ion-heavy air. Renzo dialed up his magnification and squinted through the trees. He could just make out a line of CASPers moving methodically forward and up the slope as they worked in concert to attack the left side of the line. His Alces returned fire in a massed volley of mingled MAC shots and laser bolts. Lightning split the sky overhead and clearly showed the scarlet crest of the Red Tide's livery.

"We've got to hold this flank, understand?" Renzo shouted as he moved behind the line, trying to back his troopers up as Aeryn, Nicholas, and his other officers echoed his cries. "Hold them here, Alces! This is where we stand!"

Like the inexorable tide that was their namesake, the attacking CASPers drove forward into the teeth of the Alces' defense. Their troopers fell in waves, but more kept coming on, stutter-leaping over the crumpled heaps of their fallen comrades as they blazed away with MAC and laser both. Admiration for the Red Tide's bravery wrapped around his throat, but Renzo shoved it in the box with all his other emotions and pushed it away. He'd deal with all that later.

Lieutenant Nicholas Fauls cried out and fell. His troopers moved into his position, providing him covering fire, while he dragged his wounded CASPer back from the line. Renzo started in that direction when Aeryn called out to him.

"Sir! The sergeant major!"

Renzo spun just in time to see SGM Spoljoric's CASPer fall to its knees and list heavily to its right, falling onto the smoking wreckage of the MAC that had taken a direct hit.

"Sergeant Major!" Renzo yelled, bounding over. "Carl!"

"I'm all right, sir," the sergeant major's voice answered, sounding tinny and garbled, but strong enough through the CASPer's half-blown external speaker. "Damn Reds got me right in the MAC. Plays hell with my target practice."

"Get a medic over here," Renzo said to Tom, who had just bounded up as well.

"No, sir, I'm all right. I just need a mechanic when one can be spared. I've got plenty of chems left to power my laser." As if to prove the point, he lifted his CASPer's undamaged arm and fired five shots out toward the Red Tide, who had once again begun a solid retreat under fire.

"Sir!"

Renzo looked up to see Captain John Hooper executing a perfect low bound to land crouched beside himself, Tom, and the sergeant major.

"Captain?"

"We're critically low on ammo, sir, and some of our troopers are nearly juice-dry as well!"

Renzo made up his mind and turned to his deputy.

"Tom, go see what you can get from The Strong on our right side. Anything will do, juice, MAC rounds, nanites…hell, even some water would help. But quickly, go!"

Tom got to his feet in answer and bounded up the hill and back toward the right. Renzo turned back to Hooper.

"Take what you can from the wounded…and anyone else who isn't going to be using it themselves." He didn't want to call John's attention to the fact that he was ordering him to loot the bodies of his dead friends, but that's exactly what he was doing. An ugly thing, perhaps, but no uglier than letting their position be overrun because of an excess of sentimentality. He reached out to touch Hooper on the shoulder of his CASPer, hoping to help the younger officer understand. "Just pick up what you can from anywhere."

"Here they come again, sir!" SGM Spoljoric said, firing his laser with surgical precision. Once more that high-pitched, ululating yell joined the crash of thunder from the dry lightning and the *crack* and *sizzle* of his troopers' fire as the Red Tide commander sent his CASPers charging up the hill.

Renzo surged to his feet and opened up with his MAC over the half-prone figure of his senior NCO. His rounds took out three of the lead CASPers on the charge, causing them to fall and tumble back down into the path of their comrades bounding up the slope behind them. But the disciplined Red Tide troopers kept pushing on, screaming that wildly unnerving yell the entire way. More jagged lightning rent the sky above them, deafening them all with the resultant thunderclaps. Renzo fought to keep his feet, to keep his nerve, and to keep firing.

The Tide kept coming.

Renzo could see them, an endless, seething mass of courage and destruction, forming new lines in the trees ahead, fighting meter by meter up the treacherous slope as his own Alces poured hatred and fire down on them like the judgment of all the gods. He fired until his MAC clicked empty and his temperature indicator screamed at him that he was low on water and in a potential overheat situation. Not that he needed the CASPer to tell him that. He was wet from crown to toes, drenched in sweat and stinking with the fear he refused to let into his mind. Instead, he took aim with his laser and fired—

—only to feel his suit kick him so hard in the side that he spun like a top as the rock-strewn ground tilted wildly to the side and rushed up to meet his face. His last thought before everything went dark was that he'd thought dying would hurt more.

* * *

"Colonel! Colonel! Renzo!"

It was the anguish in Tom's voice that finally penetrated the thick darkness that wreathed Renzo's mind. He blinked his eyes open to see the interior displays of his CASPer lit up like a starport on a dark night. Half a dozen warnings blinked red and yellow at him, and a high, persistent buzzing rang in his ears.

Again. Between the thunder and the battle sounds, tinnitus was starting to seem like an old, familiar friend.

He groaned and toggled off the warnings, diverting the last of his water to the suit to act as an emergency coolant while he fought to get his hands and knees under him.

"Oh, thank all the Gods!" Tom's voice echoed overhead as Renzo pushed up and rolled himself over. The ringing in his ears got louder with the effort, swelling in volume and taking on a high, ululating tone that shivered down his spine—

He looked up just in time to see a Red Tide CASPer bearing down on the clump of them, midway through a juice-burning leap. Without thinking, Renzo raised his laser and fired a burst that flashed out through the air and sliced through the midpoint of the suit. Lightning stabbed through the sky as well, proving the inadvisability of the CASPer's usual big jumps as it wreathed the attacker in blue flame and brought it crashing to the forest floor. It landed about ten meters below Renzo and skidded down the slope, fetching up in a crumpled heap next to one of the big boulders that dotted the terrain.

Renzo couldn't do anything but breathe and stare. He'd come that close to death not once, but twice in a matter of minutes. The lid on the mental box that held his emotions shifted, and all the stuff he couldn't afford to deal with threatened to spill out. He closed his eyes and breathed, shoving the lid down onto the box as hard as he could.

"Let me help you up, Colonel," Tom said, his voice barely penetrating Renzo's fog. He felt himself being lifted and set back on his feet, and once he was steady, he opened his eyes.

"Thank you, Tom," he said, in control once more.

"Looks like you took a ricochet," Tom said, pointing to Renzo's left leg. He used his external camera to sweep for damage and found that Tom was right. A seared crease in the outermost layer of armor just above the knee joint bore mute testimony to the round that had toppled him with its force. He didn't want to think about what could have happened had it been a direct hit.

"What did The Strong say?" Renzo asked, urgency flooding his tone as he remembered the errand he'd sent Tom on earlier.

"They got nothing to spare, sir," Tom said, his voice tightening up as he delivered the bad news. "They've got problems of their own with the Lone Star Company charging up the right. What's worse, Colonel Vincent is hurt in a bad way, and the rest of the line is struggling to bring artillery up the slope. They've just barely beaten off the latest attack, thanks to a crazy arm-blade charge by a new company arriving under a guy named O'Roarke. Crazy brave sonofabitch. He didn't make it, but the line held! The line sure enough held!"

"We're gonna need ammunition," Renzo said, just as Lieutenant Aeryn Mata approached.

"Sir," she said. "Nicholas…Lieutenant Fauls is dead. I've taken command of his platoon, but more than half of them are badly wounded, maybe five dead. If the Reds come up that hill again in the same strength, I don't know if we can hold them!"

"Spread the word to take ammunition from the wounded and the dead," he ordered her, as that chilling cry began to rise in the trees below them once more. "Go!"

"Here they come again, sir!" SGM Spoljoric's grim pronouncement wasn't entirely necessary, but Renzo didn't bother to tell him so. He contented himself with aiming his laser and firing into the first CASPer to come into clear view. The CASPer dropped and rolled away, but like before, another took its place.

"Make your shots count, boys and girls!" the sergeant major called out as he raised his own weapon while his half-crippled CASPer leaked jumpjuice and hydraulic fluid onto the rock-strewn ground. "Just like the colonel! Make every one a kill shot!"

Once more the Tide rolled up the slope. Once more the Alces opened fire with devastating effect. Renzo kept firing, dimly aware of his officers' shouts of encouragement to the men and women in their charge. His fuel cell indicator blinked first yellow, and then orange as each shot depleted his precious fuel reserves. Overhead, more lightning crashed, casting the grim scene in a surreal, pulsating, strobing light.

How many of these bastards did they bring to this shit planet?

Beside him, SGM Spoljoric swore and jettisoned his laser rifle attachment. While Renzo kept firing to cover him, the sergeant major crawled forward in his damaged CASPer and hauled up the corpse of a fallen Tide trooper. With grim practicality, SGM Spoljoric ripped the dead trooper's MAC out of its shoulder mount and braced it in his lap before somehow using the dangling wires to cause the thing to fire. It would have thrown him backwards from the recoil if he hadn't been braced against a boulder. But its report was a welcome addition to the chaos of death and noise boiling up and down the slope in both directions.

Renzo fired once more and noticed that the enemy was flowing left again. He dimly heard Aeryn calling out to her troopers.

"Keep it tight boys and girls!" she screamed. "Keep it tight…FIRE!"

On her command, a withering onslaught of reserved MAC rounds crashed through the trees, followed up immediately by a barrage of laser fire. The first two ranks of Red Tide CASPers faltered, but the following ranks answered with that eerie, ululating howl and charged up the slope, arm blades glinting in the web of lightning flashing overhead. Aeryn's troopers met the attacking force with a resounding *crash* that reverberated through the forest floor as tungsten-steel blades sliced into CASPers. Defenders used everything from MACs to lasers to their own steel blades to hold their tenuous position.

"Tom!" Renzo screamed as two of Aeryn's troopers disappeared under the wave of oncoming Red Tide CASPers. "Fill that hole!"

Tom bounded forward in a lightning-defying jump. He snapped open his arm blade and slashed down on the attackers as he landed in the midst of the fray. Aeryn and her top NCO charged over to join him, standing shoulder-to-shoulder and pushing back against the impossibly tenacious forces arrayed against them. All around, Alces troopers were running out of ammunition. Renzo watched as one young trooper—he wasn't sure who exactly—picked up a boulder and used it to smash the chestplate of one of the attackers, crushing the Tide driver inside.

Somehow, against all the odds, the Alces held as the Tide washed up against their line and then, once more, retreated back down the hill. As the enemy CASPers disappeared back into the trees and behind the stacked bodies of their fallen brothers and sisters, Renzo looked around in despair.

They had held, but it was obvious they couldn't do so one more time.

"Sir!" Aeryn called out as he bounded over to her position. She stood with Tom supporting her, the right side of her CASPer a smoking ruin. "Half my troopers are down, most of the rest are wounded."

"And your ammo? Power?"

"Mostly gone, sir. The left is too thin to hold again."

"Sir!" the voice came from the other direction, back toward the right. Renzo turned to see Captain John Hooper approaching. "Sir, my troopers are out of ammunition, and our fuel cell reserves are dry! Some of my boys and girls have nothing at all!"

"Sir," Tom said quietly as the rest of the officers began to gather around, "Maybe we ought to pull out."

"No," Renzo said, Vincent's words ringing in his memory. "No, we can't do that. Our orders were to hold this hill at all costs. If we pull out, the Red Tide comes sweeping up the slope and over the hill and the whole flank collapses. The Caroon civvies and all our comrades get slaughtered."

"Well," SGM Spoljoric asked, somehow managing to sound laconic even now, "what do we do, sir?"

Renzo looked around at the fallen Alces, at the survivors, all staring at him with terror and fatigue.

"We can't run away," he said slowly, as sure of that fact as he was of his own name. "But if we stay here, we can't shoot. So…let's fix bayonets."

"What?"

"Our arm blades. Fix them out, like bayonets." He looked down the slope at the piles of dead and disabled CASPers littering the ground, victims of his troopers' sustained fire. "They gotta be tired, the Reds. They gotta be nearly spent if we are. So fix your arm blades out rigid."

"You mean charge?" Captain Hooper asked, his voice cracking in surprise.

"Yes, but listen, here's what we're going to do. We're going to charge down the hill, moving across the slope as we do. We'll use Hooper's point as the pivot and swing like a door, pushing them into the fire coming from the rest of The Strong over on our right. Just like we pulled back this left side of the company. Now we're going to swing it down. We swing like a door, understand?" He looked around at his officers, at their dirt-smeared, smoke-stained CASPers. "Does everybody understand?"

"Yes, sir," they chorused, and in a tiny corner in the back of his mind, Renzo thought he could hear a thread of excitement and hope where moments before there had been none.

"Good. Mata, you take the left wing, and I'll take the right," Renzo said. Maybe if he said it enough, it wouldn't sound so crazy. "And when I give the command, I want the whole company to go forward, swinging down and to the right."

"All right, sir," LT Aeryn Mata said.

Renzo inhaled once, slowly, and focused on her CASPer.

"Move," he said quietly. She and all the other officers turned and raced back to their positions in the lines as more lightning crashed in the sky overhead. Renzo didn't know if it was the still-building ionization or the prospect of action, but something tingled through the air, infecting them all.

"Bayonets!" he shouted, and every speaker from every CASPer left in the company let loose with a full-throated roar, deep and savage; it drowned out the distant, ululating howl that had haunted them all day. All along the line, left and right, his officers echoed the command while troopers snapped their arm blades out and extended them to their furthest reach. Those who had rounds left for their MACs charged them. Others siphoned precious jumpjuice from downed friends and enemies alike.

"Stay low," Renzo ordered, listening as the command echoed down the line. He pushed back to the right, Sgt Maj Spoljoric moving in his wake. "Conserve your juice. Ready!"

Left and right, the CASPers crouched, preparatory to their first real jump. Renzo settled himself in position at the head of the formation on the right and snapped his own arm blade out to its full length. On the far left, he could see Aeryn getting her troopers formed up and in position.

"Fix bayonets!" she shouted, snapping her own arm blade out as she did. Her troopers followed suit, some of them cheering on her bravery as she stood between them and the inexorable approach of the Red Tide from below.

"Mata! Left wing, right wheel!" he shouted, borrowing a term from the parade ground training maneuvers they'd all done before leaving Earth.

"Right wheel!" Mata echoed at the top of her speaker's volume. She turned to face the oncoming enemy and crouched, her blade out.

"Charge!" Renzo called.

"CHARGE!" Mata echoed and fired her jumpjets. Unlike the earlier attackers, however, she kept her trajectory low and used the power to push forward while staying below the line of the trees. Her troopers followed suit, swinging back toward Renzo's position just as he'd envisioned. They cheered their gallant lieutenant as they drove, blades out, toward the mass of CASPers approaching up the hill.

Renzo watched, heart in his throat, and waited for the line to swing just so—

"CHARGE!" he shouted and hit his own jets. The men and women around him echoed his cry, and the roar from their throats and the massed jumpjets of their CASPers caused the onrushing Red Tide to falter.

Once more CASPer collided with CASPer among the twisted steel and tangled thickets of trees and boulders. Metal crashed on metal, and cries turned to screams of rage and pain as the Alces hacked and stabbed their way through the front ranks of Red Tide attackers. Somewhere off to the left another throaty cry rose, and a massed volley of MAC fire ripped into the Red Tide's right flank.

Renzo ducked and punched his blade straight through the chest compartment of one of the Tide CASPers, then kicked the metal corpse off before firing his jets again. Below him, one of his troopers grappled in a death struggle with a Tide trooper, and he angled himself to land within reach. A swipe of his arm blade against the vulnerable back of the Tide trooper's knee joints brought the enemy CASPer crashing to the ground.

Another volley echoed from the left, and Renzo looked up to see his Bravo squad, long thought lost, entering the fray and rolling up the right side of the attacking Red Tide.

The flankers had become the flanked.

All around him Tide CASPers flinched back from their right. Then in ones and twos, and gradually in larger groups, they raised hands and retracted their weapons, signaling surrender. For just a moment, Renzo feared that his Alces troopers' blood was up too high for them to accept, but he need not have feared. One minute they fought like demons, but the second surrender was offered, his men and women backed off and accepted.

That ululating howl was his only warning.

Renzo turned just in time to see a Tide CASPer with colonel's insignia land next to him, MAC pointed dead at his chestplate. At this range, a MAC round would rip his armor to shreds of metal and pulverize him on contact. He froze and waited.

Click.

The enemy CASPer seemed to sag as its driver retracted the empty MAC and raised his hands. Renzo raised his arm blade and held it steady, its point centimeters from the crimson crest logo painted on the chestplate.

"Shit. Your move, sir," the CASPer's driver said, voice echoing from the CASPer's external speakers.

"Come on out," Renzo said.

The Red Tide commander let out a sigh and popped the hatch on his CASPer. The chestplate slowly lifted, and for the first time, Renzo got a good look at the man who'd cost him so many lives.

"Colonel Otis Calvin, commander of the Red Tide Company, at your service," the man said. He looked as wrung out and haunted as

Renzo himself felt, his haptic suit drenched in sweat and clinging to his body as he wearily climbed out of his CASPer. On impulse, Renzo popped his own canopy and let the man see his face.

"Colonel Renzo Stewardson, Alcey's Alces," Renzo said. "I'm pleased to make your acquaintance."

Strange, perhaps, but it was true. The Red Tide had fought hard during charge upon charge, and Renzo would never say aught against their bravery or toughness. But he infinitely preferred speaking to their commander like this to further fighting.

"Wish I could say the same, Colonel," Calvin said, giving Renzo a half smile. Renzo snorted and found himself smiling as well.

"Well, I understand that. It seems your men and women have largely surrendered. I'll have your parole if you'll give it, and we can gather up your wounded to take to our medics. Is there anything else you need right away?"

"Could I please have some water?" Calvin asked.

"Absolutely," Renzo said, and turned to flag down one of his medics. The woman approached, her face worried.

"Were you hurt, sir?" she asked.

"No, I'm fine. But please give Colonel Calvin here some water and see to his men and women as well as our own. He's given his parole." Renzo looked over at the defeated colonel, who gave him that half-smile again and nodded.

"Of course, sir. Colonel, if you'll please come with me. We've water and food for you and your troopers just over here…"

* * *

That night Renzo found it hard to sleep, despite the grinding fatigue that pulled at his every thought and made him feel like he was swimming through an ocean of maple syrup. Minutes after their crazy charge, reinforcements had arrived from the center with water, ammunition, food, and nanites. Renzo had seen to it that his men and women, and the Red Tide prisoners, were properly cared for. Every one of them got a good meal, plenty of water, and whatever medical care they required. Battlefield custom held that the captured Tide CASPers were his to keep, so he sent his mechanics to ensure they salvaged as much as they could while under the watchful eye of the reinforcing MinSha company.

But even after all that, he still couldn't rest. So he found himself walking under a moonlit, lightning-webbed sky toward the medical facility and Colonel Calvin's quarters.

"Can't sleep?" Calvin asked him as he stepped in through the tiny entrance to the underground cavern that led to the Caroon settlement.

"No," Renzo said. "I hope you don't mind."

"Not at all, Colonel," Calvin said. "Come on in, I was just having the single drink your medic allowed me. Join me?"

"Sure, thanks." Renzo followed him in and sat down at a tiny camp table that held a small battery lamp and a bottle with a single cup. Calvin turned to a cabinet and rummaged around for a moment before turning back, another cup in his hand.

"So," he said, plunking the cup down in front of Renzo and pouring some of the liquid into it. "What brings you up here tonight besides insomnia?"

"I just thought...maybe you might want to talk."

"About what? The way you bluffed my company into surrendering with your insane kamikaze charge?"

"If you like," Renzo said. "Though it wasn't a bluff; I was just out of options and ammo. What else was I supposed to do?"

"You could have surrendered," Calvin said, humor threading through his tone.

"But then you'd have rolled up the entire line."

"Yep. That I would have. What I want to know, though, is how under a million suns you held off on using your Bravo Company for so long!"

"We thought they were dead," Renzo said honestly. "We thought you guys got them in your first charge up the hill."

"Huh. Damn that hill," Calvin said with feeling.

"Indeed," Renzo agreed, picturing the crumpled, lifeless CASPer of Lieutenant Fauls, and the other brave, tough men and women who'd bled out their lives under the Laupapalaiti lightning.

"You know the Zuparti army will attack again tomorrow?" Calvin asked.

"I do," Renzo said, "but we've been moved up the list for evacuation. Word from my leadership is that you and the Lone Star Company were strong-armed into taking this contract, with no way out but our evac point. That's it for us. We're leaving tomorrow, and you're coming with us. This war may continue forever, but it will do so without humanity."

"Well, hell," Calvin said, shrugging. He lifted the cup and raised it toward Renzo. "I guess I'll drink to that."

Despite himself, despite everything, Renzo found himself laughing.

"Me, too, Colonel. Me, too."

* * * * *

Kacey Ezell Bio

Kacey Ezell is an active duty USAF instructor pilot with 2500+ hours in the UH-1N Huey and Mi-171 helicopters. When not teaching young pilots to beat the air into submission, she writes sci-fi/fantasy/horror/noir/alternate history fiction. Her first novel, MINDS OF MEN, was a Dragon Award Finalist for Best Alternate History. She's contributed to multiple Baen anthologies and has twice been selected for inclusion in the Year's Best Military and Adventure Science Fiction compilation. In 2018, her story "Family Over Blood" won the Year's Best Military and Adventure Science Fiction Readers' Choice Award. In addition to writing for Baen, she has published several novels and short stories with independent publisher Chris Kennedy Publishing. She is married with two daughters. You can find out more and join her mailing list at www.kaceyezell.net.

# # # # #

The Thelosi Gambit by Quincy J. Allen

1

Karma Station

Guild Operations Sector

Mercenary Guild Negotiation Chamber

Karma station, its docks lined with vessels, filled the wide viewports of the conference room. Private Max Boudreaux stole his gaze away from the beginning of the negotiations and reveled in his first trip to Karma. A massive cargo hauler approached the dock at the near end of the facility, while two mercenary cruisers maneuvered out of their births on the far side, headed, presumably, for the jump point. At the voice of Colonel Hu, commander of Hu's Hawks, Boudreaux turned his attention back where it should be and waited for the order to begin the attack.

"I must tell you, Praeliet Tokarra," Colonel Hu said evenly, using the Veetanho's title, "we're not at all happy with the situation we found ourselves in on Kuason." Hu eyed the wealthy merchant who sat at the other end of the conference table. The commander of Hu's

Hawks was not a big man. At only 1.7 meters, with a wiry, cord-thin frame, his presence still seemed to fill any room. His black hair was cut close along the sides, with a thicker shock over the top of his head, and he wore a form-fitting uniform in the black and red of his mercenary company. His narrow, piercing dark eyes were set in angular features as he continued, "I'm reticent to undertake another contract for you, particularly if it involves the Thelosi again." He leaned back in his chair. "We still haven't found their species in any database, and I find that rather troubling. Have you informed the Union?"

"Not yet," Tokarra replied smoothly.

"Additionally," Lieutenant Yeo Jiang chimed in, "our losses were significant." She ran a hand over the thigh of her prosthetic leg, which had replaced the real one she'd lost on Kuason. She eyed the two Veetanho mercs standing behind Tokarra, their slim rifles slung. "While our initial contract afforded us appreciable combat bonuses, and we're grateful you paid in full without argument, the loss of lives, equipment, and expertise set us back in ways we could never have anticipated."

Tokarra blinked her keen black eyes several times, and then she bared her front teeth, the Veetanho version of a smile. Her smooth white fur was offset by a green sash decorated with glittering red gems that seemed to have a radiance all their own, almost as if they were subtly illuminated from within.

"I completely understand," she said in a placating tone. Her native language was instantly translated via the Hawks' pinplants. "Those events, while costly to you, were of immeasurable benefit to me and my associates. The Hawks did a marvelous job setting the tracker on that ship, and the information you acquired for us is still bearing fruit."

"I don't suppose you could be a little more specific," Yeo asked.

"I'm afraid not. I'm here to negotiate another contract—of a slightly different nature. And *yes*, it does involve the Thelosi. It's also back on Kuason, the planet where you first encountered them, but they've shifted to a more mountainous, underground location." Both Hu and Yeo tensed up. "However," the Veetanho continued quickly, "we'll be providing you with considerably more intel than before. That includes the number and disposition of forces, a rough layout of the underground cave system taken from orbital-based, ground-penetrating radar, and the location of both Thelosi dropships, which they've immersed in a nearby lake. We acknowledge we didn't provide nearly enough information on the last mission, although we didn't have much more to offer you at the time. Regardless, we *are* in a position to remedy that oversight here and now. I would also point out that your own experiences regarding the Thelosi have given you a better understanding of their tactics and capabilities…far better than anyone else we could have chosen to work with."

"Those huài dàn are bloody ghosts," Yeo blurted.

"I'm sorry," Tokarra said, "but did you say…bad eggs?"

"Nevermind that," Hu injected, placing a hand on Yeo's arm. "Suffice it to say, we're reticent to engage once again with beings who seem to have a natural ability to remain hidden, even when we're looking straight at them."

"Again, Humans have proven themselves to be more than capable of adapting to new tactical situations. I have no doubt your organization will find ways to be successful here. I have a great deal riding on it, in fact. To that end, the Thelosi in question are the same group you faced before. They are marauders from an unknown corner of the galaxy, and their piracy has had a serious impact upon business operations I and my associates deem critical to our long-term objectives."

"Why not hire a Besquith or Tortantula merc company with more punch than we have to just wipe the marauders out?" Yeo asked.

"Knowledge is power." Tokarra's reply was flat, almost emotionless. "And frankly, we know next to nothing about this species. Why invest in the long-term eradication of an enemy of unknown size and disposition, when we can glean more data through the use of specialists in information gathering. We haven't abandoned the hope that we can, perhaps, find ways to create an alliance with these beings and put them to good use. The Hawks are ideally suited to infiltration and task-specific missions on this scale. Mercenary companies of the sort you suggest are the nuclear option, whereas your organization is more closely likened to the application of a surgical scalpel."

Hu and Yeo looked at each other for a moment, and then Yeo turned to where Boudreaux and Private Azeela Mopantomobogo—AZ for short—stood behind her, hands resting casually upon their sidearms. Both privates stood somewhat stiffly, dark aviator glasses hiding their eyes, as they presented the illusion of being bodyguards. Yeo nodded once to Boudreaux and transmitted a single command via her pinplants: *"Initiate the hack."* She then then turned back to the negotiations, her attention focused on the Veetanho who might or might not be an enemy of Hu's Hawks.

Tokarra slid a large slate across the table for Hu and Yeo to examine as Boudreaux and AZ's eyes glazed over behind their glasses. The two privates dove into the GalNet side-by-side.

"We've been able to determine where that ship went, and we now want you to *capture* a Thelosi. As you can see..." the Veetanho said, but her voice was quickly lost to the two privates.

Boudreaux and AZ's attention was, instead, now focused on using their newly-installed pinplants to hack Tokarra's slate without being detected. A web of energized data filled Boudreaux's thoughts. He saw not with his eyes, but with his mind, and he could feel AZ moving with him as he navigated through the GalNet toward his objective.

"There it is," Boudreaux said excitedly as they approached the glowing nexus of a firewall identified by its digital address.

"Pulling up the slicer code now." AZ seemed to hover beside him in the orange latticework of digital streams that flowed around them like glowing rivers of gossamer web. A tight bundle of crimson threads appeared before them, hovering just at the edge of the firewall. "Initializing."

The bundle seemed to unfold around the edges, and tendrils not unlike the legs of an insect spread out and seemed to plug themselves into the firewall.

"Plugging in," Boudreaux said. As he closed the connection, a complex construct appeared within the firewall, with countless paths slowly twisting and turning in a jumbled mass. "Holy shit." Boudreaux was having a hard time figuring out where to begin.

"Just focus on the hack," AZ replied, as if she'd heard him. He had to wonder if she had.

The tendrils of the slicer code started picking and parsing through the threads within the construct. As it did, a tiny hole, little more than a pinprick, appeared in the center of the firewall. Pale white light shone through; if they opened the port fully, they'd be able to access all the data that lay beyond. The hole grew, and as it did, a glowing spark of light drifted inward, nearing the tunnel they were digging into the firewall. Boudreaux and AZ felt a warning buzz in their thoughts. The slicer code identified the spark as an alert node, and if it reached the gap they were creating, the firewall would shut down and send an alarm.

"Watch that node there," Boudreaux said.

"I've got it." AZ's presence seemed to grow larger in Boudreaux's mind, then one of the slicer's tendrils approached the alert node and began spinning a glowing blue cocoon around it. Moments later, the spark seemed to go dormant and drifted away on whatever currents shifted the interior of the firewall.

"This slicer code is really slick," Boudreaux said. "Look how it's making those alert nodes dormant."

"It's too bad we can't keep the program," AZ replied. "He said we'd only get one shot, and then the code itself would go dormant."

"Could you recreate it?" Boudreaux asked as another alert node drifted toward their breach. He initialized a tendril and sent it off to capture the alert node.

"Unlikely. Some of this code looks like complete gibberish to me…it's probably alien, or encrypted several times…or both. And the key-cypher he provided is time-coded."

They kept working, peeling away one layer of security after another as the tunnel widened…

* * *

"The modified contract is agreeable," Tokarra said. "I see no issues with your revisions to combat bonuses, casualty and death bonuses, and the clause regarding the quality of the intel we're providing you. Everything in that data packet is as accurate as we can make it, and if they still have only one ship there, the numbers you'll be facing will be consistent with our estimates, plus or minus about ten Thelosi."

The Veetanho's words filtered into Boudreaux's awareness as he lifted his mind out of the GalNet. It looked like he and AZ had finished their task just in time. He quickly called up Lieutenant Yeo via his pinplants and sent a single statement.

"Close the deal."

If Yeo received the message, she gave no indication. Instead, she and Colonel Hu looked at each other and nodded.

"As long as the intel is solid, the job is doable," Hu said without skipping a beat. "I believe we can get this done. We'll have one of them here in under three weeks."

"I do have one question," Yeo spoke up. "How do you want us to deliver the captive?"

Captive?

Boudreaux and AZ looked at each other. They'd missed quite a bit while they were under.

"Now that's an excellent question." Tokarra reached out to the slate in front of her, the one Boudreaux and AZ had just been hacking, and entered several commands. "We've prepared a device that should make transport considerably less complicated than coming home with an alien restrained in cuffs or chains." The door behind her opened, and two Veetanho wearing blue sashes rolled in a tall cylinder of dark gray metal. It was just over two meters in length, had a control panel on the front, and a clear port that revealed a darkened interior. "Once you have one of the aliens in custody, please place the captive in this confinement chamber and activate the power. The system will automatically place the occupant in cryo-stasis, and the power module should sustain it that way for at least several months."

"You certainly came prepared," Yeo said. "Makes me wonder about your motives."

Tokarra raised her nose in the Veetanho version of a non-committal shrug. "Like with any mercenary contract, we reserve the right to keep our wider objectives to ourselves." She looked thoughtful for a moment. "What is it you Humans say…? Yours is not to reason why?"

Colonel Hu chuckled. "Quite right. The new contract is solid, and you've proven your ability to pay what I consider very generous terms." He slid his own tablet across the table. "If you'll just execute the contract here, we'll be on our way."

"Of course, Colonel," Tokarra replied. She leaned forward, pressed her thumb to the imprint box on the screen, and then rose. "We'll just leave this with you," she added, motioning toward the stasis chamber.

* * *

2

Karma Station

Dock 34-Alpha

***Zhūgéliàng* Cargo Hold**

Boudreaux and AZ rolled the stasis chamber into the massive launch bay of the *Zhūgéliàng*—named after an ancient Chinese hero—with Colonel Hu and Lieutenant Yeo close behind. The jump-capable medium cruiser was the pride of the Hawks' three-ship fleet and served as their primary mission platform. The large, modified launch bay held four swept-wing LAHVs (Low Altitude High Velocity aircraft) in upper cradles. A single standard drop ship sat on the main deck, locked down but ready for rapid deployment. In addition to the familiar atmospheric craft permanently housed in the launch bay, there was a small shuttle tucked away in a far corner, one that didn't belong to the Hawks.

Several of the ship's crew stood just inside the airlock, expectant looks on their faces. Like many on the ship, they performed two or more duties, and in this case, they were the cargo handlers. The two Humans were Privates Dolan of Ireland, and Singh, a native of Nepal. Private Tokath Burr was a massive GenSha with pale white fur and a green striped pattern. Finally, there was a pair of grim-looking Lumar brothers, Privates Rok and Tolka.

"Hey, Boudreaux," Private Singh said with a hopeful smile. "Are we on?"

"And then some," Boudreaux replied a bit ominously. "The colonel will break it all down later. Right now, we need you to stow this in Jian-1." He raised his eyes to one of the LAHVs cradled above them. He always got a kick out of the designations for their drop ships. Jians were the old Chinese double-edged swords, and he had to admit, the craft did mimic that design in many respects.

"Please take great care with the stasis chamber," Colonel Hu said, stepping up. "The whole contract rests on it staying in one piece long enough for us to deliver it back to that shit-eating Veetanho."

"Sir?" Tokath said, his voice a deep rumble. "I thought she was our client."

"Oh, she is," Yeo said, shaking her head. "She's just not a friend."

"So it's another setup?" Singh asked.

"We think so," Hu said. "Go ahead and get that stowed. We need to have one last conversation with our guest."

"He's in the shuttle." Dolan pointed with his thumb over his shoulder. "He hasn't come out even once."

"No surprise there," Yeo said. "I hate being in the middle of all this, but we don't have much choice."

"That's right," Colonel Hu said. "We don't. And the longer we stand here, the longer it takes us to get ourselves out of this mess. Stow the chamber and prep for our departure. I've already notified Captain Zhou."

"Yes, sir," the deck hands said in unison as they moved over to the stasis chamber.

"Come on, let's get this over with," Hu said, making for the shuttle.

Yeo, Boudreaux, and AZ followed and boarded through the rear hatch of the small shuttle, where they found a hooded Pendal waiting for them in the relatively dark hold. The small, brown being stood there, about a meter and a half tall, it's upper and lower arms crossed. It wore a deep blue cloak with the hood pulled back, and its peculiar eyes—two on either side of its skull as well as the one in the middle of its forehead—focused on the group as they entered. There was no mistaking the blue sash across its chest, nor the distinct, tree-adorned badge of a Peacemaker.

It shifted its gaze away from Colonel Hu and seemed to peer expectantly at Boudreaux and AZ.

"Did you get it?" Peacemaker Zarikk asked, exposing a mouthful of sharp teeth.

"AZ?" Hu said, turning to the private.

Azeela Mopantomobogo was nearly two meters of deep ebony skin that seemed to absorb all the light around her. She had beautifully sculpted features, with high cheekbones and dark eyes full of strength and intelligence. She kept her hair cut to within a couple mills of her shining skin, and her smile was the sort of thing photographers and artists dreamed of.

She held out a slim data chip to the Peacemaker.

"That slicer you provided got us past the firewall and pulled all the files down." A concerned look crossed her features. "But it's all encrypted, so we have no idea what we've got."

"I'm running some encryption algorithms," Boudreaux said, tapping the pinplants on his neck. He'd chosen the full modification rather than the standard pair most of the Hawks received. He wanted as much bandwidth, processing power, and multitasking as the alien system afforded him. So far he hadn't been disappointed.

"Excellent," Zarikk said, slipping the data chip into his cloak. "I'll get my people on this immediately."

"So, we stick with the contract?" Hu asked. "This whole thing is starting to stink. Tokarra wants us to actually capture one of those aliens."

"Capture?" Zarikk asked, sounding confused. "Stand by a moment." His focus seemed to drift away for several seconds, and it looked like he was communicating via his pinplants. Moments later, he gave a sharp nod and then focused on Colonel Hu. "Yes. Proceed as we've discussed. Pursue this contract just as if the Peacemakers weren't involved. It's the only way to keep the situation in motion. We're playing the long game and need to know not only who the players are, but what their endgame is."

"You know this is another setup, right?" Yeo asked.

"Undoubtedly," Zarikk said. "We believe Praeliet Tokarra's interest in Hu's Hawks is a result of your involvement in the events that took place on Reliak IV almost two years ago."

"We did beat out a Veetanho company on that run," Yeo said. "Are you saying this is a vendetta of some kind?"

"We don't know at this point." Zarikk shifted his attention to the lieutenant. "We do have assets looking into the situation, but our best bet right now is to proceed with the mission in the hope that we can crack the encryption on the data you've acquired."

"Do you know anything more about the Thelosi? They're holy terrors during combat ops."

"No." Zarikk sounded both dismayed and deeply troubled. "What's important right now is you know the situation going in, and you've faced them before. It should give you sufficient edge to complete their task while keeping your people alive."

"Should?" Yeo asked sourly.

"It's enough." Hu cut her off. "And if we pull this off, we get paid twice. Once by that Veetanho, and then double that from your people."

"Correct," Zarikk assured him. "I don't know how long it'll take for our people to crack the encryption, assuming they can do it at all. However, once we do, and if there's anything that will help your mission, we'll do everything we can to get it to you in-system in time. However, if you don't hear from us, simply complete the contract as safely as possible and return here. I'll find you when you do."

"Then let's get moving," Hu said. "You still want us to cut you loose on the way to the jump point?"

"Yes." Zarikk moved toward the forward hatch that led to the control section of the small shuttle. "Signal me when you're ten kilometers from Karma, and I'll launch." He paused at the door. "Best of luck to you all, and know that the Peacemakers appreciate your assistance in this matter. There's something deeper going on here, and it's vital we determine what it is." He opened the hatch and went through without another word.

Hu tapped his pinplant.

"Captain Zhou, prepare for launch. We're heading out as soon as you're able." He turned to his subordinates. "We'll have our operational meeting just as soon as we make hyperspace."

"Sir," Yeo and the others said, and they exited the Peacemaker's shuttle, intent upon prepping *Zhūgéliàng* for the mission.

* * *

3

Kuason

Hawk's Orbital Insertion

LAHV-1

The air screamed by the hull of Jian-1 as it sliced through Kuason's thickening atmosphere. The deployment bay of the descending LAHV shuddered and rattled with the thunder of bleeding Gs as Lieutenant Yeo, Fireteam Cooper, and a half-dozen Hawk support technicians did their best to endure re-entry. The Mk 8, recon-modified CASPers and their occupants were securely locked into receiver cradles along the sides, while the others were merely strapped into couches at the front of the bay, feeling every shake. The fireteam's Dragonflies, quad-rotary vehicles that looked like a cross between a motorcycle and a drone, were anchored along the middle of the bay, along with several large crates of equipment. The stasis chamber, on the other hand, was secured within an armored crate at the front, where it would remain until they had their captive.

"Any luck on the decryption?" Yeo's question came in through Boudreaux's pinplants.

"Still running in the background," he replied. "I'll say it again: there are no guarantees. These pinplants you gave us are fantastic, but I may not have the cycles to crack something like this…the algorithm keeps shifting. I've restarted the damn thing three times since we left Karma. At this point, I'm not hopeful."

"Just let it run. We should still be able to get this done, even without that missing piece, whatever it is."

"I intend to," Boudreaux replied.

Soong Ha Yoon's voice came in on the comms. "Prep for high-Gs…we're about to pull out of our dive and level out." Soong had been a pilot for the Hawks for years, and of the six who flew missions for the recon company, she was by far Boudreaux's favorite. She had a natural talent for flying and always seemed to make the insertions at least a bit gentler than the other pilots.

"Copy that," Yeo replied. "Hang on, everyone."

Moments later, the nose of the long, narrow-bodied craft pulled up as the wings extended slowly with a whine of servos. The turbines kicked in, and reverse thrust jerked everyone aboard. One gravity after another piled upon their already tortured bodies, and Boudreaux felt his vision swim. He grunted over and over again, struggling to keep the blood from draining out of his skull.

The maneuver took only thirty seconds, but it felt like an eternity to Boudreaux. Drops were his least favorite part of any mission, but there was no avoiding them. When the pressure finally lessened, and the LAHV leveled out, Boudreaux let out a sigh of relief.

"That's it." Soong's voice was as even and calm as ever. "We're 1000 meters off the deck and losing altitude slowly. Thirty klicks out from the landing zone. Jian-2 is in our wake and tracking. Jians 3 and 4 are north of their landing zone and right where they're supposed to be."

"Copy that," Yeo acknowledged. "I want us to get offloaded as quickly as possible." The lieutenant disconnected her CASPer from the receiving unit and rose to her feet. Gripping a steel rail that ran the length of the deployment bay, she turned to the members of Fireteam Cooper. "Alright, folks, you know the drill and what we intend to accomplish here. The new drones should give us the edge we need."

"I hope to hell this works," Boudreaux said. He thought about Yeo's prosthetic leg. Close quarters and blind corners with an enemy that didn't show up on sensors was just asking for trouble.

"Cut the whining, Boudreaux," Yeo ordered, "or I'll give Killian's call-sign to you," she said sternly.

"Yes, Lieutenant," Boudreaux said and then shut his mouth. His fireteam leader, Corporal "Bitchy" Hank Killian, had received his call-sign not long before the first engagement with the Thelosi, and it had stuck. Boudreaux and his entire fireteam had been brought into the ranks because of the losses taken on that mission. "Bitchy" was a running joke for the entire company, although Killian seemed to wear it with pride.

"I agree," Yeo said, "separating the squads into two forces is risky, but you heard Hu in the planning meeting; there really isn't much choice. That fucking Veetanho set us up, and this is our best chance to find out why and get some payback. This will all depend upon whether or not the mods on our drones work the way we expect them to."

They better, Boudreaux thought.

* * *

The landscape was mostly forest-covered rolling hills and low mountains of partially exposed granite. Rivers and creeks cut through most of the valleys, indicating that the area, like most of the planet, got an inordinate amount of rain. A turquoise sky spotted with clouds made it feel like they were all on a hike through the woods back on Earth, but there was no mistaking the tension everyone felt as they drew nearer to their objective.

"Thank God the forest is thinner here than the last time we dropped onto this rock," Yeo said. "You newbies have no idea how bad an LZ can be until you hit Kuason in those mid-latitudes. That jungle was hairier than a macaque's armpit."

"You said it, Lieutenant." Corporal Killian's voice came through the comms loud and clear. He was at the center of Fireteam Cooper's line, with Boudreaux and AZ on his right. Privates Fujimoto Yoshiko and Keith Keenes were on his left.

The Mk 8 CASPers of Fireteam Cooper marched up the forested hillside in a wide line, with about ten meters separating each armored unit. Each of them carried a heavy case in both hands, making them at least a little vulnerable if there was an ambush. Fireteam Cooper, tasked with entering the caves from the north end, would be going in with only their rifles and sidearms. They all had the snap-out arm blades on their right arms and standard laser shields on their left arms. Their shoulder-mount MACs, unfortunately, had been removed because of the expected close quarters.

The CASPers of Fireteam Shikra, who had been aboard Jian-2, paced ahead about thirty meters, spread out along an even wider line as they ran point and scanned for any sign of movement. They *did* have their MACs and would provide suppressing fire if Fireteam Cooper had to fall back.

There was an identical formation two kilometers to the south, on the other side of the ridge, made up of Fireteams Fiji and Gabar. Fiji would be entering the caves, while Gabar supported. Heavy Fireteam Doria, with assault-equipped Mk 8 CASPers, was moving in toward the lake where the Thelosi drop ships were supposed to be. Their orders were to prevent any escape and bring down the dropships if they launched.

The forest surrounding them was light enough to allow daylight from Kuason's G-Type star to illuminate the blanket of meter-tall shrubbery that covered the area for a hundred kilometers in every direction. Although the CASPers had no trouble forging through the underbrush, the support staff had to trail behind, making their way in the paths made by the large, heavy CASPers.

As they cleared a thicker swath of forest, the rocky mountain ahead came into view. At the base, where undergrowth met stone, they spotted a cave entrance about three meters across that looked like it had been cut into the rock with mining equipment. It was far too neat to be a natural formation.

"We're just about in position." It was Staff Sergeant Kun Hsiu, who was leading the operation on the other side of the ridge. "Still no enemy contact. It looks like they're all underground."

"Copy that, Kun," Yeo said. "Fireteam Doria, are you in position?"

"Affirmative." Corporal Gan Gamyagiin was the best heavy CASPer pilot they had, and she had a rock-solid group of pilots under her command. "We're set up on the west side of the lake, with clear lines of fire to the far shoreline, and we're unobstructed for missile barrages on all five designated targets. Targeting solutions are locked in. We've had no enemy contact either. It's quiet over here, almost peaceful."

"Well, it's about to get a lot louder," Yeo said. "Fireteam Shikra, give me a defensive perimeter while we get set up here."

"Copy that," Corporal Wei replied. Moments, later the lead CASPers moved into positions that gave them clear lines of fire at the cave entrance, as well as along both sides of the mountainside.

"Corporal Killian," Yeo said, "Get ready to deploy the drones."

"Yes, Lieutenant."

"Alright, folks," Killian's voice came in on the fireteam channel. "Drop those cases and open them up. We've got sixty seconds."

Boudreaux and the others dropped their cases with loud thuds and quickly hit release levers on the top of each. With a whine of servos, the tops folded back to reveal small racks that rose up and exposed dozens and dozens of small drones that looked like a cross between dragonflies and wasps. It had taken the entire week in hyperspace to modify them to Hu's exacting specifications, but they were the secret weapon that, hopefully, would give the Hawks an edge over an enemy that had defied their sensors during the last encounter.

"I hope to Christ this works," Killian said. "I'm betting we'll have to run dark down there."

"It's all we've got, short of a blind man's bug hunt." Boudreaux eyed the dark cavern mouth ahead and then hit the activation panel on the case. "Fight bugs with bugs, I always say." He turned and gave the support technicians the thumbs-up. All six of them had just finished setting up several pieces of equipment that were the heart of a system that was supposed to keep Fireteams Cooper and Fiji alive in the tunnels. "As long as the Thelosians don't see the UV frequency we're using, we should be fine."

"It's too bad we don't know that for sure," Private Keenes added. He wore the heavy Mk 8 CASPer in Fireteam Cooper. It was actually a standard Mk 8, unmodified by Hu's requirements for the scouting rigs, with heavier armor, a bigger power plant, and stouter weapons systems.

"Looks like the drones are all online," Yeo said. She glanced at the lead technician, and he gave her a thumbs-up. "Everyone, activate the new interface and prep for action."

With a command through his pinplants, Boudreaux activated the modified sensor grid that appeared as an overlay in his HUD. The grid they normally used spread out in front of him, wrapping itself to the contours of the landscape. "System active," he said. "No anomalies indicated."

The other members of both fireteams responded in kind.

"All units, lock and load." Yeo said. All the CASPer pilots grabbed their rifles in a smooth motion, pulling them from cradles on their backs. "Cooper, move up." Yeo's voice was calm as she called out the orders, and Boudreaux knew Staff Sergeant Kun would be doing the same thing on the other side of the ridge. "Fireteam Gabar, fire at will. Fire for effect."

Boudreaux felt his pulse quicken as he and the rest of his fireteam strode forward with the *thunk* of armored feet hitting the turf. He glanced toward where he knew the lake lay and watched as a swarm of missiles rose out of the forest a kilometer away. Several seconds later, he heard the swoosh of them and watched as the incoming munitions separated into five separate clusters that arced overhead a thousand meters, and then came down in a rush. The cave entrance loomed before him, only twenty meters away.

"Boudreaux on point, with Killian behind," Yeo said. "Once you're inside, Killian has operational control."

"Copy that," Killian replied as he closed in behind Boudreaux.

"Prepare for impact." There was tension in Yeo's voice as everyone watched the incoming missiles streaking toward the earth. They were all aware of the risks...the numbers they'd crunched said there was a ten-percent chance some or all of the cave structure might collapse. Nobody wanted to get caught in it, but more importantly, they didn't want to just wipe out the Thelosi. Combat was one thing, but the Thelosi weren't an enemy, per se, they were a contract...and a recon-capture contract at that. Killing was something Hu and his Hawks didn't take lightly.

The ground shook with the impacts as the missiles did their job, sealing the other cave entrances.

"Launch the drones," Yeo ordered.

Boudreaux was only meters away from the entrance as rocks tumbled down the hillside above. More broke loose from the ceiling just inside the cave. For just a moment, he wondered if the whole system would cave in once they were inside. His legs wanted to stop, but his will—his sense of duty—kept him going. He was a Hawk, and there was a job to do, so he pressed on.

The darkness folded around him, carrying with it a sense of foreboding. Just as the swarm of drones flew past him in a cloud of hundreds, the comms lit up with a high-pitched screech across the entire bandwidth, making Boudreaux wince. He reflexively shut down the standard comm system, and the world went silent.

They're jamming, he thought, *just as expected.* He smiled and swapped over to the laser-based comm net they'd prepared.

* * *

4

Kuason

Thelosi Cave System Insertion

"Into the lion's den," Boudreaux said.

"What was that?" Corporal Killian asked.

"Never mind," Boudreaux muttered, and, with a thought, he activated the IR sensors of his CASPer. The interior of the cave brightened around him, the rough surfaces illuminated with a green tint. The small, insect-looking drones, only four centimeters long, zipped around his CASPer like water around a stone and sailed into the darkness, disappearing quickly from view. Like the Thelosi, the small machines gave off no heat, so as their frames adjusted to the cooler temperature of the cave, they faded from his IR imaging. He saw several rise toward the ceiling as their bodies cooled, and then they too disappeared, fading into the rough, rocky surface of the cave and nestling into any nook or cranny where they could find purchase.

As the small machines flowed through the cave system, a new set of images was overlaid on top of his IR view. Second by second, the interior of the cave complex filled his HUD, and as it did, dozens of moving targets appeared much deeper inside. *It's working*, he thought. Because of the light frequency and delay, the images seemed somewhat fuzzy, with finer details lost in the 3D overlay, but there was no mistaking the numerous rushing forms of Thelosi shifting about in small clusters throughout the twisting complex.

The drones were equipped with UV lasers that, in addition to carrying their comms, would sweep continuously, mapping the interior as it changed from second to second. The imaging data was then relayed from one drone to the next and back to where the support technicians monitored the equipment they'd brought. There could be up to a .3 second delay between the imaging data and what was really happening, but it was more than enough to perform the mission…at least, that was the theory. The Hawks had never done anything like this before.

The Veetanho had praised the innovative qualities of Humans, and that was about to be put to the test in a live-fire exercise that could get them all killed.

"UV comms online," Killian said. "Count 'em off."

"Cooper Two, live and alive," Boudreaux said.

"Cooper Three, receiving," AZ added.

The rest of the fireteam called in, and then the rest of Shikra checked in, followed by Lieutenant Yeo.

There were several seconds of silence while they waited for the drones coming in from the other side of the complex to link up, and as they did, Boudreaux watched the entirety of the cave complex appear on his HUD. He was relieved to see movement in several locations much further into the complex. His targeting system highlighted about thirty moving targets, obviously Thelosi, arranged in small clusters at several portions of the complex that could only be described as choke points. It was hard to get a good idea of what they looked like, but they all seemed to be between one and two meters tall, bipedal, and appeared to have six limbs above the waist, some of which looked like they flowed and undulated more like tentacles than jointed appendages.

"All teams," Yeo said, "we've got connectivity, and it looks like we're able to scan not only the enemy positions, but the enemy itself. Mission is a go. Proceed as planned."

"Roger that," Killian called out. "Boudreaux, do you see that small group off in that left-hand side-tunnel? Just after the second branch. It looks like three of them."

Boudreaux scanned the HUD image, using his pinplants to shrink the image and move it into the proper perspective.

"Affirmative," he finally said. "Second left, along that long curve, and around the sharp corner. Looks like they're arrayed behind a pretty solid defensive position."

"Seems to me they *all* are." It was Hu's voice this time. He was monitoring the whole operation from his CASPer. He'd positioned himself not far behind Fireteam Doria on the other side of the lake, ready to make any adjustments to the plan as needed.

"Well, we did just hammer the cave entrances with a missile barrage," Killian said.

"That's not what I mean," Hu replied. "Look at it. It's like they knew we—or at least somebody—was coming for them."

"We always suspected this was a trap," Yeo said with a bit of an edge.

"I think this goes beyond trap," Hu said. "It just doesn't figure."

"Do you want us to abort?" Yeo asked.

There was a pause.

"Boudreaux, how's the decryption coming?" Hu's voice carried with it a good deal of concern.

"Hold up," Boudreaux said, raising the armored fist of his Casper. He stopped in the middle of the tunnel he'd been traversing and went down to one knee, aiming his rifle down the passage. He heard Killian step up behind him and knew the corporal was taking up a position to cover him while he dove into his pinplants.

Boudreaux examined the process running in the background of his mind. This cycle had been running for thirty-six hours, and it looked like it was nearing the end. He had no idea if it would complete the decryption function or crap out at the last second like it had the last time. He held the algorithm before his eyes and watched as tendrils of the decryption protocol plucked and picked at a massive and incredibly complex barrier that looked more like a crisscrossing pattern of webs than anything else. When he'd started, it had been nothing more than a tangle, but now most of the threads were aligned into a patchwork that almost looked like the threads of woven fabric. Satisfied that the decryption was still working, he lifted out of his pinplants, but kept the process running closer to the surface of his consciousness.

"Sir, all I can tell you is that it's close, perhaps even closer than the last time it crapped out on me. If it doesn't bomb again, it could finish in seconds, minutes, or even hours. There's no way to tell until it's done, one way or the other."

"Understood, Private," Hu said. "Yeo, Killian, I want you to proceed as planned. I'm having Sergeant Kun and his teams hit the other side as hard as they can to draw most of their attention. Boudreaux, you watch that thing like a hawk. If it finishes up, you have two priorities—send the whole data packet to me and scan through that data as fast as you can for any intel on what the hell is going on here. Am I understood?"

"Yes, Colonel."

"Boudreaux, I want you to fall back behind me," Killian ordered. "Keenes, move up in that heavy. You've got point."

"Yes, sir," Keenes replied. Boudreaux heard the clomping of CASPer feet behind him as he rose to his feet. Knowing how tight the tunnel was, he moved to the side, putting his back against the curving wall as Private Keenes moved up.

"Watch yourself," Boudreaux said as Keenes passed by.

"I got this," Keenes replied. "You just make sure you get that data processed."

"Count on it," Boudreaux replied with less confidence than he felt.

"Let's move people." Corporal Killian strode past as he gave the order, and Boudreaux stepped in behind him.

Boudreaux checked his HUD again, picking out the blobby forms of Thelosi outlined by the UV scanners. They were now fully set up behind what looked like a fortified position of stacked containers and a rocky outcropping, and it looked like all of them held long objects he guessed were the fast-cycling weapons used against the Hawks during their first engagement against the Thelosi…the ones that had taken Yeo's leg off.

The fireteam pressed further into the tunnel system, each step drawing them closer to their target. They made it to the first split in the tunnels and went left. Another eighty meters found them at the second split, and again they turned left.

As Boudreaux walked, he decided to try something. He'd been ordered to keep tabs on the decryption process crunching away inside his brain, but his fireteam was walking into an enemy position defended by forces who knew they were coming. Using his pinplants, he envisioned a split between the decryption process and his HUD. At first nothing happened, but as he focused his thoughts, he felt something…*click*…inside his head, as if he'd flipped a switch, and suddenly both views were suspended in front of him.

The web pattern of the decryption process, a nearly complete cross-hatch of glowing threads, was clear before him on one side, and the tunnel system ahead stretched out on the other. They walked another thirty meters, moving through the long, curving tunnel they knew would end at the enemy position.

And then the shooting started.

The *ratatatatatat* sound of multiple high-cyclic weapons echoed through the tunnels, and as they did, the areas where the Thelosi had taken up their positions started to go dark.

"They're shooting the drones!" Killian shouted as the shooting continued. "They can see them!"

In seconds the five enemy positions were dark patches in their HUDs, and at the same time, a number of the blobby alien outlines seemed to disappear from their scanners, as if they'd melded right into the walls and floors.

"Hold position," Yeo barked. "AZ and Fujimoto, cover Killian's back. You're past those forks, and I don't want you taking fire from the rear."

"Copy that," AZ and Fujimoto said together.

Boudreaux checked his HUD and watched as the shooting continued, and the blank areas of the enemy positions expanded outward meter by meter. One of them was quickly approaching the last fork in the tunnels they'd passed.

Oh, shit, he thought.

"Everyone," Killian barked, "take up positions to protect Boudreaux. If we're engaged, we need to make sure he doesn't buy it. Understood?"

"Yes, sir!" the other privates said grimly.

No pressure, Boudreaux thought. He put his back against the wall and focused all his attention on the decryption process. The damn thing was nearly finished, and as he scanned the cross-hatch pattern of the firewall, he saw that the decryption program had focused most of its tendrils upon a single section of the web. It poked and pried at the still-knotted area, but seemed to have come to a standstill. The section glowed before his eyes, turning from the strange orange glow to yellow.

It's gonna crap out. Boudreaux was on the brink of panic. *I've got to do something.* He pushed his mind against the stubborn area of the security net, and as he did, he realized that the section wasn't part of the wall, it was the actual lock…or a keyhole. *The damn thing must be a prompt requiring a response of some kind.* Its hue was changing from yellow to a pulsing red. *That's why the decryption always bombed. It needs someone, a conscious mind to turn the key. But how?*

Will.

His only option was will alone. Drawing heavily upon the processing power of his pinplants, he dove at the glowing point of light like a hawk diving into deep waters after a fish. He felt his mind impact upon it, and as it did, he saw a small, complex pattern of lines tangled in disarray. He pushed again, pulling and pushing at them, and as he did so, he found that he could move them. One line at a time, he adjusted the tangle, laying them down in what seemed to be a logical pattern.

"They're almost on us!" Killian said. "Target any movement, and fire at will."

Boudreaux ignored the command and pushed harder at the threads. Time froze. Boudreaux laid out one strand after another as if he were straightening a bowl of tangled yarn. The pattern blazed before him, and the pulses quickened to the point where it was almost a solid, burning point of light.

I'm not gonna make it, he thought in a panic.

Another thread…and another fell before his will.

The last thread dropped into place, and there was a flash of light in Boudreaux's mind as the entire security net collapsed around him…broken.

He dove into the data beyond, pouring all his energy into scanning the files and data as quickly as he could. His brain burned with the amount of data assailing his consciousness. He portioned off a section of his mind and sent the entire data packet across the network and into the waiting hands of Colonel Hu.

"Thirty seconds to contact," Killian said.

Boudreaux sifted through data as fast as his pinplants could process them. First, he found a Thelosi translation protocol for the pinplants. After that there were hundreds of communiques between Praeliet Tokarra and a Praeliet named Litarran, mostly regarding Thelosi prisoners, and a wager. He reviewed logistics files, unit orders, comm frequencies, even a file detailing the Hawk's first engagement with the Thelosi, as well as the Hawks' mission against Veetanho mercs in possession of a Depik adviser. As his brain absorbed the data, he saw what was really going on. Rage flared within him.

"We're like dogs in a pit…" he said out loud as he installed the language file into his pinplants. He sent the same file to Colonel Hu and everyone else on the net.

"What did you say?" Killian asked.

"Corporal, we have to get out of here. We can't engage the Thelosi," Boudreaux's voice was pleading.

"What? Are you out of your god damn mind? We're in the middle of—"

"Boudreaux." Colonel Hu's voice broke in. "I want you to disarm and try to make contact with those enemy units. Surrender if you have to."

"Sir?" Killian blurted with disbelief.

"I've reviewed the data just like Boudreaux has. This is the only way out of this and keep our souls intact," Hu added.

"Yes, sir," Boudreaux said. His mouth went dry, and fear clutched at his insides. "Everyone swap over to radio frequency 21.34 kilohertz, and Yeo, have the techs broadcast this across all remaining drones."

"Copy that." Yeo's voice was just as disbelieving as Killian's had been.

Boudreaux stepped away from the wall, handed his rifle and sidearm to Killian, and turned toward the bend in the tunnel.

Open canopy, he thought and marched forward, moving past Killian and then Keenes. His canopy opened with a hiss of atmosphere, and he initialized the onboard lights of his CASPer, illuminating the dark tunnel before him. *I just made myself the easiest target in the galaxy*, he thought.

In as loud a voice as he could, and activating the PA speakers of his CASPer, he took a deep breath and spoke.

"Honored Thelosi warriors, we surrender and wish to speak. We know you want to go home, and that this conflict is not of your choosing. I repeat, we surrender."

His words were instantly translated by the pinplants and broadcast in the Thelosi language, which seemed more like a barely-audible, high-pitched squeaking chatter of random tones.

His guts churning with a storm of fear, Boudreaux strode forward one heavy step at a time. As he approached the bend in the tunnel, he raised his hands over his head.

"Their progress has stopped," Yeo said disbelievingly into the comms.

Boudreaux took a deep breath, prayed that he wasn't about to get riddled to pieces, and turned the corner. He spotted the enemy defensive position. He took several steps forward and saw two dark shadows shift behind the cargo containers, their multi-barreled weapons trained on him. He still couldn't get a good look at them, but their skin looked black, and they didn't seem to have eyes on their elongated heads.

"I am unarmed and only wish to speak," Boudreaux said. One of the Thelosi shifted behind the crates, but it said nothing. "Your people and mine are being used. Do you understand what I am saying?"

Seconds ticked by, and he picked up a series of squeaking noises that still went untranslated.

"We do not want fight you any longer," Boudreaux said. "I give you my word that we will vacate these tunnels if given the opportunity. But before we do, we would like to give you all the information we have about those who hold the others captive."

At that, a shape appeared beyond the crates. It seemed to grow out of the rock face, swelling like a bladder being filled with air, and it stepped forward. The other two Thelosi shifted slightly, and there was an exchange of squeaking that still didn't come through translated.

Boudreaux felt the blood drain from his face, and he felt ill. He couldn't help but wonder if he was about to die.

The alien stepped out from behind the crates, and Boudreaux got his first good look at a Thelosi.

The being was a meter and a half tall and stood on two legs that looked almost canine in its digitigrade formation. It's skin...*or suit*, he thought...was completely black, as if it was wrapped in vulcanized rubber. Four swaying tentacles rose up from its back and hovered around its body in slowly gyrating motions. It its three-jointed arms, it held a strange-looking weapon with five barrels, a central body and stock, and a curious grip. There was a blocky casing just aft of the trigger assembly that Boudreaux thought might be for ammunition. The alien's body was tapered somewhat, almost like an elongated teardrop that terminated in a thin neck. Its head was strangely elongated front to back, and at the top was a row of dark patches that Boudreaux could only assume was some sort of sensory apparatus. At the muzzle of its long head was a slim line, which opened as it spoke.

"We hear," it said, in a high, screechy voice, and it seemed to punctuate its words with subtle motions of the tentacles. "We understand. Blood has flowed between. You are the Foe of today..."

Boudreaux tensed at its words but remained motionless. He could barely hear the squeaking sounds of its voice, but the translation came in through his pinplants.

"You are not the Enemy of yesterday," the Thelosi said as it set its weapon on a nearby crate. "Yet will we decide whether you are the Enemy of tomorrow."

"How do you want to proceed?" Boudreaux asked nervously. *Enemy of today and tomorrow?*

One of the tentacles reached behind and then rose, revealing a Veetanho slate secured by small suction cups that lined the underside of the appendage. "The Foe will transmit all data to this. We must learn and evaluate. The Foe will then retreat from this stone and into the light. Await our word and take no further action. Any deviation, and blood will flow with the Foe of today."

"I understand," Boudreaux said. Through his pinplants, he picked up the signal of the Thelosi's slate and transmitted all the data, including their current mission objectives. Moments later he lowered his hands, which prompted the two-armed Thelosi to tense. "I've transmitted the data. We will now pull all of our soldiers back into the light and await your words." He started to turn away, but then he looked back at the alien who was now examining the slate. "Thank you," Boudreaux said.

The Thelosi paused for a moment. Boudreaux couldn't tell if it was looking at him or not. It clearly didn't have eyes in the traditional sense of the term. It lowered the slate slightly, then two of its tentacles waggled in his direction.

"It is too early for thanks," it said, "but I see that our hope for the *Sleeka*"—the word came to Max's ears as a mere squeak—"may yet find a place to sleep."

Boudreaux had no idea what a *Sleeka* was, or why it would be good for its hope to sleep, but he wasn't prepared to ask.

"Now go," the Thelosi said, "and wait."

Boudreaux turned and walked quickly back to where the rest of his fireteam stood.

"You heard?" Boudreaux asked.

"All of it," Corporal Killian said. "You want to tell us what the fuck is going on?"

"Everyone out, *now*," Colonel Hu's voice broke in over the comms. "They've cut the jamming, so you can swap over to our standard frequencies. Fireteams Cooper and Shikra, you're to take up a position fifty meters from that tunnel entrance, recall the drones, if you can, and break down all the equipment. Set up a defensive perimeter, but make it low key. Be ready if they come out shooting, but I want you all on your *best* behavior. This is no longer a combat operation, it's a first contact and negotiation scenario."

"Understood, sir," Yeo said, sounding confused.

A moment later, all the drones detached themselves from the walls, seeming to almost appear out of nothing, and they buzzed back the way they'd come.

"Oh, and Private Boudreaux?" the colonel called out.

"Yes, sir?"

"Well done."

Boudreaux paused for a moment, forcing AZ to come to an abrupt halt behind him. She thumped the back of his CASPer but didn't say anything. Boudreaux quickly started moving again, and as he clomped down the stony passage with the rest of his fireteam; it was all he could do not to throw up now that everything was over.

"Uhh…thank you, sir," Boudreaux finally said. "Glad I could help."

"What the fuck just happened?" Killian's voice came to Boudreaux on a private channel.

Boudreaux thought about what sort of response to give. There was just so much that had been contained in Praeliet Tokarra's data, and the implications were nothing less than a train wreck. And then he thought about his first words once he'd absorbed the data.

"Do you know about pit fighting? Like with roosters and dogs?" he asked.

"Of course."

"Well," Boudreaux said slowly, "us and the Thelosi…we're the dogs."

"Are you fucking kidding me?"

"I wish to god I was, Corporal."

Boudreaux kept marching forward, and with every step, the anger inside him grew.

* * *

5

Kuason

Hawk Base Camp Alpha

"Now that we've got everyone situated and ready to bug out if we have to, I'll give you the short version of what's really been going on." Colonel Hu stood in front of fireteams Cooper and Shikra just outside the cave entrance. Everyone else had fallen back to the far side of the lake with Fireteam Doria at Base Camp Beta. The dropship and two of the LAHVs were all parked there. The company had just spent the past hour shifting personnel and equipment around while getting the landing craft to positions where everyone could EVAC as quickly as possible. They still didn't have a clue as to what the Thelosi would do next, but Hu wanted them prepared. "In a nutshell, it all started on Reliak IV, when the Hawks took that Depik captive from some Veetanho mercs who, apparently, were actually working for Praeliet Tokarra. The Depik had intel on the location of the Thelosi homeworld. Tokarra and her associate wanted more Thelosi to play with, and we made that impossible."

"More, sir?" Killian asked.

"That's right, more," Hu replied. "They have only one colony, held captive and hidden somewhere, and that's the leverage they needed to get the Thelosi inside to do whatever they wanted."

"Goddamn Veetanho."

"It gets better," Hu continued. "Their plan was to keep throwing us at different scenarios they came up with as a sort of wargame, and every time us or the Thelosi came out on top, Praeliet Tokarra or her pal Praeliet Litarran won the bet they'd placed. It looks like they were testing these Thelosi in some sort of scheme to turn them into shock troops they could lease out to Veetanho mercenary companies."

"How do we proceed?" Yeo asked. "We're gonna kill that Veetanho bitch, right? Her and her pal?"

"I don't think we can…not yet, at least." Hu shook his head, and he seemed disgusted by his own answer.

"Why the hell not?" It was Killian this time, and he looked like he was ready to chew steel and spit bullets.

"Do we just go back and tell the Peacemaker everything?" Keenes asked. "It's not like we can complete the mission, which means we don't get paid. Maybe the Peacemaker will still pay us for everything we've found out."

"Who knows?" Hu replied. "I suspect he'll make good on his end, considering what we've found, but we'll take at least a small hit without the Veetanho contract. There's no way I'd ever deliver one of these Thelosi to them, even if I thought there was a way to capture one without any casualties on either side. We're mercs, not slavers."

"Amen to that," Killian said. "I like Yeo's idea. Let's just kill the two Veetanho bitches that started all this and sell their organs…I actually know a guy."

"I don't want to know why you know someone like that," Yeo said.

"There's a resolution to both of our situations." The words came from everyone's pinplants, and as they raised their weapons, searching the forest for where it had come from, a Thelosi appeared from behind one of the trees. And then another…and another. They all had their arms and tentacles up and appeared to be just standing there, their once black skin now a mottled camouflage pattern of the forest around them, and their bodies were slowly shifting to a deep green.

"Hold your fire!" Hu ordered.

"Where the hell did they come from?" Killian asked, his weapon aimed at the nearest Thelosi.

"Jesus, they're good," Boudreaux mumbled. He shot a message via his pinplants to AZ: *"We ought to put them on the payroll."*

"Everyone, lower your weapons," Hu said calmly. "If they'd wanted to start a fight, most of us would already be dead."

Everyone did as they were ordered.

Hu turned to face the nearest of the Thelosi, who was striding up with his limbs still raised.

"The *Kaenite* has reached our decision," it said. "You're a people of negotiation and war, so let us negotiate the destruction of yesterday's Foe and the deliverance of the *Sleeka*."

* * *

6

Karma Station

Guild Operations Sector

Mercenary Guild Negotiation Chamber

Privates Boudreaux and Mopantomobogo rolled the dolly into the chamber where Praeliet Tokarra sat once again at the far end of the conference table. Colonel Hu strode in behind them, with Lieutenant Yeo on his heels. As the officers took their seats, Boudreaux and AZ moved the stasis chamber around the table and along the wide windows that looked down on the Karma Station docks. When they'd gone about two thirds down the table, they lifted the back end of the dolly and set the chamber upright, with the small view port clearly visible. Tokarra bared her teeth with pleasure when she saw the dark form of a Thelosi occupant motionless within.

"I knew you could do it." Tokarra practically purred. "I've always maintained every faith in your abilities to overcome difficult situations."

Boudreaux and AZ moved back around the table and took up their positions behind the officers, standing at parade rest with hands upon their sidearms.

"I'm sure you have," Hu said with a smile. "I have to admit, the Thelosi are a clever, dangerous species. I'm still wondering where they came from…" he pulled a slate from within his coat and slid it across the table, "but I'd be satisfied if you'd just transfer the balance due into our accounts. There were two combat operations, and no fatalities."

"None at all?" Tokarra asked, sounding surprised.

"Not even a scratch," Yeo added, and Boudreaux didn't miss the snide tone in the lieutenant's voice.

"I'd love to know how you managed that." Tokarra reached out and pulled the slate closer, examining the data that broke down what she owed Hu's Hawks for successful completion of the mission.

Hu chuckled. "I bet you would…I'm afraid that's what we call a trade secret, but I'd be willing to tell you if you're willing to tell me where the Thelosi came from."

"I see your point," Tokarra said, then she pressed a thumb onto the screen and slid the slate back to Hu. "I believe we'll just have to leave those two questions unanswered."

Hu picked up his slate, checked to make sure the funds had been transferred and then set the slate down in front of him. He glanced behind him at Boudreaux and AZ and then fixed his gaze upon the Veetanho across the table.

"There was just one more thing," Hu said, and all pleasantry was gone from his voice.

Tokarra got a concerned look upon her face.

"What might that be? If you're after another contract, I'd have to say it's possible there might be more dealings with the Thelosi, but we'll need to examine this specimen and see what the future might hold."

"It's not that," Hu said. "I was more interested in knowing how much you'll be collecting from Praeliet Litarran, now that you can call us the victors in your little game."

Tokarra's eyes went wide, then she glared at Colonel Hu.

"Weapons!" she shouted.

The two Veetanho behind her stepped to the sides and raised their rifles in one smooth motion, and as they aimed them at Colonel

Hu and Lieutenant Yeo, two more Veetanho troopers opened the door behind her and strode in, their weapons held at the ready.

"Now this is unfortunate," Tokarra said. "I was hoping to draw this game out for another year at least, bleeding you Humans dry one body at a time." She let out an exasperated breath. "I'm afraid you know too much. If this got out...well, the repercussions would be severe. How much do you know?"

"A good deal more than you'd like," Hu said calmly, "but that's not a question you should be asking *me*. The real question is, how much do *you* know?"

He looked to the stasis chamber.

"*Sto'Kaito*," he barked with a strange accent that approximated the pronunciation of the Thelosi leader's name.

Praeliet Tokarra got a confused look on her face.

In the blink of an eye, two weapons slid out of ports the Hawks had installed on the front of the stasis chamber, and a long burst of rapid gunfire filled the room. All four guards slammed against the back wall, their bodies ripped to pieces by the Thelosi weapons before they even knew what hit them.

Tokarra sat there, a stunned expression on her face.

"Boudreaux, AZ...weapons, if you please."

Both privates drew their pistols and leveled them at the Veetanho, who was still blinking in shock at what had just happened. The front of the stasis chamber swung open, and her eyes shifted quickly to the occupant that stepped out, still holding two of the strange Thelosi rifles. It stepped forward several paces and placed its weapons on the table. At the same time, the door behind Hu and Yeo opened, and Peacemaker Zarikk walked in with a needler aimed straight at Tokarra's heart.

"Did you get the others?" Hu asked over his shoulder.

"Indeed," Peacemaker Zarikk said. "My associates have secured six Veetanho troopers in Praeliet Tokarra's employ."

"Then we've fulfilled our commitment to the Peacemakers as well, don't you think?" Hu said, reaching for the slate.

"There is no doubt," Zarikk said.

Tokarra's hand moved from the table, and she started to reach for something out of sight.

"Don't do it," AZ warned the Veetanho. "We'll be shooting to wound, not kill, and it's likely to be rather painful."

"Hands back on the table," Zarikk ordered. "Leave them there, or this will go badly for you."

"You treacherous vermin," Tokarra spat, but she obeyed.

"Guess she never heard of the pot and the kettle," Boudreaux whispered to AZ.

"Sto'Kaito," Colonel Hu said, "we've fulfilled our promise to you. The Praeliet is all yours."

Tokarra's eyes went wide with fear as the Thelosi commander lunged forward. He was upon her in an instant, wrapping his tentacles around her body and head. She started to scream, but when the tentacles made contact, her body stiffened, and it looked like there were small patterns of electricity running from the tentacles into her furry scalp.

Tokarra's eyes rolled back, and her tongue lolled out of her mouth. Her body quivered and shook almost imperceptibly, and within a few seconds, a trickle of blood seeped from her nostrils and dripped upon the table.

Neither the Peacemaker nor any of the Humans moved a muscle as the Thelosi rummaged around in Praeliet Tokarra's brain.

The one thing that had been missing from all the data they'd stolen was the location of the Thelosi prisoners, or "*Sleeka*" as the Thelosi commander had called them. The term didn't have a reasonable facsimile in any language, but it was a combination of 'beloveds' and 'usurped' and 'sufferers,' all rolled up into one painful idea.

Hu's Hawks had learned that and much more on their journey from Kuason.

About a minute later, Sto'Kaito released the Veetanho and let her collapse upon the table, where she lay gasping for breath. He stepped back and seemed to consider her for several moments.

"She has given me what I need." The translation came through everyone's pinplants. Sto'Kaito turned to face Hu and the Peacemaker. "I have your word that she will be detained until the *Sleeka* are free?"

"I can guarantee that," Peacemaker Zarikk said. "The Hawks are helping one of my associates capture Praeliet Litarran, who is in a nearby hotel." Zarikk's eyes fixed upon the Veetanho, and his mouth split into what could only be a snarl. "Not only are you done, Praeliet, but all of this will be presented to both the Peacemaker and Mercenary Guilds. In time, you'll tell us how deep this slaving conspiracy runs."

"I'll tell you nothing," Tokarra groaned.

"That's your choice, but I'm certain we can come up with something worse than death if you choose to remain silent."

"The *Kaenite* thanks you," Sto'Kaito said. It seemed to focus on Colonel Hu. "Your nobility and reason will not be forgotten."

"Maybe you'd consider working together in the future?" Hu asked.

The Thelosi considered the man who had once been his enemy.

"It is unlikely. We wish to reach our home once again and remove ourselves from such things." It waved a tentacle toward Tokarra. "Family and friends will be safe, and that is all we seek." It turned its strange head toward Peacemaker Zarikk. "You will keep our existence secret?"

"I'll see to it. The Peacemaker Guild has already agreed to your terms, and we're prepared to assist you in freeing the prisoners."

"Then we will await you on Kuason, once these have delivered us there." Sto'Kaito motioned toward Colonel Hu.

"There's one last bit of business, Peacemaker Zarikk," Hu said. Hu pulled up another contract on his slate and held it up over his shoulder.

"Of course," Zarikk said. He stepped forward, reviewed it quickly and then placed his thumb to accept the terms and transfer payment.

"It's been a pleasure doing business with you," Hu said agreeably. He cast a sidelong glance at Tokarra and then got up from the table. He walked around to the Veetanho and yanked the green sash over her head. He gave a quick inspection of the red jewels woven into the fabric and smiled. "I believe I'll consider a handful of red diamonds as the penalty for withholding so much intel," he said, staring down at the still-groaning alien. "These should fetch a couple million, at least." He spat once on the floor beside her and turned toward the Peacemaker. "Any problem with that?"

Zarikk's features were impassive. He glanced at the Veetanho and then back to Colonel Hu.

"None at all," he said.

"Good." Hu glanced at Sto'Kaito. "Come on, Commander, let's get you and your people back to Kuason." He then strode along the table, nodded once to the Peacemaker, and reached the door. "Hawks, we're out of here." He waited for Sto'Kaito, Yeo, Boudreaux, and AZ to walk out the door, then he turned back to the Peacemaker.

"And if you need help getting those other Thelosi, we're in," he added.

"Let me get back to you on that," the Peacemaker replied.

Without another word, Hu stepped through the door, closed it behind him, and followed his people and their new friend to the *Zhūgéliàng*.

*****

Quincy J. Allen Bio

Bestselling Author Quincy J. Allen is a cross-genre author with numerous novels under his belt. His media tie-in novel *Colt the Outlander: Shadow of Ruin* was a Scribe Award finalist in 2019, and his noir novel *Chemical Burn* was a Colorado Gold Award finalist in 2010. *Blood Oath*, book 3 of the Blood War Chronicles, was released in February of 2019, and he is working on the fourth book in that six-book fantasy steampunk series, due out early in 2020.

He has co-authored *Reclaiming Honor* with Marc Alan Edelheit in their Way of Legend series, published November 1st of 2019. He is currently working on a novel for Kevin Steverson in his Salvage universe based on the short story *Vorwhol Dishonnor.*

His short story publications are numerous, including a pro sale appearing in Larry Correia's *Monster Hunter: Files* from Baen, published in October of 2017 entitled "Sons of the Father," as well as a number of other stories appearing in Chris Kennedy Publishing's mil-sci-fi anthologies in and out of the Four Horsemen Universe.

He works out of his home in Charlotte, North Carolina, and hopes to one day be a New York Times bestselling author.

# # # # #

First Steps by Richard Alan Chandler

Kenneth Branson stood in the hot Texas sun watching the ship descend on the recently rededicated Houston Starport. The Cochkala freighter wasn't one of the regularly scheduled ones, and Kenneth had lucked out and had been able to grab the new loader—trying to run a forklift in alien freighters was often an invitation to frustration or damage claims. The loader was a bipedal framework of steel bars and hydraulic rams. The new ones used batteries instead of propane engines—the aliens often complained about the smell of the exhaust, although compared to some of the things he'd smelled on those ships, Kenneth didn't think they had any room for objections.

The freighter settled down on the landing pad, and the cargo ramp descended. One of the Customs jerks was there to make the captain sign some paperwork, but after a very short conversation, he stalked off. The crew chief waved for the rest of them to get to work.

Kenneth checked the straps holding his feet in the stirrups, pulled the crash cage down in front of himself, and cycled the joysticks to make sure all the controls were operating—standard procedure. He loved the loaders. Even the other cargo handlers who had more experience had to admit he was a natural with the machine.

There was even talk of sending him to compete in the Heavy Equipment Rodeo in Dallas this fall. That would be fun.

Thoughts of fun were dismissed, though, as a line of ambulances pulled up on the concrete apron, and a stream of men began descending the ramp. Human mercenaries returning from a contract; no wonder the ship wasn't on the schedule. They looked pretty beaten up. Most of them were bandaged in some way or another. Others helped their buddies hobble down the ramp, while still more were carried to the ambulances on stretchers. There was some incredible medical tech out there in the Galactic Union, but none of it was specifically for Humans yet, and these men paid the price. As Kenneth walked the loader up to the ramp, one of the mercs came up to him full of long-stewing anger and got in his face, poking his arm though the cage and pointing at him. The man shouted, "You baggage monkeys better take good care of my men! You drop one, and so help me, I'll kill you with my bare hands!"

Another merc grabbed the first by the shoulder. "Come on, Sarge, leave him alone."

"I'm just sayin'..." the sergeant let the threat trail off.

"I'll do my best, sir," Kenneth said to the back of the grumbling mercenary. He knew what he'd find at the top of the ramp—coffins, or body bags. He wasn't quite prepared for so many of them, though. It was grim work, and by the time they finished filling the fourth baggage train, he realized this company had probably lost three quarters of its complement.

The crates were easier to load into the trucks, but behind that was a load of loose equipment. A lot of rifles and such just thrown in a pile. That made Kenneth nervous, wondering if any of them were still loaded. The rest of the loading crew seemed to have no trouble just grabbing individual rifles and running them out to the truck, but the heavier stuff they left for him. He carefully clamped the manipulators around a huge pedestal-mounted 20mm Vulcan cannon and turned to walk down the ramp.

At the bottom of the ramp were two men. He didn't recognize the man in the suit, but the man in the uniform everybody knew, Colonel James E. Cartwright, commander of Cartwright's Cavaliers. Whatever they were discussing, though, they were still blocking the ramp.

"Uh, excuse me…"

They both looked up the ramp at Kenneth and the loader. The man in the suit immediately stepped out of the way, but Col. Cartwright just looked at him, and then there was a gleam in his eye, and a smile grew on his face. Then he stepped out of the way, but he watched as the loader came down the ramp.

"Say, son, could you stop there for a moment?"

"Sure thing, Colonel Cartwright."

"How's that thing work?"

Kenneth put the loader through the motions, explaining how, when he lifted against the straps of the stirrup, the foot of the machine came up with it, automatically shifting weight to the opposite foot. Then he showed how the manipulators could move around based on how he moved the joysticks and switches on the panel in front of him.

The colonel turned to the man in the suit. "What do you think, Jerry? What if we got some of these things and armored them up a bit? Then we could bring the big guns to those damned spiders."

"I dunno, sir," said Jerry, "they probably aren't designed with combat conditions in mind."

Cartwright walked around the loader, examining it. "What's this thing called, son? Who makes it?"

Kenneth had to look at the panel for the exact model number, since there was such a variety of equipment on site. "It's a Mitsubishi HF-22A Heavy Frame Loader." He pointed to the logo on the front, three red diamonds arranged radially to form an equilateral triangle.

Cartwright continued to circle the machine. "Ripley? That you?"

Kenneth leaned out through the bars and looked at the side of the cab. Dean Norton had struck again; most of the bright yellow panel had been pinstriped with a black marker, including—in beautifully rendered script—"Ripley," styled like the name of a fighter pilot. Kenneth didn't get the joke, but Dean insisted it was hilarious, and kept re-doing it every time the managers forced him to remove his handiwork. A shame, because he was actually quite talented.

"No, sir, I'm Branson. Kenneth Branson."

"Well, thank you, Mister Branson. You've given me quite the idea to think about."

Kenneth finished loading the truck, and then of course there was an outbound cargo ship to load. 100 tons of frozen strawberries later, he was exhausted, and the loader barely had enough juice left to make it back to the charging station. He really didn't think much about the encounter after that.

* * *

Dr. Paul Mauser, chief of Robotics Engineering at the Mitsubishi Heavy Industries complex just outside of Houston, clicked send on his critique of the company's internal white paper on asteroid mining. As long as Earth was dependent on chemical rockets or on hiring alien shuttles at incredible expense, the effort was financially impractical. And hiring alien mining companies to do the entire job would basically bleed the planet dry. They were only interested in F11, virtually unknown in the Sol System, which was part of the reason Galactic civilization had passed humanity by for so long. Iron ore and rare earths couldn't be produced in the quantities required to be profitable.

No, if Earth was going to exploit her own system, she needed her own ships. But to get the fusion drive technology to do it, she needed credits. And right now, the only real source of credits was the mercenary trade, which converted Human bodies into capital at a ruinous rate. As for how MHI was going to get their hands on those credits, he didn't have an answer. But at least he could design the robots to do the mining.

The other answer that eluded him was how to design an automated cargo-handling system that could cope with the seemingly infinite variety of alien ships. Even their common designs had so many variables due to repairs, customization, and the sheer age of some ships. That's what had made the Heavy Loaders such an instant hit, and why this facility had been built so close to Houston Starport. They could rapidly prototype and adapt the machines as needed. Specialization and customization had become his area of expertise, even as much as he hoped for a more universal solution.

He pulled up the design files he'd requested on coal loaders. Those earth-moving machines were built so low to the ground the driver sat almost prone. They'd run into one race who—at only a meter tall—didn't believe in wide-open cargo holds. He was looking for inspiration, but before he could really switch mental gears, an IM appeared on his screen. "Director Yashimoto wants to see you in his office immediately." He sighed. It was too soon for Yashimoto to have actually read his e-mail, but that wouldn't stop him from receiving his ire.

* * *

"Doctor Mauser. Good! Good! Come in. I was just telling Colonel Cartwright here about the amazing work you've been doing with our Heavy Loader line. He's very interested in having us do a project for him." Yashimoto turned to the other man in his office. "Colonel, this is Paul Mauser, the lead engineer in our Research and Development department. If anyone can realize your vision, this is the man."

The twin shocks of the effusive praise from Yashimoto and the sheer presence of Cartwright left Paul speechless. Yoshihiro Yashimoto being anything but an ass could easily be attributable to the need to make a good impression, but Cartwright was more than just a folk hero, and the reality more than lived up to the legend.

Cartwright walked over and shook Paul's hand. "Nice to meet you." Then he shoved a slate into his hands and started poking at it. Paul scrambled to keep a grip on the alien computing device worth more than his annual salary as the colonel cycled through a series of pictures of what looked like an HF-22A carrying a very, very big gun.

* * *

Jim Cartwright followed the bald and goateed engineer back to his office to discuss specifics. The place was full of odd little robot toys on shelves on the wall. Another shelf was lined with various engineering awards, and prominent in the middle was something that looked like an enormous nut.

He was pulled back from the cacophony of colored plastic by a question that sounded like English, but didn't really register.

"So, basically we're going more for Starship Troopers than Mobile Suit Gundam…"

"Excuse me?"

"Just trying to pin down the overall concept. One would be basically a powered suit of armor; the other encloses the pilot entirely inside the torso of the machine."

"Oh, the first one. The other one sounds like it would be big. And big things are easier to hit. You see, the Cavaliers specialize in heavy assault. We move fast, hit hard, and break through defenses. But infantry armor is only effective against small arms. And man-portable weapons are of limited effectiveness against some of the aliens and defenses we're running up against."

"And tanks are out of the question."

"Too big, too slow, too vulnerable to terrain."

"And crew-served weapons like that one from the pictures you showed me aren't mobile enough."

"We move them up behind our assault line to back up the infantry. Being able to deploy them faster, and to the front line, would make a huge difference."

"I can imagine. But the important question is, where are you willing to compromise?"

"What do you mean?"

"In engineering, we like to say, 'You can have it Good, Fast, or Cheap, pick two.' In terms of Good, I can see the ideal is something that fits like a suit of armor, lets a man run, jump and fly like Superman, and carry a ton of weapons. The technology isn't even close to that. It would take time and considerable research to get there. I get the feeling you'd like a much more immediate solution. At the fast and cheap end of the line, we could take an HF-22A and weld on a bunch of armor and weapons mounts like something out of the A-Team. It won't be perfect, but it will get the job done."

"Both," the colonel said firmly, "I need something I can field right away. We're getting slaughtered out there. Anything we can do to improve things for my men is worth doing. In the long term, yeah, I love what you're saying, and we can work toward that. But unless something changes, I swear sometimes it looks like the Earth is going to run out of men who can fight."

* * *

The conversation lasted hours, and in the end, Paul had more than enough information about the types of weapons systems the Cavaliers fielded, their tactics, and how the colonel would like to deploy them. Likewise, Paul had given him an understanding of the capabilities and limitations of what was physically possible, and even lent him Jim Smentowski's seminal work on robotic combat so he would understand the trade-offs between speed, armor, weight, power density, and duration. ("Sounds a lot like that Good, Fast, Cheap thing.") By the time the colonel left, Paul's mind was entirely oriented on the problem, and he found himself sketching out a development program late into the night.

Two days later, four brand-new HF-22A heavy loaders unloaded themselves from a flatbed trailer into the high-bay shop requisitioned for the project. Dr. Mauser addressed the collection of machinists and technicians recruited from the manufacturing line. "Gentlemen, we've been commissioned to transform these humble cargo loaders into the most advanced infantry fighting machine in the world. Something long in the annals of science fiction, we're going to make them real. And in the process, we're going to put Human mercs on an even footing with the nastiest aliens the universe can throw at us."

Fortunately, the loaders were already structurally strong enough to support the proposed weight of the armor. Armor plates of half-inch thick AR500 steel were delivered to the waterjet cutting shop and cut per the 3D model. Welders fashioned the parts into armor segments for each moving part of the loader, bolting them to standoffs welded directly to the loader's frame. Technicians stripped out the cargo-handling gear from the arms and installed mounts for the guns that arrived on a pallet from the Cavaliers. Mauser and his assistants modified the control systems to actuate the guns and added small LCD screens for remote sight cameras mounted on the guns. It took almost an entire day to recalibrate the balance systems. The first prototype was quick and dirty, but it would work.

* * *

Three weeks into the project, Cartwright visited the bay to see how the project was progressing.

"The biggest problem we're having is battery life," Mauser advised him. "Right now, without external power, we're only getting about 4 hours of average walking life, and simulated combat maneuvering cuts that almost in half. I have some guys working on a modified troop carrier that can keep them topped off until they dismount, and a tow-behind diesel genset they can drop as needed. It'll have to be modified to automatically change its operation for various atmospheres, but that should be doable.

"Reloading the guns is another issue. Either they need an infantryman to assist, or the driver needs to pop the canopy to reach the gun."

"It needs a bayonet," said Cartwright.

Mauser cocked his head. "A bayonet?"

"It needs to be able to fight when he's out of ammunition until it can get resupplied."

One of the welders stood up a long, wickedly curved chunk of leftover armor steel. "I could whip something up out of this."

Cartwright grinned. "How soon before we can conduct some trials?"

* * *

Two weeks later at the Cavalier's training grounds, Prototypes #2 and #3 stepped off the trailer, and the gawking began.

"It's huge."

"I don't like it."

"It's fucking awesome, I want one!"

"Needs a bigger gun, and missiles, and a grenade launcher."

"Get a round into one of those view slots, and it'll bounce around inside until it hits you."

Paul Mauser flitted nervously around the machines, checking in with the drivers. "It's our first live fire exercise. You know how to calibrate the rangefinders, right?"

"Stop worrying, Doc, we've got this."

Cartwright led Mauser up to the observation stand, and the demonstration began. First they demonstrated their range of motion, squatting down, standing, pointing the arms in all directions. Then they marched forward to the first firing line. Mauser clenched his fists, but the first salvo was right on target. The truck never had a chance. The machines made a remarkably stable fire platform.

Next they demonstrated advancing fire, and the cargo-handling legacy of the machines showed as they maintained their aim. The pop-up targets were another story. Getting the guns shifting from target to target had some definite lag. That was an inherent problem with using joysticks to control the arm movement.

The obstacle section was distinctly unimpressive, until one of the drivers improvised and bulled through the obstacles, knocking them over, and popped the blade to smash through a section of fencing. That elicited a cheer from the men observing.

All Paul could see was a long list of things that needed fixing, so he was totally unprepared when the colonel turned to him and said, "We'll take 20 to see how they operate, with a tentative contract for the 100 depending on performance."

* * *

Production at the Houston facility was turned over 100% to manufacturing the new "Combat Assault System, Personal, Mk 1," and even then it was strained to the limit. They'd never built loaders at anything near this rate before. Parts shortages were leaving a lot of units partially completed. Technicians installed systems whenever they could, which sometimes meant they had to be disassembled again when the needed parts finally came in, and this drove up costs. But that didn't matter; the payment the Cavaliers had agreed to still made this ridiculously profitable for the MHI Cargo Handling Systems division. Yashimoto was positively giddy.

After the initial demo, Dr. Mauser had addressed a few concerns. The first production units now sported auxiliary hardpoints on the shoulders where additional weapons could be mounted, either a "six pack" of surface-to-air missiles, or a 7.62mm minigun. A spall liner was added to the interior to catch the fragments of shrapnel that flake off at high velocity from the interior of armor plates even when they aren't penetrated, and bulletproof prismatic periscopes were added to the view slots, much like the commander's hatch of a tank. Additional changes were made to the control software to make it possible for the machines to actually jump. They couldn't jump very high, but the fact they could jump at all owed greatly to the code they licensed from Boston Dynamics.

The first delivery of 20 machines was almost ready when Colonel Cartwright visited again. This time he was accompanied by a young man in a brand-new uniform, who looked remarkably out of place in it.

"Doctor Mauser, I'd like to introduce you to Sergeant Branson. I recruited him to head up training on these new machines. I thought I'd bring him over to work with you guys on developing the program."

The young man nervously started to salute, when Cartwright said to him, "You don't have to salute, Doc here is a civilian." He caught himself and extended his hand.

"Pleased to meet you," said Mauser, eyeing the young man. "Would that be Kenneth Branson?"

"Yes, sir!"

"I thought so. Congratulations on your victory down in Dallas. There was a big article about it on the company website. You made us look really good."

"That's why I had to hire him. He's a natural," said Cartwright. "He's the same fellow I got the idea from in the first place."

Paul smiled at Ken. "Made you an offer you couldn't refuse, eh? He's good at that." Ken blushed. Looking across the shop, Paul shouted out, "Hey, Mark! You done loading the new code on prototype four? Give this guy the nickel tour and let him have a go at it." He turned back to Ken. "See that guy in the yellow hard-hat with 'Tonka' written on it? Go see him; he'll get you set up. Just don't shoot anything." Ken looked concerned, but he reassured him, "We don't actually have any ammo here in the factory."

The two men watched the young sergeant cross the shop floor. Paul turned to the colonel and gestured toward his office. "Got time for a Coke?"

"Always."

* * *

Training began immediately after the first batch of CASPers were delivered. A dozen of the machines squatted on the Cavaliers' training ground beneath a hastily-erected scaffolding, heavy steel cables hung from an I-beam that ran above them to the hoisting rings set in the shoulders of the mechs, and the first dozen mercs scheduled for training milled around, looking them over. They all turned as a deuce-and-a-half pulled up with another mech crouched in the bed.

The mech stood up and jumped off the truck, landing with a thump that shook the ground. It then walked up to the men and stopped. The entire front of the torso swung up, revealing Sgt. Branson. While not nearly as muscular and otherwise hardened as the mercs before him, the two-ton death machine he was riding made quite an impression.

"Gentlemen," he said without a hint of sarcasm, "I'm Sergeant Branson, and I'm here to teach you how to operate the Mitsubishi Heavy Industries CASPer Mk 1. By the time we're done, you'll be running, jumping, and shooting like it was second nature. But today, you're going to have to learn to walk all over again." He looked over the men and was surprised that almost all of them appeared to be taking him seriously. He'd been warned "there'd be one in every class," but it looked like there were two. "Pick a machine and mount up, and I'll make sure you're all set up correctly."

After making sure the men had adjusted their stirrups tightly and set their seat heights, he returned to the front. "Pull down your yokes and lock them in position." Like the seat restraint in a roller coaster, the padded bars flipped down over their shoulders and attached with a buckle to a strap at the front of the saddle. With the padded bolsters at the sides of the seat, they ensured the pilot would be properly positioned within the machine at all times. The control panel was mounted to the front of the yoke.

"We'll leave the canopies open for now. Right now I'd like to draw your attention to two controls on the panel in front of you. First is the master power switch. That's the big red Emergency Stop button. Before you touch..." One machine began beeping as it ran its self-checks. In two bounds, Branson was right up against the offending machine. He reached around his yoke and slapped the button back off. Without a word, he went back to his position. "As I was saying before Mister Jenkins here interrupted, before you touch the master power switch, look at the mode switch and make sure it's in the park position. That's the squatting pose you all started in, but it's easy enough to get knocked out of position, and if you try to stand before the gyros are up to speed, the results could be embarrassing for you, and fatal for whoever you fall over on. Now then, make sure the mode switch is in park, *then* pull the power on."

All twelve machines beeped their way through their self-checks, then the hydraulic pumps kicked in, pressurizing the system and loading the accumulators. Green LEDs lit on the control boards, indicating the mechs were good to go.

"The next mode is Idle. This will stand you up. The inertial guidance will be in full authority. This is very useful, believe it or not. If you're riding in a vehicle, or just standing guard, you'd exhaust yourself and your batteries trying to keep steady. After that is Walk, which has somewhat less guidance authority, then Run, which is optimized for fast moving, and finally Manual, which has no inertial guidance at all. We'll go through all these modes in turn, but first, engage Idle and stand up."

Eleven CASPers slowly and evenly stood up. The last, however, violently kicked, shoving upward much more strongly with one leg than the other. It tipped and sagged from the cables as the legs spasmed, digging deep furrows in the dirt and kicking rocks in every direction.

"Hit the stop! Now!"

The pilot mashed the red button, and the mech stopped thrashing. Branson walked up, livid. "Let me guess. 'I don't need no computer telling me how to walk, I can handle this myself.' Right?! You went right for the fucking manual mode, didn't you?! Well let me give you your last CASPer lesson. Put that machine in park, turn it on, and once it settles, turn it off again and get out. You're done here, Mister…" he read the nametape on the man's uniform, "… le Roi."

The lesson continued without further mishap, and soon the men were comfortable marching in place, turning back and forth, and so on. Ken figured they were acclimated enough to the lag between lifting on the stirrup and the legs coming up, and the way the machine compensated for the shift in balance from two feet to one like the original loader, only much faster. He decided to cut them loose.

"When I disconnect your support cables, I want you to walk forward, around that truck, and back to your starting position. Only the last ten feet, I want you to walk backwards. Try not to knock over the scaffolding."

It was painful to watch, as the first machine staggered in the general direction of the truck. Ken jogged over to him, taking position in front of the man and walking backwards so he could see what he was doing.

Groaning, the man—Corporal Callen according to his uniform—muttered, "It's like having fifty pound blocks strapped to your feet."

"You're fighting it too much. Lift your feet evenly, and it should keep up with you."

There was some improvement, but the machine still lurched from side to side.

"Keep your toes pointed in the direction you want to go. You're kicking way out to the sides. That's better. Keep it up, you're halfway there." He jogged back to the rest of the class. "If any of the rest of you walk duck-footed, you're going to have a difficult time. The hips twist outward to match the angle of your feet, and that affects the way your knee bends. Aside from poor balance, that requires a lot more adjustment to keep you on an even keel, and that'll eat your battery."

"Can't we just adjust the stirrups to compensate, Sergeant?"

"If you were to do that, aside from reducing your range of motion, it means your flesh and blood knee would be bending on a different axis from the knee of your leg shell. And that, as they say, would be bad. You're just going to have to work on your posture."

Eventually, all eleven CASPers had made the walk. "I'm very proud of you all. None of you managed to fall over, although that *is* pretty difficult in walk mode. There's one last thing I want to show you before we hike these machines back to the shed for recharging. Jenkins, you like to rush into things. Give that knob a twist to Run and take a lap around the truck. You might want to put down your canopy, too."

Jenkins began to move forward slowly, and a little more unsteadily.

"Yeah, just because the knob says run doesn't mean you have to run. But because I say run, you do. Pick up the pace."

Jenkins lumbered toward the truck, picking up speed until he was positively jogging, and when he got to the truck, he started turning.

Only the CASPer didn't turn, it tumbled spectacularly. Momentum carried it in the direction it had been running.

"Come on," Ken said to the rest of the class, "this is what I want to show you."

When they arrived at Jenkins' prostrate CASPer, he shouted, "How you doing in there?"

"You set me up!"

"You did better than I thought. That was probably about a five mile an hour crash. That harness should keep you safe up to around forty. Which is overkill, because the best you can make in one of these suits is about ten. But here's the thing I want to show you. Set it to park." The mech's legs retracted to a squatting position. "Now grab both joysticks and pull them straight back the same amount."

The CASPer's arms began a slow rotation, up over the head and straight back, and in a motion not possible for Human beings, continued past the "head" until they were pushing against the ground, then eventually they stood the machine up on its feet.

"Excellent!" Ken shouted. "Just like in Judo, it's important to know how to fall and how to get back up. Especially when we start training with running and jumping. Everyone should expect to get a lot of practice doing this. Okay, let's head back to the shed."

* * *

Ken was exhausted. Pretending to be tough like some kind of drill sergeant wasn't easy for him. Although when he thought about it, that's exactly who he was now.

"So only one washout," said a voice behind him.

Ken jumped to his feet and saluted the colonel.

"Relax, son. I brought you onboard for training, not soldiering. I just wanted to see how it went."

"Actually, pretty well. I've trained a lot of people on the loaders, but that's usually one-on-one, and frankly, there's usually a lot less ego involved."

"That's why I made you a sergeant, so you outrank them. But in training, the only real ranks are Instructor and Student. Even when it's my turn, I expect you to tell me what to do and how to do it."

"Yes, sir. But do you really want to do it? Those CASPers aren't exactly safe. They're missing a lot of the interlocks the loaders have."

"They're weapons; they're not supposed to be safe. Your job is to train the drivers to handle the dangers. Either way, I think my chances are better inside one of those suits than outside."

* * *

Corporal Chuck "King Charlie" le Roi was enjoying the easiest march on his objective ever. While the 0.85 G of Leatrun 4 would have made any march easier, he found a much better way that involved no marching at all. The objective was a factory on the outskirts of town. Zuul mercenaries had seized it, and the rightful owners had called upon the Cavaliers to seize it right back. It was a perfect first outing for the new CASPers. The hired dropships had set them down at the starport on the north side of the city. Most of the CASPers had been loaded into trucks. But several had been detailed to escort the caravan, including his buddy Corporal Peter Jenkins. Chuck was assigned to CASPer support.

With their short battery life and limited onboard ammo, each mech needed at least one support troop to aid in resupply and rearmament. So the CASPers on patrol each towed a small trailer with a generator from a pintle hitch on the rear of the mech. The generator supplied additional power through a quick-release power cable connected to the battery housing in the back of the machine. The trailer was also stacked with ammo cans for the .50 caliber main guns, and the 7.62 mm chainguns. Jenkins' trailer was also stacked with "King Charlie." The trailers could be easily dropped by pulling a release inside the cockpit, and Jenkins was about two more "Mush!" jokes away from giving it a test.

"All I'm saying is you could be walking a lot more smoothly if you tried. This jerk-jerk stuff is really annoying."

"Maybe if you ask real nice, they'll let you ride on a truck. Or you can walk."

"Nah, I gotta stick with you, buddy. But look at Sergeant Buckley over there, he's got it down pat. Nice and smooth."

"Maybe you can go ride with him, then."

Their banter stopped when the caravan was called to a halt at the target industrial park. The buildings were arranged in a sort of offset grid, more reminiscent of a brick wall. Toward the front, they tended to be office buildings, mostly glass and the local version of concrete.

Toward the back of the lot, the buildings tended to be simple sheet steel warehouses and machine shops. The building they were after was in the back.

The Zuul mercenaries were obviously aware of their presence. The starport could easily be seen from here, so they must have seen the dropships. They would be ready.

As the CASPers deployed off the trucks, Chuck kept a wary eye for scouts or worse. And it didn't take long before he saw a head peeping over the top of one of the offices.

"Sniper! Rooftop, three o'clock!" His warning was punctuated by three bursts from his rifle, which was rewarded by the Zuul sniper falling from the building like a scene from a classic western—if the cowboys had been anthropomorphized German Shepherds and worn modern combat armor. The shrubbery around the building was also peppered by infantry fire, just for good measure. If there were any more scouts, they'd fallen back in the face of overwhelming numbers.

Their battle plan had been worked out well in advance. As soon as the CASPers were ready, they would split into two groups and push up either side of the central row of buildings, forcing the defenders to keep their forces distributed as they were flanked. Whichever side broke through first would sweep across the defending lines, making an opening for the rest of the Cavaliers to join the party. They'd also mapped out where the ammo caches would be dropped, and paired CASPers would relieve each other as they stepped back to reload. Infantry would handle resupply and guard the flanks.

Like all good plans, it didn't survive first contact with the enemy. As Jenkins and the rest of Buckley's squad rounded the corner of the loading dock, they discovered the Zuul had used the two weeks it had taken to send for and ship out the Cavaliers to severely reinforce their positions. The perimeter of the factory had been completely surrounded by a barricade, complete with concrete pillboxes at the corners. A fusillade of light lasers was focused on Buckley, and the pillbox opened up, too. The heavy bolt from the pillbox struck Buckley's left machine gun, blowing it up as the ammo in the feeder instantly cooked off. He scrambled back just in time to avoid another bolt. His armor was covered with squiggly gouges halfway through the plate, "worm tracks" in the vernacular, caused by the movement of the lasers as they hit. They may have been well-entrenched, but clearly the unfamiliar machines had the Zuul rattled. If they'd been more disciplined, some of those shots might have penetrated.

"That pillbox has gotta go!" shouted Buckley. "He's at the end of the line, so pie the corner, two by two."

Jenkins took his place, standing back from the edge of the building, with the corner just obscuring the pillbox's line of sight. He and Callen both took a step or two to the left and painted the pillbox with their .50 cals until they ran dry, then ducked back behind the building. Before the crew in the pillbox could stick their heads back up, the next two CASPers opened up, and so on. Le Roi and the other infantrymen were kept busy reloading the burning-hot machine guns.

Running back from the ammo dump with two more boxes of .50 cal sucked, even in the lower gravity. Running back with the last two boxes sucked even more. The concrete of the pillbox had been jackhammered by the heavy fire, but it still hadn't failed, and the gunners, having been emboldened by the feeling of invulnerability it gave them, stayed at their gun and were making hits on the CASPers.

"Sarge, this is the last of it."

"Crap, what else have we got?"

"We have a ton of ammo for the miniguns."

"If the .50 won't go through it, that won't do it, either. What I wouldn't give for an RPG right now. Anything else?"

"Uh, a couple of claymores."

"Crap. Guess I gotta take the fight to them. Get me some green tape."

Buckley taped the claymore to the ruined end of his left arm and fed the wire to the clacker through the edge of his canopy. "On three, everyone with anything left, step out and give me covering fire. Keep their heads down until I can deliver this."

Thirty CASPers fanned out from the loading dock, miniguns sweeping up and down the barricade. The cacophony was deafening even through the armor. Buckley sprinted toward the pillbox, tracking the slit with both gun cameras. He plowed into the pillbox at full tilt and jammed down the detonator. A pound and a half of C-4 sent 700 tiny steel balls ricocheting around the interior of the pillbox, pureeing everything inside. Buckley's CASPer fell away from the box, landing on its back.

Inside, Buckley shook himself. "Sonofabitch, I figured I was gonna die." With nothing left of its arms, he had no way of righting the mech. He just caught a glimpse of Zuul troopers peeking over the barricades, seeing if there was a way to get at him. "Maybe I still will," he muttered as he fished around at his side for his .45.

Back at the loading dock, the men were furiously reloading the miniguns. "Sarge is still alive, we gotta get him out of there," several troopers said.

Chuck was feeding more ammo into Jenkins' minigun when Jenkins said, "Don't bother, it's down. I don't have any control of it."

"Lemme take a look." He climbed on the back of Jenkins' CASPer and examined the gun. "Looks like you took a hit through the control cables, but the gun still has power. Hang on, I have a really stupid idea."

"What are you doing?"

"Something really stupid, don't move."

Half a minute later, Jenkins heard a slap on the top of his canopy. "Okay, stand up," said Chuck. As Jenkins stood, he said, "Damn, you really can do anything with paracord and duct tape."

"Are you serious?"

"Just keep your armor between me and the doggies, and I should be fine. Now let's get Sarge. You get me out there, and I should be able to drag him back."

"Guys, we're gonna get Sarge, just give us covering fire. You ready, Chuck?"

"Let's do this."

Jenkins snapped out the blades on both arms of his mech and stepped out before anyone could talk them out of it.

"Le Roi! Jenkins!" shouted Callen. "Crap, they just went out. Stick to the plan!"

Jenkins charged toward the fallen mech, but Buckley was the only one unaware of the rescue plan. He was already out of his suit, his back against the pillbox, .45 held against his chest as he tried to peek around the corner to see if the Zuul were coming.

Jenkins and le Roi could see the Zuul were gathering to rush Buckley. Le Roi tried to hose them down with the minigun, but he only got a short burst off before they ducked back behind the barricade. "Well, crap, let's get them." Chuck turned around in his improvised sling on the hoisting rings and waved on the rest of the troops.

Callen shook his head in disbelief, then shouted to the rest, "Cavaliers! Lead the charge!" and set off for the barricade.

"Hold on tight!" Jenkins shouted. Just as he approached the barricade, he held down the jump button. The hydraulic pumps whined as the accumulators fully loaded. The machine crouched and exploded upward as the dump valves let full pressure into the leg actuators. They cleared the barricade with inches to spare. They didn't clear half a dozen unfortunate Zuul who were behind it. Chuck worked the minigun in a frenzy, firing burst after burst into the troops stationed behind the barricade now that he had a clear shot. Those who got too close were dispatched by the twin blades as they chopped up and down, pretty much the limit of their primitive range of motion, but devastatingly effective when they connected. In moments they were joined by the rest of their group. The Zuul defense crumpled soon after.

* * *

"You guys are effing maniacs, you know that, right?" Buckley said to the pair after the Cavaliers had finished securing the area. "You've gotta have Emperor Mong on speed dial."

"Eh, if it's stupid but it works, it's not stupid," shot back le Roi.

"And let's not forget that business with the claymore," added Jenkins.

"Feh, if it's stupid but it works, it's still stupid. I'm just amazed I came out of this alive. You guys nearly gave me a heart attack."

* * *

Dr. Mauser had partied in college, but even the rowdiest frat party was nothing like a night out celebrating with mercs. Singly and in groups, nearly every Cavalier sought him out to tell him what they thought of the new machines, slap his shoulder, or put another drink in his hand.

Jim Cartwright mounted the stage at the end of the bar and smacked a beer stein with something metal in his hand to get everyone's attention. A respectful silence blanketed the bar. "Just a couple of announcements. I just got off the phone with the hospital, and Lieutenant Buckley is going to pull through. They said he died for about thirty seconds, but you know Joe, he keeps coming back for more. Hopefully he won't have another heart attack when he finds out he's an officer now. In other promotions, Jenkins, le Roi, Callen, and Henderson, congratulations on making sergeant. Peterson, Mulford, and Lazarus, congratulations on advancing to corporal. And congratulations to you all for coming home with zero casualties!" He raised his glass and saluted before taking a drink as the men whooped.

After he descended the stage, Jim sought out Paul and shook his hand. "I just wanted to thank you again for all your hard work. And here's a token of my appreciation." He pressed the metal object into Paul's hand. It was a challenge coin with the logo of Cartwright's Cavaliers impressed on it. "Consider yourself an Honorary Cavalier."

"I don't know what to...Thank you. But you know, there's still a lot of work to be done."

* * *

Block 3 testing was going well. The new batteries were providing better life, and they'd been able to expand the capabilities of the shoulder mounts to add rocket launchers. Paul returned to his office to find three strangers in it, one in a suit, and two in Mitsubishi Security uniforms. The Suit was holding one of his models.

"Uh, that's a rare Strelizia Maquette. They only made a hundred of them."

"Why does this toy robot have tits?"

"It's a Japanese thing. You should see how the pilots drive it. In any case, who are you and what are you doing in my office?"

The suit put down the figure, and Paul released the breath he didn't realize he was holding when it appeared to be undamaged. "Edward Johnson, Corporate Investigations." He handed Paul his card. "When was the last time you saw Yoshihiro Yashimoto?"

Paul had to think for a minute. "In person? Huh, it's been over a month since the Block Three launch meeting. I think I got an e-mail from him on Monday…" He went to his desk. "Where's my computer?"

"That's Mitsubishi's computer, and this is Mitsubishi's office. This facility is being shut down until we can figure out the mess you people have made. How you can show the profits you've been making when you've only shipped two of the product you're supposed to be building in the last two years, and then where the money's gone. The forensic accountants are going to have their hands full untangling this. Apparently Yashimoto has been accepting payments in Galactic Credits instead of electronic transfers, which is against corporate guidelines, and a lot of that money appears to be missing."

"I had no idea…"

"As for this unauthorized program of yours, well, it does seem to be successful, but this is not what Cargo Handling Systems is supposed to be doing. While we're straightening this out, the Defense Systems division will be taking it over. And you'll be on administrative leave. These two gentlemen will be ensuring that you remove your personal property, and *only* your personal property, from this office. Although it appears we'll need some more boxes…and a cart."

"Wait, what?!"

"If it's any consolation, we've already looked into your finances, and you probably won't be implicated, but what's gone on here can't be allowed to continue. We can't have whole divisions deciding willy-nilly to abandon their business and do something else. I'm sure they'll find something else for you to do once our investigation is completed."

Paul was dumbfounded. His guts felt like they were full of ice water. Everything he'd been working on, all the good he was doing, had just been yanked out from under him.

Johnson walked out of the office but turned back at the door. "If Yashimoto does contact you, you have my card. And don't leave Houston; you need to be available for further interviews."

* * *

Chariclo—a "Centaur" Microplanet between Saturn and Uranus.

"That was pretty much the end of it for me. After Defense took over the CASPer production, they just kept cranking out the last block for years. They tried to develop a Mk 2, but it was such a disaster they almost canceled the whole program. I think the project director actually committed ritual suicide."

"That's not a normal Human behavior, not that I've heard of," said the small alien "seated" across from the terribly elderly Paul Mauser.

"It's a Japanese thing. He cost the company a fortune and couldn't stand the humiliation. It was quite the scandal, too. It was almost the end of the CASPer, until Binnig came along and took over the business. The rest is history."

"It's a fascinating history, too. Researching it for this job was very enlightening. Military history is a hobby of mine as well."

"As for me, it turned out Mitsubishi finally had the funds to buy their own ship, and nine months later, I was given a new assignment at Ceres station. I had most of my success with microgravity mining and in-situ refining technology. I hear Jim put in a CASPer museum or something with a Tri-V of me in it, but I've never seen it. I haven't been back to Earth since my accident. I did a lot of work on cybernetic prosthetics, but I never liked them myself. I just prefer it in space. I even bought this science outpost and retired to it. Most people don't even know about the Centaurs. But I love Chariclo in particular because it's the only one with its own ring system."

"It's very unusual, indeed, for such a small body to have rings."

"I like the solitude, and the gravity is so low, there's just enough that things stay where I put them. But these days, it seems like everyone can get anywhere in the solar system in a small ship. Why, a month ago there was a crew doing a documentary for the 60th anniversary of the CASPer who came by for an interview."

"That's actually how I found you. My employer is very keen on having me meet every Human involved in the creation of CASPers."

"Well, I guess you're in luck, I think I may be the last of them."

"Indeed, you're the only one on my list still alive."

Mauser closed his eyes, seemingly lost in thought. A few moments later, he looked at the alien, and asked, "You know, I don't think I've ever seen your species before. What are you called?"

"Very few Humans have. I'm what you call a Depik."

*****

Richard Alan Chandler Bio

Richard Alan Chandler lives in the Pacific Northwest with two incredibly lucky black cats. He's been everything from a Software Developer to a Taxi Driver to an Aviation Machinist. He's been into science fiction since he read his first Heinlein at age nine, and he's been playing at writing for almost as long. This is his first story in the Four Horsemen Universe.

Find him at https://www.amazon.com/Richard-Alan-Chandler/e/B00I3GOHZ2/.

#####

Unnatural Selection by Dan Bridgwater

Jesalic, commander of the Zuul Company KayHan Scout Runners, strode down the ramp of the drop ship and stared into the ruins. Turning his head, he shouted, "Karilisan! On me!" As the younger Zuul caught up, the older looked over his shoulder and continued, "This is your first contract; don't get overwhelmed. The XO is taking the rest of the company to get the camp set up, but your focus is to get into the existing security network and see where we can make it better. The Besquith gave us the mission brief, but I don't think they told us everything."

They'd emerged from hyperspace the previous day and had been contacted by the Besquith liaison, Srentaal. The discussion had focused on the specific requirements of the contract. The Runners would be providing basic security around the camp and on the perimeter of the dig site. Within the camp, things had gone missing. Slates, small boxes that contained recovered artifacts, and even food had gone astray. They had thought it simply a matter of the smaller local fauna, attracted to the new or shiny. But there was never anything on the security footage, and the Besquith themselves never heard or smelled anything that the cameras missed.

"It's all well and good to be hired to provide defensive forces, but they still won't tell us what they're doing here. I want to know."

Jesalic looked around, making sure they were alone. "Now, tell me again what you found out."

"Yes, sir," Karilisan replied. "First, they're not mercs. They seem to be a family unit and, depending on which entry in the Galnet you read, they're either paleontologists or archeologists." He looked at the ancient broken tower that dominated the landscape. "Given where we landed, I'd bet they're trying to find usable Great War tech to sell—either to other Besquith or on the black market."

Jesalic nodded. That last bit matched his own thoughts. He looked out over the existing Besquith camp and snorted. He glanced over to Karilisan and saw the rookie harbored the same doubts about the layout of the camp. "They're so used to being the apex predator," he whispered over to Karilisan, "they really don't know how to do defense. Oh, their professionals *can*, of course. They hate it, but they can. But these guys?" He gestured toward the encampment. "That just sucks. The fields of fire are cluttered, lines of sight are bad or nonexistent, all sorts of dead space, and cover right up to the walls. This isn't even 'I read a manual once' good. Something has them spooked, and they're not talking. It's time to harass Srentaal again."

Coming into the camp, they spotted the Besquith liaison. Jesalic walked over to the Besquith and greeted it with a nod. "Srentaal. We need to talk. My tech," he gestured to Karilisan, "needs access to your network. He must see your security arrangements and audit the archive data."

Srentaal looked irritated by the intrusion. "The alpha has agreed to this, but he," it pointed at Karilisan, "cannot be there unescorted, yes? If he attempts to enter the command center without me, he will be killed, as would any of you should you come in without escort," it warned.

Karilisan's hackles rose. Both races might loosely resemble canines, but if the Zuul were hounds, the Besquith were great dire wolves. Any threat from them was serious.

"Believe me, none of my pack wants your secrets," Jesalic replied soothingly. "My troops will happily patrol outside, but Karilisan hunts his prey in the computers. He can't do that out here. Also, he needs remote access to the cameras and other sensors. I don't care about your dig, but without remote access, there will be a Zuul in your center all day, every day. None of us want that."

Srentaal nodded. "I've spoken to the alpha on this, and she agreed. But just the sensors and the sensor archives. Come." Not watching to see if they followed, Srentaal began to trot toward a metal shipping container near the base of the tower.

Entering the container, Karilisan saw it had been converted into a small command center. Four large monitors above a desk flipped through different views of areas around the camp, and a second desk appeared to have a basic analysis workstation set up. He nodded his head in appreciation. The design was efficient. As he got out his slate and prepared it to integrate into the network, he turned to his commander. "This is good, sir. I'll pull a map of the surrounding area and then build a diagram of the sensor lay-down. Once I get the remote access node up, we'll be able to hit the sensor net from our command tent."

Jesalic nodded. "Good. I need to get back to our camp. The XO will have them working, but I need to set up the patrols. We need to know the area. You can call me if you need to." He paused and looked directly at Karilisan. "I don't expect you to need to." Jesalic turned and was quickly gone from sight.

Karilisan sat at the sensor station and started running the diagnostic and mapping programs. He needed to know where all the sensors were before he could look to improve the layout. He tried to focus on the task at hand, but the presence of the Besquith behind him was too much. Feeling like every hair on his spine was trying to crawl up to his head, he turned to address Srentaal. "So…you've told us of the missing equipment and the failure of the sensors to catch anything; what do you think is going on?"

Srentaal glowered and then shook its head. "At first, like the others, I thought it was some small creature coming into the camp to steal shiny things. But it was never on camera, and most of the local animals stay far from us. They don't taste good, but some of the pack have found it a pleasant diversion to chase and hunt them. So they stay away. No. I think there's something here. Something smart, not an animal. Something smart enough to avoid detection."

Karilisan thought it over. "Smart, you mean sapient? Something from…" He gestured toward the tower.

"Maybe. Some have said natives, but I doubt it. There are no signs beyond small, primitive mammaloids or reptoid life. Some have said pirates seeking to steal our artifacts. If it were pirates, I think they would have attacked us. We're Besquith, but we aren't many. But the possibility of pirates is the reason the alpha decided we needed security. We're too far from Bestald to get a proper Besquith unit, so we hired you." Srentaal paused and then chuckled. "Some of the others think we've angered some ghost or spirit, but that's stupid. No, it's something else, but I don't know what."

The slate beeped. Karilisan turned and saw that it had completed its initial sweep of the sensors. "OK," he began, "it looks like we have three directional listening stations, and nine cameras, although I only show eight displays. Did you know you have a camera down?" he asked, turning back to Srentaal.

"Nine? There are only eight cameras…"

* * *

The discovery of the unknown device brought Jesalic back to the command center, along with the alpha. It was the first time Karilisan had seen the Besquith leader. She was enormous. With her towering over him, Karilisan felt the command center was very small indeed.

"Sir, ma'am," Karilisan said. "Over the last 10 minutes, I've been attempting to access the device. It's acting like a camera, based on the protocols, but the access codes are being refused. I have a couple of programs trying to force access, and we should have something soon."

"Do we know where it is?" asked the alpha, her voice low and harsh.

"No, ma'am. Based on the return times, close, on site, but I should be in momentarily." A beep interrupted him. "We're in." Karilisan checked the slate and turned to the alpha. "With your permission, I'm going to access the feed and put it right here," he said, indicating one of the large monitors.

The alpha nodded.

The monitor blinked and reset. The display showed an image of four figures, two Besquith and two Zuul. Alarmed, Karilisan exclaimed, "It's in the command center!"

The alpha jumped and turned to the corner of the room, looking for the device. "What's the meaning of this?" she barked out angrily. She took two steps toward a blocky brace at the corner of the roof, but there was a pop, and the display went dark.

Karilisan looked down at his slate. "We have a problem."

"What is it?" Jesalic asked, turning toward him.

"The camera was switched off, and the command came from outside the camp."

Both Jesalic and the alpha started, then bolted toward the door as one. As they passed through, Karilisan could hear them speaking into their comms. The alpha's speech was low and growling, but he could clearly understand Jesalic. "All hands! Full alert! Now! I don't care where you are, get back to camp, full armor, heavy loadout. We're about to get it stuck in…" His voice faded as he ran toward the Zuul encampment.

Karilisan headed after him. As he exited the command center, Jesalic turned back.

"No! You have to stay on the sensors! Find him, whoever's doing this! If we're about to get hit, I need you in there to tell us where it's coming from!"

Karilisan stopped at Jesalic's command, and Srentaal ran into him from behind, staggering him. He recovered and said, "But, sir!"

"No! We need eyes, Karil. Get in there and tell me what I need to know."

The alpha faced Srentaal. "You as well; protect the pup." Srentaal started to protest, but was interrupted. "Pack before wolf. Protect him. This is your task."

Srentaal grunted, "Pack before wolf. Yes, Mother." It took Karilisan's arm, herding him back into the command center. Inside, Srentaal released the Zuul.

He looked up. "What now? What do we do? Wait…Mother?"

Srentaal shrugged. "You have your orders, find the intruder."

Karilisan turned toward the workstation. There was a tremendous flash, and the floor struck him.

* * *

Karilisan woke on a hard, smooth surface.

"What? Where…"

He stopped as the pain came flooding in. He raised his hand to his head, but it felt wrong—numb and painful all at once. He squinted down at his hand, forcing himself to focus. It was wrong somehow. He couldn't get the focus right. It was…it was gone. His right hand, gone. His arm ended in a bandaged stump. He wiggled his fingers and could feel them moving, but…nothing. There was no hand there.

He passed out.

When he woke again, he found himself on a rough pallet. The pain in his head seemed less, and his hand…He jerked upright and looked. It was still gone.

"Ah! You're back with us. Good."

Karilisan jumped. The voice had come from above him. Looking around, he realized he was in a small cell separated by bars from the rest of the room. Along the ceiling, he saw a maze of pipes, with several extending down the wall. Among them a deep shadow lurked.

It moved slowly, sliding easily among the pipes. "Yes. You were beginning to bore me and," the voice paused, "we can't have that."

As the shape slid toward him, Karilisan saw what seemed like several ropes trailing behind it, and several that seemed to reach before it. Finally, it emerged.

Wrogul.

Karilisan, his fur standing up, scrambled back into a corner of the small cell. The Wrogul appeared boneless, a dark-colored mass with several manipulating tentacles. Beyond their appearance, no one knew much about them, certainly not more than the Wrogul wanted them to know. They were extraordinary surgeons and scientists, but there were rumors of a more unsavory aspect to their pursuits of knowledge, a lack of morals. The thought of being captive to one, especially one who had placed him in a cell, didn't comfort him.

The Wrogul regarded him thoughtfully. "Relax, my little Zuul," he said. "If I wanted you dead, you would certainly be dead, just like the rest of your little Zuul friends."

Shocked, he tried to push back the fog in his head. All dead? His last memory was of Jesalic, very much alive, telling him to return to the command center. What had happened?

"You look confused. You took a blow to the head, so I'm not surprised. They're dead. All the Zuul, all the Besquith. Once you discovered my camera, I couldn't have them running around looking for me, now could I? They might disrupt the things I'm doing here. So, no, they had to go." The Wrogul gave a lurching sort of shrug and continued, "So I triggered the bombs. I'd placed them in and around the camp. Very thoroughly, I might add. Honestly, their security was a bad joke. Your Zuul friends were less cooperative, making a separate camp, but a couple of armed drones, and that problem went away. Yes, I thought you were all dead until I found you and the gamma." The Wrogul gestured with a tentacle, and Karilisan saw the mound of matted fur in the next cell.

"Srentaal?" he asked.

"Is that its name?" Chromatophores rippled the length of the Wrogul's body, lightening and darkening his skin. "Not really important, I suppose. It was more damaged than you were. You lost a hand and acquired a kind of interesting puncture through your back, very close to the spine." The Wrogul's tone was impersonal, as if he were describing a challenging hunt or a meal. It was an exercise to relieve boredom, or just to see if it could be done—nothing more. "But this one," he gestured toward Srentaal, "it took a chunk of ferro-plas to the skull. Damage to the temporal and parietal lobes, and a bit to the brain stem as well. Just getting it stable enough to move up here was a challenge. That was real fun." Excitement crept into his voice. "And now I have a Besquith to work on!" The Wrogul returned his attention to Karilisan. "Oh, I'm happy to have you, of course. Zuul are interesting in their own way. Pack evolution, large olfactory processing, and yet you still dedicate a good part of the brain to visual processing. That's not always the case in a predator species, you know. Interesting oxygenation index, as well. But Besquith?" The Wrogul actually quivered with delight. "The spinal structure, the muscle and bone density, the resilience of the heart chambers. Amazing! This is going to be so much fun! Oh, and Besquith are trioecious."

Karilisan looked blank.

The Wrogul saw it. "Really? Trioecy? Three sexes? You didn't know this?" His tone became that of a lecturer. "Zuul have two sexes, but Besquith? Females, males and," he gestured toward Srentaal, "gammas, who are neuter, but can become either male or female." The Wrogul pointed a tentacle at the Zuul. "You are male, of course, and functional. It might be interesting to see how a female works out. I'll think about it." He turned away and started to move toward an assortment of lab equipment.

In his befuddled state, Karilisan hadn't noticed much beyond his own cell. He now realized he was being held in a well-equipped laboratory. "Wait. You can't hold us! You must contact the Guild and either release or ransom us."

The Wrogul stopped and turned enough to look back. "Release you? Why would I want to do that? Sleep now."

Something inside Karilisan's neck clicked, there was a stinging pain, and the room faded away.

* * *

Once again, Karilisan woke on the pallet.

"Good! You're back. You need to see this."

Karilisan slowly sat up. It was like moving through mud, and it was hard to think.

"Wh-what? What have you done to me? I feel…wrong." He struggled to a seated position.

The Wrogul swung into view, glancing from the far cell back to Karilisan. "What? Oh, that. You're fine, you've just been unconscious for a bit. About twenty days, in fact. It's just the drugs and the nanites, you'll be fine. But look over here!"

"Wait, what? Twenty days?" He struggled to understand, his brain sluggish and stupid.

"Well, yes, but that isn't important. Look over here!" The Wrogul was focused on the other cell and sounded extremely unconcerned about the Zuul's confusion. "Look at her…" Pride colored the Wrogul's voice.

Karilisan looked through the bars between the two cells. Srentaal was there, but different. The Besquith was changed, recognizable, but larger, much larger than before. Its fur was darker and glossier, and where before it had outweighed him by possibly one hundred pounds, now it would outweigh him easily by at least a two hundred pounds or more. "What have you done to it?"

"Her," the Wrogul corrected. "As a gamma, she was supremely uninteresting. But as an alpha?" Once again, the Wrogul sounded proudly possessive. He turned to the Zuul. "You need to understand what I've done here. When I found you two, you were bleeding out. This one was as good as clinically dead. With the damage to her brain stem, her heart was just a spasming muscle. I stabilized that. I stopped your bleeding. I stopped her aneurism. I got you both up here alive. That is amazing! You need to be more appreciative!"

Looking back at the Besquith, he continued, "But now, instead of the simple gamma, we have an alpha. Bigger. Stronger. I triggered the transformation with tailored nanites and some hormones. Once I recovered the body of the previous alpha, it was relatively simple. Not easy, you understand, but straightforward. So now we have an alpha to play with. This is so much better."

The Wrogul paused for a moment and then added, "I'm thinking of growing my own pack. First Besquith show up, and then Zuul. If I'm going to continue my work, I need privacy. I'll have to think about it." He looked at Karilisan. "What do you think? A group of cloned Besquith for guards?" The Wrogul continued without waiting for a response, "I'd have to adapt them a bit. And of course, there would be some behavioral issues. The rage." He muttered to himself as he swung back to his equipment. "Besquith have pack loyalty. I may need to try to tweak that. I need them to be loyal to *me*. There's the size to consider as well…maybe a bit smaller? Smaller would be easier to control."

Karilisan, stunned, scanned the room. He needed to escape…somehow. The Wrogul was insane. He and Srentaal weren't sapients to this mad scientist, only lab animals. He watched the Wrogul settle in at his computer and spotted a familiar shape on the table. His slate sat next to a pile of electronics from the Besquith camp. If he could access the slate, he might be able to break out, or at least send out a distress call. He tried to use his pinplants to access it.

"Ah-ah-ah! I see what you're doing," The Wrogul turned to look back at the Zuul. "I'm in your pinplants, of course, and I see you trying to get out. I've put some of my own programming in there, so don't make me do something you'll regret…like this, for instance!"

Karilisan screamed as the stump of his arm erupted in pain. He clutched it to his chest, frantic for the sensation to stop.

"I patched you up," the Wrogul said flatly. "I had a good look at all those exposed nerves in your arm, as well as access to your 'plants. Don't screw around. In fact, I'm going to be busy for a bit, so why don't you go to sleep?"

Once again he heard a click and felt a sting in his neck, and the room went blessedly dark.

* * *

Karilisan woke up back on the pallet. He hissed with the effort of trying to sit up. Everything hurt. It wasn't like before, when he was just sluggish and groggy. It wasn't general pain, either, but sharp and specific. Coin-sized spots burned on both biceps, both forearms, several spots on both sides of his ribcage, and both thighs. Finally, his head ached with pressure that felt like it was going to split his skull.

"You may be feeling some discomfort," the Wrogul said, drawn by the hiss. "I imagine at the very least, you have a headache."

Karilisan growled a threat under his breath, just audible to the Wrogul.

"Fair enough," he said, raising two tentacles in acknowledgement. "I did some work while you were out, and I wanted to thank you."

"What?" Karilisan was confused. What had the Wrogul done?

"If you remember, we were talking about growing some Besquith for my security forces."

"We weren't talking," the Zuul ground out. It hurt to breathe. "You were babbling. You're insane, and when I get out, I'm going to tear you apart."

The Wrogul stopped what he was doing and moved over to the cell. He looked down at his captive. "You need to understand something, Zuul." The Wrogul's cold voice was full of malice. "Your continued existence is a courtesy. I enjoy having someone to talk to, and, based on your actions in the security hut, you seem smart enough to appreciate what I'm doing here."

Karilisan glared up at him. "And what," he asked through gritted teeth, "have you been doing in these ruins that's so important?"

Colors rippled through the Wrogul's skin. "What, the ruins?" Surprise tinged his response. "Oh, no. That's just messing with Great War stuff." He waved a tentacle dismissively. "Boring. Lucrative, but boring. No. What I'm doing now is much more interesting. Remember how we were talking about breeding some Besquith?" The Wrogul paused, almost like he expected an answer. "This is so much better than that. She's pregnant, and you are going to be the daddy!"

"What?" Karilisan sputtered. "What are you talking about? We aren't even the same species!"

The Wrogul waved away his protest. "That's not a problem. See, the Besquith have some traits I wasn't interested in. Too big, too psychotic, and entirely too likely to turn on me. After I looked her over genetically, I saw where I could make some improvements, and that's where you come in."

"No, still not following," Karilisan shook his head. "We are not genetically compatible. Not the same species. We can't."

Excited, the Wrogul started flashing along his tentacles. "You can't under normal circumstances," he agreed. "And that's where I come in." The Wrogul was actually twitching with pleasure. "While you were out, I took the liberty of getting some samples from you—muscle tissue, lung tissue, heart tissue. I even got a few fresh brain and spinal cells. Nothing you'd miss!" he added hastily. "From that material, I could see where you, as a species, had some characteristics that could really improve the basic genome, if we could get it to take. Your nerve tissue, for example, actually has a more efficient chemical matrix than the Besquith, and you have better fast-twitch muscles. As a species, Zuul intellect isn't all that much better, but your brain is above average, and we can use that. Obviously we couldn't do straight fertilization, so I obtained some gamete cells from some of the Besquith betas I recovered."

"You took the bodies?" Karilisan asked, horror in his voice.

"Well, yes…how do you think I got the alpha hormones? I've kept several in cryo, Besquith and Zuul both. No cellular decay at all, practically pristine! And in you," the Wrogul continued happily, "I have a live donor, which is even better!" He paused, waiting for acknowledgement. When he got none, he continued, "Anyway, after I completed DNA mapping the samples I got from you, I stripped out some of the corresponding material from the Besquith gametes and put yours in. Easy! After that, it was a matter of getting some zygotes to take. There were a lot of fails, but I only needed a few, and once I had them, I implanted them into our dear, sweet Srentaal. Congratulations! You're going to be a dad!"

* * *

Srentaal had been returned to her cell. For the first time since their capture, Karilisan saw her conscious.

"Srentaal," he hissed across from his cell. "Are you alright?"

"Who calls?" came the low growl. Karilisan backed up a little. There was an unmistakable note of hostility in her voice.

"It's me, Karilisan," he replied.

"You are Zuul. I know no Zuul," Srentaal growled.

"I should probably warn you," came the voice of the Wrogul, "she has some damage to the brain from before, remember? It's apparently interfering with her recall."

Karilisan moved toward the bars separating him from Srentaal. Suddenly the Besquith lunged, and a great clawed hand shot through the bars, barely missing him as he jumped back.

"Oh, and anger issues," the Wrogul added. "Lots and lots of anger issues. I think I mentioned there was damage to the temporal and parietal lobes, or the Besquith equivalent. That interferes with the memory and with emotional processing. I wouldn't sleep too close to her cell."

"Why is it still a problem? Why didn't you fix it?"

"Fix it?" The Wrogul hesitated, and lights trickled across his body. "Well, I suppose I could have, but it didn't really occur to me." He paused to consider the idea and dismissed it. "But really, brain reconstruction? Not interested and a waste of nanites."

"What? You could've healed it, and you didn't?" Karilisan was stunned by the Wrogul's admission.

"That's what I just said, isn't it?" Now the Wrogul sounded annoyed. "Why should I? That isn't what I'm working on, and it would have been a waste of my resources." With that, he reached into the pipes and started toward the exit. "Remember what I said. Don't get too relaxed if you're in her reach." And he was gone.

"Zuul." The growl interrupted his thoughts. Karilisan turned to Srentaal.

"Zuul," came the growl again. "Who? Are you?" The speech was broken, slurred. Like someone drunk or coming out of anesthesia. "I should…know you. Your smell. I…know it."

"I'm Karilisan. You know me. You and I worked together to defend your pack. Do you remember the Command Center? The camp?"

"Camp. Yes. Old dig. Old tech." Srentaal rumbled to herself. "Scent…I know it."

"Try to remember," Karilisan said. "Your alpha assigned you to protect me."

"Alpha? Alpha…Mother." There was a low, sad rumbling from Srentaal's chest, and in that note, everything came crashing into Karilisan. His hand, the loss of his friends, his unit…and how much worse for Srentaal? The Besquith pack they'd been hired to help was a *family unit*, beings she'd known her entire life. A quiet keening joined the rumble, and he realized it came from him.

* * *

Days passed, and they woke to find themselves still in separate cells, but now in a much larger room, at least forty feet long and half that wide. It had a tall opening, a window that had once contained glass, running its length. After the lab, the sunlight was nearly blinding.

"What's going on?" Karilisan asked, shielding his eyes.

"Natural light is better," the Wrogul's voice came from the ceiling where, once again, multiple pipes ran the length and breadth of the room. "Now that Srentaal is in a more advanced stage of pregnancy, we want better light, yes? Better for the brood…"

"What do you mean, 'advanced?' It's only been a few days," the Zuul protested.

"Actually, it's been thirty-five days. You were…unconscious for part of it. Plus, I'm helping her along. A normal Besquith pregnancy would last most of a year, and I'm not that patient. I accelerated the growth before I even implanted the embryos. I've also designed a hormone cocktail to help things along. It won't be great for her, but it'll work out."

A low growl had begun building in Srentaal's chest. It burst out in a howl as she threw herself against the bars of her cell, scrambling to reach the Wrogul. "I'll kill you!" she screamed. The bars vibrated under her assault. "I…tear…eat you…" As her anger waxed, she grew more incoherent, finally attempting to bite through the bars with her massive jaws. Suddenly she stopped, her eyes glazed. The growls and snarls lost their power as she began to slide down the bars. "Kill…you…"

The Wrogul observed dispassionately from his perch in the pipes as the Besquith folded into a heap, unconscious. The Wrogul turned an eye to Karilisan. "Obviously I've had the same access to her and her 'plants as I've had to you. A simple matter to administer a little sedative to calm her down." He seemed to think about it a little more. "You know, I hate to admit it, but you may've been right." He turned his full regard to the Zuul. "Besquith are always psychotic, but you add the damage to the parietal lobe on top of that? It might have been worth it to repair the damage, or do some work suppressing the amygdala. That would have hobbled the reaction, minimized it. In her current state? If she had anger issues before, well, they're nothing compared to what's going on now." He considered a moment, then sighed. "No, too late to fix. Any intrusive measures would risk the pregnancy, and I don't want to start over. We'll just have to get through it."

Crossing back to the Zuul's cell, he returned to his previous topic. "We were talking about the timeline. Between the work I did before the implantation and the assistance I'm giving her now, I expect we'll be looking at delivery in about three months. If I had to really get fine-tuned on it, probably just a little less. Part of this will depend on the viability of the pups. Besquith generally throw about five to seven, but I put in ten fertilized embryos. I don't expect them all to go to term, but the more that do, the more likely it'll be sooner rather than later. With that in mind, we'll need to set up a nest or, what do you call it? A den? This room will serve. But as the daddy, the least you can do is help. I'm going to allow you out to assist me, but don't get any ideas. In fact, let me remind you…"

A tickling itch started in the Zuul's stump. It rapidly became painful and suddenly…stopped.

"Like I said, between the nanites and your 'plants…'" The Wrogul paused. "It would be the simplest thing in the world to fry your mind with the pain, so it'd be best for everyone if you refrained from any stupidity."

* * *

It had taken weeks, but the room was becoming much more livable. Initially, Karilisan would wake to find a stack of extruded clear plassteel, and he worked to replace the window panes. He hated this task from day one when he realized they were being held in the upright base of the broken tower. A wave of vertigo washed over him every time he looked out over the 100 feet of empty air between him and solid ground. His skin crawled when he looked out the windows, and struggling to position the plassteel with only one hand left him exhausted.

The Wrogul tasked Karilisan with other jobs around his lair. He would remove food waste, dispose of broken lab equipment, perform maintenance on the hydroponics bay, and other dirty tasks the Wrogul didn't want to do. But it was while doing these chores that Karilisan found something that convinced him they had a chance of escape.

He was pushing a cart down a hallway when he stopped at the open door of a small room and noticed a pile of machined metal and electronic debris. At first he wasn't sure why he'd stopped, but like a blurry picture coming into focus, he suddenly realized the lettering on the metal plates was Besquith script. This wasn't ancient, broken tech. This was material recovered from the camp. After a glance down the hallway to make sure he wasn't being observed, he stepped into the room to try to search for something—anything—useful.

He was sorting through a box of loose wires when he saw it. Partially concealed under a shred of a tarp, the thin rectangle filled him with the first real hope he'd had since his capture. His slate. A familiar discoloration down one edge, the result of a plasma circuit shorting entirely too close when he was repairing a LIDAR emitter, confirmed it. He grabbed it, concealed it under his shirt, and returned to his cart.

Several days passed before he had an opportunity to examine his prize. The Wrogul had announced that he needed to acquire some samples of local fauna to further his experiments. Since he didn't trust either the Zuul or the Besquith while he was out, they would be confined to their separate cells for the day.

Karilisan waited for more than an hour before he felt confident the Wrogul had truly left. He pulled the slate from its concealment, hunched himself into a corner, and draped a blanket over his shoulders to block his actions from the camera.

He remembered the Wrogul's reaction the first time he'd tried to access his slate and manually deactivated pinplant access. He then disabled non-manual input and limited output to the 2D screen. He'd spent several days thinking about his best course of action, and he began to construct an infiltration program that would allow him to quietly snoop on the Wrogul's network. Once he knew its shape, he could hack his way into it.

The Wrogul was brilliant, but his intelligence was specific. He was a master of biological and life sciences, yet his network equipment seemed to be generic rather than purpose-built. His investigations into recovered Great War artifacts seemed to rely on examination of the object, followed by extensive search protocols through a Galnet database seeking similar items. He was a tech user, not a developer, and that reliance on off-the-shelf solutions had made it simple for Karilisan to initially detect the Wrogul's camera and then crack the security that had been placed on it. After working with the Wrogul over the last weeks, he suspected the network would have a single significant defense, but once past that, access would be open. The infiltration program he had in mind wouldn't be greatly different from some of the diagnostic tools already on the slate, just much, much harder to detect. First he'd build the program, then he'd worry about how he was going to plant it on the network.

* * *

About a month later, the 'den' was complete. Karilisan had cleared the debris and replaced all the windows. With the limited equipment the Wrogul had provided, Karilisan had been forced to use a chemical bonding agent that would need months to fully set, rather than a fusing tool that would bond the window to the frame at a molecular level. The Wrogul had stated the local climate was quite mild, and he felt little need to expend materials for anything stronger or faster.

His last task had been to run two additional cameras that focused on the area where the Wrogul expected the birthing to occur. He carefully adjusted the angles to ensure that, with their limited panning function, they wouldn't be able to observe his cell. As part of the work, Karilisan had been allowed access to the data runs and associated equipment. The Wrogul, confident of his complete access to Karilisan's pinplants, felt there was no danger in allowing the Zuul to work on the network. If Karilisan hadn't found the slate, he'd have been right. Once he had the parasite leads, he'd be able to directly jack into the data runs and insert the slate behind the network's primary intrusion defense. There would be almost no chance of detection.

* * *

About a week later, the Wrogul addressed Karilisan.

"I don't think this first batch is doing well."

"What?"

"The pregnancy. I don't think it's going well," the Wrogul repeated. "Of the ten implants, several seem to have stopped growing, and the ones that are, well, they aren't growing very fast." The Wrogul was silent for most of a minute. He came back across the room to regard Karilisan. "We'll see what comes of this litter, but I don't think your genes are adding too much to the mix. I'm going to have to go back to a purer strain for my little project." With that, he left the room.

After a few moments, Srentaal rose from her pallet and looked across at him. "Be careful, Karlsan..." She rumbled, slurring his name. "You are pack, must protect pack."

"I don't understand..."

The great Besquith pressed her forehead against the bars. Despite the time that had passed since their capture, she'd spoken very little, the damage to her brain making it difficult to find the right words. "Did you not listen?" She paused, looking into the Zuul's eyes. "The Wrogul said you are not useful."

* * *

A few days later, Karilisan was woken by an insistent buzz. Apparently the Wrogul was going to remote in today. He got up and stepped out of the cell, where the camera could pick him up.

"What do you want?"

"I have some things I need to do in the main lab," the Wrogul said, "but I want you to organize some of the gene samples I left there last night. If you look over at the long table in front of Srentaal's cell, you'll see what I'm talking about."

He moved to the indicated table. "I see them. What do you want me to do with them?"

"Well, about that…" came the Wrogul's voice.

There was a faint buzz and click behind him. As he turned, he saw the door to Srentaal's cell swing open. The Besquith started to rise. "Wrogul, Srentaal's cell is open." Karilisan said quietly, his instincts screaming.

"Yes. And she's likely to be quite angry," the Wrogul said in an insincerely sad voice. "I'm afraid her limbic system and amygdala have been stimulated by her malfunctioning pinplants all night, and she may be beyond control, but let's see what happens."

Srentaal suddenly lunged forward, and the Zuul barely evaded her grab. He dropped to the floor and scuttled to the other side of the table, hoping to keep its mass between them. When he came back up, he was looking directly into the maddened eyes of the Besquith. "Srentaal! Get a hold of yourself!" he cried out. Again he had to dodge, as massive claws ripped through the space where his head had been. Srentaal's low, gurgling growl followed him as he ran toward the door.

"Ah-ah-ah, my little Zuul! The doors are locked. You're trapped in there with the raging Besquith! Maybe you can take her! Make a fight of it!" the Wrogul's voice taunted from the speakers. There might exist somewhere an exceptionally large and dangerous adult Zuul who could take an exceptionally small and weak adult Besquith in hand-to-hand combat, but that hardly mattered. Karilisan was not that Zuul, and there were no circumstances where Srentaal could be mistaken for anything other than extremely dangerous.

Karilisan looked for anything to use as a weapon, but there was nothing. Behind him, he could hear the lab table and other equipment crashing into walls as the enraged Besquith threw objects out of her path. In a fit of desperation, he dove into Srentaal's cell, hooking the door behind him. He turned to try to brace it, and the Besquith bounded forward. She stopped, reached one hand to the bars, and wrenched it open with such force Karilisan felt like his arms were being pulled from their sockets.

She stalked into the cell and backed him into the corner. He raised his arms, but she swatted them down with numbing force, wrapped both hands around his neck, and lifted him off his feet. The claws on her thumbs cut into the muscles around his neck and collarbone as she forced his head to face her. Looking into her eyes, he saw the black pits of her pupils had all but consumed her irises. She panted hard, drool slavering between her fangs. Rage played across her face, her lips drawn back revealing the jagged teeth of an alpha predator. She trembled with suppressed effort.

"N-no," she gritted out. "Nooo! Pack…you. Are pack…" She paused, swallowing. "Pack…before…wolf. Must…protect pack." She continued to breathe heavily, spittle flying out of her muzzle. "Pack," she said again. He felt his feet touch the floor as her claws withdrew, and a trickle of blood flowed down his chest. Her hands relaxed, now just resting on his shoulders. He looked into her eyes again and saw tears. "Mother said protect," she whispered.

"How interesting," came the voice from the speakers. "I honestly thought she was going to eat you, Zuul." The speaker clicked off.

"It's no good," Srentaal whispered. For once, the words seemed to flow. "He's in my head, in my 'plants. I can never be free. Even if we could escape. No matter where we ran, he would still be in our heads. We must kill him here, or die."

* * *

Karilisan was woken by grunts and whines coming from the other cell. "Srentaal…what is it? Are you all right?" he whispered across the gap between the cells.

"It…is time," came the hissing response.

In his sleep-befuddled state, he failed to make the connection. "Time? Time for what?"

The lights came up, and the Wrogul swung into the room. "You're an idiot," he said flatly to Karilisan. "Labor has begun, a bit earlier than I expected, I admit, but since this is the very first instance of a Zuul-Besquith accelerated pregnancy, I think I can be cut a little slack."

"Wh-what?" Karilisan stammered.

"You know, I'd read that the males of many species are often stunned insensible during the birthing; I just never expected to witness it," the Wrogul said, one eye regarding the Zuul with faint contempt. "Snap out of it, idiot. You might want to be useful here."

There was a buzz and two clicks, and the doors to both cages swung open. Srentaal started to get up, but the Wrogul said, "I don't think so. In fact, it might be better if you were a little more relaxed for this."

One hand rose to her neck, and Srentaal slowly lowered herself to the floor, her eyes becoming glassy.

"I only hit her with a little sedative," the Wrogul said. "It's better if she's awake, but I don't need her to get excited while I'm in here. She might do something rash. As it is, I'll be able to use my pinplants to monitor her vitals, as well as trigger the nanites I have in her if we need to take any more aggressive steps."

He paused and appeared to be consulting his link for information. "Things look good. I haven't got clear readings on the fetuses, but everything else has been going well. Get comfortable, Zuul. Besquith labor can take a day or more."

* * *

In the end, it took less than two hours.

Karilisan, utterly drained, leaned his weight on the bars of his cell, his head resting against them. In the darkness, he could hear Srentaal keening her grief. The birthing hadn't gone well. Of the ten embryos implanted, eight had been stillborn, and another died soon after. As for the tenth...the little pup was a fighter. Smaller than a normal Besquith at birth, but clearly larger than a Zuul pup, it had come out mewling and struggling, as if trying to get to its feet from the moment it emerged. The Wrogul had perched in the pipes, watching. When it was clear that the birthing was complete, he ordered Karilisan into his cell and sedated Srentaal. He then gathered up all the pups, the one living and all the rest, and left the cell, closing the door behind him. When Karilisan saw that he was taking the live one as well, he struggled against the bars of the cell, but to no avail. The Wrogul left without a word.

When Srentaal regained consciousness, she asked the Zuul what had happened. She knew she was no longer pregnant but could remember nothing of the event. Telling her had been among the most painful things Karilisan had ever done, and the news that one pup had survived only threw her into a deeper grief when she realized the Wrogul had taken it.

* * *

Karilisan began his work to escape in earnest. He completed his infiltration program and built the parasite leads he needed to jack into the network. Now all he needed was the opportunity.

He began to fear the opportunity wouldn't come. The Wrogul had been absent from the den since the birth. While an occasional absence wasn't unusual, Karilisan could only remember one time the Wrogul had missed two days in a row. Now they were on the fourth day. Karilisan had prepared for almost any eventuality, but he hadn't considered they might be abandoned in their cells. On the morning of the fifth day, the door to the den opened, and the Wrogul entered. An autocart followed behind him.

"Well, it is interesting, and it still holds some promise," the Wrogul stated as he assumed his perch in the pipes. "Some of the desired traits didn't take. The Besquith genetics…well, it looks like some of the chromosomal patterns overwrote the Zuul characteristics." The Wrogul paused and looked at both the Besquith and then the Zuul, the disappointment evident. "But some traits took, so it's not a complete failure, just—not the complete success we were hoping for."

He keeps saying 'we,' Karilisan thought to himself, glaring. The Wrogul was the only willing participant in this nightmare; Srentaal and Karilisan were being used as source material for a twisted experiment.

The Wrogul sent the autocart over to Srentaal's cell, and Karilisan saw that it carried a small, dark ball of fur. Srentaal stood, gently reached through the bars, and lifted the furball to her chest. She turned away, slowly beginning to rock and hum.

"I expect you to care for it now," the Wrogul said to Srentaal's back. "It's your responsibility. You'll tell me if there's anything needed to keep it alive." He turned and slid over to Karilisan and said quietly, "I thought about putting it down, of course, but then it occurred to me that Srentaal needed something to, well, ensure good behavior. The pup is perfect. For the Besquith, the mother instinct is undeniable. Zuul are rational, and you'll accept the situation, but a Besquith? No, she needed something more. I need to go; I have other things I need to work on." He headed toward the exit and continued to himself, "I think I'll end up having to go with pure Besquith if I'm going to get a guard force. We'll just have to work on that pack loyalty…" the voice went on until cut off by the door closing behind the Wrogul.

There was a buzz and a click, and both cell doors opened. Karilisan quickly moved over to the other cell. "Srentaal? Let me see," he said quietly.

She turned, and for the first time since he'd woken in the cells, Karilisan saw a look of peace in her eyes. There were lines there, but she seemed almost relaxed. In her arms the small bundle of fur moved, resting against her ribs. He could see the chest expanding, contracting, as the tiny pup breathed.

"Look," she whispered. She turned it onto its back in her arms, and its paws waved as if in protest at being disturbed. "Small…but strong."

Something heaved in the Zuul's chest. He looked down on this new life, and his heart, thudding in his ears, threatened to deafen him. However strange a path it had taken, this life, this fusion of Besquith and Zuul, of Srentaal and Karilisan, was his. His responsibility, his pack, his pup. His decision was made.

He quickly turned, striding back into his cell to retrieve the slate. It was time. He'd had the last five days to think about it and knew exactly what needed to be done. There was a data run and an access node behind one of the monitors. Grabbing some adhesive tape from the lab table, he stepped over to the monitor. Reaching under and behind it, he attached the two parasite leads to the cabling and activated the infiltrator program. He verified the dataflow, and then secured the slate between the monitor and the wall. The Wrogul would have to crawl behind the monitor to have any chance of seeing it.

He then went to the Besquith and told her his plan. He'd allow the slate to map out the facility, as well as the surrounding area, if possible. The Wrogul had to have some significant transport capability, at the very minimum a shuttle. Once they knew where it was, they could steal it and head for the stargate. If there wasn't a ship to attach to, they could bribe the gatemaster to smuggle out a message. He'd seen enough of the recovered artifacts to know that he could easily proffer a significant bribe—something that would cause even a jaded Sumatozou to sit up and take notice.

He'd hoped he could raise Srentaal's morale, but she looked up from the pup and smiled sadly at him. "Not work, packmate." She was losing some of the words again. "Cannot leave. With him. Alive. In our heads, in our 'plants." She shook her head. "Not free until Wrogul dies."

He sat heavily on the pallet next to her. She was right. They could get out of the tower and halfway to their theoretical ride out, and the Wrogul could just shut them down through their compromised pinplants as quick as a thought. They were still trapped.

* * *

A few days later, the Wrogul came in to examine the pup. After taking some measurements, he cleaned his work area and secured his tools into a locking container. "I think that's enough for today," he said to the Besquith. "The pup seems to be growing quite fast, but other than that, it appears fairly normal. In fact, it's showing some very promising and unexpected traits. Once it gets a little more mass on it, we should be able to do some testing."

Srentaal answered with a low growl.

"Oh, relax," the Wrogul said, waving a tentacle dismissively. "I'm talking about measurements and reaction times. OK, maybe some blood draws, but that's completely normal! It probably happens back home all the time on Besto, or whatever your homeworld is. Normal examinations for offspring!"

"As for you..." he turned to Karilisan. "I'll be spending the afternoon at the dig. I found some interesting crystals down there that could be a data storage system. You have rations and water in here. Finish cleaning the work areas. I'll probably be back tomorrow."

The Wrogul left, and Karilisan waited half an hour before retrieving the slate. He quickly queried the infiltration program, which had made short work of the security on most of the databases. There were two areas still blocking access, Security Systems and Slate. With a start, he realized Srentaal was looking over his shoulder.

"Karsan," she said, slurring through his name again. "Sec'rity S'tems." Security Systems. "Locks."

She was right. Control of the Security Systems at minimum would give him the doors, and probably the cameras as well. Once he had that, he could get physical access to anything else he needed, and that would get them out. "I'll need to write another program," he told her. 'Security Systems' and 'Slate' had stopped the infiltrator cold. "Now that I have access, we can use his own systems to burn through a lot faster than we could before." He started organizing his thoughts. First he'd need to break the lockout, then he'd need to map out the Security database, and finally gain control of the doors and locks. It looked pretty straightforward, and he could grab sections of the code he'd written before.

"Weapons," Srentaal stated. She was right. There was no doubt they'd need weapons, as well. They had to drop the Wrogul before he realized what had happened. If he had so much as one clear instant of thought to recognize the threat, his access to their pinplants would stop them. To attack the Wrogul without weapons would be a death sentence.

He looked over at the Besquith, and he could see it in her eyes as well. There was no escape possible, especially with the pup, while the Wrogul lived. The eye contact was broken by a snuffling bark. The puppy was awake, and Srentaal glided back into her cell. "Have you named it yet?' he asked.

"Him. It is male. For Besquith, pups are all born gammas, and selection comes later. But not this one. He," she said, emphasizing the word, "is unique." She paused. "His name must honor us both, both our clans, both our species. It's important, and I must think on it. But soon."

Karilisan suddenly realized, whenever she spoke of the pup, her language problems almost completely disappeared. She returned to her cell, and Karilisan returned to his programming. Hours later, he put the slate down on the table. His mind was numb from the work, and he turned toward his own cell.

Srentaal saw his movement and asked, "What progress?"

"It's going." He shrugged. "I think I have it all in place, but I'm exhausted. I'm making mistakes. Right now I've got it attacking the Security System locks, and once we're through there, it'll start working on the door controls. But I'm forgetting something, and I'm too tired to see it. I need to lay down for a few minutes and think about something else."

"I have a name."

"What?"

"A name. One to honor us both. Taali-kar. He is already unique, but he is both of us. Taali-kar."

"Srentaal, he's beautiful."

* * *

The Zuul woke on his pallet and saw they weren't alone. The Wrogul moved through the bars and pipes of the den, and occasionally paused to check various projects.

The Wrogul looked over. "Ah! You're awake! I may actually take you outside tomorrow. I've found some items that would certainly be easier to move if there were two of us." The Wrogul continued to swing through, stopping in front of his cage for a moment and then moving over to Srentaal's.

"I see the pup is still alive. I think it will probably be sterile, but it might be worth the effort to harvest some genetic material. No telling what we might be able to gain."

Karilisan stood and leaned against the cell door. Locked. It wasn't really surprising. He doubted the Wrogul would be in here if he hadn't secured the cells first. He leaned into the bars and relaxed. "What have you found?" he asked.

"I'm not sure. It looks like part of an emitter array. It has a focusing dish. It could be communications, but it could be a weapon." The Wrogul had swung over the table in front of Srentaal's cell and continued to chatter, partly to Karilisan, partly to himself.

The Zuul started to tune him out. His eyes wandered and stopped on the slate. He'd left it out on the table. The Wrogul hadn't noticed it yet, but would that last? The adrenaline surge made it hard to think. He had to get the Wrogul away from it, and out of the den! "I worked on emitters!" he said quickly. "All the time! That might be something. I mean, I did operations, maintenance, installs...I know 'em!"

The Wrogul turned and worked his way back toward the Zuul's cell. Stopping above him, he said, "Really? That might make you useful, after all. This could be good news for both of us, because frankly, you haven't shown much value lately. I was..."

The slate beeped, and the Wrogul froze.

He turned and swung back across the den. "What's this? This shouldn't be here! What are you trying to do?" Hanging down over the slate, he turned back to Karilisan. "I see. Now that I query the systems, I can even see what you've been up to, you stupid little Zuul. I think it's time for you to die..."

The slate beeped again, and the Besquith's cell door swung open. Srentaal burst through the door and struck the Wrogul in a blur. Midflight she started to howl, and Karilisan joined her, fire in his brain and his missing hand as the Wrogul lashed out through the pinplants. Besquith and Wrogul tumbled through the air and struck a window, breaking it from the frame. They fell through and… Karilisan passed out.

* * *

He woke to a blinding, spiking headache. He rose, growling, and clutched his hand and stump to the sides of his head, trying to hold his skull together. Something was different. A smell of outside. A breeze. He looked up and across the den. He realized his door was open, and he was alone. He staggered across the room, heading for the opening where a window used to be. As he drew close, he hesitated. He didn't want to look, but he had to. He had to know. He stepped to the window and looked down.

He could just make out the bodies below. Neither had survived the fall. Srentaal's words echoed in his mind, "He's in my head, in my 'plants. I can never be free…we must kill him here, or die."

She had found her freedom and given him his.

The slate beeped again. He stared at it for a full minute, mind hardly working, before walking across to it. He looked at the readout. The network was completely open to him now. As suspected, the Wrogul had a transport. The slate database listed the specifics of a shuttle and a ship in orbit. A ship large enough to use stargates.

Karilisan looked out the window again. He was free. He had a way home. All of it a gift from Srentaal.

A quiet *wuffing* from her cell drew his attention. Out of the rags a small head appeared, yawning. The pup.

Karilisan crossed the room and gathered the pup into his arms. "Little Taali-kar, Srentaal's final gift. Come. Let us go," he whispered. "When you're older, I'll tell you of your mother…"

The Zuul left the den, cradling his son in his arms.

* * * * *

Dan Bridgwater Bio

Some of Dan's earliest memories include watching Godzilla movies and Star Trek re-runs on television. This love of monster movies and TV SciFi eventually led to his reading just about every bit of science fiction and fantasy he could get his hands on. An Army Brat and a Marine Veteran, Dan has lived on both coasts, the Midwest, Korea, and Kuwait. He now lives with his wife and daughters in Colorado, where he supports training for the US Military.

# # # # #

Fire from Fire Quickened
by Rob Howell

"Sell me the *African Queen*," I said to Peacemaker Rhan'Tlanit'Tala, my new boss.

The Cochkala blinked, and a message icon appeared on my pinplant. "Read that first."

It was a bill of sale showing a "Casablanca Enterprises" had acquired the ship.

"Who's Casablanca Enterprises?" I asked.

"You are." He flicked his tail in his race's form of a shrug. "Or rather, you have controlling interest."

"I don't recall being part of such a firm."

"I may not have your skills with electronic intelligence, Mr. Blaine, but being a Peacemaker has some power."

"How much money do I owe you?"

He named a figure. "However, I'll waive that if you pay for the upkeep, fuel, and crew costs for two years of service as a Peacemaker. It'll look better that way, anyway."

"And who are the other investors?"

"Myself and Kiial."

"He has no idea about this either, does he?"

"My nephew performed well, by all respects. It wouldn't do for his actions to go unrewarded. On GrBatch, any recognition given to him by the Foresters would be irrelevant. An uncle opening up a

Galactic corporation and giving him stock, on the other hand, is a clear sign among Cochkala of approval."

"Does that mean you approve of me?"

"I do, though I didn't make this arrangement entirely for your benefit."

"You expected me to accept your offer."

"Yes. We're going after Kukuluki the Zuparti, a task for which you'll be very useful. He has much to answer for."

I shook my head. "I'm going after HR."

"HR?"

"The people who killed my old boss."

"Ah, yes. HR. Human Resources, correct?"

"Yes."

"What a horribly inappropriate name for them, should my data prove correct."

"And what does your data tell you?"

"It tells me that the Peacemaker Guild wishes to avoid provoking them."

"The *Guild* wishes to avoid them?" My mouth dropped open.

"Yes. There are hints that Galactic influences controlled those behind your previous employer. Powerful influences."

"Hints such as?"

He pointed his tail at my sweeper. "Such as that technology."

I glanced at it. "Bullitt was a genius."

"Not that much. Your sweeper has technology the Information Guild possesses. Many steps beyond Human technology, even for a genius."

"He was a good man. He didn't deserve to die that way."

"Good beings often die, usually in a way they shouldn't. Such things are not necessarily the concern of the Peacemakers."

"I can't just let it go."

"And I can't, as a Peacemaker, assign you to cases which are not within the jurisdiction of our Guild."

"Then what do you want me to do?" I snarled. "As a Peacemaker."

"What is it you already do?" He flicked his tail about. "What was that phrase your former employer used?"

"We deal in elint, friend."

"And that's exactly what I want you to do for me. You're to return to Earth and see what you can discover about Captain Gregg."

I cocked my head. "He, too, is a good man. How's Gregg a concern of the Peacemakers where Bullitt is not? Has he dropped a missile from over ten miles up or released some sort of bioweapon I'm unaware of?"

"No. He's done nothing to warrant the attention of the Peacemakers in any legal sense. However, we know someone threatened his mother to prompt his betrayal of the Foresters on Peninnah, and we know Kukuluki was behind that attack. We also have evidence that Kukuluki attacked my nephew during his training, and *that* is definitely something the Peacemakers care about. How can we do our jobs if our families are held hostage?"

"You want me to use Gregg to get to Kukuluki."

"Yes."

"And you don't care about Captain Gregg."

"I don't. I care only about the Zuparti, who I'll investigate using all my resources. Including you. His problems are ancillary to the interests of the Peacemakers, but there might be a connection here, and that must be investigated."

"And if I can help Gregg?"

"If such actions don't hinder your primary mission, the Peacemakers care not. The Guild only cares about Kukuluki and those allied to him. We must unravel those knots before our tails are entwined."

I sighed. "You're colder than I am. I'm not sure I shouldn't quit right now. I have…debts to pay."

The Cochkala swept his tail about in a broad gesture. "What Rhan'Tlanit'Tala the Peacemaker does is one thing. What Tlanit the Cochkala does is another. There are times when Tlanit can do things the Peacemaker cannot. For example, he could send his nephew to a Human mercenary unit and purchase weapon upgrades for that unit."

He pointed his tail at me. "And consider this. While HR may be something we can't touch at this moment, we can gather information that might be useful at some future point."

"Very well."

"I believe you shouldn't hide your new employment. Being a Peacemaker opens some doors you might not otherwise be able to open, and it should provide some protection from retribution. At the very least, should someone know you're a deputy Peacemaker and still strike at you…"

"That would allow you to bring all the might of the Peacemaker Guild to bear, no matter who it was and how powerful their defenses might be."

With eyes sharp as a laser designator, the badger flicked his tail. "Precisely."

* * *

I spent the two weeks of the flight back to Earth reviewing all I had on Captain Gregg. Between what Lyons had gotten, intel from Tlanit, and downloading the Foresters' entire database, I had quite a bit.

I started with the unit database. His fitreps had been topflight. The Foresters gave him increasingly challenging opportunities over the years of his service, and he'd always served well. Thus, he'd risen up the ranks smoothly and earned several bonuses and commendations along the way.

An exemplary soldier—except, of course, when he'd sent over the electronic codes necessary to ambush his company on Peninnah. Hard to gloss over the betrayal and destruction of an entire platoon and more of mercs who depended upon him.

Weighed against his mother, though?

I turned to his family background. An unbroken line of Greggs had served with the Foresters and other merc units ever since the Alpha Contracts. All Greggs who served in the Foresters had done so with distinction. Many had reached the rank of major and moved on to larger units with more opportunities for higher promotions.

One article written just after the Alpha Contracts talked about George Edmonds and Marcus Gregg, the current Gregg's great-something grandfather. Both had tried to purchase the battle honors and history of a Royal Canadian Army regiment from the Canadian government. Each promised to use those honors to form a Canadian-focused merc unit. Marcus had even founded a now defunct non-profit to help get his unit off the ground.

Eventually the Canadian government had accepted the offer for the Foresters from Edmonds, because he had better financing. Marcus had then dropped his request, resigned his commission, and had become one of the first Royal Canadian Army transfers to the new merc unit. In fact, he was Edmonds' executive officer for nearly two decades.

Then I turned my attention to Captain Gregg's personal files. Nothing wrong or strange in his financials, not that I'd expected to see anything. No stupid escapades as a teen. Three-sport athlete. Devout student of military history, especially the transition from cavalry to armor in the early 20th century. High marks throughout school, culminating in one of the top VOWs ever. A good kid, by all accounts, though his teachers and coaches often mentioned he might be too intense, too driven.

Desperately wanted to be a merc and follow in the family tradition. That must have made his betrayal of the Foresters even more difficult. Worse, once they got you, they got you. Bastards.

I sent a copy of the record to my pinplant, and for the rest of the trip I sat in the suite that had once been Bullitt's, drank his scotch, and memorized every bit of Gregg's past.

There's not much else to do once you enter a stargate.

* * *

The *African Queen*'s shuttle dropped me off at the Houston Starport, and I went straight to the Lyon's Den.

The Lyon handed me a Ragnar's chilled to precisely ten degrees Celsius. "You look like you could use this."

"Yeah." I grabbed the rich brown ale and took a healthy drink.

"How'd it go?"

I sighed. "Well, I have a new boss."

"There was a rumor about the old one..."

"I bet." I held out my new UACC.

His eyes widened. "And Bullitt?"

"Dead."

"So it's true." He snorted. "Trust you to end up with the Peacemakers, though. That'll surprise everyone."

"Good." I finished the Ragnar's.

He gave me another.

"And give me a Macallan's 12," I added.

He raised his eyebrows, but poured out two. "To absent companions?"

"Yeah, to all those who've earned their measure of love and respect."

We drank the scotch and stared at our memories.

"Another?" he finally asked.

"No, just keep the Ragnar's coming."

"What now?"

"I need everything you have on Gregg."

"He doesn't deserve the law after him."

"I'm after the one who got to him."

He blinked. "As a Peacemaker?"

"Yes. We believe the one who threatened him also threatened a Peacemaker's nephew. The Guild takes a dim view of such things."

"I can imagine. In that case, you should stay overnight, and we can chat."

"We'll chat in the morning. I hope you have a bunch more of these." I tilted the bottle back and drained it.

He put another on the bar. "I got plenty." He chuckled. "And I'll make sure one of the Lumar shoves an anti-hangover pill down your throat when they carry you to bed."

I nodded and proceeded to earn that pill.

The next morning, Lyons knocked on my door. "Breakfast in my office."

"Ugh."

"All the coffee you could ever want."

"Ugh."

"I'll take that as a 'Be right down.'"

"Ugh." I rose, freshened up, and went to his office.

"Sweep it," he commanded.

I blinked, then I pulled my sweeper out and checked for any evidence of bugs. None. His security had always been good.

I must be hungover not to have done that automatically.

Lyons smiled. "OK, now we're both happy. I kept looking at Gregg after you left to help the Foresters. I'm not sure what happened to his mother."

"They kidnapped her?"

"They apparently…moved her to a new hospital." He grimaced. "I think my nosing around made them nervous."

"Assholes."

"Yeah."

"Heard anything about Kukuluki the Zuparti?"

"A Zuparti?" Lyons leaned back. "Well now, maybe that makes sense. There's been a bunch of Galactic credits flowing around this whole thing, more than is usually a part of something purely Earth-bound. Why him?"

"He's been one of the ones going after the Foresters, and I'd be shocked if he wasn't involved here. He's got his rat claws in too many pies for my comfort."

"The attack on the Foresters leaving the Den?"

"My guess is yes, but that's just a guess."

His eyes sharpened. "He went after the Cochkala on Bruce Peninsula. That attack always seemed odd, but if it was actually aimed at the Peacemaker..."

"Yes."

Lyons drummed his fingers on the bar. "Whoever it was, put a lot of money into attacking the Foresters. The ambush here, Peninnah, the mining colony." He snorted. "And Binnig's still pissing in their pants about whoever it was that broke into their systems."

"I never had a chance to really look into that with my sweepers." A thought crossed my mind. "That reminds me, I want to find one of my old co-workers."

"Assuming they're alive."

"I hope so. Her name's Heidi, and she's a sharp cookie. Likes chocolate donuts with sprinkles."

"Who doesn't like sprinkles?"

"Exactly."

"I'll see what I can find out."

"Thank you. And I'll see what I can find out about a nurse working at a certain assisted living facility."

"Yes." Lyons narrowed his eyes. "Be a shame if that one were to have a bad day."

"Yes."

* * *

When I got to the nursing home, I discovered the nurse had just had a really bad day, and that it was, indeed, a shame.

I sat in a pancake shop just west of the I-55 corridor in Cape Girardeau, Missouri. The local news coverage splashed garish images of an aircar that had crashed and burned. The EMTs put a body into an ambulance in that relaxed, laid-back manner of people who understand time is, for the moment, irrelevant.

The accident had occurred two nights before, but the crash had been spectacular enough it still dominated the coverage. "Police," they said, "are still investigating the cause of the accident that killed Vincent Sasaki, 34, nurse at SEMO Life Care Center."

"Strange thing isn't it," said the waitress, older but pretty, with deep blue, experienced eyes framed by laugh lines.

"What? The crash?"

"Yep." She topped off my coffee. "Haven't seen anything quite like that in a while. I mean, accidents happen and all that, but I can't remember the last time we had someone die like that. I heard the explosion inside my apartment, and it's like four miles away."

"What happened?"

She shrugged. "I guess he took off all the safety restraints and lost control."

"Poor guy."

"Yeah." She sighed. "Anyway, can I get you anything else?"

"No, thanks, I'll finish this cup and get to my client."

"Have a great day, dearie." She smiled. "Come on back while you're here."

It was a nice smile. "I will."

A few minutes later I drove my rented aircar to the SEMO Life Care Center. I walked in and inquired about their facilities for an ailing mother. While the efficient lady with perfect hair but no laugh lines discussed their options and checked my cover ID's credit, I slipped a tracking program into their system.

Then, after promising to call back, I went elsewhere to prowl through their records.

Leslie Gregg had been a resident there up until very recently. Then she wasn't. I double-checked the dates. Her record at SEMO ended a week before the attack on the recruit platoon on the Bruce Peninsula.

That's not a coincidence I believe in.

I didn't see anything in her records that raised my eyebrows, but I'm not a doctor, nor do I play one on Tri-V. After Sasaki's 'accident,' I didn't expect to find a clue on where they'd taken her after SEMO, and I didn't. No final care records. No new doctor listed. No transfer of prescriptions to a new pharmacy. Cape Girardeau had 33 assisted living facilities. None of them showed a Leslie Gregg or any patient fitting her description arriving at the correct time.

I looked at ways to transport a patient. I went through the records of both ambulance firms in the region. Neither showed a record of her. If she left alive, it had to have been in a personal vehicle.

It came as no surprise that the security systems had apparently glitched on the day of the last entry in her record. There was no video footage of the hall outside her room, or to the nearest exit, either inside or outside. In fact, all video of her room since her arrival date had been deleted. The key card records for her final day had disappeared as well. All that remained were Sasaki's notes on her charts.

I went to public records and looked her up. No death certificate or obituary. None of the local funeral homes listed her. I looked through all the freelance body transportation companies.

Nothing. She'd just completely disappeared.

I turned to Sasaki's personnel record. His time at SEMO had been exemplary, according to his supervisors. "Great with patients."

"Always on the ball." "Cares about everyone." They'd never written him up for anything. His drug tests had all come back clean. SEMO had even named him employee of the year once. His salary wasn't huge, but more than enough for Cape Girardeau, which seemed a pleasant, prosperous place to live.

I pulled his bank account from his records. It was with one of the national banks, and we already had a route into their systems. I started the laborious process of checking all his transactions.

It had a reasonable balance. Direct deposit from SEMO on the 1st and 15th. Rent and bills auto-withdrawn. Subscriptions to several gaming networks. None of the purchases seemed abnormal. Restaurants and bars, though not as frequently as many bachelors. I noted the transactions with personal accounts to double-check them on his social media.

I looked for other accounts and found two. His retirement account held a large amount, but not extraordinary, given that Sasaki had started investing early on. The other looked like a savings account. It too had a sizeable balance, but all the deposits were direct from SEMO, and he'd made few withdrawals, mostly for the biggest, baddest gaming system he could afford.

In short, it was the profile of a sensible, reliable employee who liked to game.

I logged into his gaming sites. I still had their security codes, too, of course. It was probably the first thing Bullitt's techs had double-checked every day, after all. I pulled down his records from those sites, especially his in-game purchases and comm logs.

I set my sweeper to search through those logs for repeated patterns or hints of codes. I repeated the process with his social media profiles and communicator records. Then I manually read through them all.

Two days later, I'd read back nearly ten years and had seen nothing extraordinary. The personal transactions in his bank account matched conversations with friends. My pattern recognition programs had found no hint of hidden communications within any of it. I'd only spent a few days on it, so it wasn't the most detailed search, but thus far there wasn't a hint of anything wrong with Sasaki.

So how did they get to him? Could it have been a different nurse, and maybe Sasaki discovered something?

I spent several days going through the bank records of every employee at SEMO. At least the waitress at the pancake shop had given me her comm number, because the only thing I discovered was the best way to get her to laugh, among other things.

What had Sasaki known?

* * *

I said goodbye to the waitress that Friday. No tears, just the unspoken shared knowledge this week could never be repeated, even if we happened to be in the same place again. Two days later, she'd find a mysterious message and a sizable addition to her account. Even with the expenses I'd incur with the *African Queen*, I had more money than I'd ever spend, and Laugh Lines deserved proper appreciation.

Then I went to Sasaki's apartment. The electronic lock there proved no challenge, nor did hiding my presence on the security cameras in his complex.

Getting through the police caution tape actually proved more difficult, at least without making it obvious I'd tampered with it. Then I remembered I could flash my Peacemaker badge, and I just cut it.

I started by moving everything from the freezer to the sink to thaw.

Then I went to the bedroom. It wasn't neat, but not a complete mess, either. He had a fairly normal collection of shirts and jeans to go with his work scrubs. A normal collection of shoes. One suit and a few Sunday-go-to-meeting clothes, but he clearly wasn't a clotheshorse. No expensive jewelry.

The only thing possibly out of place was an old model GP-90 and a half-empty box of 10mm caseless ammo. I double-checked his social media, though, and saw that, while he was no gun nut, some of his friends were. He'd been shooting with them a number of times.

I logged in to all his electronic devices and downloaded their histories. He had a few porn sites linked, but nothing surprising for a bachelor, and their records showed he played straight, vanilla stuff on a regular basis. I set my sweeper to compare the records on his gaming machines with those from the site servers.

I went back to the kitchen. His utensils looked well-used, and he had a variety of half-filled containers holding a usual assortment of cooking ingredients. He had a pad in the kitchen linked to recipe sites. He seemed to favor traditional Italian, which matched his grocery purchases.

The frozen items included the usual sort of things. No diamonds hidden in the ice or drugs stuffed into the ground beef. He had some cheap beer in the fridge, matched by a few cans in his recycling. He had open bottles of vodka and rum, plus around two dozen bottles of reasonably priced wine that went well with Italian food.

His living room was sterile and boring, and looked merely to be a path from one end of his apartment to his kitchen.

Of course that was where I found something.

He had pictures of his family in rotating displays. I downloaded the photos and went through them all.

The last date code for his sister Maria was two years ago. Prior to that, he'd gotten pictures from her regularly. I checked to see if he'd said something about her dying on his social media, but found nothing, though he'd stopped mentioning her at about that point.

If there's one thing these assholes have shown, it's a penchant for manipulating people out of love, not greed. They could have done it to him, too.

His contacts file listed her address in Orlando. I looked for her in the Orlando media, but found nothing. I checked the death and hospital records. As far as the government knew, she still existed and had even paid her taxes the last couple of years.

That meant I had to go to Orlando. I sighed.

I hate Orlando. I especially hate Orlando during the busy season. In fact, now that I think about it, I hate all of South Florida.

* * *

Orlando was as awful as I remembered. Tourists. Companies who tried to help tourists but didn't. People who scammed tourists. Honest beggars with their hands out. Dishonest officials who were even worse. Bureaucratic nightmares everywhere. Worst city in the worst state in the union.

As I drove my rental car through the city, I set my sweeper to hide as much of my passage as possible. It eliminated my record going through the constant toll stations, stoplight cameras, and everything else it detected. If there was ever a city I'd make sure to take my normal precautions in, this was it. I thought about 'accidentally' erasing the city's current month's data, but that'd just hurt the lives of everyday people.

I drove to her apartment and bypassed the complex's security without a problem. I started with her door records. The patterns had changed two years ago, exactly as I'd feared. Previously, the door to her apartment had opened on a normal basis. Now it only opened every few days during the middle of the afternoon, and then again after about ten minutes.

Time enough to make sure nothing had changed.

Her rent had been auto-withdrawn and had never been delinquent. I looked at the bank account. Other than rent, utilities, and a regular deposit to cover those amounts, the account showed no activity for the last two years.

I look at the source of those deposits. The account went to a shell company, and then another, and then to a blockchain linked to a tumbler. I decided to hold off backtracking this until I could use the computing power on the *African Queen.*

The last entry in her door records had been yesterday, and as it seemed unlikely they'd be back for a couple more days, I broke into her apartment.

It had all the things a twenty-something waitress might have.

Except laundry. Except half-empty containers of things that would spoil. Except trash. Except dirty dishes, either in the sink or sitting next to the couch in front of her Tri-V. I looked at her Tri-V's viewing history and found nothing in the last two years, though previously she had watched every reality show.

The assholes behind Gregg's betrayal had nested family blackmails to hide their tracks. I bet they'd fed Maria's body to some alligators at about the same time as Vincent's aircar dove straight into the ground. Unfortunately I didn't find any clue to the assholes behind it. Their method had the virtue, so to speak, of avoiding most financial trails.

I looked for other electronic devices and found none. No pad. No comm. No gaming system. Not even any photo displays like at Vincent's. Nor did I find any physical media. I went through the apartment with deliberate attention to detail.

It was as sterile as an operating theater.

I turned to the door, and that's when I found something. Or rather, it found me.

I almost didn't realize the door had started to open, so smoothly did the man behind it bust in. However, that same smoothness warned me.

I reached for my GP-90 and stepped to the side.

The man slid into the apartment, feet moving in the precise manner of a trained operator. He had sharp, dark eyes, a grim smile, and his own GP-90 already aiming at me.

So fast!

I ducked out of his shot. The low-energy flechettes, designed to avoid penetrating the walls, flickered past me. One sliced through my sleeve and along my shoulder. They thunked into the drywall behind me.

Another set slid past. And another.

I couldn't get a shot, so I kept moving away and went around a corner. Another splash of flechettes followed me.

When he couldn't see me, I jumped back to the corner just as his GP-90 poked around the door. I smacked it out of his hand, sending another round of flechettes skittering off the floor.

He launched a spinning kick almost faster than I could see.

Almost.

But my own training kicked in, and before I knew it, my GP-90 barked. The 10mm round ripped up through his center of mass, tumbling through the wall, and somewhere off into the complex's courtyard.

Time to go.

I checked the guy quickly for any devices or ID. Nothing, of course. I snapped a picture of his face and grabbed his GP-90 in case I could find someone to do ballistic tests. After making sure I hadn't left anything useful, I walked out of the apartment and to the rental.

I drove away just above the speed limit, eyes half on the road and half on the sweeper watching for any pursuit. I drove to the first hotel I could find and caught a cab to a completely different rental car place.

In another city, a wound on my shoulder might have mattered. Not in Orlando, where tourists got mugged every day. Within minutes, I had another aircar and was on the way back to Houston, having altered my transaction records so anyone trying to follow me would be looking for a different car.

I dropped the aircar off at the rental company in Houston, altering those records, too, and then hailed a cab. The cabbie looked at my shoulder, but shrugged when I asked to go to the Den. Not the first bloody trooper to wash up on these shores.

* * *

I slid the GP-90 over to Lyons as he gave me a Ragnar's.

"And what's this?" he asked, glancing at the blood on my sleeve.

I described what I'd discovered so far.

He nodded and slid it under the bar. "Go up to the room and take a shower. I'll send up a shirt and some good news."

"I can use both."

The shower was delightful, the shirt an awful Hawaiian print, and the Ragnar's in the room's mini-fridge all I could hope for. I had just kicked back in the comfy chair when someone knocked on the door.

I palmed my GP-90. "Come in."

A cute-as-a-button face peeked in. "Mr. Lyons said I should—"

"Heidi!" I jumped out of the chair. "Please, come in!"

"Mr. Blaine?" She ran into my arms and started sobbing. "Oh, Mr. Blaine, Mr. Bullitt's dead!"

"I know. I'll miss him."

We spent the next few minutes catching up. I listened intently to her description of the explosion, but heard nothing I hadn't expected.

"Heidi, I'm not Bullitt. For that matter, I'm not really Mr. Blaine. Anyway, I'm going to find out what happened to him. I got work to do while I investigate, though, and I could use your help."

She shrugged. "I'd like to help, but—"

"This will be proper employment. I'd like to hire you as part of the *African Queen's* crew."

"The *African Queen*?"

"Yes. I'm her majority owner now, and Captain Allnut—err...Captain Barkley is one of my employees."

"How can that be?"

"Bullitt left me some gifts, including the money to afford her and its crew."

"What would I do?"

"What you did before. You're one of the best hackers I've ever seen, and I'm going to need help."

She sighed. "It's all so effing much."

"I bet you've said 'holy effing poop' more than a few times."

She giggled and lowered her eyes. "Well, yes."

"Would you say that if I offered twice what Bullitt payed you?"

"Holy effing poop, Mr. Blaine." She smiled sadly. "But you don't have to. I'm going to say yes. I liked Mr. Bullitt."

"Total bastard, but I liked him, too. I'm not going to let them get away with blowing him up."

"Good."

"But for now, we have other work to do. You see, I have a new boss, too." I showed her my new UACC.

"A Peacemaker? Holy effing poop!"

"I know!" I laughed. "Anyway, I want you to go up to the *African Queen* and look through a bunch of money trails."

"Uhhh…I've never really done much of that."

"Mostly you'll be making sure you're hacking into the right accounts and overseeing some of Bullitt's programs."

She looked at me dubiously. "I guess…"

"You'll love it. Besides, these'll be useful skills for you. First, let's start with the blockchain concept."

"OK."

"These list transactions of a bunch of accounts into one ledger, thereby obscuring which account does which. I need you to use Bullitt's blockchain separation program to pull out the various accounts. Then you'll track those accounts, which may very well lead to another blockchain, or tumblers, but you're to keep going until you've separated as many accounts as you can."

"Tumblers?"

"Yeah, an old scheme from the early days. It's an account that takes in credits from a number of accounts, jumbles that money all together, and then uses it for whatever they want. It's useful as hell for money laundering. Bullitt had another program for those. Basically, his programs sift through huge amounts of data and, bit by bit, come up with connections."

Heidi sniffed and wiped her eyes. "He spent a weekend teaching me about tweaking algorithms. I thought I knew things, but holy effing poop, he was smart."

"Yeah."

"What do you want me to look for?"

"I have a file of notes on the system up on the *African Queen* listing all the bank accounts I've seen so far. You'll be looking for any connection to those accounts. All the details you can find."

"OK."

I smiled. "I can't tell you how glad I am you're here, Heidi."

A tear went down her cheek. "I'm glad you found me, Mr. Blaine. I didn't really know what I was going to do after…I mean, I had plenty of money. We all did after Bullitt left us some. But…"

"But you had to do something."

"Yes, Mr. Blaine."

"We got stuff to do, my dear. Lots of stuff. I'll be bringing you donuts for *years*."

She giggled. "With sprinkles."

"Absolutely."

* * *

After getting Heidi sent up to the *African Queen*, along with an update of new data to my notes file, I slid into my spot at the bar. "Thanks for finding her, Lyons."

"No problem. She was the easy one. I haven't found anything yet about that Zuparti you asked about. I did track down the financials of all the bastards who attacked those Foresters here. I didn't see any connection to a Zuparti or any offworlder, though I bet you'll have better luck."

"I'll add those accounts to the ones I'm having Heidi run through."

"More of Bullitt's legendary programs?"

"He really was a genius, and he knew how to make stock markets do his bidding." I sighed. "Anyway, find anything new about Gregg or his mom?"

"Not yet, though I'll keep checking. As for the GP-90, it'll take a week or two for me to get anything."

"You won't find anything."

Lyons grimaced. "Not the way they've locked this whole thing down."

"Still gotta check."

"Yeah."

I projected a picture of the shooter. "Recognize him?"

Lyons' eyes narrowed. "Not off the top of my head."

"He had training. Moved too well to be just a thug."

"I can ask around."

"Thanks." I sent him a copy of the photo.

"Where are you off to now?" he asked.

"I've been going after the way they controlled Gregg, but now that they've eliminated the Sasakis, I think that trail is cold. I think it's time to see if I can find anything up at Owen Sound. I can still claim I'm working for Elite, after all."

"Yeah, that part of the company is still working, though there's been some confusion from what I hear."

"I'm not surprised. It was always a legitimate business, after all." I finished the Ragnar's and stood up.

"Keep your powder dry."

"Will do." By dinnertime I was hailing a cab at Pearson Airport, still designated YYZ. I checked into the nearest Marrilton, pleased to find my corporate card still worked. I barely had the presence of mind to push all the locks and set up my sweeper's alarm programs before falling asleep.

I woke up the next morning far more refreshed than I had any reason to feel. I stopped by a Tim Horton's on the way over to the Forester House at Jarvis and Carlton. I dropped the box of TimBits on Corporal Stanley's desk.

He seemed very happy to see me. Too happy.

"Mr. Blaine!" He leaned around the corner. "Master Warrant Russell, Mr. Blaine is out here."

"Send him in!"

I shut the door as I walked in. Master Warrant Officer Graham Russell was standing up, offering his hand. "You're alive!"

"Of course." I looked at him with hard eyes. "I apologize for the delay in getting back to you. My schedule's been crazy of late, but I should have checked in sooner."

He shut his mouth, nodded, and waved at the seat. I sat down and started my anti-snooping programs. I asked him questions about the training software we'd sold him until my sweeper told me we were in the clear.

"You heard my company had an incident?" I asked.

"Yeah." He grimaced. "I've been helping Lieutenant Fournette with intel work, and I found out what I could."

I leaned forward. "Who have you told?"

He raised his eyebrows. "Just the officer staff."

I grimaced. "So, everyone knows."

He opened his mouth and then shrugged. "Yeah, probably."

"Well, what's done is done."

"Why are you worried?" he asked.

"I'm an intel specialist. I don't want *anyone* to know *anything*."

He smiled briefly. "What happened?"

"My boss always had enemies. It's part of the business."

"Now what?"

"Elite will continue to work for you."

"I meant for you."

"I'm going to keep helping Edmonds as much as I can."

"Good. We need it. That *victory* on Maquon," his lips twisted, "may break this regiment."

"If anyone can keep it together, it'll be Edmonds."

"Yes, sir! Tenacious and versatile!"

"Good qualities to have these days."

"Yes." He stared at me for a long moment. "What do you want?"

"I was just thinking about what I should tell you."

"Everything, of course." He smiled without humor. "But you won't."

"I don't even tell Lyons everything."

"So what *can* you tell me?"

"The people going after the Foresters aren't done."

"I already figured that."

I pursed my lips. Then I got up. "I shouldn't have come here."

"You think someone's betraying the unit."

"I didn't say that."

"You didn't have to. You're tap-dancing around things, trying not to tell me anything while clearly being worried about what I told people about you." He shook his head. "I'm not the best intel guy that's ever walked, but I'm not dumb."

"No, you're not." I paused. "You remember Cox?"

"Corporal Bag O'Dicks? Yeah. I'm still surprised he jumped in front of that rocket for the Cochkala."

"I'm not. He was actually working for the Peacemakers."

"What?" Russell's jaw dropped. He tried to say something, but shook his head. Tried again. Then he said, "I'm not sure if I'm glad he wasn't really that much of an asshole, or I feel betrayed he spied on us for the Peacemakers."

"I'd go with the first choice. That's why your Cochkala's still alive."

"I guess." Russell shook his head and grimaced. Then his eyes sharpened and looked at me. "There are more spies, aren't there?"

"Why do you say that?"

"Cox, whatever else, did his job and died saving another trooper. We wouldn't go ass over teakettle about that even if his connections to the Peacemakers became common knowledge. But someone set us up on Peninnah and here on the Bruce, and we want that asshole."

"I'm going to tell you a story, Master Warrant Officer."

"I hate stories," he growled.

"It starts with a girl—probably not smart, but not a bad girl. She had a brother. That brother was a good man. He made helping people his career, and he was good at it. However, one of his patients had a relative someone wanted to control. I think that someone kidnapped the sister and used her brother to gain control of that relative."

"My troopers would never let that happen!"

"What would you do if someone held a gun to your mother's head?"

"I—" He shut his mouth. "I don't know."

"That's really why I don't want to tell you. I need to be around the Foresters to figure out the exact chain and see if I can flip it around."

"And then we cashier the bastard."

"Oh, no, Master Warrant Officer. I think Kukuluki the Zuparti is behind it all. If I can turn this source, we have a chance to hammer that fucking rat by feeding misinformation through it."

"That isn't my way, Blaine."

"Would you throw away a weapon?"

"One I couldn't trust, yeah."

"Trust is its own weapon."

"Look, Mr. Blaine. Whoever it is, my regiment's been hammered. I'm not going to let them get away with it."

"I doubt they'll ever think that." I sighed. "Let me put it this way. You can always cashier someone, but you don't always get a chance to trap the other guy."

He grimaced. "Very well, what do you need?"

"Nothing really, just authorization to check into the performance of our software and training systems. That'll give me all the reason I need to roam around Owen Sound."

He sighed, but punched something into his system, then reached around his desk to get the pass card. He tapped it on the desk a couple of times, but eventually handed it to me. "You could probably have hacked into the system and done this yourself."

"I expect so, but it's better this way." I smiled. "Is Captain Gregg still in charge of the sims?"

"Yes."

"Might as well start there. Can you schedule an appointment?"

He punched something into his computer. "Done. Do you need anything else?"

"Not at the moment. I'll get with Gregg and go from there."

He sighed again. "I trust you, Blaine, but don't let me down."

"I won't."

As I was leaving, my message icon pinged. Heidi already had an update for me. I went back to the Marrilton and spent the evening reviewing her data.

She hadn't discovered many new accounts, but she'd gone through all we had with a much finer-toothed comb than I'd had time for. Her list included far more data on each, including biometric data and passwords.

Most had intelligible passwords, presumably because most people who used accounts designed to hide money trails didn't want to record passwords in any way.

It's amazing how many criminals use passwords like "Password123."

Most, however, had combinations someone could remember, but were still difficult to guess. "Casablanca=GeorgieIII=11111885" caught my eye. Apparently Bullitt wasn't the only one who used old movies to help hide things.

I snorted. For that matter, there's nothing to say Bullitt didn't set up that file himself.

I spent several hours correlating the data, sorting it in different ways, and looking for connections. Boring work, but I didn't have much else to do at the moment, and you never know. All I managed to achieve was to give myself nightmares where strange alphanumeric strings kept making strafing runs at my head.

* * *

I felt off the next morning, and even a Tim Horton's butter tart didn't help much. Fortunately I'd gotten two, and by the time I landed my aircar in the Owen Sound lot, I felt sharp and ready to tackle anything. Except, of course, for talking to Captain Gregg.

Who wants to talk to someone you know has been blackmailed into betraying all he holds dear, including his family's legacy?

But there was no help for it.

We met in the training facility. Elite's simulators gleamed, and their displays showed a section currently running an exercise.

He held out his hand. "Your software's been very useful, Mr. Blaine."

I shook it. "Thank you, Captain Gregg."

"We especially appreciate your specialized packages. The ones designed to simulate specific worlds and aliens."

"We do our best. We're constantly scouring updates to Jane's and other sources to ensure those aliens are armed with everything they have in their arsenals."

I plugged into the units and ran through their maintenance logs. Gregg waited patiently. We chatted over this and that while the systems passed bits hither and yon.

"Anything else here, Mr. Blaine?"

"Not unless you have something to show me."

"No, sir. Shall we return to my office and I can run through our upcoming goals and requests?"

"Absolutely."

Excellent. We can talk privately. Maybe Russell's lapse in info control will be useful, and Gregg will use the opportunity to ask for help.

Gregg settled behind his clean and organized desk. The only personal touch, other than his "I Love Me" wall, was a photo display frame changing images every fifteen seconds. Pictures of his family and dog, mostly.

"Hold on while I transfer the request file," he said.

"Thank you. I hope you'll take the time to run over those with me so we're sure to address any issues."

"Of course. Major Dozier said not to waste the opportunity, especially since we have so many holes to fill after the battle."

"Thank you. I had heard you suffered some casualties."

He snorted. "More than a few." His eyes held something…

Does he want to talk now? Maybe if…

I grimaced. "And you had actions on Peninnah and Cimarron 283133-6A as well as Maquon, right?"

"Yes."

Odd. No reaction to Peninnah. Maybe if I prime the pump again.

"If I recall correctly, you were in command at Peninnah. It's our hope none of your officers will have to deal with anything like that ever again."

His face turned into a granite mask hiding his thoughts. "Indeed."

Well, not the first time I've seen someone hide their feelings behind a wall, though it does make it hard to help.

I took a breath and glanced at the picture frame. It showed Gregg's dog perched on the top of an aircar. I chuckled.

He glanced at the frame and smiled. "He's a good dog, even if he doesn't always act like it."

"What kind is he?"

"English Bull Terrier. His name's Georgie."

I blinked at the name. "That's a real breed, right? Not a mutt?"

He chuckled. "No, these are pure-bred. I probably shouldn't spend that much getting them, but they're great with my kids and keep their training well."

"So you've had more than one?"

"Oh, yes. This is the fourth I've had."

"His name is Georgie IV?" I blinked again.

"Yes." He glanced up at me. "Why do you ask?"

"No reason. I just like to get to know my clients. I find that if I learn a little bit about their family and pets, it makes my job more enjoyable."

"Makes sense." His smile didn't reach his eyes.

"I've noticed some other Greggs in the Foresters' history."

"My family has been a part of it since it began."

"I didn't realize serving in the Foresters was a family tradition."

"Oh, yes." He eyes bored into mine. "We've *served* in the Foresters ever since day one. The Edmonds have always given us the chance to serve their family ever since the RCA decided to sell them a unit's history and battle honors. A generous gift indeed," he added almost in a snarl.

I frantically pulled the notes from my sweeper to my pinplant display. The account with GeorgieIII in the password had been part of the blockchain that had paid *into* Maria Sasaki's account. And this time, I actually noticed the account's details.

Oh, hell! The tax designation shows it was originally opened by a non-profit in the time just after the Alpha Contracts. Gregg had paid to control Vincent. It had all been a lie. Gregg faked the threat to his mom to give himself cover.

I glanced up and looked into his eyes. I had taken too much time. I realized he knew I knew.

He calmly began opening the bottom drawer of his desk.

I leapt for the door and dove out into the reception room. A 10mm round went over my back and impacted the hardened concrete on the far wall.

Gregg's orderly looked up in shock.

I rolled off to the side behind a heavy desk, my GP-90 at the ready. The corporal looked into Gregg's office door and received a round to the face for his trouble.

Gregg charged out, GP-90 blazing. His shots crashed into the desk, sending metal slivers along my ribs.

I was too stunned to return fire immediately.

More rounds impacted the desk, jamming it up against me.

I sent a couple of rounds back to make Gregg think.

The captain snarled, "The Greggs pay all their debts!" He fired a few more times, and then the outside door snicked shut.

I peered around the desk and saw no one except the faceless orderly, brains leaking on the linoleum.

I sent a message to Russell, dumping my notes and a description of what had just happened. I told him to shut everything down. I could have done it myself, but right then, I wanted to live. If Gregg hadn't stayed to pay his debt to me, that meant he expected me to die right here. Now I had to figure out how, and do it right quick.

I sat in the orderly's chair and started my sweeper, looking for all net activity in the area. A sharp pop and a burst of heat came out of his office. I glanced in to see a pile of slag where Gregg's computer had been.

My sweeper showed a bunch of programs activating on the Foresters' servers. The easiest to deal with were the relatively standard viruses. I sent my malware programs chasing after them.

We'd always anticipated this possibility with our simulators, and their anti-malware routines kicked in as well, meaning I could ignore the programs attacking them.

I started to help salvage what we could from the Foresters' servers when I saw the code directed at the armory.

"A bomb in the armory would most definitely not be a good thing," I stated to the corporal on the floor.

The orderly didn't disagree.

The timer showed less than fifteen minutes. It also looked too big to be *just* a timer. It had to include separate subroutines, and that meant traps.

Gregg hadn't been in this position to sacrifice himself. He wanted revenge, not a heroic death. That meant he had to include some sort of emergency way into the program, just in case.

My sweeper finished its initial examination and provided me with that backdoor.

I kept talking to the orderly. "At least I have a way in. Now to stop it in less than—" I looked at the timer "—twelve minutes without setting off those traps."

The orderly urged me to hurry. In his quiet fashion, of course.

A dropship broke the silence when it screamed over the building. I released a breath when I realized it hadn't dropped any ordnance.

Thank goodness it hadn't been armed.

I sent up a message to Captain Barkley to track the dropship and glanced at the timer. *Ten minutes.*

"Now, Corporal, if you know the code, you can tell me."

He refused to answer.

"How about a hint? It can't be a random thing. Had to be something Gregg could remember like the password on the bank account, right?"

Still no answer.

"Fine, keep your captain's secrets."

Nine minutes.

"Well, since you're not helping, I'm going to have to do something stupid. You might not realize, Corporal, but fifteen minutes, even at modern processing speeds, is not long enough for most brute force attacks to succeed. If he had to enter a passcode, he had to enter it correctly under stress. Might be safer to allow himself some mistakes, don't you think?"

The orderly had no answer.

"Well, anyway, I don't see much choice."

I set my sweeper searching for any relevance to the password on the bank account. It came up almost instantly. George Patton, born on 11 November, 1885.

Dammit! I should have recognized it. Gregg's senior thesis had been on Patton's armored doctrine technical papers, and Casablanca wasn't just Bullitt's favorite movie.

I set my sweeper to attack using combinations related to Patton. "Might be a good time for a prayer, Corporal." I closed my eyes and executed the program. I opened them after a moment to find well over a million attempts already without success.

I blew my breath out. "No luck yet, son, but at least we've got a chance."

Seven minutes.

I started adding all I could think of that I knew about Captain Gregg to my sweeper's attack algorithm, beginning with Georgie and all the info I could find on English Bull Terriers. I tagged Marcus and all the ancestors I knew about. Added the non-profit's name and the unit Marcus had hoped to purchase.

The sweeper now showed over a billion attempts and counting.

Three minutes.

I thought of Gregg's senior thesis and pulled it up. "Now, if it's in here, it's something memorable, don't you think? Something important to him. How about the dedication?"

I sent it over. Nothing.

"Thesis statement?"

No.

Two minutes.

"You're not giving me much help, son. Let's check the foreword." Nothing there.

One minute.

"Yes, you're right. It could be in the conclusion." My eyes widened at the Patton quote on the last page.

Thirty seconds.

"Well, shall we?"

The orderly didn't argue when I overrode the sweeper's brute force attack and copied over the quote. I double-checked to make sure I hadn't screwed it up. I'd get one chance.

I took a deep breath. "Well, Corporal, it's been nice chatting with you."

I sent, "Nobody ever defended anything successfully; there is only attack and attack and attack some more."

The timer stopped with four seconds remaining.

I started to relax, but I heard footsteps running up to the door.

There'll be time to explain later, if I have a later.

I slid my GP-90 away. I dropped to the floor, laced my hands behind my head, and stared into the dead orderly's ravaged skull.

Four Foresters burst into the office. They had their AK-218s trained on me, just hoping I'd move.

I didn't.

Thank goodness Edmonds trained his people well. Gregg's not the only one with debts to pay.

*****

Rob Howell Bio

Rob Howell is the creator of the Shijuren fantasy setting (www.shijuren.org), an author in the Four Horsemen Universe (www.mercenaryguild.org), and an editor of When Valor Must Hold, an anthology of heroic fantasy. He writes primarily epic fantasy, space opera, military science fiction, and alternate history.

He is a reformed medieval academic, a former IT professional, and a retired soda jerk.

His parents quickly discovered books were the only way to keep Rob quiet. He latched onto the Hardy Boys series first and then anything he could reach. Without books, it's unlikely all three would have survived.

His latest release in Shijuren is Where Now the Rider, the third in the Edward series of swords and sorcery mysteries. The next release in that world is None Call Me Mother, the conclusion to the epic fantasy trilogy The Kreisens.

You can find him online at: www.robhowell.org, on Amazon at https://www.amazon.com/-/e/B00X95LBB0, and his blog at www.robhowell.org/blog.

#####

Long Live the Huma by Chris Kennedy

Peepo's Pit, Karma Station, Karma Orbit

Colonel Kuru Shirazi stumbled as he walked out of Peepo's Pit. Although not normally one to consume alcohol, he had allowed one of the members of the Golden Horde to give him a shot glass of something the mercenary had called "Mother's Milk." The former gang-banger hadn't been very forthcoming over *whose* mother had spawned the devil drink, but a second one had Shirazi's vision starting to go fuzzy around the edges, and he knew he needed to beat a hasty retreat before someone gave him a third.

"What was in that stuff?" Sergeant Major Kazemi asked, moving quickly to steady his commanding officer.

"I don't know, but don't ever let me have another of them. Ever."

"Yes, sir."

They walked in companionable silence across Karma Station. Although it was late according to the space station's daily clock, a wide variety of aliens were out and about, many of which the Humans hadn't seen before. New to the Galactic Union stage, it wasn't much more than a year since the first aliens had shown up on Earth and welcomed them into the galaxy-wide polity. The aliens at the time had said that Earth didn't have anything the galaxy needed...until they saw Humans fight. After a terrorist bomb had killed the galactic ambassador, the mercenaries protecting the delegation had gone in to destroy the terrorists and found that Humans had *quite* the propensity to fight.

Although vastly unprepared for war at the galactic level, the people of Chabahar, Iran, and the military units stationed there had rallied and—while they'd lost a whole lot more than they'd killed—they'd been able to inflict casualties on the MinSha, the giant praying mantis-like aliens that had come to plunder the town. In the wake of their admittedly minimal success, the Galactics had invited the Humans to become mercenaries. They hadn't done much...but they'd done enough. Out of the thousands of races in the galaxy, only 36 would fight for money. The Humans would be the 37th.

Colonel Kuru Shirazi, Iranian Army, had put together a mercenary group called Asbaran Solutions, made up of former soldiers under his command, and had taken one of the first hundred contracts offered to humanity. Unfortunately—just like their initial meeting with the MinSha in the streets of Chabahar—humanity was unprepared for fighting the alien mercenaries, and only four of the companies had made it back. In addition to his own Asbaran Solutions, only Cartwright's Cavaliers, the Winged Hussars, and the Golden Horde were still viable organizations.

Through some cosmic joke, all four had a horse in their logo—the Asbarani were ancient Persian elite cavalry—and the leader of the Cavaliers, Jim Cartwright, had convinced the other leaders to call themselves the "Four Horsemen" after some religious story of his, and he had gotten their agreement to do everything they could to help Earth take its place among the other mercenary organizations in the stars, toasting the new group with, "The Four Horsemen for Earth!"

It made sense, though. Humanity's start had been inauspicious at best. A 4% success rate was nothing to brag about, especially since at least one of the "winners" appeared to have done so through the wildest chances of luck. As Cartwright had said, they needed to hang together, or they would all hang—or get shot—separately. They needed better equipment, and not just the gear the aliens had. Sure, more lasers and magnetic accelerator cannons—MACs—would help, but it wouldn't level the playing field considerably. The aliens were bigger, faster, stronger, and generally meaner than anything humanity could throw at them.

In addition to the MinSha, he'd seen the Besquith, giant aliens that looked like werewolves that had mouthfuls of shark-like teeth. They were said to be ferocious warriors and merchants; he knew Humans weren't ready to face the Besquith. The ones who had faced them hadn't come back. Other aliens were just as scary. Humanity needed to carefully pick their next set of contracts, while amassing new galactic weapons and working on a number of projects to help make them equal to the aliens. Cartwright had an idea about a new set of powered armor. While Shirazi was interested in it, nothing the Iranian Army had ever fielded along those lines had ever worked for more than a few minutes. He remained skeptical that such a project would work, too, but Cartwright thought, with an injection of galactic tech, something might be possible.

Lost in his thoughts, he almost tripped over the two creatures who stopped in front of him. The aliens appeared mammalian in nature and looked like the anteaters he'd seen in a zoo once, with long snouts and droopy ears. The aliens also had long, sharp claws, although whether they were for digging or tearing the flesh from someone's bones, Shirazi had no clue.

One of the creatures said something, which his translation pendant turned into, "Greetings!"

"Greetings," Shirazi said, starting to go around the aliens.

"You are a Human, right?" the alien asked.

"Yeah, why?"

"We need help and want to hire you."

Shirazi made eye contact with Kazemi, who raised an eyebrow. "You do, huh?" Shirazi asked. "And why is that?"

"We heard there was a new mercenary race, and we want to hire it," the alien repeated.

Shirazi chuckled. "Because of our military prowess?"

"Well, no, not exactly," the alien said. Both of them shifted around a little, looking uncomfortable.

"Well, why then?"

"We heard you were new, so we thought you might be a little more…affordable…than some of the other races."

"Yes," the second alien said. "Can you believe the prices some of them charge? It's almost usury!"

"Uh huh," Shirazi said. "So, basically, you couldn't afford anyone else, and you're hoping we'll give you a good deal because we're new and don't know any better?"

"Well, actually, we heard most of your first contracts didn't go so well, and no one's going to want to hire you. You'll have to drop your rates."

"Unfortunately, the anteater probably has a point," Kazemi said in Farsi, which the alien's translators probably wouldn't understand.

"That doesn't mean we have to let them know that," Shirazi replied, also in Farsi. He looked back to the first alien and said in English, which the translators understood, "Thanks, but we're busy." He looked back at Kazemi. "Let's go."

He'd only taken two steps when the second alien said, "Open skies! Now you've offended them. We'll never get them to take the contract now!"

"Wait!" the first alien called. "I didn't mean to offend you! Can we talk a moment?"

Shirazi stopped and indicated a café nearby. "Buy us a drink, and we'll talk for as long as the drink lasts."

* * *

Kefjack's Kafe, Karma Station, Karma Orbit

"That's why we need you," the alien—a Caroon—said ten minutes later as Shirazi picked up his glass to take his final drink.

He swirled the amber liquid in the glass, looking at it critically. He'd almost finished it, and he still had no idea what it was, or what it was made out of. It tasted good, though, and didn't make him lose all his senses. His eyes came back up to meet the Caroon's. "So let me get this straight. You have a uranium mine, and you think this group—"

"The Besquith Alliance."

"—is going to swoop in and take it from you."

"That's correct."

"Why would they do that?"

"Because the price of uranium has risen on the galactic exchange, and they want to control more of it."

Shirazi raised an eyebrow. "But the mine is yours?"

"Absolutely," the Caroon said. "My partner's family has had the claim filed with the Cartography Guild for many years. Now they're trying to pressure us into letting them have it for a fraction of what it's worth."

"And you think they might come and try to take it if you don't sell?"

"Exactly. We've seen them do this in the past. When they didn't get what they wanted through negotiation, they sent in mercenaries to take it."

"I don't know," Kazemi said in Farsi. "Have you seen those Besquith creatures? If they wanted something of mine, I'd be awfully tempted to just let them have it."

Shirazi nodded. "I think we'll pass," he said to the Caroon.

"But it will be *really* easy!" the Caroon exclaimed. "That's the thing—the Alliance is a new company that's still trying to carve its niche in the business world. They don't have the funds to pay mercenaries to attack something that's being defended by other mercenaries; instead, they just go looking for easier targets. Also, they're still small enough that they're worried about being reported to the Merchant Guild. Just by being there, you'll ensure they don't come. This is the easiest garrison contract ever; I can guarantee you there'll be no combat. Your presence alone will deter them."

"What do you think?" Shirazi asked Kazemi.

"I think it's too easy. My mom always warned me about Iraqis bearing gifts."

"Mine, too." He paused, then added, "Still, if it's true, this could help fund that powered armor project Cartwright is looking into." He looked back at the lead Caroon. "Let me think about it. I'll see you back here tomorrow at the same time, and I'll have your answer."

* * *

Kefjack's Kafe, Karma Station, Karma Orbit

"You returned," the Caroon said the next night. "I was afraid you wouldn't."

"And I was afraid you'd lied to me about the Besquith Alliance hitting fortified positions for economic gain. But we did some searches of the GalNet and can't find where they hit an opposed mining operation. We're in, but for twice what you offered us."

"What? We can't afford that! Then there would be no profit in it!"

"There'll be more profit than if the Besquith capture your mine and take it for themselves."

"And you'll have the good fortune of still being alive to enjoy it," Kazemi added.

A long series of negotiations followed, and in the end, Shirazi got the Caroons to come up 25%, with a combat bonus that would triple the contract's value if combat actually occurred. If Shirazi was going to fight Besquith, he was *damn* well getting paid for it.

* * *

Deployment Site, Roget's World, Kak'L'Kak System

Shirazi led the company of troops off the dropship and watched as they quickly unloaded it. As soon as it was empty, the dropship lifted to go back up to the transport for the next load of equipment.

Sergeant Major Kazemi walked over to him and made a sweeping motion that took in the local terrain. "Reminds me of Zahedan," he said.

Shirazi nodded. They'd done a lot of training in the high plateaus along the Pakistani and Afghan borders prior to first contact, and the arid, desert-like terrain was very similar. A holy site for Zoroastrians, Shirazi had spent a lot of his personal time there, as well. Low mountains ringed the plateau, too, just like back home.

He pointed to one of the mountains, about a mile away, that had a large building near its base. "That's where we're headed once our transport comes down with the next load."

"Aside from the refinery, I don't see any signs of civilization," Kazemi said.

"There aren't any. The Caroons all live underground. We'll be setting up our own civilization here. That or moving in with the Caroons underground."

"No thanks. They smell badly. I can't imagine living underground with them for six months. I'd probably never get the stench out of all my stuff."

"It's not something I want to do, either, but it'll be pretty cold here in a few months."

Kazemi smiled. "It'll have to be *damn* cold."

"It will be."

* * *

Besquith Alliance Headquarters, Bestald

"So they hired…Humans?" the CEO asked. "What exactly is a Human?"

The CEO's secretary tapped his slate. "I put together a briefing for you." He tapped it one last time. "You have it."

The CEO picked up his slate and brought up the file. After a couple of minutes, he set it down again. "They're unimpressive, to say the least. They look soft…and tasty."

The secretary nodded. "The lowest completion percentage for the first round of contracts ever. Among races still in the mercenary business, that is."

"Of course," the CEO said. Mercenary races came and went. The Besquith had consumed a couple of races who hadn't measured up. Literally. While they weren't as good at planning as the Veetanho, there were few who wanted to meet the Besquith on the battlefield. Especially at close range.

"I know we typically don't hit defended mines," the operations officer said, "but with Humans guarding it, is it really defended? We can roll through them as if they never existed, capture the mine, and erase all signs of their existence, like what happened to them on most of their contracts. The Humans don't have a presence in the galaxy yet, and they're still only probationary members, so no one will notice—or care—if one of their detachments on a far-flung planet is no longer heard from again.

"Additionally, we have experience taking over Caroon mines, and we know they're good workers. They adjust well to having us as overseers." The operations officer smiled. "And they taste good, too, when examples have to be made. The bottom line is, the mine is producing well, it's undefended for all intents and purposes, and the price for uranium just went up 5% on the galactic exchange, which will boost our profit margins even further."

The CEO considered for a few moments and then nodded. "Send two companies, wipe out the Humans, and capture the mine."

"*Two* companies? We could do it with a lot fewer troops. There's only a company of Humans. That will unnecessarily lower our profits."

The CEO nodded. "There's no kill like overkill. Paying death benefits—even a few—will lower profits even more. Send a company and bring this mine into the fold."

* * *

Base Perimeter, Roget's World, Kak'L'Kak System

"Colonel Shirazi! Colonel Shirazi!" a trooper yelled as he ran up. His breath puffed in the cold air, and his voice was somewhat muffled by the falling snow.

Shirazi and Kazemi stopped their inspection to wait for the runner, pulling their overcoats tighter around them. "Yes?" Shirazi asked after returning the trooper's salute.

"Sir! The transport just called. A ship has arrived in the emergence area."

Shirazi smiled. "Calm down. If the ship just emerged, it will take days to get here. We have time. Take a breath, start at the beginning, and give me the whole message like a professional soldier."

The soldier took a couple of deep breaths, squared his shoulders, and said, "Sir, I have a message from the transport. A ship just arrived in the emergence area and is heading toward the planet. The transport says it's a Besquith merc cruiser."

Shirazi shook his head once as he looked over to Kazemi. "It appears our friends the Caroons were wrong about whether the Besquith would attack."

"How do you know this is an attack?"

"There's no reason they'd have come here, except to get the uranium. Having come this far, I doubt they'll take 'no' for an answer." He shrugged. "I guess we can go talk to them and find out for sure."

"Sure thing, Colonel," Kazemi replied. "It's better than standing around in the cold, too; that's for sure."

The two men jogged back to the comm center with the runner in tow. "It's almost worth getting invaded just to come in here and get warm," Kazemi muttered as he shucked his overwear in the warmth of the building.

"Almost," Shirazi said. "Up until they get here, anyway."

The tech set him up with a circuit relayed through the transport. As the Besquith ship was still a long way out, there was a lag in the conversation.

"The ship is the BMS *Mauler*, sir," the tech said.

"*Mauler*, this is Colonel Shirazi of Asbaran Solutions, the merc company guarding the mine. Please state your intentions."

"This is Colonel Cahl-An of the Besquith Alliance. Our intentions are simple. We'll take your transport as our own, and we'll use it to transport all the uranium that's been mined back to Bestald. If you vacate the mine, we'll consider not chasing after and eating most of you."

"Sorry, Cahl-An, but we've given our word to defend the mine, and that's what we intend to do."

"Then you'll die screaming before my troops."

"If you come down to the planet, someone will certainly die; however, I believe it's far more likely to be you."

"We shall see."

The tech shook his head. "That's it, sir. He cut the connection."

Kazemi sighed. "That could have gone better."

Shirazi shrugged. "It wasn't any different than I expected, but I had to try."

"So, sir, what now?"

"Now we're going to fight the Besquith and become the first Human company to withstand a Besquith assault."

"I like the way that sounds," Kazemi said. "One question, though. How exactly are we going to do that?"

"Well, we've got the refinery and two days. I'm going to see what kind of shapes the refinery can make."

"Like walls and doors?"

"No, like defensive positions we can take cover behind. Uranium is one of the densest elements found naturally; that's why they use it for tank armor. It offers both resistance against shaped charges like HEAT rounds and shatters kinetic energy penetrators. Put enough of it between us and the Besquith, and they're going to have a hard time shooting at us. Maybe they'll get bored and go home."

"But uranium is radioactive. We'll be irradiating ourselves while we're covering behind it."

"Uranium-238 constitutes the majority of the uranium they mine, and it isn't radioactive, so there's probably less radioactivity than you would expect. Uranium *is* a toxic metal, but I'll bet they can put some sort of sheathing on it to protect us. Failing that, we have the medical nanites that can clean the radiation from our bodies after the fight. And besides, we only have to worry about the radiation if we *win.*"

"True," Kazemi said with a nod.

"I'll go talk to the foreman and see what sort of molds they have," Shirazi said. "Why don't you start organizing everyone for the move into the mines?"

"Ugh. I didn't think about that. Maybe we can use some of our chemical warfare gear to protect us from the smell of the Caroons."

"Maybe," Shirazi said with a smile. "I know one thing about their smell, though."

"What's that?"

"It's less deadly than the Besquith are going to be to anyone who isn't in the mines in a couple of days."

"Good point. I'll go see about moving everyone inside."

"Thanks."

* * *

Command Center, Roget's World, Kak'L'Kak System

"There they are, sir," Sergeant Will McClain said, pointing to the monitor. "Right on time. Unfortunately they're landing too far away."

Shirazi nodded. While there were flashes of the troops landing, it was impossible to see the dropships clearly through the blowing snow. They'd mined the best landing sites close to the mine, but the Besquith had landed further away. He shrugged internally. It would have been nice to get an early win by blowing up some of the dropships as they touched down. "How many, do you think?"

"Hard to tell, sir," the technician said. "I think there were at least four dropships, so maybe a company? Looks like the dropships are lifting off again, but there's no way to know if they're going back up to get more troops or just to get out of the way."

"Think they'll rush us?" asked Corporal Paul Sparks, the tech's assistant.

"Hard to know what they'll do, but I wouldn't," Shirazi said. "I'd get everybody down and organized. The weather sucks, which is going to complicate things for them." *For us, too. I'd love to hit them now, but trying to rush the monsters in the snow would make it a free-for-all that was greatly in the Besquiths' favor.*

"What's that?" Sparks asked.

"Looks like a tent going up," Kazemi said.

"I agree," Shirazi said. "Looks like they're here to stay. Stand down to the normal rotation of forces. It doesn't look like there's going to be an assault today."

* * *

Command Center, Roget's World, Kak'L'Kak System

"Looks like they're coming," McClain said two days later. The snowstorm had finally stopped, having left three feet of snow in its wake.

"What do you make that?" Shirazi asked, nodding to the screens that showed the Besquith marching through the snow toward the mine. McClain panned the camera around.

"Looks like about two companies," Kazemi said.

"That's what I make it, too," Shirazi agreed.

"Want me to thin them out some?" McClain asked.

"Go ahead. Don't want them getting too brave too soon."

"The snow is going to deaden the blasts some," he cautioned. "It may also make them less sensitive if there's ice."

"I know," Shirazi said. "Arm them."

McClain entered a command into the system, and the entire field detonated at once, filling the cameras with smoke and snow.

McClain winced. "It may also be possible that the mines were too sensitive, and the weight of the snow could set them off."

After about 20 seconds, the picture had cleared enough to see that the majority of the Besquith were unharmed. Although some of the shapes in the snow didn't get up, most did; the mines had gone off before the majority of the aliens had entered the field. The Besquith retreated back toward the tents.

"Well, that'll at least make them think about it next time," Shirazi said.

* * *

Command Center, Roget's World, Kak'L'Kak System

"Do we have anything else to make them think about this time?" McClain asked three days later.

Each day the Besquith had pushed forward, ever closer. Although the uranium walls had held, the constant impacts were wearing them away, and Shirazi knew it wouldn't be long before they failed. Although they'd set up second- and third-level defensive positions in the mine, they were nowhere as strong as the ones at the entrance to the mine.

He'd seen the Besquith rush forward several times before, and the Humans had been unprepared for their speed and ferocity. If they got into the mines, he wasn't sure they'd be able to hold.

"No," Shirazi said. "We're out of options." The drone attack had worked well and killed several Besquith before they'd destroyed the fleet of drones. Hidden in the snow, the booby traps had killed several others. By their best count, though, there was still a company of the aliens left, and, based on their proximity to the mine, Shirazi figured they would rush the mine the next day. He would have if their positions were reversed.

"What do you think?" Kazemi asked, coming to stand next to him.

"I think the wall is going to be breached," Shirazi said. "Probably tomorrow. We're down to about a platoon. We're outnumbered and outgunned. It's inevitable. You know it; I know it. Hells, even the dogs probably know it. When they rush us, they're probably going to get in." He shrugged. "There's only one thing left to do."

Kazemi looked up in surprise. "We're surrendering? You think they'd actually honor a surrender?"

"Hell, no, we're not surrendering. Not to the likes of them. We're not going to surrender; we're going to attack."

"But they outnumber us, and they have better weapons…"

"Yes they do." Shirazi smiled and tapped his temple. "But we're smarter."

Kazemi's brows knit. "What do you have in mind?"

"How extensive is the tunnel network for the mine?"

"Damn extensive, sir—you know that. What am I missing?"

"Do the tunnels only go back into the mountain, or do some of them loop around back in front of the mine?"

"They go everywhere. Back into the mountain, to both sides, and a few wind back in front of the mine entrance…" He smiled. "…right under where the Besquith are dug in." He shook his head. "They're pretty deep, though, I thought."

"I don't know," Shirazi said. "I don't know mines. But I do know we have some of the best diggers in the galaxy here in this mine. If sufficiently motivated—like if a group of aliens were about to eat them—I think they might be able to dig us to where we need to go, don't you think?"

"They just might at that," Kazemi said with a chuckle.

* * *

Command Center, Roget's World, Kak'L'Kak System

"Make ready your troops," the lead Caroon miner said. "We're starting the final phase of the dig."

"Okay," Shirazi said to his assembled troops. "It's time. Time to make a name, not only for ourselves, but for humanity as well. The other races laugh at us as mercs—hell, the only reason we got this contract was that we were the only company the Caroons could afford. But here we are, and here's where we're going to make our stand.

"Now, we could try to defend the tunnel entrance another day, but in looking at the fortifications, I don't think they're going to hold, and when they fail, it will be down to hand-to-hand combat with the Besquith. I don't know about you, but that's not something I'm looking forward to. Rather than let that happen, we're going to attack.

"Right now, the Caroons are digging a tunnel into the Besquith's camp, and are about to reach the surface. If they've done their jobs right, we'll come out right behind the tent we've identified as their barracks, where the dogs are resting comfortably, getting ready for their assault on us tomorrow.

"We're going to hit them there and wipe out as many as we can, then kill any of the stragglers who won't surrender."

"Do you think there'll be any who will surrender?" Kazemi asked from the back.

Shirazi shook his head. "No, I don't. If you see a Besquith and it doesn't have its paws in the air, shoot it. In fact, shoot it several times just to make sure. You've all manned the wall and seen how much damage they can take. If you put one down, make sure it *stays* down."

Shirazi smiled. "If we all do our jobs well, when the sun rises, humanity will be the winner here on this planet, and we'll be one more step closer to being taken seriously by the aliens. Any questions? No? Then grab your gear and follow me."

Shirazi turned to the Caroon and said, "Lead on."

The anteater-analogue dropped to all four feet and loped off quickly, and the Humans had to double-time to keep up. The Caroon led them to a part of the tunnel system Shirazi had never been in before, and, looking at the walls, he realized why—they hadn't existed until today. The boring machine they used had just finished digging out the tunnel, and the Caroons were still spraying sealant on the walls in places and installing shoring where needed.

The Caroon Shirazi was following didn't stop for any of this activity; he charged past it as if it was of no matter. After another minute, they came to a small spur. "Wait here," the Caroon said, indicating the side passage.

Shirazi signaled his men to go into the passage, which was almost the exact size needed to hold all of them. Shirazi nodded in appreciation. *The Caroons really are excellent diggers.*

A minute later, a machine trundled backward from up-tunnel. The massive vehicle was the boring machine, Shirazi saw as it passed on its tank-like treads. Its front was an interesting mélange of boring bits, lasers, and scoops for picking up the rock and sending it back behind it. Despite its size, though, it rolled quietly, with a minimum of noise

Still, the noise reverberated in the tunnel, and Shirazi winced, hoping against hope the Besquith hadn't heard it.

As soon as the machine passed, the Caroon was back, and he waved the Humans forward again. Shirazi smiled; even the Caroons were trying to be quiet. Of course, they'd have to be idiots not to realize their lives depended on the Humans' success.

Shirazi led the troopers forward to the end of the tunnel, where two ladders had been propped up into a 10-foot-diameter tube that extended up toward the surface. The floor underneath the shaft was covered in foam, with a number of Caroons standing around, shifting nervously.

The lead Caroon motioned for the Humans to mount the ladders, and Shirazi stepped forward and looked up into the shaft. Near the top of the ladders, a Caroon waited on each, holding a mining laser. The shaft was still sealed above them.

"What do we do?" Shirazi whispered.

"Climb up the ladders on the back side from my men," the lead Caroon replied. "Breach is imminent. As soon as you're ready, they'll drop the plug."

Shirazi nodded, and his eyes swept the men nearby. Their eyes met his, and he could see the fear in them. They all nodded, though; they'd heard and were ready.

Shirazi gave them a smile to strengthen their resolve. "Let's teach them why they need to fear humanity. For New Persia and Earth!" he said in a stage whisper.

He turned and went to the closest ladder, going up the back side from the Caroon until he couldn't go any farther. Although the ladders were nearly vertical, it still took most of his strength to hold himself in place, and he hoped it wouldn't be long.

He looked down at the lead Caroon, who nodded and moved back out of the way. The Caroon above Shirazi turned his laser on and went to work. From his new perspective, he could see the area above them had already been prepared; very little cutting was necessary to finish it. Within seconds, the center of the roof fell away to drop onto the foam below it. If he hadn't been right above it, he wouldn't have heard it hit.

The Caroons standing around leapt forward and pushed the tops of the ladders away from the walls they were braced on at the top, and Shirazi found himself now on the "up" side of the ladder. The Caroon on the other side of the ladder dropped his laser—caught by one of the Caroons below him—and jumped off to land on the foam. It was so well choreographed, Shirazi had to wonder if they'd practiced it before.

Once the ladders were free, they telescoped, extending up beyond the mouth of the shaft. The ladder came to rest on the lip of the shaft, and Shirazi climbed as quickly as he could to the top. There, not 15 feet away, was the barracks tent. The tunnel was easily within three or four feet of where he'd asked them to put it. *Amazing.*

He looked down into the shaft, gave them a thumbs-up, and crawled the rest of the way up the ladder. It was snowing again, but he barely noticed as he started forward to the tent. He couldn't hear any noises coming from it or around the camp.

His men flowed forward like wraiths, their white camouflage blending in with the snow. Shirazi collected his squad and moved toward the command tent, while Kazemi took his squad around to the entrance of the barracks tent.

* * *

Besquith Base, Roget's World, Kak'L'Kak System

Kazemi motioned his squad forward as he led them around to the entrance of the barracks tent. Outnumbered two-to-one by the Besquith, he knew his portion of the assault would help determine the outcome of the attack. If he was successful, the Humans had a chance of achieving victory; if he wasn't, they would all be dead before the sun came up.

Even though they hadn't seen any of the Besquith roaming around the camp in the middle of the night, the snow swirling around helped hide his force and gave him a sense of security. They reached the entrance undetected. Kazemi reached for the hatch, but it started moving on its own.

"*Someone's coming!*" he whispered as he jumped to the side.

The alien stepped out of the hatch and turned away from Kazemi to shut it. It saw the rest of the squad and opened its mouth to call a warning, but then Kazemi was on its back, and he looped his left arm around the Besquith and jammed his combat-armored forearm into the monster's mouth.

Rather than try to flip the Human off, the Besquith bit down on his armor, and its rows of shark teeth crushed it.

"Kill it!" Kazemi gasped in pain. He jabbed his knife repeatedly into the alien's back, but it didn't appear to have any effect.

The creature was taller than Kazemi's six feet and far more massive, and it leaned forward slightly, lifting Kazemi from the ground, and began shaking, trying to throw him off. Kazemi had to drop his knife to hold on.

After a couple of seconds it paused to get a grasp on Kazemi, and Sergeant Ghorbani stepped forward and shoved his knife into the Besquith's throat all the way to the hilt, then ripped it out to the side. The alien fought for another few seconds, then it collapsed. Kazemi picked up his knife and cut the Besquith's throat the rest of the way, just to be sure.

"You're hurt," Ghorbani said, pointing to the blood dripping from Kazemi's mangled arm.

Kazemi looked down. It hurt—a lot—but blood wasn't spurting, and it didn't look like any of the arteries had been hit. "No time for it," Kazemi said. He waved the rest of the squad forward. "Let's go."

The tent was a giant open bay, with rows of cot-like beds lining both sides, and heaters interspersed to fight off the cold of the Roget's World winter. The door had been open for a while, and the cold air was starting to cause the troopers to shift in their beds. He shut the hatch after the last trooper entered and pointed toward where the soldiers needed to set the satchel charges they were carrying.

The men snuck forward, placing the charges throughout the space. It would have been better if they could have just knifed the Besquiths in their sleep, but after his short struggle with the one at the door, Kazemi was glad they hadn't opted for that strategy. He didn't see how the ten members of his squad could have killed almost 30 of the Besquith without one of them alerting the rest of the group.

Corporal Ardavan had just placed the charge in the farthest corner when the Besquith in the bed next to him sat upright and yelled, "Intruders!"

Ardavan tried to run, but the alien sprang from bed, cutting off his escape.

"Humans! Intruders!" the Besquith shouted again. The other Besquith began sitting up in their beds.

"Run!" Ardavan yelled, retreating to the satchel charge he'd just placed as he drew his hypervelocity pistol. "Get out of here."

Kazemi opened the door, and Private Sasani and Corporal Mazandarani ran through it into the cold. He could see the rest of the men had been cut off by the Besquith. Some had drawn their rifles, and others their knives or pistols, but all were moments from being killed in horrific ways. There would be no escape for them.

One of the Besquith turned toward the door, saw Kazemi, and shouted, "More of them at the door."

Kazemi knew two things; his group was overmatched in this fight, and if he failed to kill the Besquith troopers, the rest of Asbaran would be overwhelmed, too.

He dove through the doorway and triggered the explosives.

* * *

Command Tent, Roget's World, Kak'L'Kak System

Shirazi and his squad had made it to the command tent unopposed, and the squad stacked up outside the door. "Quietly," he reminded them, "until you need to go loud." He triggered the door open, and the men flowed forward, only to find themselves in an airlock-like space, probably to keep the cold air out. The fact that the outer door was unlocked or didn't require a code was sloppy. Or, Shirazi realized, probably just indicative of how little the Besquith feared them.

Hopefully we'll change that right now, he thought as he stepped to the controls of the next door.

The men got ready again. He nodded. "Here we go."

He toggled the door open, then he rushed forward with the rest of the squad at his back.

The tent was about a 30-foot square, with consoles lining the perimeter of two sides. Several Tri-V monitors showed the mouth of the mine. Most of his attention was taken up by the three technicians monitoring the equipment and the larger Besquith in the command seat overseeing the operations.

"You're late—" the Besquith in the command seat started to say as he turned. Two things happened simultaneously to interrupt him, though—he saw Shirazi at the same time a massive set of explosions rocked the tent. "Intruders!" he roared. "Kill them!"

"Fire!" Shirazi yelled in response, and he leveled his laser rifle and fired.

Unfortunately the alien leader was faster than Shirazi had expected, and the shot went wide as the Besquith exploded from his seat in a blur of motion. Some of the technicians weren't as lucky; he saw laser bolts from his troopers spear into them.

All he got was a glimpse, though, for the leader was immediately on him, slashing down at him with its razor-sharp claws. Shirazi brought his rifle up and blocked the attack, but the force of the strike snapped the stock. He threw the half in his right hand into the alien's face and drew his knife as he deflected the alien's follow-up attack with the rifle half in his left hand.

The alien swatted the rifle away then swiped at the knife, impaling it in his palm. The force of the blow ripped the weapon from Shirazi's grasp. The Besquith's lips pulled back from its mouthful of shark's teeth in a snarl—or maybe a smile; Shirazi couldn't tell—as the alien pulled the knife from its paw.

"You're mine now, Human," the Besquith said, dropping the knife to the side. It slashed out with its other claw, catching Shirazi unprepared as it ripped across his face. He fell backward, blood filling his left eye.

"No!" yelled Sergeant Will McClain as he dove onto the alien from the side.

The Besquith was more massive than McClain had expected, though, and his attempt at a tackle left him hanging off the alien's side as it stood, unmoving. The Besquith slapped McClain to the ground and stomped on his head. The armor shattered with the force of the blow, as did McClain's head. He jerked once and went still, but his sacrifice had given Shirazi the time he needed to draw his hypervelocity pistol.

"Don't move!" he ordered, looking down the barrel at the Besquith.

The alien leapt forward, but this time Shirazi was ready, and he fired. The round went through the Besquith's eye at four times the speed of sound, snapping its head back and dropping the alien in place.

Shirazi scooped up his knife and turned, but the other aliens were down, along with most of his squad. Only Corporal Paul Sparks was still standing. Both spun as the doorway opened, only to find Sergeant Major Kazemi, Private Sasani, and Corporal Mazandarani.

"Everyone else?" Shirazi asked.

Kazemi shook his head. "The Besquith woke up, and we had to blow the charges early. Most of the troops were trapped in the barracks when the charges went off."

"Did you get them all?"

"All of the ones in the barracks. I have imagery of 31 before the charges went off. A couple survived the blasts, but we put them down."

"There were four in here; that's 35."

"And our latest estimate was 38?"

"Yeah; we're a few short."

"They must have had a—"

With roars of challenge, five Besquith shredded the sides of the command structure with their claws and sprang into the tent. Shirazi and Kazemi each killed one as the aliens charged, then the other three were on top of them.

Corporal Sparks screamed a challenge and stepped forward, firing his rifle at the aliens. He shot one, then the Besquith behind it ripped out his throat with a swipe as it went past.

Shirazi fired again, taking a chunk out of its arm, and the Besquith turned on him. He fired again, but the alien dodged and then slapped his pistol away. Shirazi stepped back, drawing his knife, and fell into a defensive stance.

The Besquith leaped forward, and Shirazi tried to backpedal, but a body on the ground caught his feet, and he fell over backward. The alien trooper grabbed his shoulders and rode him down. Shirazi jabbed at the Besquith with his knife, and after several tries, finally found a joint in the trooper's armor. The Besquith roared into his face, and Shirazi pulled on the knife, trying to cut deeper.

"I will eat you now," the Besquith swore, ignoring the wound, and it leaned forward, its mouth open, trying to get at Shirazi's neck. Shirazi brought up his other arm and got his forearm across the Besquith's forehead, momentarily stopping the Besquith's forward movement.

Shirazi could feel the Besquith's hot breath in his face as it pulled on his shoulders, trying to draw him close enough to bite. Shirazi could feel his arm growing weak—the alien was incredibly strong—but the horrific sight of the creature's rows of shark teeth moving ever closer to his neck gave him an adrenaline boost to hold it off a bit longer. He pulled the knife from the Besquith and dragged it along the alien's armor, searching for another opening.

The Besquith reached forward, sliding its arm around the back of Shirazi's head. Shirazi could feel his strength waning, but then his knife found the creature's armpit, and he drove the blade in. The alien pulled back and roared again, and Shirazi allowed himself to be pulled forward so he could thrust again, driving the blade in as far as he could.

He must have hit something vital, for the creature's eyes rolled into the back of its head and it fell forward onto Shirazi. Unprepared for the monster's sudden collapse, he wasn't able to direct the body to the side, and it fell onto his face. He was able to turn his head slightly so he could breathe—barely—but the stench of the Besquith threatened to overwhelm him. The weight of the alien, plus all of its armor and other combat gear, bore down on him, making breathing even more difficult. He tried to push the alien off him, but the weight was more than he could move on his own, and he struggled feebly, feeling himself grow weaker with each attempt, as his oxygen-starved body failed him.

His vision narrowed, and his breath came in shallow gasps as he realized he was going to die there. Even though he'd killed the Besquith, it was going to have the final laugh in whatever hell it was currently in, as its dead body killed Shirazi in turn.

Shirazi struggled to draw in a breath, but was unable, and everything grew dim. Just before the darkness closed, the Besquith was rolled off his chest, and air once again filled his lungs. His head rolled to the side to see Kazemi on his knees next to him.

"Bastards are fucking heavy," Kazemi said with a grunt. He struggled to his feet, then moved back a step as blood from one of his wounds dripped onto Shirazi. "Sorry 'bout that, sir."

Shirazi tried to sit up, but wasn't able. Kazemi leaned forward, offered him a hand, and pulled Shirazi up to a seated position. He looked around with his one good eye, then shook his head. Kazemi was the only being left standing, although Shirazi had no idea how; he had more cuts and holes than Shirazi could easily count. Only the older soldier's fierce determination held him erect.

Shirazi reached into a leg pocket, pulled out a med-kit, and handed it to him.

"S'all right," Kazemi said with a slur. He pointed to Shirazi's face. "You use it, sir."

"Take it, you hard-nosed bastard. You're hurt worse than I am."

The senior enlisted took the dispenser and sprayed a couple of his worst wounds, and a hiss of breath escaped his lips. "First time using one?" Shirazi asked.

Kazemi nodded; it seemed like that was all he could do.

"Burns a little, doesn't it? Shirazi added with a smile.

"Compared with that, all the fires of hell are little more than a feeble campfire." He shook his head as he leaned forward to put his hands on his knees. "Given a choice between doing that again and outright dying, I think I'll take the latter."

After a second, Kazemi rose. "Ready to get up?" he asked.

"Yeah," Shirazi said, and Kazemi helped him to his feet.

"I have to say, sir, that sucked," Kazemi said, motioning to all the bodies around the command center.

Shirazi shrugged, overwhelmed by the slaughter. "It could have been worse, I guess."

"Oh, yeah? How?"

"They could have broken into the mines, captured us, and eaten us alive." He shuddered as a vision of the Besquith leaning forward over him ran through his head.

"That would indeed have been worse."

"And we're still alive, with our honor intact. We didn't run, nor did we give in to the Besquith. Even better, we've shown we can win a straight-up fight with some of the galaxy's best troops. People will want to hire us because we've shown we can win. More importantly, we now have some credits we can spend on better equipment, which will help increase our odds in our next engagement."

"So you want to continue with Asbaran Solutions?" Kazemi asked. "Even though it's just you and I remaining?"

Shirazi nodded. "We'll reconstitute our forces. We'll re-equip and rearm. We'll go forward, and like the Huma bird, we'll rise from the ashes and be reborn. In fact, that'll be our new logo."

"A Huma bird?" Kazemi asked.

"Yes. What could be better? We're down, but we're *not* beaten. We'll rise again, and we'll show these Galactics why Persia once ruled on Earth. We have a fighting spirit that won't be broken. Long live the Huma, and long live Asbaran Solutions!"

* * * * *

Chris Kennedy Bio

A Webster Award winner and three-time Dragon Award finalist, Chris Kennedy is a Science Fiction/Fantasy/Young Adult author, speaker, and small-press publisher who has written over 25 books and published more than 100 others. Chris' stories include the "Occupied Seattle" military fiction duology, "The Theogony" and "Codex Regius" science fiction trilogies, stories in the "Four Horsemen," "Fallen World," and "In Revolution Born" universes and the "War for Dominance" fantasy trilogy. Get his free book, "Shattered Crucible," at his website, https://chriskennedypublishing.com.

Called "fantastic" and "a great speaker," he has coached hundreds of beginning authors and budding novelists on how to self-publish their stories at a variety of conferences, conventions and writing guild presentations. He is the author of the award-winning #1 bestseller, "Self-Publishing for Profit: How to Get Your Book Out of Your Head and Into the Stores," as well as the leadership training book, "Leadership from the Darkside."

Chris lives in Virginia Beach, Virginia, with his wife, and is the holder of a doctorate in educational leadership and master's degrees in both business and public administration. Follow Chris on Facebook at https://www.facebook.com/ckpublishing/.

# # # # #

They Called Him Pops by Kevin Steverson

Chapter One

Petes' Dive Bar

Parmick

Parmick System

"Yep, I knew them boys," Waldon said.

He brushed a little mine grit off his coveralls and took a sip of his beer. It wasn't very cold, but it was colder than when the original owner ran the place. Ol' peg-legged Pete was a stingy man, and everybody knew it. Good riddance to him. Ligtarny, the new owner, ran a respectable establishment.

"Knew who?" Pullnerth asked. He wiped his mouth with his arm, the fur soaking up the liquid. He loved the Human beer, but unless he used a straw, he tended to spill some when he drank it.

"Yeah," Ligtarny asked, his translator stretching out the word. He hopped over the bar and landed without spilling the pitcher he was holding. "Who? Are you saying you're familiar with the Peacemakers who put a stop to Barlung?"

The Jivool sitting across from him wiped his mouth again and said, "Waldon, you're a fabricator of lies. You don't know any Peacemakers. You've been here for fifteen years. I've worked with you on the mine equipment through all of them. From when it was barely operating through when we suffered through the last owner."

"Aw, hell, Pully," Waldon said, "that hurts. You cut me deep. I thought we was friends."

"We are," Pullnerth said, "you're my best Human friend. But that doesn't give you a pass on telling a lie. If you'll admit it's a made up story like so many of your others, that'll be different."

Ligtarny filled both of their mugs, poured himself one, and sat down. His knees stuck up near his head as he had his feet in the seat with him. Resembling a toad from earth, he blinked one of his huge eyes and looked at Waldon. He enjoyed the Human's stories, lies or not.

"Wait," Waldon said as he leaned back, "let me get this straight. If I tell you from the start I'm making up a story, you're good with it. But if I tell you something that's just as all-fired crazy, but true, you have a problem with it? What in the hell?"

"Telling stories is an art," Pullnerth explained. "An artist is free to embellish. Telling a story while pretending it's true in order to trick a being into believing it is wrong. That's dishonest, and you'll be called a fabricator of lies. In my clan this is looked at the same as one being a litigator of laws, or a repairer of teeth. Both are necessary, unfortunately, but no one looks forward to spending time with them."

Waldon took a drink and then realized what he had been called. "Wait. What? Are you calling me a dentist or…or a *lawyer*?" he asked, narrowing his eyes. "'Cause you know them's fightin' words where I come from."

"Yes," Pullnerth said without hesitation. "Unless you reveal the story to be fiction before telling it, you are both of those, in my eyes. Like dealing with them, I would prefer to know about it from the beginning. They're necessary, but don't let it be a surprise. I'll need to know in advance so I'm mentally prepared to deal with it."

"Damn, Pully," Waldon said, "next thing you know, you'll be calling me a politician."

"No," Pullnerth explained. "They lie every time they speak. You don't do that."

Waldon choked on his beer. He managed to swallow half the mouthful while the rest dripped down his coveralls as he laughed and coughed at the same time. He wiped his face and grinned. Politicians. It was the same all over the galaxy, on Union or non-Union worlds.

Ligtarny turned one of his eyes to each of his friends. It was getting good. When they started calling each other names before telling a story, he knew it would be an interesting night. He glanced around to ensure his employees were doing fine. His bartender was pouring a drink, the waitress was busy taking an order, and security was seated in the corner with a bored expression, so he turned back to his friends.

"Fine," Waldon said, raising his hands, palms out. One of them was a mechanical hand, the metal completely exposed below the cuff of his long-sleeved shirt. It was an older model, but it had been expensive when it was built.

He said, "If I make a story up, I'll let you know. I'm telling you, though, this one is true. I knew them boys."

Still seeing disbelief on the Jivool's face, Waldon explained, "Not the Peacemakers. Lord knows I don't care for revenuers. I knew them two Pushtal."

"Politician," Pullnerth said. He crossed his arms, daring Waldon to deny it.

"Ok," Waldon said, throwing his hands up in resignation. "I knew the man who raised them. I didn't really know the Pushtal. They were knee high when I left the Aspara System."

"Half-lies," decided Pullnerth. "You're still a politician, only now you're one that keeps getting re-elected."

"Well, thank you for that," Waldon said, "I think." He drained his mug, grabbed the pitcher with his shiny hand, and refilled it. "Now do you want to hear the story or not?"

Ligtarny's tongue came out, looped up, wiped one of his eyes, and disappeared back into his mouth. "I do," he said. He leaned forward and nodded quickly several times, his excitement obvious.

Waldon shuddered. "Blah! Why do you do that?" he asked the Naylorn.

"I must," Ligtarny answered. "I cannot clean my eye with a digit. The pad will stick to it and irritate the eye." He smiled, his toothless mouth stretching across the width of his face, and shrugged.

"Tell us this half-lie," Pullnerth said, "you tooth-pulling, legal-speaking, career politician."

Waldon held his beer up in salute and said, "You're lucky we're friends, Pully, or I'd give you the ol' one-two."

He took a long drink, set his mug down, and wiped his mouth one last time. Staring off in the distance with the memories coming back to him, he began to speak.

* * *

Chapter Two

Pete's Dive Bar

Town, Parmick

"They called him Pops," Waldon said. "Pops McCoy. It wasn't his real name. His real name was Milton Gene McCoy. Of course, if you called him that, you better be ready to fight. Only his family back home on Earth, in the north Georgia mountains, called him that."

Ligtarny asked, "He didn't wish to be called by his given name? Why?"

"He never said," Waldon answered, "and I never asked. Besides, when I first met him, he was already in his late sixties. 'Pops' fit him."

"Isn't that an advanced Human age to be mining in a place like the Aspara system?" Pullnerth asked.

"Yeah," Waldon said. He took a sip. "It was, but Pops didn't act like it. I swear he was the toughest man I ever met. Maybe it was the treatment he got so he could pilot a CASPer. I don't know. If he did get the treatment, it was way back when. Probably not as refined as what they get these days."

"Those war machines made the difference here on Parmick," Pullnerth explained to the bar owner. "Without them, you wouldn't own Pete's Dive Bar."

Ligtarny nodded, raised his mug, and said, "Then let us drink to the CASPers and those who operate them."

The three of them raised their mugs. Several of those sitting around them raised theirs as well. The waitresses who worked in the establishment under the previous owner were out of work mercenaries. They owned and piloted the mechs and aided the Peacemakers in ridding the colony of Barlung and his mining operation. Now it was run by a Caroon corporation after a series of explosions deep in the mine during the revolt revealed a new vein of red diamonds. The miners received fair wages and a much better working environment under the new owners.

"Ok," Waldon said. "No more questions, you're throwing me off. Where was I? Oh, yeah. See, what had happened was...."

* * *

Asteroid Ring

Kanora Moon

Aspara System

Waldon Baines reached for the piece of pipe floating near his head. He slid it on the end of the wrench and slipped his feet into the straps he'd just screwed to the cutter. Using his legs and the extra length of the bar for more leverage, he managed to finally loosen the last bolt on the outer housing. Once he had it out, he'd be able to replace the power amplifier and get it working again.

"You gonna fix that thang or what?" Pops asked. He had a hand on a strap in the hold, watching. "We need to get it back out there on that rock. They's bound to be a vein or two of the good stuff on it."

"I'm trying," Waldon said as he moved the housing. "It would be a lot easier to fix if we went back to the planet. Working in microgravity isn't easy, you know, especially when my power wrench is broken."

"Aw, hell," Pops dismissed with a wave of his free hand. "If'n I was your age, I'da done had it fixed."

"Nope," Waldon said, "you wouldn't. If you were my age, you would still be in a merc unit somewhere. Or with the Galactic Haulers."

"Same thing," Pops murmured.

"Wassat?" Waldon asked from deep inside the cutter.

"Nuthin'," Pops said. "Get that other'n connected so we can get it back out there. We're taking a chance as it is. Dang pirates out here stealing folks' loads. Two weeks ago, over near Nylin Moon, ol' Stinky got plum robbed. They emptied his hold while him and his partner were down on the surface."

Waldon stuck his head up out of the compartment and said, "Stinky probably left his hold open. You know he doesn't bother closing it when leaves in that mini shuttle."

Pops ran a hand through his thinning flat top haircut. "Yeah, you're probably right. He don't close it 'cause he might get locked out again. Damn fool."

"Your ship is in a little better shape than his," Waldon said. "I doubt whoever's sneaking around would try it with the *Naydeen*."

"Someone tries to rob me," Pops said, "and they's a dead sumbitch."

"I hear ya," Waldon agreed.

He kind of doubted it, though. Pops was an old man. There was no other way to say it. Waldon had known him for several years, and Pops was every bit of seventy. He still worked out on the exercise equipment in the spare berth, and got around like he was much younger most days, but the years were there.

* * *

Chapter Three

Kanora Moon

Aspara System

Pops adjusted the angle of the cutter and stepped back softly. He made sure not to move too far from the machine as it cut into the cliff wall. His tether to the shuttle had several more yards of cable, but it was best to be sure. The small moon he and Waldon were mining had some gravity, enough to hold him down.

As a precaution, he'd fired two anchors into the soil from the belly of the shuttle when he'd landed. If he needed to get off the surface quickly, he could blow the restraining bolts on them. He hoped he never needed to. They weren't cheap.

If this new location gave up more of the moon's gold like the last, it would be time to start thinking about upgrading his equipment. The cutter was an old, outdated machine, along with the shuttle he used to bring it down from his ship, *Naydeen*. The Caroon mining exploration ship was solid, but she was old, too. Half the surface scanning gear didn't work anymore. A lot of what he did was now guesswork. Like this location.

Pops checked his environmental status. The readouts appeared on the inside of his helmet and still allowed him a clear view through the front. He had several hours before he would need to swap out his oxygen scrubber and another day of power left. The rest of his equipment may have been old, but the suit he owned to work where there was no atmosphere was not. He'd used most of the profits from his last strike to purchase it. There were several companies across the galaxy with suits designed for Humans, as well as many other races. They weren't cheap, but they were better than most brands made on Earth.

Pops heard the static and crackle that usually meant a call coming from Waldon. It happened twice more with no call following. Deciding Waldon was probably working on the communication gear or the settings, Pops forgot about them and eased over to check the cutter's progress.

* * *

Naydeen

Waldon yawned and checked the fuel status. It was good, and the F11 tanks on *Naydeen* were half full, so there was no need to worry. Pops would be back in a day or so. The shuttle had several spare oxygen scrubbers for his suit and the ability to recharge its power cell. He was bored. He drained the last of his pouchful of protein shake and settled back in the seat.

He considered working on his power wrench. It would occupy him for most of the day. For the last couple of years he'd worked with Pops as his general mechanic and only crew member. It wasn't a bad gig. Every now and then when they made a good haul of precious metals, he got a bonus in addition to his pay. He had a few credits saved now, and all his debts were paid off. He could deal with the boredom if it meant finally getting ahead.

A bonus was coming for sure this month. They had nearly half a cargo container of gold in the bay. Pops had been right. They'd hit a vein of the good stuff once the cutter was running again. Hopefully the old cutter would hold up long enough to see if they got lucky again. It would be nice to have a full container to sell.

The proximity alarm went off, startling Waldon as he was dozing. He looked at the screen in front of him and realized it didn't show him the ship's sensor screen. He'd left it on the internal systems check. Whatever ship was out there, it hadn't been detected until it set off the alarms. That could only mean one thing. The ship was about to be locked with another, and probably boarded.

He hit the button on the comms to warn Pops. Before he could say anything, the signal dropped off. He tried it twice more and realized the ship was being jammed. He thought it had to be the same pirates who'd robbed Stinky.

Waldon reached for a strap and pulled himself out of the control seat. He quickly swapped the screens to show what was outside the ship. Near the rear of Pop's ship was an old freighter. It wasn't much more than twice their size, so the profit margins on hauling legitimate goods was close to zero. No wonder they'd chosen pirating instead.

He felt the ship shudder when the boarding tube connected with the cargo ramp. They'd force it open or cut their way in. Either way, that gave Waldon a little time. He pushed off the bulkhead toward the back of the control compartment and the hatch. Pops kept a small armory hidden in a panel in the passageway between berths. Depending on the race attempting to gain entry, having a weapon might mean surviving the raid. If they didn't take the whole ship.

He made it to the panel before the boarders gained entry. He decided he had time to put on one of the emergency suits stored in the same false panel. He'd hold off on the helmet and sealing his suit until he had a little more information on the unwanted guests. He clipped the helmet to his side and grabbed a flechette rifle. The darts would damage most suits and cut deep into flesh, but they wouldn't cause an outer hull breach.

Before he closed the panel, he activated the lock-hatch protocol. Several hatches leading to the control compartment slid closed and locked. The hatches couldn't be pried open because the sides of each were within the bulkheads. If you didn't know the code and where the override panel controlling them was located, the only way through would be cutting them. Waldon was no longer annoyed at Pops for being suspicious by nature and insisting he knew about all the security features installed on *Naydeen.*

Thankful the suit had magnetic boots, Waldon made his way to the cargo hold and crouched down behind the waist-high, half-full container. He set his rifle down and held his helmet in his hands. He waited to see if the boarders would enter wearing their own suits, or if the connecting tunnel was pressurized with atmosphere. It didn't take long for him to find out.

With a series of screeches, the small hatch in the center of the ramp was forced open an inch at a time. Whoever was doing it had a powered prybar. Waldon checked the display on his forearm. There was no loss of pressure, and the oxygen content remained steady. He put his helmet down and picked the rifle up. Unless they'd scanned the ship before boarding, he'd be a surprise. Especially if they'd been watching for the return of the small shuttle normally stored in the bay adjacent to the cargo hold.

Once the hatch was open enough, the first boarder put a bar in place at the bottom of the opening to keep it from closing and slipped through. Waldon hesitated. He was surprised to see the orange and black of a tiger. The pirates were Pushtal. *This is not going to be good,* he thought. The Pushtal had a reputation for being ruthless. Once they found him, they *would* kill him, leaving no survivors.

He fired the rifle...and missed. He was a technician and a mechanic, not a trained soldier. The dart hit the ramp and ricocheted back to hit the container he was hiding behind. Waldon fired three more times, and the final shot hit the pirate in the shoulder. It dropped below his angle of fire. As he stood slightly to take another shot, he was spun around by several of the same type darts hitting him in his upper arm.

Waldon fell to his side, bleeding heavily. He looked at his arm. The suit was ripped open, and he knew the muscles were torn up pretty badly. The blood was dark, quickly soaking his sleeve and running across his chest as he lay on his side. Feeling lightheaded, he reached up and pulled the tab below his armpit, enacting one of the suit's tourniquets, and passed out.

* * *

Pushtal Ship *Ragged Edge*

The Pushtal growled softly as his mate dug in his shoulder with one of her claws. After a moment she pulled the flechette from the bleeding hole. Several of the crewmembers watched as the rough surgery was performed. They nodded in appreciation of their captain's pain tolerance. None of them would have cried out, or so they each thought.

"Damn that Human," Kilthak said. "I should have shot him again instead of leaving him to bleed out."

"He's surely dead," his mate consoled him as she wrapped the shoulder. "He was hit in the arm and the chest. There was much blood over his upper body. I don't know how much Humans have inside them, but he was covered in most of his."

Kilthak reached up with his good hand and ruffled the fur between her ears. "You're right, Meetha. The pain is made all the more bearable with the thought of the gold in our hold. We'll be able to upgrade and hire more crew. Perhaps the down payment on another ship is possible."

"Two ships is the beginning of a fleet," she answered as she gathered her things to leave him to his decisions.

"Blythin, target the engines," Kilthak decided. "If we can't get to the operations center, no one will. Let it burn into the moon. The type of ship I have in mind will be better suited to our needs than that one, anyway."

"Firing two missiles now," answered his younger brother.

"Take us back into the asteroid field while we plan our next move. The fools in this system continue to be ripe for the slaughter," the pirate captain said.

* * *

Chapter Four

Pops picked up a rock and threw it at the cutter. It bounced and went sailing off in the light gravity. It didn't make the cutter start working again, but it made him feel better. He eased over to the break in the cliff to see if there was any sign of gold or platinum. He didn't see any, not even traces of the type of rock found near veins of gold. Once Waldon fixed it again, he'd try somewhere else. *Hell, maybe we'll find red diamonds*, he thought. *Nah, I ain't that lucky.*

He opened the panel on his forearm and called Waldon. There was no answer. He tried several times, then decided to move the cutter back into the shuttle and try again with the shuttle's communication system. A mineral in the area he was mining could be blocking the transmission.

"Probably the same dang thing that kept me from getting his call a while ago," Pops said out loud. No one was within hours of him to hear him.

The cutter wasn't hard to move. The lack of gravity helped him. He made sure to move slowly and deliberately. With his tether still secured in the cargo hold, he engaged the reverse spin on the two anchors, and they twisted themselves out of the rock and dirt. Once they were free, he made his way into the hold and closed the ramp. After it was up, he retracted the two tie-down anchors.

He tried again to call Waldon from the cockpit of the shuttle. There was still no answer, and he was concerned. Waldon was on the same time schedule he was, so at worst, he was taking a nap. The incoming call had always woken him before. Pops pushed the shuttle past the recommended thrust as he left the thin atmosphere of the moon.

When he reached the designated orbit of his ship, he entered it and chose a direction. He'd catch up to *Naydeen* in no time. He watched his sensors for signs of the ship. Once he'd made a complete orbit, he knew there was an issue. Either the ship was gone, or it was damaged and drifting closer and closer to the moon. It would take some time before there would be an issue with burn in, but if Waldon was hurt, or worse, he need to get to it fast.

He dropped lower in orbit and made the trip again. On his eighth pass, closer to the moon each time, he caught a flicker of something on the edge of sensor range. He entered the adjustments into the helm and pushed it even harder. He flipped the shuttle and began slowing, timing it to match the drifting ship.

When he got within viewing range, he saw the damage. The engines were destroyed. Very little atmosphere was venting from the powerplant, though. The compartment had sealed itself, by design. His sensors indicated the ship still had some functioning power, but no mobility.

Pop's slammed his fist on the console. Thinking quickly, he landed the shuttle on top of his ship and engaged the magnetic landing pads. Once the two were locked together, he increased thrust, and slowly pulled the ship from its descending orbit and up into open space.

When the movement was nearly stopped, he disengaged the magnetic pads and flew around to the side of *Naydeen*. He activated the shuttle bay door, and to his surprise, it slowly slid open. He landed inside, shut down the shuttle, and waited for the bay to seal and regain pressure. Once the indicators showed it held steady and was safe, he moved as fast as his old legs could carry him. The magnetic boots of his suit kept him on the deck. He had to find Waldon.

He found him lying in dried blood, his suit crusted with it. His knees were up, the soles still connected to the deck. Fearing the worst, Pops knelt beside Waldon and felt for a pulse. He found it. It was weak, but it was steady. He pulled the nanite kit from his thigh pocket and opened the hard case.

He felt Waldon's chest and could find no penetration signs in his suit. When he checked his arm, Pops noticed the discoloration of Waldon's hand. Shaking his head, he probed the upper arm. He knew the tourniquet was the only thing that could have saved his friend. It hadn't saved his arm, but it had saved his life. He injected the combat nanites above the tourniquet, knowing they'd begin to heal the end of the part of his arm that was still alive.

Pops moved Waldon to his berth and inserted a line for a bag of artificial blood to make its way into the unconscious man. It had been years since he'd had to do that type of first aid. Still, he was happy with the results.

He sat by his friend and waited with a bulb of water ready. A half hour later, Waldon stirred and moaned. Slowly he opened his eyes and blinked. His good hand reached across, only to be stopped by the IV line pulling.

"Take it easy, Wally," Pops said, "you'll pull the dang needle out. It took me three tries to get it right. You might be a bit bruised there."

"Thanks, I think," Waldon whispered. "I'm just glad to be alive."

"Who did it?" Pops asked. "Who's the sumbitch what needs killin'?"

"It was a Pushtal," Waldon said. His voice broke, and he tried to lick his lips.

"Here," Pops said as he held the straw of the bulb up for Waldon to drink. "Sorry. I shoulda done that already."

"Thanks," Waldon said, his voice stronger. "I said, it was a Pushtal. They're the pirates."

"Well, hell," Pops said. "Them's the sumbitches what are fixin' to die, then."

Waldon looked down at his hand. He tightened his lips in a grimace. "That one's gone, I guess. Not much use for a one-armed mechanic."

"Bullshit," Pops argued. "I seen plenty of mercs operate with a fake 'un. After I kill them bastards and get the gold back, I'll buy you the best on the market."

Waldon brightened. "Really? That's great. There's one that'll allow you to attach tools to it. Screwdrivers and sockets. I'll have a power ratchet on me at all times. If I can get more attachments, I don't need the synthetic flesh. That'll save some credit."

"We'll get you whatever you want," Pops said, standing. "Don't you worry 'bout the credits none."

"I think I hit one," Waldon said, after a moment.

"You did," confirmed Pops. "I seen the blood near the ramp. You rest now. I need to see about the engines. It looks like she took a missile or two."

"Well, dang," Waldon said. "Just when I had all three running good."

"Three?" Pops asked. "You got the backup engine running?"

"Well, yeah," Waldon said. "I been tinkering with it. I haven't been running it 'cause we ain't needed it. If they fired missiles using sensors to target the engines, we still got one. It ain't as powerful as the others, but it'll land and take off from Aspara."

* * *

Chapter Five

Pops sealed the passageway to the power plant and put his helmet back on. Once he was in the green on his readings, he disengaged the safety override and opened the hatch to check on the engines. One was worse than the other. The missile aimed at it had hit it directly. The other engine was damaged, but not beyond repair, given time.

He lifted the deck panel that led to the small compartment below and looked around. The backup engine was undamaged. The light in the bulkheads below came on when he lifted the panel. They were in business. He closed the panel.

He used four cans of emergency sealant spray and sealed the powerplant where the missiles came in. The damage had been too great for the automatic systems to completely seal it. It would still need repair, but it was safe as long as they didn't put too much stress on the hull of the ship. As he took his helmet off, he wondered why there wasn't more damage than he could see. The missiles hadn't exploded on impact. Instead, they'd simply penetrated and did kinetic damage.

"That's how they get most of their ships," he said out loud. "They damage 'em, but not more than can be fixed." He looked around the compartment and realized he'd been talking to himself more and more these days. *I'm getting old and crazy,* he thought. *Nah.*

Pops made his way to the control compartment and sat down at the helm console. He stood back up and took his protective suit off. He put his boots back on and paced back and forth, thinking, skinny legs in the tight bodysuit constantly moving. Suddenly it dawned on him. He knew where the pirates were hiding. He went to Waldon's berth.

"Hey," Pops said as he stepped through the hatch. "You reckon you'll be alright for a few more hours, or you want I should take you down to the planet and see a doc?"

Waldon looked over at Pops, his eyes glassy. "I guess. The nanites are doing their thing. Some of them must have released a painkiller, 'cause I feel fine. We know there ain't no worry about infection now." He made an effort to focus his eyes. "What the hell are you wearing? That suit liner is skintight. Your knees are bigger around than your thighs."

"Never mind my dang knees," Pops said. "I'm talking 'bout skinnin' cats."

"Well, I can wait," Waldon said. "Why? What do you have in mind?"

"I think them sumbitches is hiding in the asteroid belt," Pops answered. "I aim to go give 'em what for."

"Good," Waldon said, nodding slowly. "The sooner you do, the sooner I get an arm. This one is dead, you know. Doc's gonna have to saw it off." He started to sit up straighter. "Say, you want me to fly? I can do it with one arm, no problem."

"Hell, no!" Pops exclaimed. "You're higher than a circling buzzard. You'll get a feller killed. We'll hit every asteroid in the belt."

"Well, okay then," Waldon said, settling back. "What's the plan?"

"I'm gonna fine tune the sensors and find 'em," Pops explained. "The dang sensors won't find us heavy metals on the surface of a moon through rock anymore, but I bet they'll find a big ass ship floating among them. We just need to get close, and I'll pay 'em a visit in Lucille."

"Your mech?" Waldon asked. "You're really gonna attack their ship with your Mk 7 CASPer?"

"Damn right I am," Pops confirmed. "She stays charged with a rack full of missiles on one shoulder and the MAC on the other'n."

"But I haven't seen you run that thing in the last three years. Well, ever." Waldon argued.

"That's 'cause I ain't as young as I used to be," Pops said. "Besides, I ain't had a reason to climb inside. I been saving her to send to a great niece one of these days. Her grandma tells me she's sweet as sugar and mean as a snake at the same time. I'm betting she takes the VOWS one day and scores better than I did. Anyway, it's like riding a horse; it'll come back to me."

"Well alrighty then," Waldon murmured as he started to doze. He opened one eye. "I'll help you fix her if you wreck her. I'd hate for you to send her to your kin all busted up."

* * *

Chapter Six

Pops eased *Naydeen* along the edge of the asteroid ring, not that the ship could move at anywhere near the speed she did with her main engines. He moved slowly to allow the sensors time to scan. He didn't think the Pushtal ship had the same capabilities his did, so he wasn't concerned with them sensing him.

The screen he was watching flashed. A steady tone came from the overhead speakers. He checked the shape to compare it to the footage and readings in the security file. It matched the ship that had docked against *Naydeen.* He eased away from the closest asteroids on the edge of the belt and set the auto pilot. It was time to break out his pride and joy.

He made his way to the shuttle bay by pushing off bulkheads and using hanging straps. When he got to the bay, he edged along one side until he reached a certain panel. He pushed on the upper corner, and a small, unseen door opened. He punched in his code, and the entire panel slid back several inches and shifted to the side, out of sight. In the ready room, his CASPer waited for him.

He climbed in and checked to ensure the programmed diagnostics were up to date. Everything was in the green on the center screen. He reached out and unplugged the line running to the maintenance counter behind him. He initiated startup and sealed himself in. He adjusted his straps and settled himself. Pops McCoy was back in the merc business—for one more contract, anyway. Plus he'd hired himself, so... *Whatever,* he thought.

* * *

Pops used a little over half his jumpjuice avoiding meteors on his way to the ship's location. It wasn't as difficult as he'd thought it would be, because they were mostly big ones and not the unpredictable small ones spinning everywhere like around the system's fifth planet. That other ring was a nightmare. It was no wonder the pirates had decided to hide among these. It was relatively safe, as long as the pilot paid attention.

He checked his readings one last time to ensure he had enough power and fuel to make it back to his ship. He decided it would do. He oriented his mech toward the rear of the small freighter and gave his thrusters a tap with his feet. Still undetected as far as he could tell, he waited until he was in range to fire all his rockets at once. They'd know about him now, if they didn't already.

Every missile hit the ship's thrusters. The glow winked out as the engines shut themselves down like Pops figured they would. *Safety third*, he thought as he continued to glide across the distance to the ship. The ship floated toward a meteor, but at the last minute the maneuvering thrusters fired, moving it away slowly and gaining some semblance of control.

Pops flipped his feet around in time to slow himself with a small burst from the mech's thrusters. He hit the cargo ramp of the ship feet first. He bent his knees to minimize the impact, but he still felt it in his old legs and back. He maneuvered to face the ramp and fired his MAC several times. Once he could get a grip on the jagged edge of the holes, he used the mech's strength to pull parts of it open. It wasn't long before he was in the hold. Several Pushtal in environmental suits fired rifles at him. The darts bounced off the CASPer's armor, causing little damage. It didn't take him long to kill them all.

He stomped toward the front of the cargo hold, but an emergency door slid down, covering the ramp and resealing the hold. Some one else was still alive in the ship. He ensured the magnets were engaged and popped the hatch of his CASPer. He climbed down and picked up one of the Pushtal's rifles. He checked to see it was still loaded with flechettes and went deeper into the ship, clearing compartments and berths as he went, using the few straps he found and pushing off bulkheads in the microgravity.

He didn't encounter another Pushtal until he got to the operations compartment. She nearly took his head off with a swipe of her claws. The only reason she missed was because Pops had reached down to rub a sore knee before hitting the panel to open the hatch. She opened it from inside. He fired on instinct, and several darts hit her thigh. Others hit her chest as he raised the rifle.

The obviously female Pushtal lay there bleeding and breathing heavily as he searched the ship's bridge. There were no more left. The pirates operating the ship were a skeleton crew. He'd killed them all. Well, except the one bleeding at his feet as she slowly rose in the lack of gravity. He put a foot on her to hold her steady.

Pops looked down without pity. They got what they deserved, as far as he was concerned. He'd take his gold and leave the ship to be destroyed by meteors. He didn't want it. It stank of unwashed Pushtal. As he turned to leave, he heard her whisper the same thing, over and over. He stopped and tilted his head. He didn't understand her.

She looked up, pleading with her eyes. She stopped whispering and looked at him in concentration. Finally, with difficulty, she spoke in his language. It was just one word, but it rocked him to his core. She said, "Babies."

She whispered it again and died. Pops moved like he never had before. He hit his head several times as he made his way through the unfamiliar ship to the berthing area. He searched each one carefully but didn't find any Pushtal cubs. He stopped and hung by a torn strap in the passageway between all of them and listened.

He almost missed it. A soft growl followed by a hiss. He pushed himself into the berth he thought it had come from and checked the panels on all sides. In the back corner, one sounded hollow. He noticed a scratch mark on a seam. He reached down, took out his antique folding knife, wedged it where the tip of a claw would go, and pried the panel open.

In a box were two small Pushtal cubs. They were rolling around, playing. They looked up when they realized the lighting had changed. Pops reached down and scooped them up. He realized they couldn't see him very well, as their eyes had only recently opened. They sniffed his hands as he slowly made his way to the cargo hold.

Occasionally he had to hold them together against him with one hand as he used a strap to continue moving. They used those opportunities to continue their play-fighting. One or the other almost slipped away several times.

When he got to the hold, he moved over to the cargo container holding his gold. He made sure it was closed tightly before he located the panel to override the emergency hatch. He climbed up his mech while holding the two cubs together by the scruff of their necks, backed into the cockpit, and tucked the cubs into the open zipper on his skinsuit.

Flinching from their claws, he shut them all in and moved over to hit the release. When the hatch slid up, he pushed the cargo container out the hole. He followed after it, hoping for the best, and with a good grip on it, he fired the thrusters and made his way to the edge of the ring.

Getting out was easier than coming in, because he didn't have to worry about being noticed. Slowly, using nearly all the jumpjuice he had left in small bursts, he reached the shuttle bay of *Naydeen*. It was a tight fit with the shuttle, the waist-high container, and his mech, but he managed to close the bay door.

He opened the cockpit of his CASPer and stood in the seat, one foot tucked under a strap. He unzipped his bodysuit and pulled the cubs out. He was sure he was bleeding in several places. As he held them at arm's length and wondered what he was going to do with them, he noticed they were both males. One of them shivered, and Pops realized it was still cold in the bay after being open to space for so long. The atmospheric pressure was right, but the heaters hadn't warmed it to the ship's normal setting.

He pulled the cubs close and held them against him loosely. One started purring, causing the other to follow suit. Pops spoke out loud, only this time he wasn't talking to himself.

He said, "Boys, I'm naming one of you Ricky, and the other'n Keaton."

* * *

A Year Later

Pops sat back in the booth and looked across the table at Waldon. Without thinking about it, Waldon reached up and scratched his eyebrow with the shiny metal finger of his bionic prosthetic. True to his word, Pops had bought the best on the market, along with dozens of tools and attachments, for his young friend.

Beside him and between him and the wall, Ricky played with the menus and the condiments. It didn't take him long to figure out how to swap lids. His brother Keaton had a small slate and was playing a game. They were a little over knee high and growing fast. Both wore pants and matching Jacksonville Generals t-shirts.

"Ah sure hate to see you go," Pops said, "but I understand. You want to work on mining equipment on a planet for a while. Somewhere other than the backside of the galaxy."

"Yeah," Waldon said. "I had enough of ship life. I mean, I 'preciate you giving me a job and all, but it's time I moved on, I reckon."

"I hear ya," Pops agreed. "I'm thinking I might take a little break and show the boys where I'm from. Let 'em run around the woods in the North Georgia mountains fer a bit."

The door to the café opened and several obvious mercenaries walked in. They all had a patch of some type of whirlwind or something on their sleeve. Two of them sat in the booth backing up to Pops. Ricky stood on his tiptoes to look over the seat at them.

The one on the other side motioned with his head to the bigger of the two. He looked over and noticed the young Pushtal. He reached up and shoved Ricky in his face, knocking him back and down against Pops' table.

"Boy," Pops asked, concerned. "You alright? You need to be careful. Come here, don't cry." He held Ricky tight, rubbing his back as he sniffed against him.

Several customers of various races looked over at their table. When a young one gets hurt, it's everyone's business in a small place like Aspara Town. Waldon motioned for Pops to lean closer.

"That big merc pushed Ricky off the back of the booth," he whispered.

Pops' hand froze, and a look came over his face that scared Waldon. Truly scared him. "Take off your arm, Wally," Pops said in a whisper that allowed no other option.

Waldon reached over and unlocked his arm from the elbow down. The bionic arm was easily detachable at that point in order to connect the various attachments. He handed it to Pops.

"Don't worry about denting it," Waldon whispered. "That alloy won't bend."

Pops nodded and sat Ricky down in the seat beside his brother. Keaton was still oblivious to everything around him, lost in his game. He stood up, turned around, and held the arm behind him out of sight.

"Hey, big 'un," Pops said. "Did you just lay a hand on my boy?"

The big man looked up and sneered. "Your boy? I shoved a no-good Pushtal in his damn face is what I did. You're lucky we're in a place that makes us check our weapons at the door, or I'd have put a .45 round between his eyes. Damn things'll grow up and be pirates, or worse."

The entire room went silent. Pops stared at the man and said, "One, you put a hand on my young'un. Two, you threatened to kill him. So…I'm gonna put a hand on you, and then I'm gonna kill you."

The big man stood up and towered over the skinny old man. The man sitting with him put his arms up across the back of his seat and snickered. Several more members of the merc unit elbowed each other, expecting to be entertained.

Faster than most in the room could believe, Pops whipped his hand around holding the prosthetic and smashed it against the side of the merc's head. The man dropped like an empty sack. Before anyone could react, he slammed the arm down on the man's throat. Already unconscious, the man never drew another breath.

The other merc in the booth scrambled to get out of his seat until Pops slapped him across his face with the hand hard enough to loosen teeth. The man froze as blood trickled from one side of his nose.

"What's your name?" Pops asked.

"Miguel," answered the man in a nasal voice as the blood came faster.

"These your boys?" Pops asked waving the hand around at the other mercs. He leaned forward and read the patch. "Miguel's Monsoons, huh?"

The man nodded and didn't say a word, his eye on the metal hand moving around as Pops spoke. He wasn't ready to die at the hands of an old man…by a hand in his hand.

"I tell you what," Pops decided. "You gather this group of merc wannabees and get the hell out of Aspara System. Don't look back, and don't come back. You hear me?"

"Hey!" one of the men shouted. "You can't just…"

He didn't finish his words. One of his buddies elbowed him to silence when the rest of them noticed every patron in the café other than the mercs stood with forks, knives, and spoons turned backward, looking at them.

"Who was that?" one of the men whispered as they shuffled outside.

His buddy answered, "They called him Pops."

*****

Kevin Steverson Bio

Kevin Steverson is a retired veteran of the U.S. Army. He is a published songwriter as well as an author. He lives in the northeast Georgia foothills where he continues to refuse to shave ever again. Trim…maybe. Shave…never! When he is not on the road as a Tour Manager he can be found at home writing in one fashion or another.

#####

Bushwhacked! by Terry Mixon

"Anyone have a guess why we're here?" Commander Rick Betancourt asked over the rim of his beer mug. It wasn't the best brew he'd ever had, but it was far from the worst. It was only a tad sour, but still had the hint of hops. It would do.

While he waited for his crew to shrug noncommittally, he looked around at the bar. Yankor's Retreat advertised itself as a merc bar, but in reality it was just a dive with delusions of grandeur. Like the beer, it was mostly right, but the furnishings looked a bit worn. So did the patrons.

As far as mercenaries went, there were a couple, but the majority of the beings seemed to be starport workers and transients. That meant the place was half full of just about every species imaginable.

He and his people were the only Humans in sight, other than a couple of what looked like maintenance technicians in the back corner. They wore grungy coveralls and seemed intent on their drink and a game they were playing with some oddly shaped dice.

"Shouldn't you know why we're here?" Adrian Vanderbilt, his helm officer, asked with a smug grin. "After all, you called this meeting."

"Does this actually rise to the level of a meeting?" Lacey Sturtevant, their scanner officer, asked with a grin. "'Hey, let's go have a beer' isn't exactly a business invitation, if you know what I mean."

"Couldn't we have picked someplace a little cleaner?" Kimberly Livingston, *Hermes'* chief engineer, complained, her face showing her distaste for their surroundings. "I'm pretty sure we'll need a good decontamination once we get back to the ship."

"I hate decontamination," their rescue specialist, Andrew Nesbitt, said gloomily. "I smell like a Besquith peed on me for two days after going through one."

Kim raised an eyebrow in a tight arch and scrunched her nose even further. "And exactly how would you know what *that* smells like? Have you been holding out on us, Andy? Kinky."

A rumble of laughter made its way around the table as Andy turned red. The man didn't bother trying to argue because long experience had likely taught him it would be a losing battle. The more he resisted, the more his friends needled him.

That's just how things were aboard the search and rescue ship *Hermes*. They didn't stand on rank and position. Even Rick's supposed rank was mainly for show. His people were all adults and, when it came time to save lives, they were the best at what they did.

Which, he had to admit, really didn't explain why they were sitting in this dive waiting for an old friend to come calling. He'd tell his people what the meeting was all about, except he didn't know himself.

When Major Kelly Hawke of the Lions had sent him a message requesting a private meeting, she hadn't explained precisely what she had in mind. Still, his ship and the Lions had a good track record, so he'd been willing to listen.

"If I knew what she wanted, I'd tell you," Rick said, keeping his voice intentionally low. While he had no reason to believe anyone was listening in on them, it always paid to be careful when talking business in public.

"I always keep track of what's going on in near space, so I'd have seen any of their ships listed as in system," Adrian said. "I gotta say having her pop up out of the blue seems suspicious."

Rick had to agree.

Since they were in transit between their last job and the system where they'd take up their next one, he had no idea how Hawke had even known where to find them. That spoke to something going on behind the scenes. Had the Lions had something to do with the job they were on the way to work?

They weren't listed in the contract, but that might not mean anything. The offer could have been made to him so no one would connect the larger mercenary organization with the transaction. If that were true, then it meant the Lions wanted something from *Hermes* and her crew without drawing attention to that fact.

Well, he supposed he'd find out pretty damned quick. Hawke had promised to be here at the top of the hour, and a check of his watch told him the meeting time was upon them. One thing you could say about Hawke was that she was punctual. And a badass.

Right on cue, he saw her come through the front door, dressed in casual clothes but with a slug thrower strapped to her hip. She might not have been wearing a Lions uniform or battle rattle, but she was every inch a damned Marine.

Everyone in her general vicinity turned to watch her as she stopped, hands on hips and head swiveling to look around. Her presence had so large an impact that it took Rick a few seconds to realize she wasn't alone.

Standing behind her were two men, one of them known to him, and the other not. Lieutenant Antwan Malave was a junior tactical officer on one of the Lions' ships. The other man was an older, slightly balding blond man Rick hadn't seen before.

Rick raised his hand and Hawke turned toward their table, a smile lighting up her face. He rose to his feet as she approached and extended a hand, which she promptly ignored and pulled him into an exuberant bear hug. One strong enough to make his ribs creak.

Considering he'd never had anything more than a professional relationship with the Marine officer, her personal display of affection was surprising. Not unwelcome, though.

Being the captain of a ship was a lonely business, and her hard-muscled body pressed up against his felt good. And, he admitted, the fresh, clean scent of her hair kind of melted him inside.

The hug brought her lips right next to his ear. Since that was obviously her intent, he wasn't surprised when she whispered to him, though the caress of her warm breath against his ear sent a shiver down his spine.

"Pretend like we're old friends," she said, so softly that he barely heard her. "I'll explain once we've settled down."

Taking her cue, he put his hands on her shoulders and pushed her back, grinning. "Damn, Hawke, it's good to see you again. When I heard you were in system, it just made my day. The crew and I said we'd make a party out of meeting up with you and your boys."

She grinned back, seemingly genuinely pleased. "That's *exactly* what I'd hoped would happen. After all, who doesn't like a good party? You remember Antwan."

Rick extended a hand to the man. "I'm glad to see your arm is better. It was broken up pretty good last time we met."

The young man grinned, his teeth white against the darker shade of his face. "That's what good medical care will do for you. I'm glad to have the use of it back. It's no fun being a one-armed bandit."

Rick laughed. "I'll bet. It's rough to be a tactical officer with one hand tied literally behind your back."

"You have no idea."

He turned his attention to the unknown man and extended his hand again. "Rick Betancourt, captain of *Hermes*."

"I'm Chappa," the man said with a slight smile.

"I don't think I've heard that name before. Which part of Earth is it from?"

"It's from up Massachusetts way," Hawke said before Chappa could respond. "And it's not his real name. It's his old call sign."

"Yeah," the man said with a smile. "My real name is Chris Kennedy. I used to be with the Lions back in the day as a pilot. I decided to retire when things got a little too exciting for my taste. Now I fly cargo and passengers out of the port. Oh, and I write in my spare time."

Rick raised an eyebrow. "A writer? That's pretty cool. What kind of stuff you write?"

"Science fiction, with a lot of real-world mercenary fighting mixed in. It's surprisingly popular."

"I'll have to give it a look. So what's with the name?"

"He's called Chappa because 'Chappaquiddick' wouldn't fit on his nametag," Hawke said with a smirk, once again interrupting the man. "While he was one of our best pilots, he had a girlfriend problem."

Rick gave them all a quizzical look but just gestured toward the empty seats at the table. "Why don't you sit down and tell us all about it while we order another round?"

Once they'd settled in, Chappa shook his head. "I didn't have a girlfriend problem. It's more like the girlfriends had a problem with me."

"Chappa's what we call a skirt chaser in the business," Hawke said smugly. "His problem is, the aerial dance of love he imagined always turned into a dogfight. You see, he likes to string along more than one girl at a time. When they find out, they tend to go…weapons free."

While Rick was digesting that information, Lacey snorted in amusement. "You sound like one of those old fighter pilots I used to read about."

Chappa spread his hands and smiled widely. "What can I say? I love the ladies, and they love me back. It's hard to say no when somebody interesting comes along."

"So, what's the record?" Antwan asked, his expression curious. "How many women have you had on the string without them realizing you weren't dancing alone?"

The question seemed to make Chappa a little uncomfortable. "A gentleman never tells."

"I heard it was five," Hawke confided in a falsely low tone designed to carry to everyone at the table. "Then, when they all figured out they were being played, they set him up. He thought he was showing up for a date with one, but another of them was waiting for him.

"At first, he figured he'd just misremembered who he was supposed to meet. Then the others showed up as a group, and things got *really* tense."

Chappa's eyes narrowed. "I never told anybody that story. How did you hear it?"

She smiled and leaned toward him a little. "One of the ladies was my Marine. Once I heard what was going on, I felt the need to offer my…tactical advice. As a Marine officer, I understand the value of a good ambush."

Chappa sat back, his mouth falling open. "*You* were behind that? Holy shit, I thought I was a dead man."

"Just remember, you can't have a booby trap without a booby. You brought it on yourself."

That gave everybody except Chappa a good laugh.

"Maybe it's a good thing you retired after all," Rick told the man. "Hawke's not exactly the kind of woman you want to cross a second time. Or even once."

He turned his attention to the Marine officer. "While it's sure as hell good to see, I have to confess I feel a little ambushed, too. How did you know *Hermes* was going to be here?"

She gave him an enigmatic smile. "The Lions may have had something to do with that. Now before you get angry, the job you signed up for is absolutely legit. No kind of skullduggery there. Everything is exactly what you agreed to in the contract.

"What I'd like to do is offer you a second contract on the down low. One that's not going to inconvenience your people at all, but is going to help the Lions, and put a good chunk of change in your pocket for going to the same place you were already going to. We just want you to take a small cargo along with you."

"What kind of cargo?" he asked, not bothering to keep the thread of suspicion out of his voice.

"The kind of cargo I don't want to talk about in a bar. Nothing illegal, just valuable, and requiring discretion."

"I'll need more information before we take this discussion any further," he said firmly. "Trust only goes so far."

She considered him for a couple of seconds and then nodded. "Scoot back from the table."

Confused, he did as instructed, and was surprised when she rose smoothly to her feet and sat in his lap. While she certainly wasn't the first woman to do so, it was an intimate sort of thing that he hadn't been expecting, and he was suddenly far too aware of her body for his own comfort.

Once again, she leaned forward and put her lips next to his ear. "I don't want anyone to hear what we're moving, so my apologies for this...less than professional seating arrangement. We've got a bunch of red diamonds that are destined for the Lions to pay off an old contract.

"The ship it came on, a cruise liner from Desvorat, had a little bit of trouble getting the diamonds up to orbit. Basically, somebody tried to steal them. We were lucky some folks on the shuttle happened to foil the attempt.

"We don't want to have anyone else try, so Admiral Lyons sent me to expedite the delivery in a less public manner. Your ship just happened to be in the right place at the right time."

Moving cargo around the Union was a complicated business, he knew. The larger the ship, the less F11 each jump required. That often meant getting something from point A to point B was anything but a straight line. More often, the route was quite circuitous.

He could see how a message might get to the Lions before the actual cargo. Particularly if something were moving slowly because it was heavily guarded. Red diamonds, depending on their size, helped denote the denominations of Union currency. It was almost like having money, so other than F11, it was one of the most valuable resources around.

Hawke reminded him of where she was sitting when she adjusted herself in his lap and made him realize he was having a *strong* physical reaction to her touch. Flushing, he realized he needed to get her back into her own seat before the situation took unprofessional to a whole new level.

Before he could say anything, she grinned at him. "Why, Rick Betancourt, is that a weapon in your pocket, or are you just happy to see me?"

He flushed a deep red, and she hopped off of his lap with a laugh before he could say anything, returning to her seat.

"You really should buy me dinner first, don't you think?" he asked, his voice a bit hoarser than he'd expected it to be.

"We can arrange that," she said, her eyes twinkling. "I didn't say anything last time we met, but I think you're a handsome guy. While I'm certainly not off duty, we're not in the same chain of command, if you know what I mean. Why don't we talk later?"

To say his crew's eyes were huge was something of an understatement. And from the way Malave was gawking at Hawke, he'd never seen anything like that from her either.

The only one who took the whole thing in stride was Chappa. He just grinned.

Rick cleared his throat. "Perhaps we should finish our beer and go somewhere a little bit more…private. To talk."

"Uh huh," she said, her voice just a little husky. "Talk. I'm more than ready to hear what you have to say."

He was about to stand when someone stepped up next to the table and dumped a pitcher of beer straight over Chappa's head.

* * *

Rick sat there stunned as Chappa leapt to his feet and stared at the red-headed Human woman who'd seemingly appeared from nowhere, and now stood glaring at him, empty pitcher in hand.

"The hell, Arlene?" the pilot demanded.

"You rat bastard, cheating son of a bitch," the woman ground out between clenched teeth as Rick and the rest jumped up from their chairs. "There can't be ten Human women working outta this starport, and you still found someone else to screw? I can't fucking believe it."

Rick suppressed the urge to laugh. He felt bad for the man, but he'd apparently brought this down on himself.

Chappa backed slowly away from the angry woman, his hands raised in supplication. "It's not like that. Julie and I are just friends."

"Julie!" the woman screeched. "I'm talking about *Ellen*, you cheating whoreson!"

With that, the woman hurled the empty pitcher at him and stalked toward the exit, her back stiffly straight, and her head held proudly high, as if daring anyone to say anything to her.

They all stood in stunned silence as they watched her go.

"She's kinda hot," Andy said sotto voce. "Can I get her number now that she's available?"

Lacey elbowed the rescue specialist. "Down, Lothario."

"All right," Hawke said with a dark chuckle. "We should probably get out of here before somebody comes looking to make Chappa pay for that beer, since I'm sure Arlene didn't buy it."

Rick looked back along the path the woman had come from and spotted the table she must've snagged the pitcher from. None of the spindly beings there seemed inclined to demand a replacement for their drink, perhaps thinking it well worth the price of the show.

Still, fair was fair. He pulled out a credit chip that would cover the cost of a replacement and made sure the bartender saw him leave it on their table as they headed for the door.

Hawke shot the drenched pilot an amused grin as she led them down the street toward the nearby port. "You haven't changed one damned bit, Chappa. I'd ask how you could possibly manage something like this, but I really don't want to know.

"What I *will* do is remind you that you're on the clock. You're being paid for this job, and I expect you to keep an eye out for any of your many girlfriends swooping in for revenge. Speaking of that, what are the chances we're going to see Ellen or Julie tonight?"

Chappa hunched over as he walked, his hair sticking out wildly in every direction now that the beer was starting to dry. "They work at the starport just like I do. Neither is supposed to be on shift, but you never know."

Rick looked over his shoulder to make sure no one was following them and then edged a little bit closer to Hawke. Time to get this back on track. "So you want us to pick up this shipment, take it up to *Hermes*, and then deliver it to the Lions?"

She nodded, never slowing her long strides. "I understand it's convoluted, but the contract you signed to provide search and rescue is in the same system where the Lions will meet us.

"All they had available to send to escort the shipment was me, a few of my people, and Antwan. We had to take civilian transport to get here in time, and we only managed it because we knew where the cargo would be passing through.

"I've got all the codes and authorizations to divert the shipment. The admiral doesn't think the first attempt on it was a random act of piracy. It's a lot of money, paying off a long-standing contract, and, frankly, I wouldn't be surprised if the first attempt to steal it wasn't a covert attempt by the people who originally hired us to get their money back."

"Really?" he asked with a frown. "Who pays cash? And if you don't get the money, does it really count as payment?"

She shrugged slightly, hunching over slightly at the chill wind. "I didn't write the contract, and I didn't sign it. Neither did the admiral. This was something his brother agreed to before he died ten years ago. It's taken a long time to finish the work, and the terms of the payment were spelled out in the contract.

"In any case, rather than have a fight about getting the payment sent again, we wanted to make sure it gets to where it's supposed to go the first time. That's where you come in. I'm going to sign for the shipment, we'll load it on Chappa's shuttle, and he'll take it up to *Hermes*.

"All you have to do is deliver it—and us—to the Lions when you arrive at your destination. At that point, you'll start your normal contract as though none of this ever happened, except you'll have a nice chunk of change in your account that you hadn't counted on. I've got it all written up if you want to look it over."

They ducked across the street as a group and left the area around the bars. The lighting in the area became dimmer, and the elements were now spaced further apart, leaving pools of darkness between the posts. That made him nervous.

"I'm going to want to see that contract," he confirmed. "I'm willing to give you a little leeway because I trust you and the Lions, but before we take possession of something like that, I want to see it spelled out."

"I'll send you a copy," she said with a nod. "It's a standard contract that even includes combat bonuses, if they're needed. Just in case you run into any derelict battleships you need to shoot anybody with."

He shook his head at her grin. "I'm pretty sure that was a one-time deal. Send it to my slate, and I'll check it out as we walk. Do you think we're in danger of someone trying to take it away here at the port?"

"I certainly hope not, but I've got people to back us up. They don't have their full kit, but trust me when I say they'll be up to defending us if someone comes along looking for trouble."

He brought out his slate and read through the contract once she'd sent it to him. Just like she'd said, it was standard. Pick up the cargo, load it aboard *Hermes*, take it to the target system, and deliver it to the Lions. It also included language about transporting Hawke and her people back with him.

They had plenty of space aboard *Hermes*, so that wasn't a problem. The ship was also fast, so if somebody decided to get after them in normal space, they'd have a decent chance of escaping.

At last he nodded and signed it. "Everything looks good. Here's to hoping we don't have the kind of problem Chappa had. Speaking of him, what's his part in all this again?"

The woman shot a smirk at the rumpled ex-Lion. "We're using his shuttle because he's a known quantity. He's not going with us. He's got his own mess here to clean up."

He nodded. "Adrian, I want you to take the rest of the crew back up to *Hermes* in our shuttle. We'll catch up with you once we've got the cargo. As soon as we board, I want us headed for the stargate. We'll get there a little bit early, but I'd feel better in a crowd of ships waiting for transit."

"You got it, boss," his pilot said.

Rick turned his attention back to Hawke. "I sure hope I don't regret doing this."

"Me, either," she said. "Are you packing?"

He shot her a disdainful glance. "I'm in search and rescue, but I'm still a merc. I've got a concealed piece, just like the rest of my people."

"We'll upgrade you when we get to the starport," she said. "In a situation like this, it's better to be obvious about the downsides of causing us trouble. Having a *real* gun on your hip goes a long way toward making sure nobody's rude."

He sure hoped nobody was going to get *that* rude. With all his bravado about being a merc, his job wasn't killing people. It was saving them.

That one time with the battleship had been a fluke. He didn't want a repeat of having to inflict violence upon people trying to kill him and his people.

But if it came to fighting or dying, he knew which way he'd jump.

* * *

The trip to the shuttle port proved uneventful. With everything at stake, Rick kept expecting trouble, but other than some workers getting off shift, they didn't see anyone at all.

This starport was laid out pretty much like every other one he'd seen. It was designed to get people and cargo down from orbit and disembarked in an organized fashion. For different species, that occasionally meant different things.

In this case, the passenger side of things was a lot prettier than the cargo side, because paying passengers complained when things weren't up to their standards. Once they were past where outsiders normally visited, everything became utilitarian and more than a bit scruffy.

It was also smellier. The air was heavy with the mixed odors of fuel, sweat, and other less identifiable things. Personally, Rick preferred it this way. It was honest.

The four of them might've looked a little out of place walking through the cargo side, but none of the workers gave them a second glance. They had pallets of cargo to move from Point A to Point B and only cared about things that affected their schedules.

"I can't say I'm familiar with this side of the starport," Rick said to Hawke as they walked around a loader carrying a stack of crates that looked more than a little unbalanced. He gave it extra room. "Where exactly does one pick up high-value cargo, and how far away is it from Chappa's shuttle?"

Hawke didn't slow her pace, dodging around people and cargo alike with ease. "We're going to the shuttle first. That's where my people are waiting. Once we pick them up, we'll go to the portmaster's office for the cargo."

"And it's safe in storage there? I'd have thought you'd be worried about someone stealing it."

"I paid extra to have it kept in high-security storage. If somebody steals it before we sign for it, the starport is on the hook to pay the entire value of the cargo, which is almost as good as getting it delivered to the Lions in the first place.

"We weren't able to get that kind of insurance on the liner. It cost a pretty penny here, but the peace of mind is definitely worth it."

The area they were entering now was made up of open pads for shuttles and small buildings where said shuttles could be stored. This obviously catered to those who owned their own vessels. The smell of fuel became a lot more pungent.

The shuttle Hawke led them toward looked to be in surprisingly good shape. With the way things had been going, Rick halfway expected Chappa's shuttle to be a flying wreck. Instead, it was sleek and clean. Stylish, even.

"You've got a nice ride, Chappa," he said over his shoulder at the other man.

"With the amount of money I have to keep dumping into it, it oughta be," the man grumbled. "Owning a shuttle is a lot like owning a boat or recreation vehicle. The damned things are money pits."

The hatch to the shuttle was open, and the ramp was down. Two burley men in unpowered armor stood there, rifles in hand. Rick didn't know them, but Hawke walked right up to them.

"Everything still good, Ray?" she asked.

The man on the right nodded, his short black hair glistening in the light. He had to be using some kind of hair product. As short as the man's hair was, Rick couldn't imagine why.

"All clear, Major," the man said in a surprisingly deep voice. "We had a couple of people approach, but nothing suspicious. Just lookie loos curious about what we were doing. I told them that wasn't any of their business, and they moved on."

The Marine officer nodded. "Good enough. Get your squad in order, Corporal. We'll be leaving two people sealed up inside the shuttle to wait for us while we pick up the cargo. Everyone else is providing overwatch to make sure we get back here without any problems."

"Copy that," the man responded.

Hawke turned to face Rick. "If you'll come with me, I'll get you outfitted in a manner befitting a *real* merc."

"Not much outfitting needed to just hand me a gun belt," he offered as they went into the shuttle.

The inside of the vehicle was open, and there were a half dozen men and women in unpowered armor waiting inside. Considering shuttles were meant to move cargo, they didn't take up much of the available space.

Hawke stopped him next to a small stack of boxes and offered Rick a smile. "I have something a little bit more…thorough in mind. Take off your shirt."

He raised both his eyebrows meaningfully. "We've circled back around to whether or not I should get dinner first."

"Armor, hot stuff. I've got something you can wear underneath your shirt. Your pants are safe. For the moment."

Honestly, he wasn't certain whether her teasing really meant she was interested or not. That was one of the problems in the dance between men and women. It was hard to tell what the other's intentions really were sometimes. The line between flirting and come on wasn't always a bright one.

If he assumed she wasn't really interested, and she was, that would be one thing. If he assumed she was interested and he was wrong, that could be *very* awkward.

He undid his shirt and pulled it off as she opened one of the boxes. It held a mixture of equipment, including torso armor that looked like it was made to be concealed. It also held a pistol belt with a weapon and magazines.

Hawke hefted the armor, but paused before she put it in place. "You've been holding out on me, Betancourt. Those abs are definitely something to be proud of."

"Is that all I am to you?" he asked, his tone cool. "Just a piece of meat to be assessed for how pretty it is?"

Hawke laughed and grinned. "I like you, Rick. You really do know how to play the game. Arms up."

She slid the armor into place and quickly tightened its straps. Once she was done, she stepped back and appraised him.

"That should do. Once we get you strapped, you won't look so…naked. Not that I think I'd mind seeing you naked."

It was his turn to laugh. "You are such a tease."

She stepped up until their noses were almost touching. Her green eyes studied his and he could smell her hair again. Or was that her skin? Whatever it was, it had the effect on him she'd no doubt intended.

"While I have been known to tease," she said softly, "I only do so with people I actually have an interest in. Play your cards right, and maybe you'll get a chance to find out what's underneath *my* armor."

That shot his internal temperature straight up. It took everything he had to avoid swallowing visibly. Instead, he just widened his smile and said nothing.

After a few moments she stepped back with a knowing smile, grabbed the weapons belt, and handed it to him. "Standard sidearm and ammunition, locked and loaded, safety on. Let's hope you don't need it. Once you're all set, we'll head to the portmaster's office and pick up the cargo. Simple and straightforward."

He wasn't certain about how problem free this was really going to be. That depended on whether someone tried to take the cargo away from them. If they did, things would get very ugly, very fast.

Since planning for everything to go smoothly wasn't the way to achieve success, he pulled the pistol from its holster and verified that it was locked and loaded, and the safety was on. He then reholstered it and nodded at her.

They headed back out into the starport, eyes watching their surroundings closely. They'd be safe on their way to pick up the diamonds, he suspected. It was the trip back that would have all the complications, if there were going to be any.

* * *

As Rick had expected, the trip to the portmaster's office went off without a hitch, although everyone was on high alert just in case.

If the sight of armed and armored Marines—even in civilian clothes—moving through the port caused a stir, it wasn't readily apparent. With the two Marines guarding the shuttle, Hawke, Malave, Chappa, and he were surrounded by half a dozen men and women as they entered.

The beings around them seemed to dismiss them without a second glance. Perhaps seeing something like this wasn't all that uncommon after all.

The office itself was just as utilitarian as the rest of the cargo port. There was a long counter set at one end of the room, and a number of beings were working behind it. One of them was Human.

The woman looked up and smiled at the group as they came in, but her expression darkened when she saw Chappa.

"Oh, crap," the man said, freezing in his tracks.

"Is this Julie, or is this Ellen?" Rick asked into the ringing silence.

"Lydia."

Hawke turned and gave Chappa a hard shove. "What's with you? Are you broken? How in the world can you sleep with *every single woman* you come across?"

"Well, I didn't sleep with you."

The Marine officer's eyes narrowed dangerously, and she poked a finger into Chappa's chest. "If you'd tried, I'd have cut it off. You're a damned train wreck."

Without waiting for him to respond, she turned away, shaking her head in obvious disbelief. With an audible sigh, she walked up to the counter with Rick at her heels.

Once there, she smiled at the other woman. "Let's get this out of the way right up front. I hired Chappa for his shuttle. Whatever problems you have with him, don't take them out on me. I had no idea what the hell he was up to here."

The woman behind the counter looked like she still wanted to make an issue of it but closed her mouth and took a deep breath before nodding. "Because I can't be sure, I'll give you the benefit of the doubt. What can I do for you?" Her tone was notably cool.

"I'm just here to pick up my cargo. It's in the high-security vault. Here's my paperwork."

Hawke pulled out actual *papers* and slid them across the counter to the woman.

Lydia picked the paperwork up and read it closely, her eyes narrowing and then going wide. "Oh. I see."

The lingering antagonism in the woman's face melted away, and she became all professional. "I've got a few more things for you to sign, and I'm going to need your biometric data to confirm your identity. Once that's done, we'll release your cargo."

"Bring it on."

The woman produced some additional paperwork and handed it to Hawke with a pen. The Marine officer started filling it out.

While she worked, Rick looked around, trying to gauge how the place normally operated. There were perhaps a dozen other beings in the room, all seemingly intent on their work, though Rick had to admit more than a few were sending looks toward the Marines guarding the door. He didn't see anything alarming in their gaze, but that wasn't his specialty, either.

The process of getting the cargo released to Hawke wasn't a quick one. He supposed that made sense, considering how much it was worth.

Once the paperwork was complete, Lydia disappeared back into the building, and returned twenty minutes later with a small cart holding a small container. It was armored and locked.

Four Oogar, tall and purple, towered behind the woman, heavily armed and armored. They were obviously there to protect the cargo until it was released into Hawke's custody.

Lydia presented a slate for Hawke to sign for the cargo, but the Marine officer waved her hand. "Before I do that, I need to see that the contents are intact. I have the codes, and you're more than welcome to watch, but I'm going to look inside that container."

"That's acceptable," the woman said. "Be advised, the cargo is not officially in your possession until you sign for it. If you attempt to take it without doing so, you'll be treated as a thief. Nothing personal, but that's the way it is."

"Good enough."

Hawke knelt beside the container and tapped in a long code. The lock beeped, and she opened the lid in such a way that the others in the room couldn't get a good look inside.

Rick looked down over her shoulder. The container was *filled* with red diamonds of various sizes. He didn't know what to think. He'd never seen so much money in one place before. It felt unreal.

A glance at the counter revealed that Lydia shared his opinion, because her eyes were huge. She said nothing, however.

Hawke closed the lid and relocked the container. That done, she dusted her hands off on her pants, stepped over to the counter, and entered her biometric data into the slate the woman offered to her.

"That's it," Lydia said. "The port hereby relinquishes control of this cargo to your care and is no longer responsible for it. I suggest you take it wherever you're going quickly."

"That's my intention," Hawke said with a cool smile. "Let me give you some advice in return. Chappa's trouble. He's never going to change his ways. To show my solidarity with the rest of the women in the galaxy, I urge you to pass along word of just how unfaithful he is to each and every one of them you meet, just in case he might ever come across them.

"He's going to try to convince you this was all some kind of big misunderstanding. Don't believe it. Leopards don't change their spots. He's going to try to get into the pants of anything that's remotely biologically compatible. Never doubt it for a second."

Lydia's eyes shifted over to where Chappa was standing by the door. The man couldn't hear what was being said, but it was obvious he recognized he was the subject of their conversation, as he turned so he wasn't looking toward the counter.

"I just can't believe how *good* he was at juggling all of us," Lydia muttered. "He had *at least* five of us on the string at the same time. I even know some of the other women. We had no idea."

"He's sly. He might be a lot of fun to hang out with, but if you've got an interest in anything resembling fidelity, he's not your guy."

With that, Hawke stepped away from the counter and gestured for the Marines to come over. "Here's the plan. We get back to the shuttle as quickly as possible and take off directly for *Hermes*. I'll push the container while you keep watch."

She turned her attention to Chappa. "As soon as we get back to your shuttle, I want you to get clearance and get us off this planet before another one of your damned girlfriends catches up with you."

"Ex-girlfriends," he grumbled. "I might as well relocate. It's going to be too hot here now."

"What you do on your own time is your business," Hawke said briskly. "I will say I thought you had better sense than this. You shouldn't pee where you sleep."

When she made to grab the handle on the cart, Rick waved her off. "While I'm armed, I might not be the best one to keep an eye out for trouble. Why don't I push the cart while you make sure nobody jumps us?"

"That works," Hawke readily agreed. "Now all we have to do is get to the shuttle and get to your ship. Easy peasy."

Rick certainly hoped she was right, but the hair on the back of his neck was standing up now. He wasn't going to feel comfortable until they were safely in hyperspace.

* * *

From the moment they stepped out of the portmaster's office, Rick felt as if he had a target painted on his back. Part of him thought everyone around knew he was pushing a cart containing riches beyond the wildest imaginings of any single individual.

Thankfully, no one paid them the slightest mind.

The shuttle wasn't parked all that far away from the portmaster's office, but they were now moving more deliberately. The armed men and women around him had upped their game and were watching for threats with far more intensity than they had been just half an hour before.

Things went smoothly enough that Rick was beginning to think they'd make it all the way back to the shuttle without any trouble.

The Human woman who stepped out from behind a stack of cargo containers directly ahead of them disabused him of that notion. She wore unpowered body armor and hefted a wicked looking rifle of a design he wasn't familiar with.

In the middle of the rising tension, before the woman in front of them could say a word or they could respond to her presence, Chappa threw his hands up into the air. "I've never slept with her! I don't even *know* her!"

The woman briefly closed her mouth and stared at Chappa in shocked confusion. "What?"

Then she shook her head and forcibly refocused her attention on the rest of the party.

"This is the end of the ride," she said in a low, sultry voice that was at odds with her obvious intent to rob them. "I'll be taking that cargo now."

With that, four Blevins stepped out to back her up, also armed with the same kind of rifles. A sound off to his left drew Rick's attention in that direction, revealing at least one person was up on top of a nearby stack of cargo containers, lying flat with his weapon covering Rick and his friends.

Where there was one, he had absolutely no doubt there were more.

"We have you surrounded, and this time we intend to get what we came for," the woman said with a grin on her face. "Circumstances may have conspired to keep us from getting it last time, but you have no choice if you want your people to live. Give us the diamonds, and we'll let you walk away. Resist, and we'll kill every single one of you before we take what we want."

Rick's fight or flight responses were warring inside him. He wasn't sure what the best course of action was, but it sure looked like they were screwed.

Hawke seemed unconcerned. "I don't think you have a firm grasp on the situation. You think you have the upper hand, but in fact you don't really understand the game. Has anyone ever told you that fighting a battle is a lot like a game of chess in the preparatory stages?

"We always wargame everything we can think of to come up with appropriate responses and countermeasures. Another thing we do is leave an opportunity for an enemy to make a mistake because they've misread the battlefield."

She smiled coldly and put her hands on her hips. "In fact, that's a big part of fighting. Using misdirection to lure the enemy into committing their forces to an area they think gives them an advantage, but in fact leaves them vulnerable. Basic stuff, really.

"So, let's flip this on its head, shall we? I'm going to give you one chance to lay down your weapons and surrender before things get really, *really* ugly. Do yourself a favor and think long and hard before you reject my offer, because I won't be making it again."

In his head, Rick thought that was just about the craziest thing he'd ever heard. They were screwed.

He knew exactly how many Marines they had on hand and, except for the two back at the shuttle, this was it. Hawke was bluffing, and if he could figure that out, he was pretty sure the woman could, too.

Judging by her smile, the woman's opinion matched his. "My people have been watching your shuttle. We know *exactly* how many people you've got and where they are. Unless you'd like my people to cut you down, put your weapons on the ground and step away from *my money*."

Hawke shrugged, seemingly unconcerned. "I think we'll give that a hard no. Execute Houdini."

Rick wasn't certain what he'd expected to happen, but the immediate effect of the Marine officer's words shocked him.

All around them, the cargo handlers who had been busy ignoring them minutes earlier suddenly pulled weapons and trained them on the woman and her four companions.

Elsewhere in the stacks of cargo, he could hear voices shouting for people to put their weapons down. Not everybody complied, because there were a few shots, but there was much less violence than he'd been expecting.

That didn't mean they were in *no* danger, because one of the people looking down on them from the cargo containers opened fire, sending hot slugs slamming into the Marines who'd drawn into a protective circle. They of course responded in kind.

Everything devolved into chaos as the woman and her companions used the distraction to duck sideways and open fire on their unexpected ambushers. Rick shoved the cart forward as fast as he could, determined to get out of the line of fire.

In this suddenly target rich environment, he still found himself the subject of interest for one of the shooters. A slug ricocheted off the armor underneath his shirt, sending him staggering forward into the cart handle. Another couple of shots struck the cart itself.

"To the shuttle!" Hawke shouted as she fired at the person on top of the cargo containers. "Withdraw! Withdraw! Withdraw!"

Rick lost track of the main enemy and her minions, but he didn't mind. It wasn't his job to fight. He was more than happy to leave combat to the professionals.

All those cargo handlers who had suddenly produced weapons must have been Hawke's people. He'd never even considered the possibility that she'd placed extra people around them. That's why she was an expert in combat and tactics, and he wasn't.

The fact that they were escaping didn't mean they were out of danger. He could hear shouts and shots behind them, and Hawke was busy receiving information through an earbud and giving commands controlling the retreat.

There were a number of sirens sounding in just about every direction, so Rick knew security forces would be on the scene quickly, but that didn't mean they were clear yet. They had to get aboard Chappa's shuttle and get off the ground.

Almost inevitably, another obstacle appeared just as they were about to reach safety. Three Human women stood just short of the shuttle, whose ramp was now down, their hands on their hips and their eyes aflame with righteous indignation as they spotted the pilot.

The one in the center was Arlene from the bar. If Rick was right, the other two would be Julie and Ellen. They looked like they were there to rain holy hell down on the man who had wronged them.

Just perfect.

While Rick was all in favor of the man getting his just desserts, they needed to get clear before the bad guys caught up with them. Or the cops, for that matter.

"Everybody into the shuttle," Hawke snapped. "We don't have time to sort this out. Chappa, as soon as we get the ramp up, you take off. I'll deal with any repercussions. Tell control this is emergency takeoff plan Zulu, and it's already been filed."

The pilot looked uncertain at that and seemed afraid to approach the angry women, but a couple of the Marines interposed themselves and forestalled any immediate fireworks. Chappa bolted past them and into the shuttle.

"Ladies, you're going to have to catch up with him later," Hawke said firmly. "The situation is far too dangerous for you to be here."

At that moment, the woman who had tried to ambush them shouted something as she came around the corner behind them, her minions in hot pursuit.

Rick saw her and pushed the cart forward. Time to get the hell out of here.

As he ran, bullets ricocheted off the shuttle, and the Marines knelt, returning fire. The three women wisely ran for the nearest cover. Unfortunately, that meant they raced into the shuttle right behind him.

As soon as he was out of the direct line of fire, Rick started strapping the container and cart into place. If they were going to take off quickly, he didn't want any of this coming loose. That could prove fatal.

The Marines with them backed into the shuttle and closed the hatch even as the ramp began rising. Some of them were injured, but it didn't look like they had any life-threatening hits to worry about.

Hawke spent two seconds staring at the three women before she shook her head and gestured for her men to secure them as she did the same for herself. "We're going to have to take them with us. We've run out of time."

"We're not going to be able to get off this planet," Rick said as he strapped himself in beside her. "Security is going to be sending people after us, and control is going to deny us permission to take off."

"Wrong. Money talks in the Union, and I paid a lot of it to the right people so they'd give us permission to take off no matter what happened. The security forces are aware we're transporting valuable cargo, and we were concerned we might be attacked. Our reputation is good here. They'll let us take off."

True to her words, the shuttle lifted off a few seconds later, pressing them sideways with the force of its acceleration.

Within a few seconds, Rick started to relax. Unless the enemy was going to use missiles, they were safe from being brought down at this point.

"Were those people in the port yours?" he asked as he tried to calm his racing heart.

"Local hires and port security," she said with a shake of her head. "That's why I know security isn't going to be coming after us. They have plenty of witnesses of their own who'll tell them who started things.

"I'd say we're safe for the moment, but I'm not sure they don't have the ship in orbit or at the stargate. Until we're in hyperspace, I'm not going to relax."

He considered her for a few seconds. "Is there a reason you didn't tell me about all this?"

She smiled slightly. "Never lay all your cards out for everyone to see. It's the ace you have up your sleeve that's going to win the game."

"So you cheat."

"When it comes to fighting?" she asked with a laugh. "Early and often."

He joined her with a chuckle of his own.

After a few seconds, she continued, "Chappa's a good pilot. He'll have us docked with *Hermes* soon enough. Once we're aboard, we'll strike out for the stargate. I seriously doubt they're going to try anything in open space, because the system defense forces here won't take very kindly to that."

Rick let his eyes roam over to the three women they'd inadvertently picked up. "What are we doing with them? We can't take them with us. Or we shouldn't. I suppose we could if we have to."

Hawke's smile grew wicked. "It would be inappropriate for us to remove any of these upstanding citizens from this system. So, being the kind soul I am, I'll order Chappa to stay in orbit until everything gets sorted out and then take them back down to the port. I figure that should take *at least* six hours. Just to be safe, you understand."

Rick laughed. "You're a cruel woman. You know he's just going to keep himself locked on the flight deck, right?"

She turned to the Marine on her other side. It was the big man she'd spoken to when Rick had arrived at the shuttle earlier.

"Ray, before we disembark on *Hermes*, I want you to have Collins plug into the systems on this shuttle and disable the operation of the door leading to the flight deck. I don't want any locks able to work and no way for Chappa to be able to secure himself inside."

"There's always the manual lock," the man said. "Can't override that."

"You're resourceful. Figure something out. If you damage anything, we'll pay him a little extra as a bonus. I don't want him to have the opportunity to escape the karma he's so richly earned."

"Yes, ma'am. I'll take care of it."

With that, Hawke turned her attention back to Rick. "There. Problem solved."

"That's only one set of problems," Rick countered. "Now you've got a new set of challenges to overcome."

She arched an eyebrow at him. "What have I missed?"

"Now you're going to have to figure out whether you're teasing me or not. As soon as we get into hyperspace, I think we should have dinner and discuss our...situation."

Her smile widened. "Are you having a *situation*, Rick Betancourt? Oh, my. Well, lucky for you, I'm a problem solver."

She leaned toward him, her eyes looking deeply into his. "And just to make things crystal clear, I'm looking forward to the next hundred and seventy hours in hyperspace. I'm sure the two of us can come up with something to...fill the time."

Yep, that was pretty clear.

"It's a good thing I stocked up on some of the higher end foodstuffs," he admitted with a smile. "If I have my way, we might not be coming out of my cabin anytime soon."

"I like the way your mind works," she said in a low, sultry voice. "I think we'll be working to become *very* good friends over the next week."

With that, she leaned back in her seat and closed her eyes, that promising smile still on her lips.

Rick tried to relax, but his mind was abuzz with the adrenaline from the fight and thoughts of the delights lying ahead. This was absolutely not what he'd planned for today, but now that it was happening, he found himself content with where things were going.

His final thought on the matter was about Chappa. He had no idea what the future held for the man, but if the fiery women who'd confronted him were good examples of the kind of women he liked to date, he was going to be in for an *extremely* long trip back down to the surface.

Rick suspected the pilot would beg them to take him with them, but it wasn't his place to save the man from the consequences of his own behavior.

In fact, he might just be able to make it *worse* for Chappa.

He smiled a cold grin. As soon as they arrived at *Hermes*, they'd break orbit and head for the stargate. That would give everyone a chance to clean up and calm down.

Chappa would think he was going to get away without having to face the women, right up until the moment Rick asked Hawke to have her Marines escort the pilot and his passengers back to his shuttle.

If Rick waited for the right time, they'd be half a day clear of everything in the system. A long trip for Chappa, but a rewarding one for the women. It was cruel, but sometimes justice had to have a sharp edge for someone to learn a lesson.

Would this change how the man behaved? Probably not, but that wasn't Rick's problem.

The benefit to him was that not only was justice served, but Hawke would think it was *hilarious*. It would also put her in an *excellent* mood to set off a week of getting to know one another in private.

Yes, he'd be bushwhacking the pilot, but it was for a good cause. A *great* cause.

With those amusing and pleasant thoughts on his mind, he settled back to think about what Hawke and he might be doing over the next week. This was going to be a fine trip, indeed.

* * * * *

Terry Mixon Bio

#1 Bestselling Military Science Fiction author Terry Mixon served as a non-commissioned officer in the United States Army 101st Airborne Division. He later worked alongside the flight controllers in the Mission Control Center at the NASA Johnson Space Center supporting the Space Shuttle, the International Space Station, and other human spaceflight projects.

He now writes full time while living in Texas with his lovely wife and a pounce of cats.

# # # # #

The Mushroom Farm by Casey Moores

His passion for stargazing originated from his days as a Boy Scout on Earth. In far simpler times, he'd laid in open fields, on top of ridges, the back of his truck, or even on his roof. His company included friends, family, and even, as he'd gotten older, more than his fair share of pretty girls. The surrounding terrain differed greatly from the cool, crisp mountain air of his hometown. It lacked trees entirely, but wasn't as "alien" as one might have imagined. It reminded him of a childhood trip to the southwest.

All the light brush and the hot, dry air resembled Death Valley. Then, as now, he'd laid his bedroll outside in the open and gazed up at the endless points of light. None of the constellations he'd memorized existed here, but it didn't bother him. He made a game of creating new constellations, a chance to utilize the artist inside him. In the weeks he'd been on planet, he'd created quite a few. He found those each night, and then attempted to find more. One night he envisioned a great space battle with Super Star Destroyers, X-wing fighters, and even a Deathstar. The next he found Cerberus, the Hydra, Medusa, and all the great monsters of Greek mythology. That particular night, he'd unsuccessfully tried the old 21st century Pokémon.

Instead, he discovered gorgeous mermaids, a Kraken, a giant shark, and the like.

He slept in shifts by day, and usually stayed up all night. Peaceful and relaxing, just how he liked it. As he squeezed peanut butter paste out of a tube onto a crumbly, dry cracker, he smiled. It was, for now, the retirement he'd dreamed of.

Semi-retirement, he reflected, as the sensor suite beeped inside his shell. The "shell," as he called it, was his personal design. The large camouflaged disc, constructed with composite material, blocked both his heat signature and electronic emissions. A harness inside allowed him to comfortably hang face down, yet stretched out so the disc lay flat and unobtrusive against the flat plains. A series of eight robotic arms allowed him to crawl slowly through any terrain the long, oval shield could fit through. The series of sensors poked out all along the sides and fed into two slates that hung right in front of his face. He stuffed the cracker into his mouth, rolled over through the netting shroud, and crawled under his shell. Glancing at the slate, he sighed and launched a micro-drone toward the source of the seismic anomaly.

It had been a hard sell to Colonel Coultrup, the commander of The Regulators, to employ a live scout, but he felt poised to prove his value. Electronic sensors either saw something, or they didn't. They could process a great number of possibilities, but in the end, they reported based on their programming. Anyone familiar with those constraints could fool them. They had no instinct.

He adjusted his earpiece and tapped on the slate to select a secure HF channel. He'd found archaic means of communication, while incredibly scratchy, were seldom noticed.

"Actual, Umbra." While awaiting a response, he rolled up and secured his bedroll. Then he stretched his legs and arms into his harness. The shell became an extension of him.

"Umbra, <static> Actual. <yawn> Go ahead." The colonel had, hopefully, spun up his staff. Calls from Umbra were rare.

"Heavy roller headed your way. Should hit your sensors in about thirty-two mikes, but they'll probably process it as a supply barge. It's not. I'm sending imagery of KzSha on board. Suggest full alert. Will continue to monitor. How copy?"

"<static> possible inbound <static> Tree Zero Mikes, was that? Copy alert, <static> on it."

"Good copy, Umbra out."

Heavy paranoia remained in his mind. The straightforward attack vexed him. Even without him, sensors would have flagged it with plenty of warning. Similarly, the watch CASPers alone would've noticed far enough out to get everyone suited and on the line before it approached weapons range. Was it a diversion? Was there an orbital attack as well, or a hidden ace somewhere he couldn't see, some big weapon? No obvious answer presented itself, so he crawled toward the mine and flipped through his sensor array and data feeds in search of a clue. With a couple swipes on the slate, he deployed his other two micro-drones toward the left and right aft quadrants from this current attack, looking for flankers. As they flew, he checked on the unit.

The feeds showed the Regulators already deployed around the mine, so the old scout turned his attention back to the KzSha. Canceling the auto track and retaking control of the first tiny drone, he zoomed in for another look as the barge rolled forward. It hit the sensor line and, either as planned or in response to the Regulators' deployment, the KzSha flew out from the large hauler. The first few rose up and fired off missiles, at very long range, and grabbed laser rifles to join the rest. Only about half deployed; the rest, oddly, stayed inside.

The swarm sporadically fired lasers at near their maximum range, as if attempting to goad the defenders into wasting their own ammunition. Coultrup wisely held their fire to make every round count, even as some of the laser fire scored a few lucky hits. Umbra focused on the reserve group, still sitting idly in their hauler. Only a few rifles remained in the group. Most of the undeployed wasp troops carried melee weapons. Stun sticks, large crowbars, and a good number of what he knew from medieval history as man-catchers, long poles with open pincers at the end. Did they plan to enslave the Human mercs? He dismissed the idea. Considering their lack of firepower and numbers, it simply didn't add up.

"Actual, Umbra. A large reserve is undeployed, heavily armed for melee. I think they mean to close quickly. Remain cautious, there's some trick we're missing."

"Copy, Umbra, you know what to do." *Figure it the heck out,* Umbra translated. A series of explosions marked Coultrup's order to fire. Missiles arced out and exploded across the wide swarm of giant wasps who flew to meet them. Umbra watched from a distance on one of his slates, as if watching a movie. His little robot spider did all it could to get him closer to the unit, but he knew it would all be over, one way or the other, before he made it. His rifle would make little difference anyway. His contribution was the intel. Drones two and three were reaching max range and hadn't found anything. There was no flanking force, no "Ch'i," as Sun Tzu would have said. The deception lay elsewhere.

Up and down the CASPer line, MACs opened fire…and then almost immediately ceased. The missile fire stopped as well. He swiped on his slate to bring up Coultrup's view of the CASPer's vitals (a view Coultrup didn't realize he'd hacked into.) The CASPers were shutting down. Few still fired laser rifles into the approaching swarm. He heard Coultrup give an order to cease fire with main weapons. A third of the unit was still powered, but armed only with laser rifles and blades, they were too few to stop the swarm. The KzSha spread out wide and concentrated fire on the powered CASPers. The Regulators tossed a few K bombs toward the large, armored hornets, which were only minimally effective, as the enemy spread out.

"Umbra…Actual." The colonel's tone said everything.

"Go ahead, sir."

"I guess we know the trick, now don't we? Look…this won't last much longer, so record everything you can. Get out of here and get it to the first Horseman who'll listen. I imagine they're pulling this on other Human mercs. I'm sure you still have some contacts. Good luck, Umbra, I'm glad I hired you."

"Wilco, sir." In the Tri-Vs, the doomed always gave a big speech. They'd say how proud they were to serve and spit out a litany of flowery BS. Real life seldom played out that way. Words wouldn't help. He knew his new mission.

The surviving CASPers extended blades and, on the colonel's command, launched toward the mass of wasps. Seconds after jumping, each one lost power, and they fell back out of the sky in unison, useless hunks of metal dropping like dead birds. Umbra almost lost his bearing at such a pathetic sight. He'd seen worse, much worse in fact, and a lot closer up, but this might've qualified for second place.

* * *

Umbra's three drones watched from different points on the wall, completely unobserved. He'd planned to watch and record until all were killed, slowly exfil to another mining town, and hop a ride to the starport. Curiously, most had survived. The KzSha hadn't dispatched them in their metal tombs. Instead, they'd cracked the CASPers open and herded the surprisingly high number of prisoners into a rough formation. The Regulators wouldn't be worth ransom, and prisoner taking seldom made economic sense. KzSha did take slaves, but Human mercs made poor slaves. Even after the defeat, Umbra remained confused.

The cleanup and security of the KzSha unit focused entirely inward. These were some cocky bugs.

Two new creatures departed from an inner compartment in the large hauler. Hopefully they'd provide him answers. One was certainly a Veetanho, the large albino mole rat thing was unmistakable, especially since all mercs knew the infamous Peepo of Peepo's Pit. This one was shorter and fatter than Peepo and, instead of goggles, it had a single monocle strapped to its head. Zooming in from a good angle, Umbra identified an asterisk or sphincter looking spot in place of an eye.

The other creature rolled along in a motorized wagon filled with water. What looked to be a large octopus occasionally flashed a pattern of light along its skin. A few taps on his slate identified it as a Wrogul, a creature common to the Scientist Guild and seldom seen outside of it.

One of the KzSha placed an overturned fuel barrel in front of the formation and lifted the Veetanho up onto it. Some unseen microphone projected its voice.

"Humans, I am General Vo. You may be wondering why you're alive. You likely haven't heard yet, but it's been determined that Humans pose a great danger to the Galactic Union. Your reckless mercenary bands will soon be disbanded, and your planet will shortly be under new leadership." Umbra subconsciously tensed up a bit at this news and with one hand searched data feeds for any related information. There was none. Was something drastic about to happen on Earth? "You've caused quite a disturbance in our Union and greatly unbalanced the Mercenary Guild. The great question is, 'Why?' Your physiology offers no great advantages…" *Look who's talking, rat,* Umbra thought.

"…and most of your population is hardly smarter than the average insect." A few KzSha turned to regard it as soon as their pendants had translated its statement, but none showed any emotion. Not that Umbra would recognize KzSha emotion.

"One of your more intelligent kind has blessed you with these impressive fighting machines, but as you've just seen, they come with great limitations which are easily exploited by the strategically minded." It gave a smug little smirk as it stated this. "Weapons and armor, as you've seen, don't make a species into great mercenaries. Neither does a mindless bloodlust, a trait your kind seems to have an abundance of. No, it takes something that by all appearances your species lacks. Which brings us back to the question of why. I would venture to say it is your *occasional* unpredictability. That's my own personal theory. You frequently contradict good sense and strategy. Your reckless and unplanned behavior can occasionally catch your opponents by surprise.

"Everything, however, has a pattern, a method, or a design. Our only difficulty with your race, so far, has been determining that pattern. And that, my dear volunteers, is why you're still alive. I'd like to take this opportunity to applaud the contribution you will soon be making to our understanding your kind. With your assistance, perhaps we can someday help develop Humans into productive participants in our Galactic Union." It nodded to the octopus, who didn't acknowledge it. It raised its short little arm and motioned the prisoners toward the haulers, at which point the KzSha prodded and their antenna flashed, translated by their pendants as directions to move. There were spontaneous attempts by the defeated Humans to grab at the stun batons or pull on the man-catchers, but all were met with electric jolts or hard smacks. One ballsy man attempted a rush to obtain a laser rifle, whose owner reflexively shot him. After a shout from "General" Vo, another KzSha, likely a sergeant, raised a pistol and killed the KzSha who'd fired. Apparently they were under strict orders to keep their test subjects alive.

Umbra recovered his drones one by one and moved his shell away. As he did so, he closed his eyes, took a deep breath, and organized his thoughts. Despite his promise to Coultrup, there was no way he was leaving them here.

First, his unit was being taken somewhere for study. Visions of 20th century concentration camps came to mind. He considered the sickest, most depraved, vile horrors the Nazis had visited on their fellow man and contemplated how much worse a morally disconnected alien species might do. Visions of vivisections, cybernetics, bioweapons, and psychological experimentation filled his head. These troops would be subjected to that.

Second, they hacked CASPers. One could only assume this capability could become widespread and, as such, was an enormous danger to all Human merc units. That had to get out before they were all destroyed.

Finally, the news about Earth. This was, putting it mildly, the most disconcerting. If this hadn't happened yet, then he must do what he could to send warning. If it had happened, it meant there were no mercenary units to call for, no official rescue he could send for. Mentally, he canceled all thoughts of hiring a merc unit to come get them. Anything related to the Mercenary Guild was suspect. That even ruled out a "sort of secret" Combat Salvage, Search, and Rescue (CSSAR) unit he knew of. This really only left him one option.

He sent a requisition request through GalNet to Kit'd Foh Shipping for a "Fungal Agricultural Kit—Expedient" and then added a few remarks. He could only hope the "company" was still in business.

* * *

Durree plodded along, head buried in his slate. Normally, he would rush back into his cool, climate-controlled office trailer but, in this instance, distraction slowed him. The supply shipment should have been a routine matter of matching the list of crates ordered to the stack of crates that had arrived. Rarely did this take more than a few minutes, and issues were usually confined to parts mismatches or incomplete shipments. Never, in his time as Head Manager, had he encountered such a large shipment he hadn't ordered.

A large, unordered shipment threatened the survival of the operation. The great mines they explored had long ago been emptied of the valuable ore and existed simply as ready-made quarries and treasure troves of recyclables. Barely worthwhile enough to turn a profit.

Some were still actively mined for rare or heavy metals, some had found deposits of various fuels, but the profitable mines were appropriated by some entity with the funds to hire mercs. Durree's masters weren't willing to make such an investment. Thus, his job necessitated some profit, but not *too much* profit. To remain inconsequential, but still productive. Too much expenditure, even if unintended, and they were sunk.

Reaching out with one hand somewhat absentmindedly toward the door to his office, he turned his head back to regard the shipping crates. "ACME CORP" stood out in large, block, Human letters on the sides. On his slate, the company displayed as a small Earth-based company that delivered rare, expensive items. The catalogue seemed difficult to find. Whoever designed the GalNet site for this company hadn't made it user-friendly. He wondered how they got any business at all. Being near-sighted, he squinted and held up an eyepiece to take one more good look at the crates. By the description, it appeared as if the company's entire stock might have been shipped here. The crates were full of something called "kingpins."

Dismay, and then anger with his underlings overtook him. He'd given explicit instructions the crates were, under no circumstances, to be opened. As a major error of someone else's doing, he didn't want to be made liable for the shipment by tampering with it before returning it. Yet one sat opened and, by the look of it, already nearly empty. His hunchbacked neck extended forward as he strained to identify the contents. It looked like seats…

"Are you coming in?" Instinct almost drove him to extend his massive claws in shock. On the other hand, the cool, soft manner in which the creature spoke calmed as much as its sudden appearance alarmed. A tall, lightly tanned, hairless, bipedal creature stood immediately next to him and held the door open. Durree dropped his eyepiece, and it dangled on its chain.

"Human, I presume? Are you responsible for this misdelivered shipment?" Shivers ran along his spine, and he fought to maintain composure. Humans were known as a very rash and deadly species. One wrong word and they might spontaneously start shooting everything.

"Yes and no, sir. May we talk inside?" Though the words themselves processed through his translator pendant so he could understand them, he could feel the calm, yet powerful voice of the being. It was mentally relaxing, but emotionally terrifying, all at once. His confused emotions left him unequipped to do anything other than what the Human suggested. A tremor went up and down his dark brown fur, and he plodded inside on stubby legs. The tall, muscular, bald Human motioned to his seat, and his legs took him there. Leaning back into the wide black leather cushioning, Durree set down his slate and stared, wide-eyed and dumbfounded. The man sat as well, and, as Jivool seats had no backing, his posture was ramrod straight, yet still tranquil and nonchalant.

"The *shipment* (his emphasis seemed to indicate some kind of joke Durree didn't understand) wasn't misdelivered. You, of course, didn't order it. Yet ordered it was. I imagine the one who did order it will be with us shortly. In the meantime, I have a proposal. There's a substantial potential for profit for you if you agree." The man reached into his thin, dark gray jacket. The Jivool's hands tensed and clasped onto his desk in a death grip, expecting a large caliber weapon. The man drew out a long brown tube of plant leaf. In smooth, well-orchestrated movements, he proceeded to clip one end with a small metal contraption, and then swapped it for a match, which he used to burn one end of the tube. He'd seen other species "smoke" before, but this was particularly potent. The silence that lingered while this operation played out served to build tension in his shoulders. He mused his shoulders had become MAC proof.

"Life is about choices. We can rub each other's shoulders, or kick each other in the nuts. Your call." With these words, the icy blue eyes of this menacing creature stared at Durree and burned holes straight through him. There was no doubt whatsoever that he meant what he said. The large hunchbacked bear jumped an inch at a knock on the door.

The hairless demon rose and moved to open it. Another Human, this one much more gaunt, somewhat twitchy, and with thin wisps of gray hair, entered. The two grabbed each other's hands and nodded.

Baldy stated, "Am I to understand you ordered a mushroom farm?"

The wrinkly one replied, "Only if it was Kept In The Dark…"

"And Fed Only Horse Shit," Baldy finished. "Patches…good to see you. Sorry for the delay. There was a major situation at Karma as we were looking for a ride out. Your warning was a bit too late. Seems Human mercs are going to have to lay low for a bit. In any case, we're here now." He sighed, and they moved toward separate chairs. "You look old. I thought you'd retired?"

"I'm both, Bull. I thought *you'd* retired, though you haven't aged a day." This one's voice was a little higher pitched and scratchy.

"I did. Still just an honest merchant. Sorry to hear about—"

"It happens, Bull, and it was time. Let's get to business," Patches stated flatly. Bull nodded and held eye contact a moment longer.

"Understood. I was about to finish my profit-making proposal, if you wouldn't mind." The large bald one, "Bull," turned to re-engage

Durree. "As I was saying, you have a choice of unexpected profits, or the immediate failure of your little operation. My assistant will be in shortly to discuss the details. When we've settled the details of the merc contract you'll be submitting," he raised a hand to prevent Durree from interrupting, "we'll need it to go out immediately."

The door opened and a slender, brown-haired Human entered without warning. By the scent, Durree could tell this one was female. Her dark green jumpsuit was adorned with an "Acme Corp" patch on the right shoulder, and one over her left breast that seemed to identify her as "SKYFAB."

"Patches, this is Archie, my lead pilot." The two shook hands.

"The new turnkey?" Patches asked cryptically.

"We'll see," Bull responded. "Go ahead, Archie."

She gave a quick nod and a friendly smile to Durree.

"Sir, they've got six air skiffs we could use. They need major maintenance and mods, but Skippy's on it. Problem is, they're VMC only," (the translator only gave letters, Durree could only guess at the meaning), "we're short on what we need to upgrade them, and nothing here is big enough for what we need. I'll draw up a plan to hit up the starport for proper shuttles and some quadcopters." Raising both eyebrows gave her the effect of having bigger, rounder eyes. If he wasn't so terrified, he might have found it adorable.

Bull casually glanced at Durree. "We'll have to charge those to you initially. Don't worry, we'll keep good records and reimburse you as soon as our delivery is complete." He stood up. "Thank you for your time and cooperation, Head Manager Durree. Patches, Archie, let's head back into my office to talk."

It was several minutes before the poor Jivool mining manager moved. He felt certain his cooperation had been assumed, and he was expected to comply with whatever insane request they forwarded to him. *Hiring a merc unit? Buying shuttles?* He had the autonomy to do so, but not the budget. Even so, as soon as the corporate office made a review, he'd be fired and maybe even executed for all he knew. On the other hand, the psychopathic Humans would certainly execute him if he failed to follow their directions.

As a separate thought, the older Human had obviously not arrived with the others, so how'd he gotten inside the compound? Were his Zuul guards completely worthless? With only questions and no solutions, he could work out no alternative. Somehow, they'd completely usurped his quiet, simple little mining operation.

* * *

The commander's "shipping crate" contained a long conference room. A long, thin desk with built-in slates ran down the middle, with chairs on either side. A refreshment area was set up along the far backside. In the middle, on the left side, halfway down, was a projection. Patches stood by it and pointed around.

"So you know this is the starport here, this is us…and there's the hole they were moved to. All the equipment wound up here, in this one. As you can see, the whole of the plains are riddled with these massive mining holes. Generally 500-1000 feet straight down, around a hundred feet in diameter. Most've played out and been abandoned, including our target. Now…there're several groups out there with different claims mapped out. There hadn't been any intrusion from one group to another for recorded history.

"For some reason, about a year ago, one of the companies hired a large unit of KzSha for 'defensive operations.' Naturally the others got suspicious. Because most mines are only marginally profitable, there was no one to defend against, and because, well, they're goddamn KzSha. The whole thing sparked a bit of a merc hiring race, and the Regulators pulled the contract for the border against the KzSha's employer, here. The whole thing smells of a setup to get a Human merc unit there where they could be taken, just like they were. I've already explained their purpose." His eyes lowered with a sigh. "That about brings us to where we are."

Bull nodded, expressionless. "Thank you, Patches. As soon as this is over, I need you back out there, all right?" He nodded to the brunette. "Obviously time is of the essence, everyone. Archie?"

"Yes, sir." She nodded. "We've got ten of these ancient junk skiffs they use here. They only fly them during the day and when there isn't a sandstorm. We've got two dropships that can lead the formations and two quadcopters for the infil. One issue is, these cheap POSs basically use something resembling AvGas, if you can believe it. They normally have the range to get from here to the starport, but they won't have the range to hit the objective and continue. I'm planning one from each formation as a tanker to top them off right before crossing the fence. Otherwise, we've planned a dozen semi-random routes. We'll train so each formation is familiar with the other's tasks so they can be interchangeable the night of. That said, with your concurrence, sir, I'd like to get my pilots going running the simulations."

"Hold off; we still have a few issues to discuss." He leaned forward to make eye contact with a fit, younger, bearded black man halfway down the table. "Whiskey, do we have a target for my buddy yet?"

The man leaned forward and spoke fast and animatedly, especially for this crowd. "Yes, sir, there were four strong possibilities, but based on distance, placement, estimated response times, and strength of the defenders, this one here wins." As with the others, the target he referred to illuminated as he spoke.

"Has that been pushed through our host?" Whiskey nodded. "Okay then. That sets the 'H' hour. Tara, you find some space in these tunnels for a range yet?" A short but heavy-set pale-faced kid spoke up in a Boston accent and annoying nasally tone.

"Yes, sir, I've actually got a few. They seriously strip out the ring on each level and move on, so there's huge empty spaces. I say we move these crates down there ASAP." The large stern bald man nodded and gave a quick glance around the room.

"Do it. D10..." Now he looked intently at a taller bald man. Unlike Bull, whose skin was smooth and totally devoid of hair as if it had all been polished off, Distelzweig had an intentionally shaven bald head and finely-trimmed, full facial hair. "Where are we on the toys?"

"Illuminator's good to go. I'm still playing around a little on the Rupert design since the conditions are a little unusual." He turned to look at the lead pilot. "Archie, I know it doesn't need to be said, but you guys gotta nail the timing and placement on this. I've got a run-in procedure that should help, but serious—" Bull cut him off.

"You wanna come sit in this chair, D10?" Silence. "Or go over and sit in hers?" The entire retinue held their breath. "They know their job, D10. Work on yours. Figure out Rupert and start production. Better get it right...nobody loves you more than you." Slow exhales began, followed by small chuckles all around as the crowd relaxed a little. D10 tensed more.

"Sir, do you mean…" Bull shot metaphorical lasers from his eyes.

"Were you planning to slap us a good game and wave us off? You're going with Archie to make sure the swarm works. Put that survival instinct to use. Get. It. Done." He turned to regard his favorite pilot. "Archie, in addition to the simulator runs, I want you guys to get some actual experience flying to and from the starport. Make the rounds to the Jivool's other mines and try not to highlight this one. Come up with a good excuse, maintenance shakedowns, parts runs, compass swing, or something—is that still a thing?—use up the whole list if need be. Learn the land. Remember, the map is not the territory. I want to desensitize them, so make your flights a regular thing. But remember Rule Two—no one sees a Human. Bring some Jivool with you, let them do the talking and trading."

"Yes, sir."

Whiskey raised his hand. "Go ahead, Whiskey."

"Sir, do we have to wait for your buddy to show up?" Grumbles and groans built up around the table.

"I remember my first op," Archie teased.

"Please," Bull said. "Proceed, Whiskey."

"No, seriously, a good plan today is better than a perfect plan tomorrow, right?" Whiskey glanced around the room, looking for support. "Those guys are down that hole dying right now. Can't we do this any faster?"

Bull raised the quieting hand again and waited several seconds after silence returned.

"I appreciate your position, Whiskey," he said, "but there's a right way and a wrong way to do this. I've been on the other end of the wrong way, right, Patches?"

Patches stared through Whiskey and nodded solemnly.

"We're doing this the right way," Bull said. "Anything else?"

"Yes, sir," Whiskey replied. The rest groaned again and were again silenced by a gesture from Bull.

"Go ahead," Bull said genuinely.

"Sir, one last item's been bugging me. Even if we maintain a decent level of surprise, how do we get a team in fast enough to secure the package before it's terminated? Obviously that'll be their first priority once they realize what's happening." The entire group started to nod uncomfortably, as they'd all been thinking similarly. "A jump won't work, the ship can't hover as they jump in, it'll get taken out. High-altitude would be suicide for a number of reasons, and..." Bull put his hand out gently, palm down, and motioned him to stop.

"Excellent question, and I know you've all been wondering about that. Let me ask...how many of you know any history related to the American Vietnam War? There're some great lessons learned from that entire conflict, but let me tell you about one in particular..."

* * *

Vo loved how her doctor worked. Being as its "name" was a series of light flashes that translated to something horrendously unintelligible when processed through the pendants, Vo had taken to referring to it as "Mengele" after a brief look through Human history. The original Mengele had sounded like a brilliant and thoroughly unappreciated man. Humans were so poor at recognizing genius.

In any event, Vo had one major concern. She worried Mengele would deplete the Humans a little too quickly. The first dozen hadn't survived the cybernetic grafts, and none so far had survived the bioweapon experiments. Even the psychological tests seemed to take their toll. Once a Human's mind was broken, it seemed nothing would repair it. They were so frail in every way.

Mengele assured her refinements were made with every necrosis. Even so, if the trend continued, Vo feared she might have to travel to Karma Station and recruit more volunteers from the newly arrived prisoners. Peepo would take that as failure, despite any progress made. Vo didn't want to make that request. She reworked the efficiencies in order to get more out of each Human. Psychological tests first, mild cybernetics next, and, if it was still alive, it could be used to test either bioweapons or major cybernetics. This created a new issue in that psychological tests took a great deal of time. They had time, but Peepo required periodic results.

Overall, it was a delicate balancing act. That aspect of it thrilled Vo. It was what she was made for.

Her comm link buzzed, and she answered. It was Zrr'tk, the commander of the KzSha unit.

"I gave orders not to be disturbed unless we were under attack," she barked.

"General Vo, a Lumar merc unit arrived in system and just commenced an assault drop. Their target looks to be our base of operations, where our spoils and remunerations are kept."

"Okay...so shoot them down." Honestly, what was their commander's purpose?

"General Vo, per our contract, we have minimal surface-to-air assets. Our plan for this contingency was to draw reserves from the surrounding mines. I'm requesting permission to do so."

"Fine, then, do what you need to do." Morons. "Wait! Do NOT draw reserves from this station, nor from Station 17. Understand?"

"Yes, General Vo. I'll keep you appraised. Zrr'tk, out."

That settled, Vo considered the implications.

* * *

Archie carried the moniker "SKYFAB," short for "She'll Kick Your Fucking Ass, Bitch." The others assumed she was "just" a pilot when she'd started as a merc, but after seeing her handle herself in a brawl at a remote station's bar, her compadres had inquired. She reluctantly explained her parents ran the infamous Laughing Coyote Xeno-centric Martial Arts School. The legend had grown substantially by the time she hired on with Bull. Everyone assumed that was why Bull had tracked her down.

"No, seriously, I was told you straight up knocked out a Besquith on Vega Station. How the hell'd you do that?" Opie, her navigator, named for an uncanny resemblance to an ancient TV character, was chattier than she preferred.

"Classified. How far have the INS solutions drifted?" The shuttle they flew, Cherry One, relied on two ancient independent inertial navigational systems, i.e. gyrocompasses, for navigation. Aside from dead reckoning, which they were also doing, the planet and their equipment offered them no other options. In fact, the shuttle and the quadcopter, Banana One, following them were the only ships that were capable of navigation. The skiffs, Apples One thru Five, and Lime One, the refueler, flew in formation behind them. The skiffs had no such systems, and they hadn't prioritized rigging them up. Thus, the formation relied mostly on the two INS systems on Cherry One, the single system on Banana One, and dead reckoning from all involved. Umbra/Patches planted a few navigational beacons to help, but they were only visible on the slates, an ergonomic difficulty. The "navigator," essentially the non-flying pilot on the shuttle, periodically referenced them as a triple check.

"About 240 feet so far. I'll run a radar update off the next turn point, just make sure to offset it. You're going to tell me about the Besquith someday." The major trouble with INS systems was that incredibly small inaccuracies increased over time. You could tell they drifted when they started to disagree with each other on their position. The entire team was somewhat boggled they relied on ancient navigational sources, but they accepted they'd acquired the cheapest, most immediately available junk. By now, they were somewhat used to it. Members of this "shipping company" didn't last long if they complained about the difficulty of tasks. Bull didn't permit his people to say, "no, because…" when faced with an issue. He expected to hear, "yes, if…" followed by a solution and plan of action.

Archie strained to see into the darkness, even with state-of-the-art night vision. Lunar illumination was minimal, and the constant dust limited visibility. Her course was as accurate as they could determine, but the scattered rock formations and low ridgelines could end the operation in tragedy. Her head panned back and forth to maintain a solid night flying scan.

"Time status?"

"We're about 40 seconds late right now; winds are hurting us. I'm gonna turn you early at the next point to shave that off." Normally a change in airspeed could help to make up lost time or lose extra time, but such changes were impractical in a formation of eight moving slower than the shuttle was meant to fly. Off-course maneuvering was the best option. She felt ecstatic that, after an hour and a half of flying, they were still within one minute of their time over target.

The radio silence remained the most unsettling aspect of the operation, even amongst the formation. Communication was limited to a simple set of light flashes, using lights imperceptible to KzSha, which communicated simple concepts, such as "navigation error," "propulsion trouble," and "require set down." A "mission abort" call, a rare event, would only be supplied by Bull, i.e. Greenleaf One, via a single, encrypted radio transmission.

Doubts about the success of their part or someone else's part crept in occasionally. What if they caught Umbra hacking the individual sensors? What if they weren't perfectly coordinated with the Lumar assault? Furthermore, they considered the miserable ending to the story Bull had told. Was that a possibility? She cracked her neck to the left and right and forced the doubts out. Cherry One would be on time, on target. Everything else would be what it would be.

"Sooo, Besquith story time?" Opie asked. With a chuckle, she gave in.

"Okay, fine, so it wasn't so much what *I* did, but what he did to himself, with my help…"

* * *

Half an hour later, it was time. The formation now trailed them by three thousand feet. The doors were open, the illuminator was prepped, and they approached the target. Archie looked out to the spot where the mine lay and made one last sanity check. Navigation was leading them just to the right of it, so it must be off a little. The ridgeline, with a canyon beyond, was a couple miles off to the left. That checked. The spot itself was darker than she envisioned. There was a slight glow from another spot ahead and to the right.

"Two minutes."

"Swarm, swarm, swarm."

The threat circle of the enemy's air defense ring had been shrunk significantly with regular civil flights pushing the bounds of its auto-tracking. As predicted by Bull, they were afraid to highlight themselves by accidentally launching on what appeared to be unarmed mining skiffs. This allowed them to get pretty close, but soon the game would be up.

To counteract, a few small crates, casually "lost" during previous passes, cracked open and swarms of small, plastic toy drones flew out in advance of the raid.

"One minute."

"Stand by!" The entire crew tensed and gasped audibly. "It's the wrong one. *Ours* is that one!" She looked at him and pointed. "See the pattern of the mines? In route study, you mentioned these two were close together. Well, this one is here, ours is there. See the slight glow? There're lights in that one." As she spoke, the blanket of tiny drones lit up at the other mine as well. Tracers burst out from nowhere, and missile batteries rotated wildly, failing to lock onto anything. Tiny flashes came from the small explosive charges of the drones hitting the guns and batteries. He processed for a second.

"Shit, you're right. Aim for it and set up, uh," the wheels spun inside his head, "thirty yards left. Left of center, that is. Thirty seconds! Fuck, we're late."

By "late" he meant by twenty-four seconds. In this unit, that was a disaster. The cockpit went dead silent for an eternity. The ground rushed by, and the hole in the ground, the hole of their objective, came up rapidly. Archie found herself holding her breath, recognized her muscles were tensed up, and she relaxed with a slow breath out.

"Ten seconds."

She was further right than he said, too close to the center. Gingerly she eased the ship left. Thirty yards lay just inside the edge of the hole. She fixed it. Her course and altitude were dead on.

"Five seconds."

"Execute, execute, execute." That was the one and only call they repeated over the radio.

"Illuminator active," called the crewman from the ramp.

"Okay, set up for Rupert deployment. Commencing teardrop. One minute!"

* * *

The complex, like all the others, was essentially a perfect round hole cut straight down, four hundred feet down in this case, with levels of reinforced concrete rings all the way down. The first few rings going downward had been used administratively, and the mining tunnels generally shot out randomly on the lower levels.

A KzSha guard stood on the second ring in the darkness and looked down the massive shaft. He and the others had been alerted due to the attack on their base of operations, but they'd been ordered to maintain the blackout as a precaution. None seemed to feel in danger of attack, and their Veetanho contract holder would certainly not release them from guard duty. Moreover, sensors would alert them well before any aircraft or ground troops approached the mine. Which made the guard confused to see the anti-air artillery light up, followed by a flood of tiny flashes, and a shuttle passed just to the side of the top. As it did so, something fell out the back. Brilliant, erratic, headache-inducing light exploded from the object and drifted, unnaturally slowly, down the center. Some reverberating, piercing noise emitted as well and overwhelmed his echolocators.

He shook his head and struggled to regain sight. As his vision started to clear, he tried to make out what the other guards said. The lights on their antennae flashed with confusion and pain. He realized the lower levels were starting to experience what he had.

Something hovered over the top of the great opening. Straining to regain focus, he thought he could make out a quadcopter moving into the mine. That couldn't be right, a quadcopter wouldn't fit. Nevertheless, it attempted to do just that.

It loitered for just a moment at the top, seemed to lose power, and dropped down into the deep, dark hole. Sparks scraped at one spot a hundred feet down, and the aircraft began to tip. A jet flared up for a split second to correct it back upright. The guard watched it spark a few more times, with a corresponding flare each time. Just before it crashed, a series of jets fired off, slowing it somewhat before it crunched down hard at the bottom. He considered how absurdly crazy this whole sequence was playing out when the shuttle passed overhead again. This time a couple dozen troopers fell out the back and deployed parachutes to slowly drift down the center, firing sporadic laser fire. Each carried another, albeit smaller, flashing light on its shoulder. Taken altogether, they made it near impossible to see or communicate. However, even while he squinted, they were remarkably easy to shoot. He and the other guards lit them up and riddled the jumpers with laser fire. The poor little creatures drifted limply down. Surprisingly, some still occasionally fired, only to subsequently get shot up again. As he looked down to observe them, he found a substantial gunfight occurring down below, where the crashed ship lay. The blinding illuminator remained active, so he drew back before the headache resumed.

What idiotic attack plan called for crashing a ship down a hole and releasing a bunch of helpless troopers into a killing field?

Searchlights came on all around the ring. An attack in progress meant the blackout order was rescinded. Flashes from the top ring promptly shattered the searchlights. Unobserved attackers had already infiltrated the top ring. The guard clearly identified laser shields pop up around the periphery, and flashes of laser fire erupted from beside them. He and the other guards shifted their fire from the jumpers in the shaft to whoever was behind those shields. Curiously, he recognized a steady pattern in the laser fire coming from the shields. Straining to see through the intense flashing, the parachutists, and the general chaos, he realized he couldn't make out any actual soldiers. Had all of these things been elaborate diversions?

This was his last thought. A figure in black, attached to a rope, swung in from above and shot him in the head.

* * *

The KzSha guards at the bottom of the pit were dispatched easily, blinded as they were by the powerful illuminator. All of the assaulting troopers were equipped with goggles that filtered out the spectrum the illuminator used, so the KzSha couldn't see very well, and the attackers could. The guards spaced up and around the ring were too distracted by the dummies falling down the center to notice enemy troops rappel down the sides until it was too late. Reinforcements wouldn't be coming as all were committed to the unit's primary base. Running down the narrow, unlit tunnel away from the battle, the cyclopic Veetanho reflected on events.

Vo found herself impressed on several levels by the audacity of the Human attack. She imagined the KzSha must have somehow allowed a Human to escape during the initial attack. This Human must have avoided contracting the variety of diseases they'd unleashed on Human mercs, which was curious, as the rest of the unit had been infected until cured (most of them) by Mengele. In any case, this Human must then have found a way to message a Human merc unit. No, that wasn't right, as the Human merc units were, by now, all neutralized. The sneaky Humans must have created units outside the authority of the Merc Guild. That would be another crime to bring to the Guild's attention.

The Lumar attack had obviously been a distraction from this operation. That the attack had actually been successful in its own right was irrelevant to Vo. The success or failure of the KzSha contract or her miner puppets meant nothing. This became especially true as she enacted her evacuation contingency.

The failure of the sensors to detect the inbound ships was no mystery. Constant interference from the sandstorms and frequent disruptions by indigenous, unintelligent life forms provided plenty of cover. Some sneaky Human must have approached and disabled them. The illuminator impressed her as well. It would not work in most other circumstances, which is likely why no one had previously bothered to develop such a species-specific weapon. In this situation, however, dark of night, focused field of view, it had practically incapacitated any KzSha that remained in sight of it. They'd reversed the killing field of the shaft.

Crashing the quadcopter was absolutely inspired. It was exactly the sort of irrational act that proved Vo's hypothesis. Doubtless, the Humans had worried that by the time they infiltrated to the lowest level, their prisoners would have been killed. A reasonable assumption as, indeed, her orders specified exactly that.

The waves of dummies that followed afterward were downright absurd, but provided enough additional distraction to her idiotic guards that she didn't think a single actual Human had been shot at.

Unfortunately for the Humans, Vo had recognized the pattern well in advance of the attack. For one such as her, the signs were obvious. The purchase of the ships hadn't gone unnoticed by her well-paid eyes at the starport. Although they tried to hide the flight paths of the ships with regular supply runs, Vo had immediately recognized that there was no reason for such a great number of runs. It was simply not plausible that the failing mining operation would suddenly require such great inventory. Besides, they neither delivered ore nor acquired supplies at a rate commensurate with the added runs. Finally, she'd received forewarning of the contract for the Lumar unit as soon as it had arrived in system. That final piece had spurred her to enact the exfiltration plan. Her suspicions were confirmed when communications became jammed shortly after the KzSha reported the attack. Hours before the spectacular assault on Station 13, Vo had wisely, and quietly, moved the prisoners via this very tunnel to Station 17. They were now loaded on her shuttle awaiting departure.

It was quite a trek on her personal transportation roller. However, the sounds behind her receded, which meant she'd escaped pursuit.

She'd gone back in an attempt to retrieve Mengele and its research, but the stubborn alien had actually called her a "paranoid albino rodent" and refused. She promptly shot it. Its loss would be a great setback to the research, but she would find another. In fact, she knew of another Wrogul who called *itself* Mengele.

One issue still bothered her. There had been one shuttle, one quadcopter, and a random collection of skiffs involved in the assault on Station 13. However, the Humans, through their Jivool intermediaries, had purchased *two* shuttles, *two* quadcopters, and a good number of skiffs. Redundancy indicated a good plan, so had they simply ensured they had backups in the event of mechanical failures? Maybe they'd gone to support the Lumar attack. That *would* explain the attack's success.

She approached the end of the tunnel and parked the transport. In the near dark, she wondered why she couldn't hear the sound of her shuttle's engines. It should be ready to depart as soon as she stepped on board. Her monocle picked up a faint red light up ahead. It flickered out. A moment later it glowed hot, and again slowly faded. A strange scent of smoke was detectable in the air. Her approach slowed when she began to make out a large shadow attached to the point of light.

"I imagine you're the one in charge down here? Coultrup's troops tell me there's a chubby one-eyed mole rat running things." Vo raised her pistol rapidly, but the blindingly quick, bulky Human had already closed the distance and broken her wrist with a quick chop. Her pistol dropped, and she slammed against the wall with a hand to her throat. He raised his other hand, which carried a cigar, and tapped his earpiece.

"Actual checking in, radio silence rescinded. All ground teams, check in." She struggled uselessly as she heard the responses crackle over another radio somewhere in the opening ahead.

"Blueboy up, zero kilo, one whiskey, twisted ankle, negative contact on package." A pause. "Greenleaf up, zero kilo, zero whiskey, objective secure, negative contact on package." As the next voice chimed in, she could hear the actual voice coming from just around the corner. "Redwine up, zero kilo, zero whiskey, objective and package secure. Seventy Eagles all accounted for, per Regulator Six."

"Copy all," the gruff muscular man holding her said. "Air units, check in." Two "Cherries," five "Apples," five "Peaches," and two "Limes" all checked in, seemingly with no issues.

"Firebirds up comms?" he asked. After a pause, he stated, "Pass my regards to Jopo on a job well done. Tell him I'll have a glass of Seemuck waiting when we meet up."

The man ceased his communications, pulled the cigar from his mouth, and gave a long, pained sigh. He glared at Vo with a hint of anger. "Seventy Regulators left…there should have been a good deal more."

"How did you pay for all this?" Vo inquired, ignoring the implication.

"Simple enough. The Firebirds—that'd be the Lumar—are getting paid on their spoils, which you know are quite substantial. Basically stealing everything the KzSha stole, plus everything you paid them. The Jivool are getting paid in a controlling interest in this entire mining plain. At least, everything you controlled."

"And how did you know I'd be coming here?" She squeaked out. A couple troopers approached, and the big man released his grip so they could secure her limbs. He walked beside them as they dragged her toward her shuttle.

"I imagine you Veetanho have a rich tradition of learning from your history?" He took a drag from his cigar and continued, "A long time back, on Earth, there was a war in which a large number of prisoners were held at a place called Son Tay, and their compatriots were worried whether they would survive their captivity. They were held in a compound close to the enemy capital, but nonetheless, they made a rescue plan."

Her captors carried her into what had been her own shuttle to the loud jeering of the large group of unfettered, rescued Humans. They quieted immediately when the big man simply put his hand up. Vo struggled.

"Don't you worry, they'll contain themselves unless I give them the go ahead."

Swallowing nervously, she passed through a gauntlet of angry ex-captives to reach a seat up front. They placed her in her very own seat and strapped her to it. The big man sat down next to her and took another puff.

"Sir, I don't believe smoking is allowed on these aircraft," remarked a younger, blue-eyed man with a full head of brown hair. His nametag identified him as "Neil." The big man gave him a quick glance and the scarcest of smiles, said, "Noted," then took another drag.

"So they came up with this audacious plan to retrieve their people. One part was a massive, distractive air raid. The biggest issue was saving the prisoners from execution. They worked out a plan to put a team down into the compound quickly and secure the prisoners before they lost surprise. The best way they could see to do this was to crash a helicopter straight into the compound. It's a rare pilot who can crash in an intentional, specific way. Follow-up teams landed outside, and the whole thing went off with zero killed in action, just one wounded. Twisted ankle, just like we had tonight."

"That's very interesting, Mr.—I'm sorry, what should I call you?"

"Bull works."

"Mr. Bull."

"Just Bull."

"Bull it is. Anyway, it's very interesting, we Veetanho would say 'history repeats itself,' but you haven't told me how you found me *here*." Certainly she'd find a way out, or her kind would come for her, so the more information she could collect, the better.

"Well, you see, the tragic part of this entire operation—they called it Operation Ivory Coast—is that despite how incredibly successful they'd been at flying so many aircraft deep into enemy territory, striking into the heart of the enemy, and doing so with no more than a twisted ankle, the whole thing was actually a failure in its intended mission. The prisoners had been moved well before the raid happened. A great tactical success, but an intelligence failure.

"The similarities came to mind when we began planning this. So in honor of the lessons learned, I made sure we repeated the successes of Son Tay without its failure. Looked into what contingencies you might have. And I'm glad we did. Seems not only did we find our people, but we found all their equipment hidden down this hole as well, and their payment. Much less well defended, I might add. I almost wish I would've stayed with the other group and had more personal opportunity to utilize my weaponry. No matter, here we are." She strained to see toward the flight deck, wondering why they still hadn't bothered to lift off.

"So what now? I mean, Human mercs are outlawed, Earth is under our control; let's face it, you have nowhere to go." She couldn't help but sneer, but he didn't even bother to look at her.

"Well, Colonel Coultrup will have to settle for merging his company with the Firebirds, just to be legal. Their contract keeps them here for a while, so they can hang out for a spell and lay low until things are sorted. Time to start addressing the psychological and physiological damage you've done."

"And you?"

"Well, we are, after all, just simple merchants. I guess we'll get back to it. Seems like right now there might be a whole lot of business out there for us."

"The Mercenary Guild won't stay blind to your operations. You're quite obviously operating outside their authority and against Galactic law. I don't think 'Acme Corp' can keep this charade up much longer."

"Acme Corp? What's that? Before we came here, we were Stark Industries. Now...I think we'll be the..." He glanced off into air for a moment, cocking his head. "Ace Tomato Company. Yeah, that sounds good. All registered legally with the Merchant Guild, all too temporary in nature to ever warrant a review."

"Looks like you've thought of everything." The monocle turned to regard the prisoners. "And what becomes of me?"

* * *

"Well, I have half a mind to start running some psychological tests on you, maybe use you to test bioweapons, or maybe even just vivisect you for fun." Vo turned an even lighter shade of white. "But it occurs to me I just told you everything, like I'm some kind of 20th century Earth vid spy villain, my vanity getting the better of me. If that's the case, you're guaranteed to escape and spread the word about us. I can't have that."

Bull looked around at the twisted mess of freaks the mercs had become. There were a myriad of attempted "enhancements," a variety of biological grafts, cybernetic experiments, and some otherwise untouched but clearly insane.

One had a Goka shell grafted to his back. *Useful, if he doesn't go crazy and kill himself.* Another had tentacles where her arms should be. They hung limply to her sides, lifeless. Several had Veetanho-like goggles fused to their faces, replacing their eyes. Their heads turned back and forth, evidently seeing *something*, but God knew what.

"You know, ever since Humans agreed to this absurd endeavor, we've been subjected to a never-ending onslaught of the worst meat grinders this galaxy has to offer. We've done what we could to hold our own, and we've learned quite a lot. The Horsemen, of course, are the front line, pushing us to new heights, and fighting the major battles. Leading the Charge. Killing Aliens, Getting Paid. Planning, Preparing, Striking. Holding What You've Got. But there are a lot more of us out there than just the Horsemen. Smaller units, getting fed to the grinder constantly. Most think there's no one there to stand up for them when things go bad, no one there to help them out. Well, obviously, here we are. Here to pull them out of hell. And sometimes…when I get the chance…I try to get what little payback I can manage."

He reached over and popped her restraints, then grabbed and lifted her with one arm.

Facing the recently rescued prisoners, he shouted, "Regulators!" They went silent and turned to stare as one. Bull turned back to stare into Vo's monocle.

"Go ahead!" He tossed her to them.

* * * * *

Casey Moores Bio

Casey Moores was a USAF officer, as well as a rescue and special ops C-130 pilot for over 17 years—airdropping, air refueling, and flying in and out of tiny little blacked-out dirt airstrips in bad places using night vision goggles. He's been to "those" places and done "those" things with "those" people. Now he is looking forward to a somewhat quieter life where he can translate those experiences into fiction. He is a Colorado native and Air Force Academy graduate, but has also become a naturalized Burqueño, planning to live in New Mexico forever.

# # # # #

Jaws of Defeat by Jon R. Osborne

A Bjorn's Berserkers Story

Bear Town, New Mexico, Earth

"Doesn't this sound too good to be true?" Captain Heimir Jonasson challenged, breaking the silence in the conference room. "The Eosogi are offering half again the going rate for a straightforward job. What's the catch?"

Commander Bjorn Tovesson III tamped down his rising ire. Captain Jonasson had served under Bjorn's father for ten years, so he knew the mercenary business. The veteran officer was also a pain in Bjorn's ass.

"The Eosogi offered a premium if we can get boots on the ground 10 days from now," Bjorn replied. The contract text floated in the corner of his pinview, mirrored by the Tri-V display in the middle of the huge antique conference table. "In addition, the contract contains multiple bonus clauses."

"They don't expect us to live long enough to collect," Jonasson remarked.

"It's a huge payout to crack the HecSha siege," Captain Jake Wirth added. "The Eosogi are up to something."

"Of course the weasels have a trick up their sleeve," Bjorn countered. If an Eosogi was breathing, it was scheming. "I included legal fees in the payout."

Captain Marian Boggs, the newest captain at the table, peered at the holographic contract. "We're committing all six companies?"

Bjorn nodded. "Everyone except the training cadre. We overwhelm the HecSha mercs and force them to capitulate. The lizards prefer to save their hides when a battle goes down the shitter."

"All six companies will eat into the payout since half again as many mercs get combat pay," Jonasson groused. The Berserkers normally fielded four companies on a contract to allow for the three Rs—rest, repair, and replace. Off-rotation mercenaries received residual payouts based on the overall firm's profit—a fraction of combat pay.

Too few troops risked the mission, and too many troops cut into the earnings. Bjorn resisted the urge to tell Jonasson to pick a side. "Eight hours until departure. The first wave loads in four."

"Six companies in eight hours?" Jonasson frowned.

"Did I stutter, *Captain* Jonasson?" Bjorn glowered at the older man. Father's friend or not, Bjorn was a snarky remark from kicking the captain's ass.

"No, Commander."

"Everyone has their assignments; get to it." Bjorn remained seated as the officers filed out of the conference room.

Captain Bill Hawkins remained behind. Hawkins served as Bjorn's second-in-command. "You think Heimir will pose a problem?"

"His negativity influences some of the other officers," Bjorn replied. Bill had joined the Berserkers at the same time as Bjorn, and the two had remained best friends throughout their careers. "I don't care how much experience he has; this will be his last mission. He can retire with a fat payout from this job."

"What if he doesn't want to retire?" Bill asked while scrolling through his tactical slate.

Bjorn fidgeted with the Mjolnir pendant hanging amid bear claws over his chest.

"He has a choice—retired or fired. My old man retired four years ago, and I'm sick of Heimir double guessing me. He knows damned well we have four companies staged for deployment. We'll need to bust ass on the other two, but it's doable."

* * *

"I hear you're leaving us with a skeleton crew," Stefan lisped from behind his desk in the office reception area. The white-haired man had served as the commander's secretary since before Bjorn had joined the Berserkers twenty years ago.

Bjorn grunted and headed for his office, thinking commands to Bettie, the battlefield tactical intelligence, through his pinplants. A logistics dashboard replaced the contract in the corner of his pinview, giving visibility to the progress of the loadout.

Bjorn glanced at the sidebar in his office but dismissed it. With eight hours until last lift to orbit, the last thing he needed was to crack open a bottle. He should have grabbed some coffee from the reception area.

"You looked as though you could use this," Stefan said from the office door, bearing a steaming mug of coffee. "The meeting didn't go well?"

"The usual bullshit. Jonasson reminding everyone I'm not the veteran commander my father was. I came close to calling out the *sukin syn* right there." Bjorn gratefully accepted the coffee.

"If it's any consolation, he gave your father a hard time," Stefan remarked. "It's in Captain Jonasson's nature. I'm not saying it makes him right, but try not to take it personally."

"Thanks, Stefan. I'll try to remember that." Bjorn checked the shipping assignments. Captain Jonasson would have 170 hours to harangue him in hyperspace. It would make for a long week.

* * *

EMS *Nanook*, Moloq, Cimaron Region, Peco Arm

"No sensor hits in the threat box," the sensors operator called while Bjorn's stomach was still settling from the emergence from hyperspace.

"We emerged 27 degrees off optimal vector," the helmsman announced. "The other trio of transports are 21 degrees off."

"Sensors, keep your eyes peeled. Helm, initiate separation and plot a one-G course for planetary orbit," Captain Breslin ordered. Bjorn stayed out of her way at the rear of the bridge. Breslin knew the operation.

The deck shuddered as the two transports attached to the *Nanook* disconnected their docking clamps. Since increasing the mass of a body meant it required less energy to remain in hyperspace, ships traveling to the same destination routinely docked with each other.

"One-G course plotted, Captain. We'll reach orbit in 22 hours," the helm reported. A display showed a countdown clock.

Captain Breslin glanced to Bjorn. Every hour gave the enemy a greater chance to prepare. With any luck, by the time the HecSha learned of the Berserkers' approach, it would be too late.

"Stick to one G, Captain. Hopefully they'll mistake us for commercial traffic," Bjorn said. Through his pinplants, he asked Bettie to relay the sensor data for the planetary approach and orbit. Enough ships traversed the system to keep the Berserkers' transports from flashing a big warning sign, but six of them together could raise suspicions.

The acceleration alarm sounded thirty seconds before the fusion torches ignited. Faux gravity tugged Bjorn down into his seat.

* * *

Siege Command Camp, Moloq

Commander Vosst glared at the distant walls. Whatever they protected wasn't worth the 60 days he'd spent trying to breach them. The Gtandan Cartel who'd hired his HecSha mercenary unit had seriously underestimated the Eosogi defenses. The wall bristled with lasers, anti-missile batteries, and shield generators.

The standoff ate further into his profit margin every day. The Gtandans had sent word they'd hired an assault force to storm the wall and break the stalemate. It meant less loot for his troops, but sitting on their tails in the ruined suburbs outside the walled town garnered them nothing.

"Commander! One of our satellites spotted a group of transports emerging," a technician hissed from a nearby makeshift console. "They're on a one-G approach vector."

Vosst peered over the technician's shoulder. "Any identifiers?"

The technician zoomed in on the image of the lead transport. An image of a hairy, hulking mammal decorated the side of the vessel. This must be the shock troops. Vosst remembered big, savage mammals from the briefing message.

"How long until they arrive?" Vosst asked.

"Assuming standard maneuvering—21 hours," the technician replied.

Vosst nodded. Plenty of time to prepare. He'd maintain the routine bombardment schedule—pausing the sporadic heavy weapon probes of the town defenses could alert the target.

* * *

JMS *Unbridled Rage*, Moloq Emergence Point

"Report!" Klet'usron roared. The commander of the mercenary force Unbridled Rage hated the transition between hyperspace and normal space. It made his fur stand on end.

"No threats," one of the Pendal manning the three consoles in the front of the CIC replied. "I read a single fusion plume between us and the planet."

"We emerged 107 degrees off ideal vector," the second said. "Shall we correct course and make for the planet?"

"Of course!" Klet'usron replied. He debated increasing the planned acceleration. It would only shave a pawful of hours and wear down his troopers. He dismissed the idea. Besides, it could alert the defenders that the Jivool weren't traders. "What's the status of our other transport?"

"It's on a trajectory 204 degrees off ideal approach," the first Pendal stated.

"They're correcting course to join up with us," the third Pendal added.

"Proceed as planned," Klet'usron ordered.

* * *

EMS *Nanook*, Approaching Moloq Orbit

"Anyone challenging us?" Bjorn asked from his CASPer. His Tri-V displayed the feed from the bridge, and Bettie fed supplemental data to his pinview. Civilian orbital traffic gave their approach vector a wide berth. "The HecSha must have ships somewhere."

"The HecSha may have used landing transports," Captain Breslin replied. Starships small enough to land couldn't carry as much and required more power to stay in hyperspace. "They could have used a jump rider, and it's lurking in the traffic. In that case, their ship won't pose a threat, since they wouldn't risk their ride home."

"I hope you're right," Bjorn remarked. A countdown in his status display showed 20 minutes until dropship launch. Captain Jonasson's paranoid remarks nagged at Bjorn. What game were the Eosogi playing?

* * *

JMS *Unbridled Rage*, Approaching Moloq Orbit

Klet'usron snarled as the comm chimed. Seventy grumpy Jivool crammed into two Besquith-built dropships. Even with the roomy Besquith design, it made for cramped conditions. The scene mirrored the opposite side of the transport, where Jivool loaded into another pair of dropships.

"What?" Klet'usron expected one of his junior officers to ask the same inane question their peers posed over the last few hours.

The Pendal sounded unmoved by Klet'usron's tone or volume. "We have an update. The fusion plume preceding us toward the world turned out to be six transports. They're braking for orbital insertion as we speak."

Other mercenaries! If they broke the HecSha siege, Unbridle Rage would go home empty-handed. "Can we catch them?"

"No. We could gain on them by reducing our deceleration now, then braking hard as we reached orbit, but they'd still arrive an hour before us."

"Do it!" Klet'usron ordered. "Can you identify what race owns these ships?"

"It's difficult to say. The largest appears to be a Besquith mercenary transport, three are Zuul designs, and we haven't pinned down the remaining two," the Pendal replied.

"Humans," Klet'usron rumbled. The clawless primates used whatever technology they could get their hands on, building almost nothing for themselves. The stark exception was the *Masu'Jiv*, the Iron Bear. The armored shells made a puny Human the equal of a Jivool warrior. Six ships full of *Masu'Jiv* would prove challenging.

However, Unbridled Rage could catch the Humans between themselves and the HecSha. Iron Bears or not, the Humans would fall.

* * *

Siege Command Camp, Moloq

"I read 20 dropships descending to the vacated air transport hub ten kilometers east," the technician stated.

Vosst nodded. Landing out of reach of the Eosogi's anti-aircraft weaponry was prudent, even if the new arrivals erred on the side of caution. He turned to his officers. "Have our soldiers arm up. As soon as the reinforcements reach the siege line, we'll hit the city defenses full force and follow our allies in." He pointed to the map. "Move our currently off-cycle artillery here. Once the defenders are distracted by the new arrivals, we'll pour concentrated fire on this section of the wall."

"Won't clustering our artillery pieces invite focused return fire?" one of the officers asked. A sensible question—the HecSha had lost several heavy weapons over the initial days of the siege.

"They'll have something else to hold their attention. Once we overwhelm their defenses, it won't matter," Vosst replied. Twenty dropships would contain enough shock troops to swamp the defenders. Too bad the Eosogi jamming would prevent Vosst from coordinating with the new arrivals until they drew close.

* * *

Berserkers' Landing Zone, Moloq

Bjorn jogged down the dropship ramp, his CASPer's armored boots clanging on the metal. The rest of Bruin Alpha trod behind him—two dozen charcoal grey CASPers with mixed mission loadouts. The ramp for Bravo platoon clanged to the tarmac and another 25 CASPers filed out. Casanovas, troop rumblers, and logistics rumblers formed up.

The CASPers would hang onto the vehicles until they were within two kilometers of their destination. Other mercenary commanders thought Bjorn crazy for the number of vehicles he fielded, not to mention infantry, but the rumblers could cross ground twice as fast as a CASPer without wearing out the troopers.

'BTI: Battle space updated. HecSha units arrayed within 90 percent of projections.' The battlefield tactical intelligence highlighted the enemy units.

'Bettie, how are the HecSha reacting to our arrival?' Bjorn asked through his pinplants. Recon flyers and UAVs circled overhead and relayed their data to the command rumbler. The HecSha lagged on responding to the Berserkers' landing.

'BTI: Seven heavy weapon vehicles are relocating. There is a 67% probability troops are massing in these two locations.' Two empty parking lots covered by camouflage netting blinked on the map. It made no sense. The HecSha acted as though they were preparing to assault the city, not engage the Berserkers. Did they think they could take the city before the Berserkers arrived?

"Captain Breslin to Bruin Actual!" The message icon indicated extreme priority.

"Go ahead, Captain," Bjorn said.

"Two transports roared into orbit and belched dropships," Captain Breslin stated. Sensor data accompanied her message. "You have 20 minutes before eight Besquith *Torszult*-class dropships rain on your parade."

Loki curse it all! Bjorn switched channels. "McCain, we've got inbound bogies. You're in charge of the air defense. Your priority is to protect the LZ and our rides home."

"Roger. We'll keep the gunboats on high guard," Captain Mike McCain replied, chomping on a cigar. "Do you want to send the birds back to orbit?"

"Only if necessary. We have four anti-aircraft rumblers at the LZ." While the dropships were vulnerable on the ground, sending them back to orbit could leave the troops with their back to the wall if this went south. Bettie flashed the data on the *Torszult* in his pinview. Each could carry a platoon equivalent of Besquith. It could add up to 250 Besquith howling for their blood.

Bjorn opened the command channel to the company captains. "The shit has hit the fan. The HecSha have reinforcements inbound 20 minutes out. I'm guessing Besquith, Jivool, or Oogar based on the dropships."

"How many?" Jonasson asked. Bjorn could hear the 'I told you so' in the older man's tone.

"Probably 250," Bjorn replied. No point in sugar-coating it. The Berserkers fielded 200 CASPers. Add in 300 infantry and 40-plus Casanovas, they could readily handle the incoming assault, but it didn't account for the HecSha's 800 infantry plus heavy weapons.

Bjorn allowed the cursing across the channel for ten seconds before cutting in. "Running isn't an option. We need to play the cards in our hand."

"Sounds like a Dead Man's Hand," Jonasson remarked.

Bjorn ignored the comment. "Bruin, Grizzly, and Polar companies will assault the new force. Kodiak and Ursus will hit the HecSha. Owlbear will eliminate the HecSha heavy weapons."

"You'll have 150 CASPers and two dozen vics against 250 Besquith?" Jonasson remarked. "You're crazy, kid."

"That's *Commander* to you, Captain Jonasson," Bjorn countered. "I'll lead the forces against the newcomers. Captain Jonasson will command the attack on the HecSha."

* * *

Jivool Dropship Rage-1, Moloq

"We have sensor and visual data on the enemy forces," the SleSha copilot reported. Reconnaissance drones ahead of the dropships swept for threats. "Their landing zone is on the edge of the target settlement's air defense envelope. In addition, they've deployed defenses around their landing craft."

Spite tempted Klet'usron to order the destruction of the enemy's dropships. His forces would have to attack by ground—a lucky shot against one of his dropships would cost the Unbridled Rage an eighth of their forces before the battle commenced. However, any troops he committed to attacking the landing zone were troops he couldn't deploy against the Humans and their *Masu'Jiv*. Better to overwhelm the Humans and leave them an avenue of retreat. The contract hinged on taking the objective with no bonus for forces defeated.

"Put us down near the quickest route between the Human forces and the main HecSha encampment," Klet'usron ordered. "Have you succeeded in contacting the HecSha?"

"Negative. The defenders are jamming comm channels," the co-pilot replied. Its antennae straightened. "If we sent a recon drone close enough, we could relay a signal and punch through the jamming."

"Do it!" Hopefully the HecSha would realize the Humans were attacking.

* * *

Bruin Actual

"Owlbear One to Bruin Actual. We have visual on the enemy reinforcements," Captain McCain called over the command channel. "We're looking at two companies of Jivool shock troopers."

Bjorn rattled in his CASPer as the Casanova he clung to jumped a curb. "This may be the first time I've been disappointed not to see Besquith on the battlefield." That explained why the new arrivals didn't go after the Berserker landing zone. Besquith would eliminate a route of escape so they could kill more enemy. The Oogar were plain mean. The Jivool were the smarter of the three. They would prove harder to bait than the more ferocious aliens.

The column of rumblers swung onto a wide, deserted avenue. Most of the inhabitants had retreated to the walled perimeter, leaving the surrounding town empty save for those too stubborn, foolish, or poor to seek safety. Whatever the Eosogi protected behind their walls and emplacements, the HecSha's employers wanted captured, not destroyed.

Bjorn checked the map. Symbols showing the Jivool crept along the road leading toward the siege line. Bettie overlaid intercept options. Bjorn chose one that would leave them a couple of minutes before the Jivool reached them.

"Here's the plan," Bjorn called over the channel to the officers and NCOs of the three companies in his task force. He indicated a point on the shared map. "The Casanovas will drop us here. Bruin Charlie and Delta will fall back to provide supporting fire from here and here." Two more points blinked on the map. "Polar Company will sweep around and harass the Jivool LZ. We might force them to send some of their forces back to defend the dropships."

Bjorn knew his officers had done the math. Half again their number in heavily-armed Jivool shock troopers meant a lot of Berserkers would die. None voiced any opposition.

* * *

Kodiak Delta Three

Charlotte Wicza listened to Sergeant Lexi Taylor repeat their mission orders. Command had tasked their platoon with taking out the anti-aircraft battery protecting the south side of the siege encampment. The squad's goal was the targeting array. Lieutenant Olinger instructed Taylor to take the squad around while the rest of the platoon kept the lizards pinned down. They'd get close enough to plant a demo charge or use heavy weapons to wreck as much hardware as possible.

Taylor hunched low as she moved forward toward the operation station, but paused in front of Charlotte. "You good, Wicza?"

Charlotte nodded. This was her first deployment. In training cadre, some of her fellow trainees laughed at her diminutive stature, especially when they found out she'd enlisted in infantry. At 155 centimeters, she couldn't operate a CASPer. "I won't let you down, Sergeant."

"I know you won't, soldier. Sergeant Eddings told me you were her best pupil." Sergeant Taylor continued forward and peered over the operations specialist. "Three minutes, people."

* * *

Siege Command Camp

"Commander, the pickets have reported between 15 and 20 vehicles inbound," the technician stated.

Vosst nodded his approval. The sooner they could launch the assault, the better. "What's the status of the heavy weapons?"

"They'll be ready in fifteen minutes," the technician replied. "Aerial recon drones show an incoming force from a separate landing zone. These appear to be Jivool shock troops."

"Jivool—big hairy mammals. We're expecting them." Vosst's thoughts froze. "Second force? Show me the disposition of these forces!"

The technician tapped at a slate, and the holographic map updated. The first force marked with blue symbols split in half, part continuing to the siege line while the remainder moved to intercept a blob of green markers.

"Oh, no," Vosst hissed. An explosion rocked the camp as the cracks of hypersonic projectiles and the snaps of lasers filled the air. A whistling noise preceded a detonation in front of the command tent, spraying debris and shredding the ballistic fabric.

Vosst opened his command channel. The squeal of jamming greeted him. "All forces to the outer perimeter! We're under attack!" Electronic horns scattered around the camp hooted three times. For the duration of the siege, the Eosogi hadn't tested the HecSha's external defenses.

"You!" Vosst pointed at a waiting courier. "Tell the artillery captain to turn his weapons outward! Go!" The lizard scurried out of the tent as another rocket screamed overhead.

* * *

Ursus Company

"What the hell happened to comms?" Captain Heimir Jonasson demanded. The battlespace on his tactical slate froze.

"The Eosogi are jamming comm frequencies," the operations specialist of his rumbler reported. "I'm receiving intermittent near-field pings from the closest vehicles."

"Guess we do this the old-fashioned way," Captain Jonasson grumbled. Outside, CASVs opened fire with a mix of magnetic accelerator cannons, heavy lasers, and rockets. "There's our cue. Drop the ramp and hit the ground, people! Follow the vics in and shoot anything scaly!"

Infantry squads poured out of their vehicles and pressed toward the enemy perimeter. Only meager return fire opposed them. The kid was smarter than Heimir gave him credit for, or he'd guessed lucky. Horns in the siege camp sounded three blasts. It would take the enemy moments to gather behind the rows of crates placed to provide cover.

Time to get to work. "Let's go, Berserkers!" Around Jonasson dozens of infantry roared and surged toward the perimeter in the wake of four Casanovas and a pair of armored squad transports.

* * *

Bruin Actual

"Bill, take two platoons alongside the factory to our right," Bjorn told Captain Hawkins. The small industrial building would screen the CASPers from view while the remaining two platoons drew out the Jivool.

"Roger." Hawkins didn't waste time on chatter as he led 50 CASPer troopers to the right.

"Remember, Jivool may resemble big dumb bears, but they'll shoot you if you stand there waiting for them," Bjorn stated over the company channel. "They may outnumber us, but we're Berserkers! We're big damned heroes! What do they say about heroes?"

"Valhalla Awaits!" 150 voices chorused over the comms.

Two blocks away, a massive mob of armored bears carrying huge guns rounded the corner.

"Attack!" Bjorn bellowed, firing one of his rockets into the middle of the oncoming throng. A barrage of rockets trailed his, exploding across the front ranks of Jivool.

Some of the Jivool paused their charge to shoulder long canisters. The weapons belched flame, and clusters of rockets arced toward the

Berserkers. Two CASPers per squad mounted anti-missile lasers, but the short range and multitude of rockets exceeded their capacity. For every rocket lazed out of the air, another reached the Berserkers. Several icons winked red, then black on Bjorn's tactical dashboard, and twice as many blinked yellow.

As the Jivool passed Hawkins' position, the remaining CASPers opened fire. The withering fire took its toll, but far too few Jivool dropped. Still, the 150 Jivool were caught in a crossfire.

"Sukin syn!" Bjorn swore. "Bill! Watch your six!"

A hundred Jivool clambered over the wall behind Hawkins' platoons.

* * *

Polar Company

Captain Jake Wirth cursed fate and the gods. Jivool drones took out two Casanovas with rocket fire and damaged two others. Laser fire from the Berserker vehicles downed several of the unmanned craft, but the threat slowed the advance on the landing zone.

"Captain, I'm reading shields on the Jivool landing craft," the operations specialist reported.

"Dammit." Wirth glanced at the tactical dashboard. Losses mounted in Bruin and Grizzly companies. "All units, fire by squads on these targets." He tapped on the slate, wishing he'd taken the offer to get pinplants. "MAC-armed vehicles, use boron-filament jacketed rounds." The special ammo would pass through shields on a clean hit, but they sacrificed penetrating power against armor. Hopefully the sound of projectiles raining on their hulls would panic the dropship crews and cause the Jivool to recall forces to defend the landing zone.

"After the first volley, all laser-armed vehicles move out. Vehicles from Platoons Charlie and Delta, proceed to the main assault. Those from Alpha and Bravo will move to support Bruin and Grizzly." Wirth's finger flew across the surface of the slate as he updated way-points.

"Sir, what if the Jivool double back to defend their landing zone? Won't we run into them?" the operations specialist asked.

"We'll run them over," Wirth replied. Over the channel he ordered, "All vehicles—fire!"

* * *

Unbridled Rage Assault Force

Klet'usron listened to the report from the landing zones. "It's a feint to draw off numbers. If the landing craft are endangered, launch and find a safe haven. Otherwise, let the Humans think their ruse worked."

Fire from the left flank halted as the troops Klet'usron had sent around the factory engaged the Humans. Klet'usron hoped to catch the Humans in a crossfire, only to blunder into the same trap. The tables turned when his flankers arrived.

"Heavy weapons teams, engage the Human vehicles!" Heavily armored six-wheeled vehicles poured laser and accelerator cannon fire into the Jivool ranks. If the Humans had fielded more of the vehicles, they could have turned the tide.

* * *

Kodiak Delta Three

Sergeant Taylor halted the squad as a dozen HecSha scurried past to reinforce their fellows facing the main assault. Charlotte spotted the antenna of the targeting array a hundred meters away while they waited. A quartet of weapon emplacements surrounded the array—two anti-aircraft lasers and two missile launchers.

"We need to get closer," Sergeant Taylor hissed, ducking behind the row of crates. She stood head and shoulders taller than Charlotte. "If we engage, Corporal Horner will take Team Two to the array, regardless." Everyone nodded an acknowledgement. It meant Team One, led by the sergeant, would buy them time. "Pichelli, take point."

Private Pichelli nodded, poked her head around the corner of a crate, and gestured for the squad to follow. She led them through a maze of crates and tents, weaving a path inexorably toward the array antennae. At one point the squad froze to let another group of hissing HecSha rush past.

The squad halted as they rounded a supply tent 20 meters from the array. They had a clear view of the array and the operator station. They could also see the squad of HecSha milling around the base of the antennae tower. Hissing erupted behind the squad as another knot of lizards stumbled into them.

"Go!" Sergeant Taylor shouted, opening fire on the closest HecSha.

Charlotte dashed to her right, getting out of the line of fire from her teammates while gunning down the HecSha furthest to the right.

A third of the HecSha fell before they recovered their wits. Some dove for cover, while others charged the Humans.

One of the reptilian aliens lunged at Charlotte. Bullets sparked off its combat armor as her hurried shot drifted off center.

"The Humans send hatchlings?" the HecSha hissed as it batted aside Charlotte's rifle.

Charlotte's combat boot slammed into the underside of the lizard's jaw. The alien's severed forked tongue flopped to the ground as the HecSha roared in pain. Charlotte dropped back two paces and put the HecSha out of its misery.

Pichelli dashed forward with a K-bomb, but a lizard crouching behind a slab of metal popped up and shot her. The K-bomb thudded to the ground, unarmed. A grenade slammed into the sheet of metal and detonated. The blast sent the HecSha behind it flying and bounced the K-bomb toward the shed at the base of the array.

Charlotte drew a bead on the K-bomb. "Fire in the hole!" She fired her gyroc and dove behind a crate. The armor-piercing warhead in the 30mm rocket served as a detonator for the K-bomb. Explosions shook the ground, and the shockwave slammed the crate into Charlotte, sending her rolling across the pavement. Metal shrieked as one of the legs of the antenna tower buckled. The array quivered, then collapsed.

* * *

Owlbear Bravo Three

"Owlbear One to Bravo Flight. The ground-pounders knocked out anti-aircraft targeting on the south approach."

"You heard the captain," Lieutenant Gideon called. "Blain, you're with me, and Hernandez, you're with Hassinger. Remember, north of our objective remains hot."

"Hang onto your lunch, Ben!" Sergeant Brian Hassinger spun the *Grissom*-class VTOL attack flyer in a gut-wrenching turn. The turbines shrieked as Hassinger pitched the craft forward and accelerated. His gunner stifled a curse. "Hernandez, you going to keep up with me?"

"Only if you promise not to get lost this time," Hernandez replied from Bravo Four.

The four attack flyers reached the siege lines in two and a half minutes on a curved path. Hassinger spotted the flashes of battle to the left, but focused on their flight path and the ground below. Targeting sensors scanned for threats and the heavy weapon emplacements.

"We've got some fire from the ground," Corporal Samson called from the turret. "Returning fire."

The rotary cannons buzzed and gouged twin furrows through buildings and pavement. The infantry may have knocked out the main batteries, but nothing kept the HecSha on the ground from grabbing a gun and taking potshots at the lightly armored flyers. A rocket streaked past close enough for Bravo Three to fly through its exhaust plume.

"So much for the infantry keeping the lizards occupied," Hassinger groused.

A staccato of rounds peppered the underside of Bravo One. One of the duct-fans sheered away, and the craft burst into flame, trailing thick white smoke. The Tri-V display painted multiple infrared laser trails to the same vehicle.

"Ben, calliope at 11 o'clock!" Hassinger slewed the flyer and angled for maximum lift. Infrared showed a spray of lasers pass below them as the multi-barreled weapon swung around.

Corporal Samson didn't bother complaining about Hassinger jerking the craft while he tried to draw a bead. If they flew steady, they'd die. "I've got him."

The rotary cannons sawed an arc of 20mm rounds across the enemy vehicle. The truck exploded, sending flaming debris across an empty park.

"We lost Lieutenant—" Sergeant Blain was silenced as another calliope stitched his *Grissom*. Bravo Two tumbled, trailing smoke from several holes, including the shattered canopy.

"Shit! Hernandez, hit the deck!" Hassinger rolled the *Grissom*, adding the duct-fan thrust to the pull of gravity for several seconds before righting the flyer. "How many of those fuckers are out there?"

The crew-served weapons didn't need the targeting array against the flyers if the lizards had time to spot them and bring the weapon to bear.

"Hernandez, how many times have they busted your chops for buzzing Black Mountain and San Augustin Pass?" Hassinger asked.

"Not enough for me to stop," Hernandez replied.

Both flyers swooped low, following a wide road as they screamed between the tallest buildings. The computer plotted a new course to their objective zone. Hassinger banked the *Grissom* close enough to a building that the fan thrust blew out windows.

"They can't shoot us through the buildings." Hassinger chuckled.

"Try not to scrape me off on a traffic light," Samson called from the chin turret.

* * *

Bruin Actual

"Charlie and Delta, support the flanked CASPers!" Icons winked out at an alarming pace as the Jivool engaged Hawkins' platoons at point blank range. In another minute, the sides would mix too much for the Casanovas to readily pick targets. "All CASPer squads, drop back to the next intersection. Use your jumpjets so the vics can take their shots."

Bjorn triggered his jumpjets and launched into the air. A Jivool grabbed the boot of the trooper next to Bjorn and slammed the CASPer back to the ground. A second Jivool fired point-blank into the canopy of the fallen CASPer. Another icon winked out.

Bjorn fired his arm-mounted laser. The weapon was less powerful than his MAC, but it wouldn't throw off his flight. The Jivool with the gun staggered back and dropped his weapon. The first Jivool grabbed the dropped gun and fired at Bjorn, but missed.

CASPers thudded to the street, cracking the pavement with the impact of their landing. Those closest to the Jivool kneeled and fired. A second line of CASPers fired over the first. K-bombs and rockets sailed from further back.

The Casanovas killed every Jivool they hit, but they lacked the numbers to break the Jivool charge. The ursine aliens surged over and around their wounded and dead, only pausing to fire rocket clusters. Some of the rockets streaked toward the rumblers, but their anti-missile defenses picked off most of the rockets. A lucky shot punched through the housing protecting the laser on one Casanova's turret, but the others pocked armor or fell around the vehicles.

Twenty-five CASPers had fallen, and twice as many Jivool littered the street and the factory yard. If the bears got past the CASPers, they'd slaughter the infantry.

"Kodiak One to Bruin Actual, we're pinned down." An explosion muffled Captain Jonasson's voice. "There's too many lizards."

"Bruin Actual. Captain, I'm counting on you to take the sieging forces. Find the HecSha commander and force him to surrender. We'll buy you as much time as we can."

"They're grinding you to hamburger. Get out of there!" Jonasson yelled.

Symbols shifted on the map in Bjorn's pinview. "We've got these bears. Do your job, Captain. Bruin Actual, out." Bjorn highlighted streets branching off the intersection behind the CASPers. "Split up north and south."

"Great idea, boss, but what if the bears don't want to walk into another crossfire?" Hawkins asked.

"They'll get some encouragement," Bjorn replied.

* * *

Kodiak Delta Three

Charlotte shook her head. The ringing in her ears muted the sound of nearby battle. She grabbed her rifle and rolled into a crouched position. The ground wobbled a little as she steadied herself and peeked around the crate.

Sergeant Taylor skewered a HecSha on her tactical sword. Half the squad held the lizards bottle necked at the gap between two large shipping containers. A building protected the south side of the clearing and the wreckage of the tower obscured the other half. A VTOL gunship streaked overhead trailing flames.

Charlotte lined up on one of the HecSha rushing Sergeant Taylor, picking the second closest, and put three rounds into him. The third in line spun awkwardly to face Charlotte. Two bullets of her next three-round burst struck true.

Despite the shouts, hisses, and gunfire, Charlotte heard the metal on the container next to her flex. She fired a burst upward, the bullets sparking off the shipping container and forcing a HecSha to retreat.

Taylor recovered her rifle from the ground and dove aside as others from the squad poured fire into the entrance. The sergeant signaled them to fall back past the wreckage of the tower. A grenade bounced into the gap between the containers and met with surprised hissing and scrambling feet. The grenade belched thick black smoke.

Charlotte wove through the twisted superstructure of the tower. Behind the squad, tentative shots probed the smoke, but the HecSha didn't venture through. The squad formed up past the crumpled control shack for the targeting array. Two soldiers were missing, and Baxter dragged Corporal Schrier.

Charlotte adjusted her helmet. "What now, Sergeant?"

* * *

Siege Command Camp, Moloq

"Why isn't the artillery firing on the enemy forces?" Vosst demanded after a panting courier had returned to inform him the artillery captain would execute his orders.

"Our troops are too close to safely fire on the enemy," the technician replied, pointing at a swarm of icons on the holographic map. Enemy infantry surged over the defensive barricades before the HecSha could man the perimeter. The HecSha slowed them with sheer numbers, but the Humans renewed their assault and could reach the command center in a matter of minutes. "If he fires, we'll hit our troops."

"We'll hit their troops as well." Vosst glared at the courier. "Tell the artillery captain to open fire immediately!"

The courier fled, only for another to replace him. The smaller HecSha bowed to Vosst. "The tanks will arrive in five minutes, but the sergeant said four tanks wouldn't stop the Humans."

"The tanks aren't for fighting the Humans," Vosst stated. "They're for making it to the shuttle that'll take me off this wretched rock if the Humans prevail."

* * *

Owlbear Bravo Three

Buildings blurred past at 200 kilometers per hour. HecSha below gaped helplessly as the *Grissoms* flashed by. One more intersection, and they'd have line-of-sight on the artillery weapons. Sergeant Hassinger threw Bravo Three into a twisting loop, vacating the intersection two seconds before Hernandez followed suit.

Vehicles sporting multiple rocket launchers, enormous magnetic accelerator cannons, and heavy lasers filled a parking lot. At least the *Grissoms* weren't flying down the barrels of the artillery.

"Why aren't those pointed at the walls?" Samson asked. The weapons faced outward, away from the fortifications.

"Because they're about to smoke our buddies! Time to wreck some shit!" Hassinger's fingers skipped across the weapon controls. "Weapons hot. Ben, anything looks at us, scrap it."

Hassinger lined up the targeting reticles on a rocket battery and one of the huge cannons, delegating two rockets each. He dropped a targeting laser on what looked like a command vehicle for a guided missile. With a jerk of the trigger, five exhaust plumes raced toward the targets.

Another volley streaked from Bravo Four. Hassinger jinked the *Grissom* aside. His canopy darkened as a rocket struck something volatile. A runaway rocket from one of the stricken launchers flashed past. Hassinger spun the *Grissom* as they side-slipped around the exploding vehicles and aimed another barrage. Small arms fire pinged off the undercarriage, answered by bursts from the rotary cannons.

"Bravo Four, you still with me?" Hassinger called as the second volley triggered another wave of destruction. One of the rockets struck an ammunition trailer, sending a mushroom cloud skyward accompanied by smaller explosions.

"*Por supuesto!*" Hernandez replied. "I'm out of Christmas presents, so I say we head back to the LZ."

"Sounds like a plan. Last one there buys the beer."

* * *

Unbridled Rage Assault Force

The Humans fell back, using the buildings for cover to lure Klet'usron's shock troops into another crossfire. Did the Humans think they were fighting Oogar?

Klet'usron sent fifty troops into the light industrial building to the right with instructions to blast their way through the wall adjacent to the Humans. He would devote enough firepower to hold the left flank and catch the Humans on the right in a pincer.

"We'll reach the position adjacent to the Humans in two minutes," the leader of the breaching team reported.

"Execute without waiting for my order," Klet'usron instructed. Between the shaped charges turning the wall into duracrete shrapnel and 50 Jivool shock troops, the Human flank would buckle.

Several explosions boomed in the direction of the siege forces. Another thunderous detonation rattled the windows of all the buildings. A mushroom cloud accompanied by continuing smaller blasts rose a few kilometers away. It wasn't nuclear, but something large exploded.

Klet'usron tried to shake the noise out of his ears—half buzz and half whine, similar to a swarm of heavy electric motors. Klet'usron spun around. A dozen more armored fighting vehicles roared along the street toward his forces massed in front of the intersection. The rumblers opened fire.

* * *

Ursus Company

The HecSha yielded ground a bloody meter at a time. Captain Jonasson guessed they had another two hundred meters to reach the command center. If the Berserkers captured or killed the HecSha commander, they could end the battle. An enemy laser grazed his left shoulder. Jonasson stripped off the smoldering pauldron from his infantry armor. Burning pain accompanied the stench of cooked pork. If not for the armor, he'd have lost his arm.

"Captain, get down!" the squad medic called, brandishing a trauma nanite applicator.

"We've got to keep moving." Jonasson spotted the lizard who'd shot him and returned the favor. The HecSha disappeared in a spray of bullets. "Hit me with the bots."

Jonasson flinched at the first detonation, fearing the enemy had finally turned their artillery on the Berserkers. A second and third blast followed, two kilometers distant. *KABOOM!* A pillar of fire gouted into the sky, morphing into a mushroom cloud as the blast sucked smoke upward. Rockets streaked into the air and detonated, reminding Jonasson of First Contact Day fireworks.

"Don't stand around gawking!" Jonasson shouted over the company comm channel. "Those fireworks were the lizards' big guns. Forward!"

* * *

Kodiak Delta Three

Charlotte Wicza picked herself up off the pavement. The heat of the blast felt like a blazing campfire even at this distance. Dust and debris rained down. Lucky for the squad, they'd sheltered next to a stout building before the explosion.

Charlotte scanned for enemies. She didn't spot any HecSha, but a hover tank slammed into an abandoned storefront a block away. Charlotte gestured for the sergeant's attention and pointed to the tank.

Sergeant Taylor crept to the wreckage of a civilian vehicle and peered over the hood. Charlotte followed and watched the tank attempt to extricate itself. A second tank glided into the intersection and crashed into the first tank.

"Those aren't headed for the fight," Sergeant Taylor remarked, checking her tactical slate. "They might be going to fortify the command center."

"Sergeant, you're not thinking about taking on those tanks, are you?" Charlotte asked. They'd used their explosives taking out the targeting array. Even their armor-piercing gyrocs would bounce off the tanks.

HecSha climbed out of both armored hovercraft to yell and hiss at each other.

"We don't need to take out the tanks," the sergeant said. "We just need to take out the crews."

* * *

Bruin Actual

Were the damned bears waiting for an invitation? Bjorn scanned the local map in his pinview. Could they circle the factory obscuring his team? He ordered the rear-most CASPers to cover their six. This Jivool commander was smarter than the average bear. He'd try something clever.

Bjorn's gaze fell on the building next to the CASPers. "Move away from the wall! Get across the street!"

Thoom! Thoom! KABOOM! The distant explosions shook the ground, and the last one sent a mushroom cloud rising into the sky.

Before the tremors faded, three detonations sprayed chunks of reinforced duracrete from the factory wall, leaving huge holes. Had the CASPers remained against the wall, they would have taken the brunt of the blasts.

Bjorn grinned as he grabbed a K-bomb. "Surprise, *sukin syn*!" His techs had modified his Mk 7 CASPer to complement his cybernetic left arm. Bjorn pitched the 2-kilogram K-bomb at the speed of a fastball into a Jivool's face, striking with the force of a 12-gauge slug. The bear staggered backward into his fellows, and the K-bomb detonated.

Other Berserkers fired rockets and tossed grenades into the breeches. The Jivool surged into the intersection, splitting to engage both forces. Instead of finding the Berserkers on Bjorn's side rocked by the surprise attack from the factory, the Jivool rounded the corner to face a ready foe. Heavy weapons fire erupted from the direction of the landing zone as additional Casanovas joined the fight.

The Jivool pressed into the CASPers to keep the armored fighting vehicles from picking them off. Bjorn grabbed the enormous CASPer-scaled battle-axe from its mount and cleaved into the closest Jivool. Another Jivool grabbed for the axe on the backswing, so Bjorn pumped a pulse from his arm-mounted laser into the bear. He kicked the ursine alien away and fired again. Another bear took the fallen alien's place.

Icons winked out, but the Jivool dropped faster. Bjorn scanned the swirling melee for the enemy commander. There!

'Bettie, mark current target QB and maintain lock.'

'BTI: designating target QB.'

* * *

Siege Command Camp

"Where are my tanks?" Vosst hissed. He'd already dispatched a courier to the shuttle to order the crew to prepare for evacuation.

"The battle may have cut them off, or damage from the blast may have obstructed their path," the technician replied. "The enemy is only 50 meters away!"

The tanks could carve a swath through the Human infantry, but they had to get here first. A squad of HecSha fled past the command tent. Shouting Human voices carried over the din of battle. Vosst peeked through the shredded ballistic cloth of the tent flaps. A light personnel transport was parked 10 meters away. It wouldn't provide the protection of a tank, but it would get him to the shuttle.

Vosst dashed across the street. Gunfire erupted around the corner, and something buzzed over his head. Reaching the vehicle, he wrenched the door open. A laser pulse incandesced against the door, burning off two of Vosst's fingers. A bullet punched through his ankle, sending him sprawling to the pavement.

Vosst rolled onto his back and stared down the barrels of weapons. Vosst raised his hands, or what was left of them. A grizzled, grey-haired Human held up his hand and barked an order. It took a moment for Vosst's translator to sync to the Human's language.

"Hold your fire," the Human in charge commanded. "Looks like we found the top lizard."

* * *

Bruin Actual

The battle devolved into a swirling, chaotic melee. The Jivool swarmed among the CASPers on both flanks. CASPer troopers flipped out molybdenum-carbide arm blades and slashed at anything with fur. Jivool ganged up to tackle CASPers and overbear them, then used their heavy guns at point-blank on the prone armored suits.

Bjorn switched his battle-axe back to his left hand and carved a path through the snarling mob. Thirty-five CASPer icons showed black, and twice as many glowed yellow or red. The Jivool at the rear of the pack fired rockets at the approaching Casanovas. One armored rumbler swerved into a building and burst into flame. Two other CASVs ground to a halt, blocking half the street and creating a traffic jam.

A Jivool seized Bjorn's laser shield and wrenched it away. Bjorn punched the bear with his freed right fist and split open the alien's chest with his axe. Bjorn kicked the furry corpse to wrench his axe loose. His Tri-V display highlighted the "QB" fifteen meters away. A pair of Jivool charged, intent on tackling him. Bjorn was familiar with blitzes and spun away from the right bear. The left one grabbed Bjorn's augmented arm. Bjorn dropped his axe, taking half the Jivool's foot off as the blade struck the concrete. Bjorn caught the Jivool's arm in a bone-crushing grip and bodily slammed the huge ursine into its partner. The impact sent both bears sprawling.

Bjorn snatched his axe off the street. Ten meters. Bjorn's teeth rattled as a heavy slug spalled his canopy armor and another damaged a hip actuator. Five meters. The Jivool commander spotted Bjorn and brought a heavy magnetic accelerator cannon around.

Bjorn slapped the gun aside with his axe as the Jivool fired. The armor-piercing penetrator grazed the left side of Bjorn's CASPer, prompting more warning indicators.

Bjorn spun his axe into an overhead arc and whipped the heavy weapon down. The blade cleaved off the Jivool's right arm below the elbow. The appendage and the MAC crashed to the pavement. The alien commander stumbled backward, clutching the stump. Bjorn raised the axe in a reverse stroke, catching a lunging Jivool under the jaw.

"Ursus One to Bruin Actual. We have the HecSha commander." Static hissed and popped from the jamming despite the relays the Berserkers used. "The lizards have thrown in the towel."

Bjorn activated his external speakers. "I'll give you one chance. Your soldiers fought well, but you cannot win the day. The HecSha commanding officer has capitulated. Stand down and live to fight another contract."

The Jivool glared at Bjorn from the pavement. Bjorn had carefully avoided the word "surrender." "I accept." The Jivool gave a high, mournful roar. Other Jivool echoed the cry. The clamor of battle dwindled.

"Give the Jivool a chance to break off," Bjorn ordered. "Polar Company, open a lane back to their LZ. As soon as the Jivool back off, tend to the wounded." Bjorn's eyes landed on the bear's severed arm, prompting him to flex his cybernetic hand.

* * *

EMS *Nanook*, Moloq Orbit

"Come," Bjorn called in response to the heavy thud on his office door.

Captain Jonasson squeezed through the hatch. The last two days had aged the man five years. "Commander. Do you have a minute?"

Bjorn set down his slate. He welcomed the break from composing the condolence messages to the families of Berserkers fallen in battle. He'd finished a fifth of the 125 missives. "I suppose you're here to remind me that you warned me."

The older man studied Bjorn a moment before answering. "No, I don't need to tell you. You kept taking these high-risk contracts, so it was bound to catch up to us. Even when you snatch victory from the jaws of defeat, you can get bit. Was it worth it?"

"Depends on who you ask. The CEO of the firm would tell you we made out like bandits once we forced the Eosogi to honor the contract in full. The leader of 125 men and women who won't see home would tell you we paid for the black ink with red blood.

"My father warned me against this day," Bjorn continued. "'You're going to lose people every contract,' he said. 'Don't let it crush you, but don't become callous.' I didn't realize how hard it would be until this contract."

Jonasson took a deep breath. "Once we get back to Earth, I want to muster out. I know I still have four months left on my contract, but I'm willing to pay—"

"Granted. I'm not going to invoke the early discharge clause in your contract," Bjorn interjected. "You've been a pain in my ass, but you've earned every credit, especially on Moloq."

"Thanks. You're doing your father proud."

Bjorn nodded. "I hope so."

"What are you going to do next?" Jonasson asked.

"Take a garrison contract somewhere so we can lick our wounds and rebuild our ranks. We lost a quarter of our manpower, and a third of our CASPers got destroyed or heavily damaged," Bjorn replied. "Hopefully somewhere with a decent bar. I have a lot to think about."

"I'll let you get back to work," Jonasson said. "Thanks, Commander Tovesson."

Bjorn picked up the slate after Jonasson departed. Condolence message number 26. He definitely needed to find a bar.

* * * * *

Jon R. Osborne Bio

Jon R. Osborne is a veteran gamemaster and journalism major turned science fiction and fantasy author. The second book in the Jon's The Milesian Accords modern fantasy trilogy, "A Tempered Warrior", was a 2018 Dragon Awards finalist for Best Fantasy Novel. Jon is also a core author in the military science fiction Four Horseman Universe, where he was first published in 2017.

Jon resides in Indianapolis, where he plays role-playing games, writes science fiction and fantasy, and lives the nerd life. You can find out more at jonrosborne.com and at https://www.facebook.com/jonrosborne.

# # # # #

No Good Deed by Alex Rath

Intergalactic Haulers Transport *Stone Mountain*, Azure Orbit

The journey to Azure had been smooth. Sloan had his doubts, given the state of the galaxy, but it seemed like the Peacemakers had put a stop to the worst of it. He was glad to be away from Earth, though. The tension that still existed after the Peacemaker-enforced cease-fire between the Mercenary Guild and Earth took effect was thick. Even on Earth, things were unsettled, and some people were still choosing sides.

"Shuttle docked, and we're closed up, Captain," Sergeant Janis Dean reported from the bay of the *Stone Mountain.*

"Thanks, Janis," Sloan responded from his command chair on the bridge. "Lock everything down. I guess we'll just be waiting a few days."

"Maybe not, sir," Lieutenant Omar Mitchell suggested from his communications station.

Sloan raised an eyebrow and looked at Mitchell. "You know something I don't?"

"Something you should see, sir. Sending it to your screen now."

Sloan looked down at the small screen deployed in front of him and read the message. "The code check out?" he asked.

"It's an older code, but it's still good, sir."

Commander Roger Wilson, Sloan's XO, stepped over and read over his shoulder. "What do you think, sir?"

"I don't think we can ignore it. It doesn't feel right, but…"

"What about Sergeant Baker? She'll be done before we even make it there."

Sloan considered. The reason they were here was Sergeant Carrie Baker of the Golden Horde. Captain Markus 'Spartan' Nicolos, also of the Golden Horde, had contracted the *Stone Mountain*, out of his own pocket, to transport Sergeant Baker to the Wrogul at the Cerulean Clinic so they could heal her and then bring her back.

"Omar, let the clinic know we have to take care of some business. We'll be back to pick up Sergeant Baker as soon as we're able. Copy Captain Nicolos and Colonel Enkh, just in case."

"Yes, sir."

"Let's get moving toward the gate. Best course to the Zaotov system," Sloan ordered.

"One jump, sir. Getting it set up now," his navigator responded.

Sloan tapped a combination on his screen to raise Lieutenant Nancy Moore, the commander of the squad of CASPers he had on board.

"Yes, Captain?" she responded.

"Looks like we've got a mission. We've got an SOS in the Zaotov system. It's at least a month old…but we're still going to check it out. You've got one jump to get the team ready."

"We'll be ready, sir."

"You're not going to tell the crew?" Wilson asked once the channel was closed.

"That we just got a message from *Valdosta,* and we're going to the rescue? No. I don't want to get their hopes up."

Sloan leaned back in his command chair and chewed his bottom lip. It felt good to be on the way to do what they were supposed to be doing, but the timing felt wrong. His was the only ship left in the Intergalactic Haulers, as far as he knew. According to that message, there were more of the Haulers out there, and they needed help. Not long ago, the Haulers had been the go-to company for search and rescue for mercenary units in trouble. Now their own leader, callsign Snowman, was missing in action.

* * *

Intergalactic Haulers Transport *Stone Mountain*, Hyperspace

"Something feels wrong about this," Wilson observed as he pulled himself down into a chair in Captain Sloan's office after several days in hyperspace.

"I know," Sloan sighed, "but we can't ignore it."

"It could easily be a trap."

"Frankly, it probably is. Someone out there doesn't like us very much, but I'm not going to ignore a chance to find them!"

"Woah, I'm not saying we should."

Sloan sighed again and nodded. "I know, Roger. I'm sorry. This is all just such a cluster. Between you and me, I'm not sure what to do from here. I know we're not the only ones looking for Snowman, but we're probably one of the few looking for him who don't want him dead."

"What about Peacemaker Francis?"

Sloan rubbed his chin. Peacemaker Jessica Francis was Snowman's, James Francis', daughter. He'd never met her, but he'd heard she was a firecracker, just like her dad.

"No idea where she is. I've sent a message off to the Peacemakers to try to reach her, but they aren't much in the mood for talking these days."

"And Spartan?"

Sloan grinned. "No idea where he is, either, or when he'll be available again. I know if I were Colonel Enkh, I certainly wouldn't have him sitting around on his hands. He's one dangerous sonofa-bitch, and honestly, I'd never ask the Golden Horde for help with this. I'm not quite sure what the Horsemen think of Snowman right now, and I'm afraid to find out. We might only still be here because we helped out one of theirs."

"You think they'd do something?"

"I think Colonel Enkh would personally strangle anyone who screwed with their plans right now, and I don't want to risk being in the wrong place at the wrong time. The best place I can think of to be is anywhere other than Earth right now."

Wilson eyed Sloan critically. "I've never seen you like this."

"Like what?"

"Indecisive."

Sloan nodded. "You're right. You've never seen it. Here's what I know for sure, Roger. We're going to check out this distress call, deal with whatever it is, then go back and get Sergeant Baker and take her back to Earth. From there, I'm open to ideas."

"I think we need to track down Peacemaker Francis. She's the only other person we can really trust."

Sloan glanced at the countdown clock on his wall display. "Ten hours to arrival. Get the first teams in their racks. I want everyone well-rested when we get there. CASPers in the dropship ready to go. Just in case."

"Yes, sir."

* * *

Intergalactic Haulers Transport *Stone Mountain*, Zaotov System Emergence Point

The experienced crew of the *Stone Mountain* showed no indication they noticed the sensation when they transited out of hyperspace, but they all felt it.

Sloan watched as his crew performed their tasks. Immediately upon emergence, scanners went hot and looked for anything in the system. Communications reached out to the stargate crew to check for any known distress signals and find out who had been through Zaotov recently.

"Gate control is useless as usual, sir," Mitchell reported.

Sloan hadn't expected any different, but one could always hope.

"I've got an active distress beacon on the third planet," Wilson reported. He turned to face Sloan. "Sir, it matches *Valdosta*'s signature."

Sloan leaned forward in his chair and gave orders. "Best course and speed to orbit. Roger, have Lieutenant Moore and her squad hold tight and launch as soon as we're in the dropship's range. Lieutenant Mitchell, see if you can raise any survivors on comms."

The mood on the bridge was tense but hopeful. Finally, after so many months, they'd found another of the Intergalactic Haulers' ships. Sloan still didn't want to relay the information to the entire crew. Something wasn't right, and he knew it. The *Valdosta*, as far as he knew, had been on a mission with *Macon*, Snowman's command ship. What did make sense, though, was that *Valdosta* could be on the ground. She was a frigate, meant for just that purpose.

As they grew closer to the planet, Wilson stayed glued to the sensor station. "Looks like CASPers and multiple dropships on the ground. No signs of an ongoing firefight, but there's plenty of damage. There's a lot of interference, so I can't get a solid read on anything."

"What kind of interference?" Sloan asked as he mirrored the display to his slate.

"Undetermined," Wilson answered, troubled.

"Can't reach anyone on comms. Just static," Lieutenant Mitchell added.

Sloan chewed on his bottom lip while he considered the situation. It wasn't unheard of for them to send people into the unknown to follow a distress beacon, but he wasn't the only one who knew that.

He raised Lieutenant Moore, who was standing by in the dropship. "Lieutenant Moore, I need to give you a full brief on this situation, because I don't know what I'm sending you into. The distress call we're receiving appears to be from *Valdosta*." He paused to let that sink in. "We can't get a clear picture of what's going on down there, so I don't know if it's them or not."

"We're ready for anything, sir," Moore responded confidently.

"Hold position until we're in orbit and can get a better picture."

"Yes, sir. Holding launch for further orders."

Sloan closed the channel and fixed his eyes on Commander Wilson. "Find out what's down there."

* * *

Intergalactic Haulers Transport *Stone Mountain*, Zaotov-3 Orbit

Several hours later, Sloan had established orbit above the third planet in the system, directly above the continuing distress signal. "Well?"

Wilson shook his head. "This is one nasty planet. Electromagnetic storms are all over the surface. Can't think of a worse place to be. I can't get any clear definition, sir. Comms can't get through, and neither can our sensors."

"But the distress beacon can?"

"Strong single-pulse signal, sir. It's burning through the storms."

Sloan licked his lips as he looked at the readouts. "Send the dropship. If something doesn't feel right, they turn around and come home without dropping the CASPers."

"Yes, sir."

* * *

Intergalactic Haulers Dropship, Descending to Zaotov-3

Lieutenant Moore double-checked that her squad was latched in and gave the go signal. She felt the magnetic landing pads disengage and then acceleration as they headed for the planet.

"What's the plan, boss?" Corporal Mack asked.

"We'll do a fly-by to see what's what and then make a call from there. Captain Sloan is a little nervous about this drop."

"Thank you for flying Intergalactic Haulers," the dropship pilot came over the comms. "Today we'll be flying through this horrible atmosphere as safely and quickly as we can and then executing a low altitude fly-over of a potential LZ which will include several high-G turns, so sit tight and hold on to whatever you can reach."

"Smartass," Moore mumbled.

"You wouldn't have it any other way, ma'am," the pilot came back. "Seriously, I can't see shit through this interference, so I'm going in hot. I don't want to be a target. These storms are going to play hell with everything."

"Copy that."

Moore grunted a few moments later as she felt the first of several high-G turns the pilot executed. He was flying like he was trying to avoid flak, and she was okay with that. There were too many unknowns on this drop. Finally the flight leveled out, and she felt a slow bank, but even that wasn't smooth. She could hear the fury of storms even through the thick hull of the ship. "Status?"

"I got a clear look at what appears to be a frigate on the ground. Some CASPers moving around, and a lot of fires burning."

"Was it the *Valdosta*?"

"Could be. No way to know for sure. Your call, Lieutenant. I can take you back up, or find a spot to put you down. Ummm, just so you know. I've lost contact with *Stone Mountain*."

"Shit! Okay, put us down a few klicks out. We'll walk in to check it out."

"Copy that, ma'am. I saw a clearing with a valley leading into where the wreckage is. Touchdown in two."

Moore switched to the squad-net. "Okay, folks, we're going to put down a little ways away from the wreckage and walk it in. Something's fishy, but we gotta check it out."

* * *

Intergalactic Haulers Transport *Stone Mountain*, Zaotov-3 Orbit

"Sir, I've lost contact with Lieutenant Moore's dropship," Mitchell reported. His voice was calm as befit a professional, but everyone on the bridge frowned.

"I can barely see them on sensors. Probably just the storms," Lieutenant Commander Aruan added. She turned her attention back to her station, then exclaimed, "Contact! There's a ship coming out from behind the second planet, headed our way."

"Shit!" Sloan tightened the straps that held him in his command chair. "General Quarters! Mitchell, hail that ship. Let's find out who else is here."

The lights around the ship turned an amber color as the alarm sounded, and the men and women of the *Stone Mountain* ran to their battle stations. Their most significant advantage was that this transport had more bite than some might think. Sloan hoped whoever was coming had underestimated their capabilities.

"I've got them," Mitchell said and switched the audio to the bridge's speakers.

"Welcome, Intergalactic Haulers, to our party, thrown just for you," a voice came over the ship's speakers. "We had hoped the illustrious Snowman himself would respond to our invitation, but it seems he's still playing the coward and hiding somewhere."

"Who are you, and what do you want?" Sloan demanded.

"Who we are isn't important. All you need to know is, we've put a lot of effort into this, and you'll have to pay the price for your commander's betrayal of the Human race…unless you tell me where James Francis is."

Sloan muted his side of the comm. "What is it?"

"Just a frigate, sir," Auran said, confused.

Sloan grinned a bit at the way she'd said it. Most transports wouldn't be happy to see a frigate approaching with bad intentions.

* * *

Zaotov-3, Surface

Moore frowned in the cockpit of her CASPer as she lost comms with the dropship. She could still barely see the jets, but the storm cut their comms range to almost nothing. It would fly circles close by and come overhead now and then, but she and her five other CASPers were on their own.

Her sensors usually provided visibility for several kilometers, but the storms were putting a stop to that. "Stay tight," she said over the squad-net. "I don't know how effective our comms are going to be in this mess. Horne, you're on point."

"Copy that, ma'am," Sergeant Caitlyn Horne responded.

The squad walked up the valley toward the wreckage, where the distress beacon was still transmitting. Horne took the lead position, Corporals Mack and McKnight spread to the left, Specialists Freeman and Snider to the right, and Moore brought up the rear herself in a modified diamond formation.

"Keep your eyes on those hills around us…if it wasn't for this damn interference, we'd spread out more," Moore grumbled.

"I can jump up and have a look, LT," Freeman suggested.

She considered Freeman's offer. She was always the first to jump if something dangerous needed to be done and was usually successful.

"Okay. Head on a swivel."

Freeman triggered her jump jets and landed on top of the hill to their right. Moore heard a burst of static when she attempted to communicate and frowned. It didn't sound like interference, it sounded like—her thought was interrupted when Freeman's CASPer exploded.

"Stand fast!" she ordered before the rest of her squad could charge up the hill. She didn't know what had hit Freeman's CASPer, but she knew whatever it was had done the job. Her jaws clenched, and she assessed her surroundings. No cover; they were in a valley and were obviously being watched, with nowhere to retreat to. They were screwed, unless…

She looked up to see the dropship flying toward the source of whatever had killed Freeman and dared to hope. High-velocity MACs and rockets fired from the dropship at something she couldn't see behind the hill. What she did see were the anti-air missiles that flew up and struck her ride home. The dropship broke apart from three missile impacts before it fell below the hill's peak.

Suddenly the comm interference died out, and a male voice transmitted to all of her CASPers. "Surrender, or you're all dead."

* * *

Intergalactic Haulers Transport *Stone Mountain*, Zaotov-3 Orbit

"Let's draw them in a bit," Sloan said calmly before he opened his mic. "I don't know where Snowman is, and if I did, I sure as hell wouldn't tell you, whoever you are."

"That's a shame, Captain Sloan," the voice said.

Sloan raised an eyebrow.

"Yes we know who you are, Captain. We also know your CASPers are on their own, since my men on the ground just shot your dropship down. Keep that in mind while you consider your next course of action. We'll be approaching your ship in one hour. Prepare to be boarded and surrender your vessel."

The communication channel closed, and Sloan scowled. "Any word from the surface?"

Wilson shook his head. "No, sir. Still can't get through. We did pick up a pretty good size explosion, though. Based on what our mystery frigate captain said, I'd guess it was our dropship."

Sloan closed his eyes and thought. He still had one assault shuttle, but no other way to get to and from the surface, so he didn't dare send it out while that frigate was still out there. "Moore's on her own for now, then. We need to deal with this frigate before we can do anything about what's going on down there."

"She's tough, sir. She'll be fine," Wilson reassured him. He almost sounded like he believed it himself.

"Heightened energy readings on the frigate's weapon positions. Based on the design, it's laser heavy," Aruan reported.

Sloan wished he had Spartan and his troopers here for this one, or better yet, more of the Haulers, but he was on his own. He wanted to know who was after Snowman, but he didn't think trying to capture anyone on the ship was an option. They'd have to throw everything they had at it and try to take it out as quickly as possible, but he wanted to lure it in just a bit closer before they showed the strength of *Stone Mountain*.

"We can't miss. Let them get as close as they're going to get, then give them everything we've got," Sloan ordered.

"Yes, sir."

* * *

Zaotov-3, Surface

"Well, this sucks," Snider summed up the situation succinctly as he scanned the area. "What's the plan, LT?"

"Given that they've shot down our ride home, and what they did to Anita, I'm going to guess they're not bluffing," Moore responded. She'd never thought she'd be in a position where she had to surrender. "Let's take it as a good sign they didn't just kill us all. They must want something."

"Sure, but what?" Mack asked.

"One way to find out. Horne, you got your holdout?"

"Always," she answered.

"I'll never make fun of you for carrying that thing again," Mack promised.

"You're so sweet, Corporal Mack," Horne said in a girly voice that didn't suit her capabilities.

Moore grinned to herself. Even in the face of imminent surrender to an unknown enemy, her team could take her mind off of it, even for a second.

"So what do we do? Put our arms up?" Moore asked over the open channel.

"Eject your hardpoint weapons systems. We see one arm blade or shield extend, you all pay the price," a voice answered. "Look to your right if you have any doubts."

She did and had no doubts at all. A dropship hovered behind a squad of CASPers on the hill to their right. Ten CASPers and a dropship against her five CASPers. Snider had summed things up perfectly.

"The dropship will come over and land. You'll board and lock in just like you know how to do. Clear?"

Moore sighed. "Eject the hardpoints. We'll do as you say."

All the members of her squad removed their shoulder and arm-mounted weapons and set them on the ground. They were all meant to be easily detached and re-attached if maintenance or swapping out was necessary. She'd never expected to use them like this.

The dropship flew over a bit clumsily, and she winced as it hit the ground harder than necessary. Whoever was piloting the thing certainly wasn't a professional with any company she knew about. That could work in their favor. She led her squad onto the otherwise empty dropship, and they hooked in like they would for any other transport.

It took a few more minutes than it should have because a few of the hookups were broken. In general, the inside of the dropship looked like something from a junkyard. Moore took a closer look at the interior of the ship and saw holes in the hull in various places, probably MAC hits, that hadn't been patched. *Maybe it* is *from a junkyard*, she thought.

"Very good," the voice spoke again as the door closed. "Now exit your CASPers, and close the cockpits behind you."

"While the dropship is moving? Are you nuts?" Moore snapped.

"You'll be fine."

"No way. I saw the way this hunk of junk came in. If you want to kill us, go ahead, but suicide by amateur pilot isn't on my list of things to do today."

Whoever it was giving orders apparently wasn't ready for an argument, which gave her time to think. The man who'd been talking to them sounded confident, but she wondered how much of that was false bravado. They had some weapons systems, and they'd taken a cheap shot at Specialist Freeman. They took down a dropship, but that didn't require skill so much as having some heat-seeking missiles and pointing them in the right direction.

"Fine, you can stay in your CASPers," the man finally responded. He sounded frustrated.

The dropship lifted off, and she grunted when it violently pitched left, then right, before finally stabilizing its flight.

"Shit! I've been on combat drops through AA that are smoother than this asshole's flying," Snider quipped on their squad-net.

Moore quietly agreed but didn't respond. She was already thinking of ways out of this mess. They were down to just their arm blades and whatever was stored in the leg compartment of their CASPers, which was inaccessible for now. She was sure the first command once they landed, if they were still in one piece by then, would be to exit their CASPers. She had as long as the flight took to decide if that was the time to fight.

* * *

Intergalactic Haulers Transport *Stone Mountain*, Zaotov-3 Orbit

Sloan went to his office while they waited for the frigate to approach. He had his crew running extended sensor sweeps of the system. It didn't make sense for there to only be one frigate in the system. He grunted as he remembered the frigate Spartan's team had taken in the Trua system. That was a lone frigate, too, but they'd had orbital defenses to help there.

He read over the information he had about the model of the frigate approaching them and was confident they could take it out, but it could definitely hurt them if they didn't disable it with one shot. Lieutenant Commander Aruan and Commander Wilson were working together on a firing strategy, given the frigate's course and probable position when they'd have no choice but to fire.

The benefit of knowing exactly what was coming was they knew where the fusion plants were. In most battles it didn't matter, because targeting anything that specific was nearly impossible. In this case, though, the *Stone Mountain* was in a fixed position in orbit. The frigate would have to be very careful if they fired, or risk hitting the planet—which, Sloan hoped, was still prohibited.

Of course, he thought, given that there are no contracts at the moment, these people might not care about the letter of the law.

With nothing else to do but wait, he went back through recent contracts the Intergalactic Haulers had completed to try to figure out who might be so pissed off that they'd gone to so much trouble to draw them in.

* * *

Zaotov-3 Surface

The dropship flew for about ten minutes, which matched the mapping she'd stored from their fly-over. She didn't have a good picture of the area thanks to the storms, but now that she'd taken time to examine it more closely, it looked like what used to be a settlement.

They felt the dropship starting its approach, and once again the ship took what seemed like unnecessary and jerky turns.

"Hey, LT, can we get captured by someone who knows how to fly next time?" Snider asked.

"I'll see what I can do just for you, Specialist," Moore responded, which gave everyone on the team a chuckle. *Good. Keep your spirits up. This isn't over yet,* she thought.

The dropship hit the ground hard, jarring them all in their CASPers. She estimated they would all probably be dead or suffering from broken bones if they'd actually been loose in the cabin.

Without being prompted, she unhooked her CASPer, and the rest of the team followed suit. They stacked along the sides of the hatch at the rear of the ship like they were going to come out into a combat zone, which they were.

"If you're thinking of trying to fight your way out, I'll remind you that you're outnumbered and outgunned," the man said over their comms.

"If you fight like your pilot flies, I like my odds," Moore snapped.

"No one else has to die today."

Moore frowned. That didn't sound like a merc.

"What do you want from us?"

"The major will explain everything if you'll come out without a fight." The confidence in the man's voice was wavering. He seemed to be begging them not to fight.

Moore wasn't much in the mood for talking after seeing two people she considered family killed, but they didn't have much choice. She figured they could probably get at least one or two of them clear, but even if the pilots were amateurs, ten CASPers against her five meant some of her team would die. Still, she felt the balance of power tipping.

"Okay, open the door, let's talk."

The hatch of the dropship opened, and she got a good, close look at what they were up against. The squad of CASPers arrayed around the dropship, the same ones she'd seen before most likely, were a motley crew. An assortment of Mk 5 and Mk 6 CASPers stood before her, and all of them looked like they'd seen better days.

She led her team slowly down the ramp and took the opportunity to get a good look at their surroundings. They'd landed in the middle of the settlement she'd seen on the fly-over video, and it was a mess. Behind them was the wreckage of a frigate-sized ship, but it had been there for years. There was no way it was the *Valdosta*. The only structures that looked remotely sturdy were two pre-fabs that had been set up on top of the rubble. Even they were barely serviceable by her standards.

Off to the side she saw an old AA missile vehicle, which had probably been what took out the dropship. The missile rails were empty. That was good. She saw at least fifteen CASPers littered around in various states of destruction, so at least her dropship pilot had taken some with him.

"So where's this major of yours?" Moore asked.

"In there," the man responded, and pointed to the better-looking of the prefab buildings.

Good, now I know which one of you is in charge, she thought. She was tempted to order her team to attack and destroy the building the major occupied, but part of her was curious. She checked the readout on her CASPer, and the air outside was breathable, but it wouldn't be pleasant.

She took a step toward the structure, and the three CASPers with arm-mounted MACs pointed them at her. "No funny business," the man warned.

Funny business? What is this, a bad movie? Moore thought.

"Stay near the dropship; that might be our ride home," she told her team on the squad-net as she walked toward the structure. It only took ten steps in her CASPer to get there, but she wanted to spend as little time in this atmosphere as necessary.

"You're not seriously going to go in there?" Corporal Mack asked.

"Yes, Corporal. I want to know what's going on down here. Maybe we can end this without anyone else dying today."

She put her CASPer into standby mode and popped the canopy. The first bite of the acidic atmosphere hit her throat, and she winced. She quickly climbed down and jumped the last bit to the ground before she went into the building and shut the door behind her.

Tentatively she took a breath and was relieved to find that the air inside was more tolerable, though not perfect. The furnishings were sparse, and everything had a purpose. She saw a small transmission dish, which would be how they kept in touch with the ship in space. She also saw what she recognized as a jamming device, adding to the already harsh conditions of the planet to stop them from communicating with *Stone Mountain*.

There was a man behind a desk, on which several slates were propped up. From where she stood, he didn't look like a CASPer driver. He couldn't be more than 20. To her, he was just a kid. She didn't miss the fact that there was a projectile pistol sitting on the desk within easy reach.

"Welcome to Zaotov, Lieutenant Moore."

She raised an eyebrow and crossed her arms over her chest. "Right. Who are you, and what do you want?"

"Major Jeremy Palmer," he said as he stood and extended a hand.

She glanced down at it but made no move to shake his hand. "What do you want?"

He sat awkwardly and tried to project an air of confidence, but Moore saw straight through it. This boy was out of his depth, and he knew it. "We have what we want, you and your team."

She rolled her eyes. "Okay, kid. Why are we here? You went to a lot of trouble to get us here, now what?"

"Now we wait. Once *Vengeance* has disabled your ship, I'll get further orders."

Moore couldn't help but chuckle and shake her head. "You're out of your element, kid. Look, have your friends outside go away; we'll borrow your dropship and leave. You get to live. It's a win-win. I don't know who talked you into this stupidity, but if you tell me who they are, I'll go slap them for you, free of charge."

Jeremy burst up so quickly, his chair toppled over. He snatched up the pistol and pointed it at her, thrusting it like a knife to accentuate his words. "I'm the one with the gun, lady! So shut up! One word, and my team will mow your CASPers down!"

She grinned. She'd gotten through what Jeremy was trying to be to what he really was. He sounded like a street thug trying to steal her pocket credits. The hand that held the pistol was shaking. This kid had never seen real combat.

"Why don't you put that down, Jeremy," she said smoothly as she walked forward. She just needed to close ground a little bit to get the advantage. "I'm unarmed, right?" she asked and uncrossed her arms to hold them out to the side.

Indecision was painted on his face like a neon sign. Whoever had put him up to this had told him it would be easy. Moore intended to make it anything but.

She smiled and folded her hands behind her back, using the opportunity to click the emergency transceiver in the small of her back twice. Her team would be on alert, ready to move if things went sideways. With that transmission, they would be selecting their targets and positioning themselves to attack. They had to hope their skill would balance out the numbers.

"Keep your hands out where I can see them!" Jeremy shouted and shook the pistol at her.

She shrugged and let her arms fall to her sides. "There, better?" *Just a few more steps*, she thought.

"What's your status down there, Major?" a voice asked from the comm system in the room. Jeremy glanced over at it and gave Moore the opening she needed.

As soon as his eyes left her to look to the side, she leaped over the desk at him. She used her left hand to push his right hand to the side just as he pulled the trigger twice. The shots were loud in the confined area. She followed through and tackled him. Because of the chair that had fallen behind him, they both landed awkwardly and rolled.

She stayed in contact with him to prevent him from getting room to turn the gun toward her. They fought for control of the pistol, but she managed to get into position to knee him squarely in the groin, which took the fight out of him long enough for her to get the pistol and roll away from him.

She came up to one knee and aimed at his chest with the pistol in both hands. "You move, you die." It was only then that she felt the pain in her left shoulder. The sonofabitch had shot her.

* * *

Upon hearing the two-click signal from Lieutenant Moore, the team got ready. Corporal McKnight had already assessed the situation and marked targets for each of the troopers. Primary objectives were three CASPers with mech-sized laser rifles that could be taken and used. For himself, he selected the nearest mech, which had two K-bombs.

The Intergalactic Hauler troopers wandered a bit away from the shuttle.

"Hey! Stay where you are!"

"We're not used to standing still; just stretching our legs, so to speak," McKnight responded.

"Yeah, well…stop it."

"Okay, okay," he said. He checked, and everyone had managed to get into position. The odds were still against them, but experience could trump firepower in the right circumstances.

Seconds later two shots rang out from inside the structure, and they jumped into action. The element of surprise was on their side. They knew something was about to happen, but their captors thought everything was under control.

McKnight left everyone else to their jobs and focused on his own. He ran toward his target CASPer and extended his arm blade. The Mk 5 CASPer he was after was slow, and the trooper inexperienced. Before the old CASPer could even respond, McKnight drove his sword through the cockpit, killing the occupant, and snatched the K-bomb belt from the mech.

He caught one of the enemy CASPers bringing a MAC to bear from his peripheral camera and turned with the enemy mech still skewered on his blade. He used it as a shield as the enemy unloaded. If the occupant of that CASPer hadn't been dead before, he definitely was now.

Around him, Snider, Mack, and Horne had been successful in disarming their targets, and all now held laser rifles. They'd disabled the CASPers they'd taken them from and fired with full effect at the still-standing enemies.

One of the reasons the Mk 5 and Mk 6 CASPers hadn't lasted was they were vulnerable to laser fire. The Mk 6 was slightly better, but only if the coating was maintained, which it obviously hadn't on these mechs.

In less than two minutes, the battle was over, and only the Haulers were left standing. Everyone but McKnight had taken some damage. "Status!" he demanded over the squad-net.

"Took a few MAC rounds. Nanites are working on it," Snider grunted. "I love to hate these things."

"Left arm's out. Mechanical issue," Horne answered. "Otherwise, all good."

"I don't…" Corporal Mack sounded weak. "Shit…got me in the back. I've locked my legs to keep me up, but I'm not going anywhere."

McKnight frowned. He could hear the pain in Mack's voice and knew he needed a medic, but they were a long way from help. "Keep an eye on them. I'll secure this hunk of junk," he said as he walked around the dropship.

Snider triggered the speakers on his CASPer. "All clear, LT."

* * *

Intergalactic Haulers Transport *Stone Mountain*, Zaotov-3 Orbit

"Captain, we've got a transmission from the planet. It's Lieutenant Moore," Commander Wilson said from the door of Sloan's office.

Sloan pushed himself out of his chair and onto the bridge. He pointed up, indicating to put the comm on speakers. Lieutenant Mitchell nodded.

"What's your status, Lieutenant?" Sloan asked.

"Situation pacified, Captain. Corporal Mack needs a medic pretty badly. The rest of us are a little banged up, but we'll survive."

"What the hell happened down there?"

Moore summarized the engagement, highlighting the loss of their dropship and Specialist Freeman. "I'm in their command building, if you can call it that, with control of their radio and the jamming equipment. I've got their ground commander at gunpoint."

"Well done, Lieutenant. We've still got a bit of a situation up here. Any idea what this is all about?"

"No idea, sir. The ground commander is a damn *kid.* I don't think anyone down here knows what's going on. We've got control of their dropship, too, though I'm not sure it's safe to fly out of the atmosphere."

"Understood. Hold your position, Lieutenant. I've got this frigate to deal with."

"Yes, sir. We'll be standing by. Moore, out."

Wilson grinned at Sloan. "Told you she'd handle it."

"So you did," Sloan said as he pulled himself into his command chair and strapped in. "Our turn, I guess. Time to engagement window?"

"They'll be in the optimal position in about 30 minutes, sir," Aruan responded without taking her eyes from her station.

* * *

Zaotov-3 Surface

Jeremy sat, then leaned back against the wall as Lieutenant Moore finished her conversation with Captain Sloan.

"So what are you going to do with me?" he asked.

"That'll be up to Captain Sloan, once he deals with your friends up there. Want to tell me what this was all really about? What the hell are you doing here?" she asked and leaned back against the table.

"Not exactly safe on Earth, in case you haven't heard. Not that the almighty Intergalactic Haulers give a shit about Earth," he spat.

She flinched as if she'd been struck. "Are you joking? Look, kid. I don't know what line you've been fed, but we've rescued and recovered more Human mercenary companies than you could ever imagine."

"Sure, that's what you tell everyone. Then you peddle the technology to the Mercenary Guild so they know how to beat us! That's why Earth is doomed! That's why my parents are dead!"

Moore tilted her head and examined Jeremy for a moment. "How long have you been out here waiting, hoping one of us would come by?"

He shrugged noncommittally and focused on the ground. "A few months, I guess."

"The ship up there too?"

He nodded.

"Son, the war is over. The Horsemen came back to Earth and put a stop to it…well, I guess you could say the *Peacemakers* put a stop to it. But it's over. There's a cease-fire in place. We were there before we came here." She felt sorry for him now more than anything. He'd been fed a line by someone with a grudge and believed every word of it.

"You're lying! The Guild won! He said so!"

She shook her head gently and was about to tell him more, but the comm device came to life again. "Dammit, Jeremy, answer me! What's the status down there?"

"That your boss?" she asked.

He nodded again.

"What's his name, son?"

"Captain Duke," he answered. She could tell he was starting to doubt his decisions, and not just because she was holding the gun.

She activated the comm device. "Captain Duke? This is Lieutenant Nancy Moore of the Intergalactic Haulers. Your people down here have lost."

"What? That's impossible! Where's my nephew?"

Moore raised her eyebrows and looked at Jeremy.

"I'm here," he said loud enough for the pickup to hear him.

"I'll destroy your precious transport, then come down there and kill every last one of you personally if you harm one hair on his head!"

"I doubt that very much, Captain Duke. He's bruised, but otherwise fine. If you want this boy and the other kids back, that's fine, but you need to stand down and give up this…whatever this is."

"Never! I've made it my life's mission to track down Snowman and the rest of your little band of traitors and make you pay for losing Earth!"

"Earth isn't lost," she said calmly. "The war is over—well, in a cease-fire at least. Enforced by the Peacemakers after the Four Horsemen came back to Earth to liberate it."

"Lies! The so-called Four Horsemen are as bad as you traitors! They left us when we needed them most!"

She sighed and shook her head. "You're behind on the news, Captain, and we're not traitors. I don't care what propaganda you've heard or have been spewing. If you want, I can have Captain Sloan send you an information dump of the latest news from Earth."

"Right, and let you send some kind of program to make our ship shut down or something? No chance! I'm going to destroy your transport, then I'll deal with you."

"You'd better bring professionals if you survive that long. I don't have time for rookies. Goodbye, Captain." Moore shut down the transmission. "He's going to die today," she said to Jeremy.

"But he has a frigate! You just have a transport!" he cried as a tear rolled down his cheek. He'd finally realized the gravity of his situation.

"Not *just* a transport, Jeremy. An Intergalactic Haulers transport. Do you know what we do? The kinds of situations we go into?" She shook her head. "A frigate isn't a match for the *Stone Mountain*, I'm afraid. If he'd attacked from range with missiles, maybe he'd have had a chance."

"It's a laser frigate," Jeremy said quietly.

"It's about to be a ball of plasma, Jeremy."

"You've got to tell him! Stop him!"

"I can't do that. Give your uncle a tactical edge? No, he's going to learn the hard way. Don't screw with the Haulers."

"Dropship's pacified, LT," McKnight said over the speakers. "It's not spaceworthy."

"So you're stuck here with us," Jeremy said sullenly, staring at the ground in front of him again.

"We'll see," she said.

"Want me to bandage up your shoulder?" he asked suddenly.

She blinked and glanced at her shoulder, then shook her head. "I've had worse," she said and knocked on her cybernetic left leg.

* * *

Intergalactic Haulers Transport *Stone Mountain*, Zaotov-3 Orbit

"Frigate is adjusting course, and the shuttle bay doors are opening," Aruan reported.

"Fire all weapons," Sloan ordered.

Aruan checked her target points for the tenth time, and then activated the weapons systems. Along the length of the *Stone Mountain*, laser and particle accelerator arrays opened fire. With the range and plenty of time to calculate the impact points, the result was devastating.

One moment a shuttle was deploying from the frigate; the next moment the ship had a hole clear through from one side to the other. In the middle was what had been the fusion plants. They weren't destroyed so much as they'd simply ceased to exist. The shields on the frigate were weak and only stopped the first few pulses from the assault. The rest cut through the hull like a hot knife through butter.

The crew members close to the impact point never knew what hit them. The rest of the frigate was intact, but without power, and more importantly, life support.

"Cease fire," Sloan ordered into the silence of the bridge. They'd been in more than a few combat situations, but this had been the most one-sided battle they'd ever fought. The enemy frigate never even got a shot off.

As they watched, explosions went off along the length of the frigate, followed by a massive blast at the center of the ship. The *Stone Mountain* shuddered as pieces of the ship struck them, and damage indicators lit up.

"Damage report!" Sloan demanded.

"Damn shrapnel came in like slugs. We've got a few decks open to space, casualties. Damage control teams are on the way," Wilson responded immediately.

"We good to launch the shuttle?"

Wilson tapped on his console a few times, then nodded. "Yes, sir. Minimal damage to the bay. It's operable."

"Send it down to get our people; send medics, as well."

"Prisoners?"

Sloan considered for a moment. He was tempted to leave them there to rot, but he sighed and nodded. "Bring back anyone who wishes to surrender. Leave them there if they want to stay. Lieutenant Mitchell, tell them we're on the way."

"Yes, sir!"

* * *

Zaotov-3, Surface

"Thanks, Omar. We'll be waiting," Moore answered after Lieutenant Mitchell notified her that the assault shuttle was on the way down. "Decision time, Jeremy. You can come with us, or stay here. The same goes for your friends. Frankly, this doesn't seem like the kind of place I'd want to settle down, but it's your call."

"What will you do with us?" Jeremy asked sullenly.

"That'll be up to Captain Sloan, but you did shoot me, in case I need to remind you. Not to mention you killed a damn good trooper and shot down a dropship. You're not exactly in a situation to bargain for leniency. Frankly, I'm surprised he didn't just order me to leave you down here."

The door opened, and Corporal McKnight walked in and closed the door behind him. "Well, this is cozy. What's the plan, LT?"

"Shuttle's on the way down. If any of the prisoners want to come along, they can."

He nodded. "Well, he's your only prisoner. None of the others made it," he said with a frown. McKnight didn't like needless deaths.

"Damn," Moore swore.

Jeremy closed his eyes, and the tears came in earnest. His chest heaved as he sobbed.

"That's the major?" McKnight asked.

Moore nodded.

"Right. Okay, I'll get the team ready for evac."

"Come with us, kid. You'll never survive down here alone," Moore suggested.

He wiped his eyes with his sleeve and pushed himself up to his feet. He looked at Lieutenant Moore, and his mouth worked, but he couldn't find words. Eventually, he nodded.

* * *

Intergalactic Haulers Transport *Stone Mountain*, Hyperspace

"Good job down there, Lieutenant," Captain Sloan said. He'd had her come up to his office once they had repaired the ship enough to get back into hyperspace toward Azure.

"Thank you, sir," she responded. "I just wish we hadn't lost Anita…Specialist Freeman."

He nodded. "I know. How's Corporal Mack?"

"Still in the med bay, sir. Doctor Wells said he should make a full recovery."

Sloan tilted his head and leaned back in his chair. "What's on your mind, Lieutenant?"

"What are your plans with the prisoner, sir?"

"That. Well, he is responsible for killing one of your troopers, shooting down my dropship, killing its pilot, and shooting *you*."

"Sir, this is nothing," she said and gestured to her shoulder.

"No, it's not *nothing*, Lieutenant. And to your question, I haven't decided yet. You have a suggestion?"

"Give him a second chance, sir."

He pursed his lips. "Second chance at what?"

"Being a good trooper."

"You want to recruit him?" Sloan asked, surprised.

"I want to let him pay for what he's done constructively, sir. I just get the feeling he's never had a chance."

"Hm. I'll take it under advisement. Thank you, Lieutenant."

She stood and saluted, then pushed her way out of the office.

* * *

Intergalactic Haulers Transport *Stone Mountain*, Azure Orbit

Captain Sloan, Commander Wilson, Lieutenant Moore, and Doctor Wells were all waiting when Sergeant Carrie Baker walked off the shuttle that had brought her back to the *Stone Mountain*. She was back in her Golden Horde uniform and looked as good as new.

She snapped to attention at the bottom of the ramp. "Permission to come aboard, sir?"

"Permission granted, Sergeant. Welcome back. Good to see you on your feet."

"Good to be back on my feet, sir," she said as she cautiously stepped onto the deck and the magnetic boots locked down.

"It's going to take a while," Doctor Wells said. "You've got a lot of therapy in front of you, Sergeant."

"You must be Doctor Wells; I recognize your voice," Carrie said with a smile.

Wells nodded. "I am. I have the report from the clinic…it's amazing."

"Guess I'm lucky the colonel wanted me back."

Sloan cleared his throat, and the rest of the welcoming committee left the bay. He walked over and offered his arm. "Disengage those boots, I'll get you to your quarters."

She flushed, embarrassed by her weakness, but did as he suggested. "Thank you, sir," she said as she took his arm.

He nodded and walked as she floated along beside him. "It wasn't Colonel Enkh."

"Sir?"

"I'm not sure if he meant to tell you this or not, but…well, I'll answer for it if he doesn't like it. It was Captain Nicolos who paid for all this."

"Paid for…all what?"

Sloan grinned. "He personally contracted us to bring you here and paid for your treatment at the clinic."

"How did he—"

"I have no idea," Sloan interrupted her question. "And I'm not about to ask. None of my business. Ah, here we are. Your quarters. I've set you up with an officer's bunk. The gym is right down the corridor, which I'm told you'll need for your rehab."

He pushed the hatch open on the small room, and Jeremy snapped to attention. "This young man is Jeremy. He'll be your personal assistant and will fetch anything you ask for while we get you back to Earth. He's paying off a bit of a debt to my crew and me."

"Sir, I'm fine with a standard bunk. I don't want to put anyone out," she said, flustered.

"You're not, Sergeant. I'm afraid I lost the woman this bunk belonged to in an engagement. The details aren't important. You need anything at all, you let Jeremy here know, and he'll take care of it. Get some rest, Sergeant. I'll get you back home. I'm sure Colonel Enkh needs all her people right now." Sloan nodded and left Carrie floating there in the room with Jeremy.

"So," she asked as she looked over the young man wearing a uniform with no rank insignia. "What's your story?"

* * * * *

Alex Rath Bio

Alex Rath is a long-time fan of science fiction and fantasy books and gaming, going back to his youth when he started playing Dungeons & Dragons, Traveler, and BattleTech, among many others.

From there, he took his creativity to more online games than can be remembered by writing character backgrounds, stories, and game-related fiction for MUDs and graphical MMOs. Now, he channels his creativity into books.

In addition to his gaming background, Alex has been an IT professional for 25+ years. He has worked as a programmer/developer, webmaster, information security specialist, and solutions design specialist. This background allows him to incorporate some technical savvy into his stories, while his experience interacting with non-technical customers allows him to do so in a way that isn't confusing or 'too technical' for a layperson to understand.

Alex is enjoying writing in the Four Horsemen Universe, the Fallen World Universe, and the Salvage Title Universe. He is also working on new universes of his own creation.

Alex lives in Columbia, South Carolina with his family. Follow Alex on Facebook, https://www.facebook.com/alexrathauthor, or his website, https://alexrathauthor.com/.

#####

Freedom of Maneuver by Kevin Ikenberry and Casey Moores

The ferocity of the attack stunned Maya Inoue. All the Marauders' intelligence suggested the Avaka rarely carried weapons and preferred close quarters combat with their opponents. Reports discussing swarm tactics also compared the unarmored mammalian anteaters to the giant armored spiders known as Tortantulas. While mercenary units of all species feared the giant spiders, the Avaka rarely received their due. The Marauders had laughed at the comparison. No one laughed as Private Andrew's screams blotted out the frequency.

The Avaka swarmed over the downed Mk 6 CASPer. Their razor teeth gouged the armor as if it were tin, and the crazed mammals burrowed inward to rend Andrews apart with crunches and splatters. As she raised her hand cannons to fire at them, sudden memories of hacking her parents' Tri-V and watching horror movies at the age of ten filled her mind. One movie, the last she'd watched until several years later, featured a swarm of rats chewing their way through a crowd of victims. She shuddered at the memory, but her training and experience as a mercenary had changed such entertainment to status quo within a few months.

The image of Hex, her lover, suffering the same fate flashed across her mind. She shook aside the thought. Hex was several hundred meters to the south with First Squad, and as far as she knew, in a much less desperate situation.

He's fine, Maya.

You still need to talk to him.

Now's not the time.

Maya shook her head violently and concentrated on marching the CASPer forward. Hand cannons blazing, she carved through the anteater-like aliens piled on top of her dying soldier. As she did, her MAC cannon swung around to her line of sight and unloaded on the horde flanking the doomed CASPer.

"Hammer, Ghost Two. One KIA. Withdrawing in your direction, over." Instead of charging into the mass of Avaka, she held her ground. If she didn't change the withdrawal plan, the wave would engulf her squad in a matter of minutes.

I'm not waiting for Hammer to make up his mind.

She selected her squad frequency. "Alpha Team, prepare to bound forty meters north. Bravo Team, covering fire. Bound!"

"Moving!" Sergeant Lam called from Ghost One-Three. A sudden thundering noise followed the transmission as the pair withdrew. Avaka tracers carved into the sky, but her feed showed no casualties. She rapidly popped three K-bombs across the line in front of them. The grenades finished Andrews and flattened a dozen meters'-worth of the inbound flood.

"Set!" Lam called over the frequency.

"Bravo Team, bound!" Maya called as she staggered back. Another thunder of jets announced the departure of the next pair. Her ammunition and weapon status indicators flickered from green to yellow.

"Angel's Three and Four rolling in on the tree line with nape," she heard Maven report on Lemieux's command channel. The flyers screamed along the thick-forested hills east of their defensive line. The close air support aircraft would burn a line of napalm and stem the flow of mutant murder rats.

"Bravo Team, set," the next team reported. As the closest anteater scrambled within a few meters of her, Maya fired her jets and jumped back behind her squad.

"Ghost Two, withdraw another four hundred meters," called the Marauder's commander, Marc Lemieux. "Pull back to us. Once you reach the line, jump across us to the far side. We'll be waiting."

"Roger," Maya answered. Second Squad continued bounding backward toward whatever surprise her boss had prepared. Short on ammunition, she carefully picked her targets and aimed deliberately. Her squad's weapons kept the enemy at a comfortable distance. Occasionally an Avaka laser flashed. A few pulses hit their targets, but none caused any serious damage. If they carried anything heavier, none of the Marauders had witnessed it yet.

On one particular bound, she risked a look toward Hex's area of responsibility and jumped far lower than she expected. Touching down on severely sloping ground, Maya almost tumbled backward down the hill, but lifted the CASPer's toes and pitched the machine forward before it did. Under control, she glanced up to see the squad arrive in Lemieux's valley. They took one more collective bound backward and over the line abreast formation of tanks.

"Second Squad is clear," Maya reported and changed frequencies. "Cease fire. Reload and get ready for the next move."

The tide of frenzied Avaka poured over the ridgeline her squad had just occupied. The mass rolled forward, down the hill, and directly at the four tanks parked at the base of the depression. Her instincts screamed at her commander to fire at the encroaching enemy, but her head told her he was correct to wait. The distance between the anteaters and the tanks diminished rapidly.

All at once, the tanks belched immense loads of flechette into the ranks of the Avaka. The first twenty ranks of unarmored, furry aliens disappeared in an instant. Fur, blood, bone, and viscera rippled back along the line. Undaunted, the enemy mercs surged forward over the mess. After another moment, the tanks again unloaded their canisters of death into the next wave. And again. And again.

Maya and her squad calmly popped the few survivors of each blast. In under a minute, the flood stopped. The crazed beasts had thrown themselves against the wall of shrapnel until there were no more. Their battle lust eliminated any reason.

"Marauders, we stopped the middle thrust, all squads report in," Lemieux called out.

"Hammer, this is Ghost One-Five, we're still in the thick, pulling toward Panzer Platoon," an unexpected voice called out.

That wasn't Hex.

"SITREP. Where's Ghost One?" Lemieux called over the frequency. There was no response, and Maya felt her blood run cold.

"Hammer, Ghost One is down."

Hex! No!

* * *

Hex Alison nestled his face into his lover's long brown hair. In contrast to his unkempt, longish mane, her clean hair smelled wonderful. Had he the option to bury his face in her hair and live there for the rest of his life, he would have traded the mercenary life away in a heartbeat. She almost elbowed him in the nose when she sleepily raised an arm to separate him from her hair.

"Dammit, Maya! You're gonna knock me outta the bed," Hex protested. "Can I at least have some blanket back?"

"No," she said curtly, somehow combining cute and callous in the single word. He struggled, pulled at the sheets, and unsuccessfully attempted to make himself comfortable again. The bunk was tiny enough, definitely not designed for two, and the magnetized edges of the sheet alone weren't enough to hold him against the mattress in microgravity. However, as had now become routine, Maya monopolized the blanket.

"You know," Hex began, "when we first got together, you were content to let us lump together in a big sweaty mess once we finished, well, you know."

"Yup," she said without budging. "That was then. Now, you're too warm. We stay sweaty, and that makes me itchy and cold, so I need more blanket. You're like a furnace; you should be fine without it."

"Yeah, but I might drift off the bed," he countered. "I have to shove my arm out to brace myself until it goes numb. No one can sleep like that."

"Well, if you've cooled and dried off, I guess you could snuggle me for a bit," she teased. Taking the invite, he gently nudged her arm back out of the way, pulled the blanket off the mattress just long enough to tug it over himself, and nestled his way back against her as tightly as he could. The two spent a few uncomfortable moments as they shifted and wrestled until he could get one arm underneath her head. She wiggled her hips back against him.

"But there's the problem," he breathed against her neck. "Once you're all snuggled against me, I get all excited, and we start all over. Can't we just sleep a little?"

Maya rolled awkwardly in the cramped space, careful to avoid striking him, and turned to face him. "Bastard," she joked, as the two closed tightly together again.

"You know you…like it," he stated, careful to avoid the other word.

"I…keep my mouth busy before I say something stupid," Maya purred, and drew him into a long, deep kiss.

She wants to say it, Hex thought. Should I say it? Or should I wait until she says it first? I just want us both to say it and get it over with.

"You're like a narcotic, sometimes," she announced when they came up for air.

"A narcotic, yeah?" Hex asked. "Not a narcissist?"

"You and I both know that this unit only has room for one narcissist," she said. Maya's hips ground around as she worked on raising the stakes.

A pounding noise echoed through the tiny room. The pair simultaneously grumbled a lamentation.

"Speak of the devil—" Maya started.

"—and he appears," Hex finished. "Why can't he use the intercom like a civilized Human being?"

"Because he's a Neanderthal," Maya answered. Hex pushed away and struggled to get his jumpsuit on. He hated how the damn things made it impossible to hide his current condition.

"Coming!" Hex shouted, to which the intruder responded with another bang. Maya buried herself under the blanket.

"Didn't you facilitate him hooking up with our resident dirty Tri-V star?" Hex whispered. His answer came in the form of a nonchalant shrug underneath the blanket. Later on, he knew she'd give him shit for calling Maven, her friend and the Marauders' lead pilot, a porn star.

Even if I think she looks and acts the part.

Finally dressed, Hex braced himself with one arm and reached the other out to tap on a keypad next to the door. Small electric motors slid the hatch open.

"Hex." Marc Lemieux grinned. His eyes carried the annoying gleam they got when he thought he'd made a great deal. Without awaiting a reply, he said, "Get suited up and meet me in the briefing room ASAP. Time to get to work. I got us a contract."

Lemieux smirked and pushed off to float away. "You, too, Maya!"

"Yes, sir," Hex blushed and called after him, and closed the door. "Dammit, he knows?"

Maya pushed out of the bed and searched for her clothes. "There are no secrets in the Marauders. You didn't know that?"

"Hmm," Hex grunted and grabbed his boots. "Wonder what it is… I just hope it's not another damn defensive contract."

"Yeah," she agreed. "We're a mobile unit, meant to maneuver. How does he not know that?"

"I knew there was a reason I loved you," he said carelessly. The temperature in the room dropped twenty degrees, and time froze. The two quietly stared at each other for an eternity before silently dressing themselves, lost in their own thoughts.

That didn't go as expected.

* * *

"Sorry, Hammer, this one ain't working out either," Lieutenant Colonel 'Big Lou' Auletta stated. Big Lou was one of the few holdovers from when Pierre Lemieux, Marc's father, had run the company. "There's not enough room in this pass."

Hex stood nearby, watching Big Lou's MX-721 Greengold tank wobble atop the boulder it had been high-centered on. The treads spewed rock and gravel forward as they attempted to gain purchase. One of Hex's soldiers moved their CASPer forward and pushed down on the rear of the tank, while being careful not to stand immediately behind it. As the treads caught the rocky soil, the tank backed away from the boulder and settled to the ground with a loud thump. Big Lou stood in the commander's hatch and slowly directed the vehicle back to where the other tanks waited.

"The whole ravine is full of boulders this size. I don't even think the CASPers could clear them." Auletta sounded disgusted.

"Copy, Panzer Lead," Lemieux said. "Ghost One, what do you think?"

"Concur, Hammer," Hex answered. "Even if we moved all the CASPers in here to lift them out, I'm not convinced we could move them all."

"Damn, it really looked like that pass would be open." Lemieux grunted in frustration. "Angel Lead, you got eyes on? Can't you see these things before we get to them?"

Hex looked up to the Sky Raider, a Maki-made, Human refitted, wide-fanned, close-air-support flyer. Maven droned lazily overhead to locate a decent passage for the tanks.

"Hammer, Angel Lead," Maven responded in her standard 'cool pilot 'tone. "I'm not seeing much more than our preliminary imagery showed. You've got maps; it all looks the same from up here. We need better sensors."

"Maps aren't the territory, Angel Lead," Lemieux stated in his mentor voice. "I sent you up there to get better eyes on, to see the actual terrain. Are you telling me you can't?"

"Affirm, Hammer," Maven answered. "Maps aren't the territory, as you've told us. But imagery is imagery, and my mark one eyeball isn't much better at resolving the three-dimensional nature of the surface than our imagery showed. From up here, I don't get enough depth perception, and those boulders you keep running into just blend into the ground cover."

"Fine, Angel Lead," Lemieux retorted in disgust. "If you're useless up there, then head back and refit. Put yourself back on alert."

"Wilco, Hammer," Maven answered.

The flyer cut sharply right and rocketed back to the staging area they'd set up just outside the quiet city. Hex's attention drifted back to the mission's goal—defending Fr'henk City. As he watched the pair of flyers head off, his eyes were drawn to the city. Quiet was an understatement. Air traffic was non-existent; vehicle traffic was minimal. Not a single road extended from the city. The shiny new metropolis appeared to have sprung from the ground spontaneously, and few seemed to have moved in since. The starport had the occasional burst of activity, but that was about it.

What are we really defending?

"Hammer, Panzer Lead on command private," Lou grunted, clarifying that he was speaking on a channel available only to Lemieux and his section leads. "This isn't gonna work, boss."

"I don't want to hear negativity from my head tank driver, Lou," Lemieux responded. The line went silent for a moment, a sign that Lemieux was conferring with Lucille, his command analysis program. "Lucille says there are still four possible routes, and there's still a seventy-three percent chance at least one pass is usable. We need to get the tanks up on the key terrain."

"Boss, even if we get in there, who's saying we can make it back out if need be?" Lou argued. Hex watched as the column behind Lou's tank backed out, spun on its treads, and moved up the narrow ravine through which they'd entered.

"Concerns noted, Panzer Lead," Lemieux replied. *And disregarded*, Hex heard in the subtext. "We're not ceding the high ground. Keep it up."

"Roger, Hammer," Lou replied.

"Hex, per the brief, didn't we have a ninety-two percent chance of finding three tank-worthy paths through the hills?" As Maya spoke, Hex checked his comm status screen. It stole his attention from the hill he was marching down, and he nearly stumbled. The two hadn't had a serious talk since his verbal slip nine days prior. They still shared the same berth, which Lemieux didn't seem to mind. Despite his best intentions to slow things down, she still coaxed him into bed whenever she felt like it. Who was he to resist? But otherwise, they'd only made insignificant small talk in the brief moments when they either dressed or undressed. Even their post-coital conversations, previously profound and extensive, had dwindled.

"Ghost Two, go private." As he said it, he noted with curiosity that he was already on a private channel. He couldn't recall selecting it. Embarrassed that all of First Squad had seen him waver, Hex refocused on traversing the hills. The primary job at the moment was to remain ahead of the tank columns to scout the pathways. "Nevermind, I see that now, but...how did you switch me to private? And why?"

At least we're actually talking.

"Last night I gave maintenance a hand and set up remote access to your comms," she said with pride. "I can literally switch you to whatever frequency I want at the touch of a button. Anyway, back to my original question, didn't we have a better chance of finding a way through?"

"Yeah, but that was then. This is now," he answered. "His little data analysis whatchamahoozie missed the boulders that are littering the paths. Resolution on the imagery wasn't good enough to see them, and we need new sensors. Maps vs. territory. Look, Maya—"

"With the odds rapidly decreasing, why are we still pushing into the mountains?" Maya interrupted. "It's CASPer heaven for us until we run out of jump juice, but there's little chance the tanks will do anything but get stuck in the passes."

"Yeah," Hex said. "Lemieux believes he has to hold key terrain because of Clausewitz. Look, Maya, while I'm impressed with your comm hacking abilities, please don't go rearranging my comm setup in combat, okay?"

Unless you wanna talk about what I said in the berth? he thought with a heavy dose of sarcasm.

"Well, you'll still hear the other freqs, you're just transmitting on this one," Maya replied defensively. "So how do we convince Lemieux to move us back where we're all mobile? Is there some other ancient strategist or tank theorist we can quote or something?"

The burly CASPer driver dug into his memory. The only tank strategist he'd studied was Guderian. While perfect for the German-trained Lemieux, the only Guderian maxim he recalled was, "When the situation is obscure, attack." The surrounding terrain prevented such a strategy.

Surely there's something better? Keep thinking.

"Ghost Two," Lemieux called out. "Anything good your way? I'm showing you're cresting a ridgeline above a very promising valley."

"Crap, Hex, he's right, this valley looks great," Maya said over their connection. Her voice was low and tinged with defeat. "Should I lie about it? If we make him think there are no good passages, maybe he'll back our tanks out of this deathtrap."

"No, he'll head there anyway 'cause he doesn't trust anyone who gives him bad news...and you'd better answer him now," Hex said.

"Yes, Hammer, this way is clear," Maya reported.

"Finally, some good news," Lemieux stated. "Panzer Lead, I'm taking my column into that valley, it'll allow Command Platoon to get further forward. You keep digging through those other passes with First Squad; move to support however you can. Wait, belay that. Ghost One, take First Squad. I want you to bound all the way forward and check out where the ridgeline meets the forest and scout some pathways for Panzer Platoon."

* * *

The crest of the ridge gave Hex pause. Waves of ridges, hills, and canyons in the high ground they'd traversed ended right where Hex stood. As Lemieux kept saying, the map was not the territory, and Hex witnessed the territory in awe. A vast forest of thick red-skinned trees covered in large blue-green leaves spread out from the edge of the hills and ran off as far as the eye could see. If a more gorgeous sight existed anywhere on Earth, he didn't know of it. The escarpment ran several kilometers to his left and right. The dichotomy between the forest below and the rocky cliffs was both stunning and viable for defensive positions. Or it would be, if it were possible to bring the tanks up.

"Hex, it's Maya again." Her tone was unusual, almost sheepish. "Yes, we're on private."

"Go ahead," he said curtly and continued his scan of the forest.

"Look, I know...we've been avoiding something," she whispered.

"What do you mean?" His heart raced suddenly. A gust of wind rolled through the trees off in the distance, which rustled all the leaves in swirls and waves.

"You know what I mean," she stated. His muscles tensed, and he closed his eyes.

"Ghost One, report," Lemieux cut in. Hex switched to the command frequency.

"There's an escarpment at the forward edge of the forest, Hammer," Hex reported. "It looks like a good position if we can get the tanks up. Cover and concealment along the main avenue of approach, too. Our fields of fire are better here than anything else we've seen. Any chance we can get the Angels over here to nape a clearing along the edge?"

"Good copy, Hex," Lemieux responded. "I'll look into it."

Hex swapped back to Maya's private channel. He double checked to verify the setting was right before speaking. This was not a conversation he wanted to accidentally broadcast to others.

"Is this the best time, Maya?" Hex asked. He looked to his left and stared at a remarkable, exquisitely layered cliff face further to the south. "We had a full week in transit, and you never talked about it that whole time. Do we really need to do this now?"

"I'm sorry," she said. "Maybe it's just that I feel safer here, inside my armored shell. Look, I'm sorry I didn't say anything. You know, I'm not like Lemieux or Maven, I'm not some broken wing that just needed a good lay."

"Your silence, and avoidance, said otherwise," Hex said bitterly.

"That's not fair, Hex, and I could say the same for you," Maya replied. "These things, these 'merc romances,' they start as flings, then things get real, then things don't work out. Come on, we've both seen this happen more times than we can count. When have you ever seen it work out?"

The squad frequency crackled to life in Hex's ears. "Wow, there's a lot of wind out there," Private Espinoza called out.

Hex looked out and saw a great deal of wind wash through the trees in the distance, slowly drifting toward them. Hex didn't respond to his soldier's statement. Instead, he listened. The wind was calm by his position.

"The wind here is kinda strange, isn't it?" Private McQuitty remarked. "Calm here, and stormy out there."

"You're strange," Private Sullivan teased.

"I just don't see how this works out in the long term," Maya continued on the private line. "I mean, remember Jessica and Marc? They seemed so perfect together, and then it all went to shit the longer they were together."

"You're one to talk, Brony," McQuitty retorted.

"Hey, it's a perfectly normal hobby," Sullivan said defensively. "It's not as uncommon as you think, and the various incarnations of the show have some very compelling storylines."

"Anyway," McQuitty said, reclaiming the conversation. "I was talking about the wind. Isn't it odd how it just sort of rolls slowly toward us like that? I mean, to cause that kind of disturbance in the trees, it'd have to be a strong gust, but it's not moving all that fast. Plus there's three separate lines moving along through the trees, as if there's three perfect, strong, but slow-moving gusts."

"I like you, Hex, and I don't want things to change," Maya said. "But they will change; they always do."

"Wait," Hex said. His attention solely focused on the breezes McQuitty mentioned, he barely heard Maya continue.

"We've waited over a week, Hex! If we don't have this talk now, then when?"

"Wait!" Hex shouted. "We have inbound. We'll talk later!" He switched to the command channel. "Hammer, Ghost One, we've got inbound!"

"Shit, where?" Maya queried. Hex ignored her private frequency in favor of the command channel.

"Three lines moving through the forest; the southern one's coming for us, middle one's half a klick north, last one's a full klick north," Hex explained. The movement in the trees was only a few hundred meters out from them. "Where are the Angels? If we nape that line like I asked for soon-ish, it could stop the whole damn thing."

"Are you sure, Ghost One?" Lemieux asked. "Lucille isn't showing anything coming this way."

"It's not plugged into our sensors or camera feeds, Hammer. It won't see shit." Hex swapped to his squad channel.

"First Squad, on me, jump to those cliffs to our south, we'll hold them there where they can't scale the wall," Hex ordered and swapped back to command. "Damn sure, sir, maybe the trees are blocking the sensors or something, I don't know. But it's definitely not the wind coming for us."

"Well, you're my forward eyes. Keep me informed," Lemieux directed. "Panzer Lead, how's your progress?"

While the other units chattered away to pass reports and receive direction, Hex turned his attention to his immediate concerns.

In relative unison, the group of CASPers fired their jumpjets and maneuvered the hundred plus meters to perch atop the cliffs. They lined the edge, careful not to get close to where rock might crumble, and prepared to fire.

"Third Squad, move to meet First Squad at the cliff. Use the boulders back from the edge as cover."

The red, blue, and green of the forest shook violently as the disturbance approached the front. At the base of the cliff, maybe sixty feet down, a rock outcropping extended a hundred yards to the tree line. A deluge of rodents broke out from the forest and charged straight at the rock wall.

"Light 'em up!" Hex shouted. First Squad unloaded on the Avaka with chain guns, MACs, and lasers. Within fifteen seconds, Third Squad ambled into position and added their firepower to the massacre. "Hold back on the missiles and K-bombs until things get a little hairier, pun intended."

The furry mass of Avaka absorbed the incoming fire indifferently. Almost immediately, the forward edge of the flood disappeared from view below them. The hair stood up on Hex's neck.

There's a rock wall here, and they're still coming straight for us.

He cautiously moved the CASPer closer to the edge and leaned forward. A laser pulse from somewhere below barely missed him, and he drew back instinctively. Then he leaned forward again to confirm what he thought he'd seen. Subconsciously he pointed the MAC on his left arm directly to his front. An Avaka appeared below him, mere feet away. It caught Hex's first round in the face. The head splattered, and its corpse tumbled backward toward the forest floor and a snarling mass of Avaka.

"First Squad, back!" Hex shouted. He brought up both hand cannons and carved across the front rank of rodents. On the command net, he reported, "Hammer, Ghost One, they can climb vertical walls."

"What? That wasn't in the brief," Lemieux protested. "Are you sure about that?"

"Bound backward, guys," Hex told his squad. In practiced, prearranged pairs, First Squad fired their jets and jumped back. "Well, Hammer, I'm watching them do it as we speak."

"Okay, Ghost One," Lemieux responded. "Lucille's confirming your report."

Good to know you trust me now that your computer agrees with me.

After a short pause, Lemieux kept talking. "There's three prongs to their attack."

I already told you that.

Lemieux paused again. Hex imagined the gears of his commander's mind clunking into space. "You guys try to slow that group down and fall back toward Panzer Platoon. Panzers, find some open space and set up a firing line with Third Squad. Second Squad, keep moving forward toward the middle column and try to draw them to us. We'll deal with the northern column once we've stopped the southern two."

"Panzer Lead copies."

"Ghost Two copies."

"Ghost Three copies."

Hex fired controlled bursts with his chain gun into the approaching furry, toothy blanket. When the first two pairs were clear, he and Private Fronczek jumped back. The jets provided great displacement, but they'd run out of juice quickly if they continued to retreat in that manner. He directed them to make a walking retreat as much as possible, and to only jump if they came up against a dropoff.

He heard Maya report in.

"Hammer, Ghost Two. One KIA, withdrawing…" Hex missed the last bit as his mind wandered. Maya'd witnessed one of her privates getting taken down. It was all part of the business, but he couldn't shake an intense anxiety, which overpowered his other thoughts.

If the rats are close enough to take one down, they're close enough to take them all down. Move faster, Maya.

"One, watch your step!" Fronczek made the call just as the ground gave way beneath Hex. Lost in concern, he'd backed up against a wide ravine.

Stupid! he thought as he tumbled backward. Attempts to catch his fall and right his balance failed. The CASPer struck rocks at the bottom with a crunch, and he blacked out.

* * *

"Hammer, Ghost Two requests to begin a recovery effort on Ghost One," Maya stated, doing her best to keep the urgency out of her voice.

"Denied, Maya," Lemieux answered, intentionally using her name instead of her callsign. "Third Squad can handle it after we deal with that southern prong. Head north and drag that group toward me so we can repeat what we did here. I'll search for a better site to line them up from this direction. You go catch me some Avaka. That's an order."

Was it her imagination, or was Lemieux intentionally messing with her emotions? Was it a stupid test of her subservience to his orders? He knew about their relationship, and he had to know what this was doing to her. Was he taking some sick satisfaction in this?

"Yes, sir," she replied in the coldest voice she had. She immediately switched to the private channel she'd set up. Simultaneously she moved as directed and tried to pull up diagnostics on Hex's CASPer. No link came up, and no data populated in her feed.

"Hex! Hex! Godsdammit, you son of a bitch, answer me!" Maya shouted frantically into her comms. Still she maneuvered according to Lemieux's orders and found the highest terrain to establish a line of sight.

"Hex! You miserable bastard, you answer, do you hear me?" She switched to her squad. "Second Squad, I'm setting a rally point. Lam and Bennett, move right and set security. Conserve jumpjuice as able. If you make contact, move back immediately, I know we're all short on ammo. Carlin, Branch, with me."

She watched the other two march off into a lower area, probing for a good way through. She led her pair up to another hill crest to attempt another call.

"Hex, if you're fucking with me, I will straight up kill you!" Maya tried to blink away the tears that built in her eyes. A few dripped down anyway. "You said you loved me, and I heard you. I'm sorry I didn't say it back. I just, it's just…I love you too, Hex. I do. You're amazing and wonderful, and you're the one I want, but I don't want to ruin things. That's stupid, isn't it? I should've let you die knowing that, and now I can't. Why is it the fucktards like Lemieux get to live long enough to screw up a good thing with someone as incredible as Jessica, but when people like you and me find something real, fate destroys it immediately? The universe really is a shitty place, isn't—"

"I'm fine, Maya," Hex grumbled. His position suddenly popped up on her digital map. "Just took a tumble into a ravine. I've been a little distracted, I guess."

"Oh, thank gods, you big dumb asshole," she said, exasperated. Her data feed pulled up information on his system's status. A few reds, but nothing critical. The clouds in her head parted, but she continued to tremble for a while. "I'm sorry I picked now to talk. Just focus on getting out of there."

"I know I'm supposed to say something witty," he said, "but I'm a little too nanite-addled to think of anything."

"If I wanted clever banter and double entendre, I'd be banging Lemieux by now," she quipped. "I prefer my grumbly bear."

"Well, I appreciate *that* imagery," he replied. "Speaking of imagery, is Lucille tracking the northern approach? I have a theory."

"Can we dwell on the fact that you're alive, and I love you for a moment?" Maya asked as she pulled up the imagery Lucille fed into Lemieux's command tank.

"Ghost Two, ma'am?" Private Branch called. "Is there a reason we've stopped?"

Maya realized she'd stopped moving her CASPer forward. The other pair in her squad had stopped, following her standing order not to space out too far.

"Yes, you love me, and I love you, it's awesome, and we can discuss this in more detail later," Hex said in a tired rush. "I'd better check in with Lemieux."

While Hex reported in to his boss and gave a personal sitrep, Maya kept Second Squad still as she checked the feed on the northern assault. Whereas the southern two approaches had climbed up and over anything and everything to get at the Marauders, the northern one funneled along a network of valleys. The path of least resistance. The difference, she quickly deduced, was that there were no Marauders up there.

"Hex?" Maya called out.

"Maya, look, I'm sorry I was short with you, but—" Hex started.

"Shut up. We'll talk about that later," she quipped. "Was your theory about the northern attack that they stayed in the low spots? 'Cause if so, you were right. They really are mammalian Tortantula, they charge at whatever enemy they can find, and since there wasn't one up there yet, they took the easy path."

"I knew it," Hex shouted. "Crap, uh, I'm getting busy down here, can you relay to Lemieux?"

"Yeah," Maya said. "But take care of yourself, you got something to live for, remember?"

"Can't forget," he answered. "Love you."

"Love you, too," she replied. Despite being low on both ammo and jump juice, Maya grinned as she marched her troops toward the next horde of armor-rending murder rats.

"Angel Three's run's complete," LeCrone reported to Lemieux on the command channel. "We naped as much tree line as we could, but the Avaka were already through. We're Winchester, RTB for rearm."

Winchester. Out of ammo. Our fault. Our idea to nape the tree line, and now they've spent their ammo when they could be naping the Avaka.

"Angel Three," Hex called, "en route RTB, get a visual recce of the northern group. Scope out how easy they'd be to strafe?"

"I give the orders, Ghost One," Lemieux interrupted. "But yeah, Angel Three, do that. Angel's Five and Six, you ready to launch?"

"Affirm, Hammer," Lieutenant 'Coop' Livingston replied. "Fired up, on standby."

"Hammer, Angel Three," LeCrone reported. "They're lined up nicely right now. Rats in a barrel."

"Great news!" Lemieux called. "Okay, Coop, you two heard him, go rake the bastards."

"Wilco, Hammer," Livingston answered. Maya resumed the march through the hills, intentionally keeping a slow pace. Things would go much better if Second Squad could hold off long enough for a strafing pass. Angel's Five and Six called airborne. Third Squad reported their final jump past Panzer Platoon. Lou argued Panzer Platoon's line appeared poorly oriented, and Lemieux chastised the complaint. Maven requested permission to do a follow-up run on the northern group, which Lemieux approved.

"Maya, Hex on private," her very-much-alive man called. "Do you think our honey trap worked out?"

"Shouldn't you focus surviving your way back to the lines?" Maya scolded. "Why didn't they tear you apart like they did Andrews?"

"They really are mammalian Tortantula, Maya," Hex answered. "Fronczek dragged the little devils away from me. Burned up serious jumpjuice doing it, but the rats stayed focused on those who shot at them. Anyway...honey trap?"

"Oh, yeah," Maya responded. Earlier discussions had led to the conclusion they might use Maven to influence Lemieux. Their boss was a decent manager, average tactician, and horrible leader. "They're kindred spirits in terms of baggage, and both masters of the casual merc relationship. Yeah, I'm certain Maven won that whole exchange. We can trust her."

"Angel Five, commencing run," Livingston called. "Wow, this is just like a gunnery sim, they're all lined up."

"Copy, Angel Five, happy hunting," Lemieux said.

"Leave some for Angel One, Angel Five," Maven called. A half second later, she screamed, "Missile launch! Break right, Angel!"

The lead flyer exploded in a tiny ball of fire. Angel Six broke sharply away from the cloud of debris, banked away from the valley of Avaka, and dove to terrain mask in the hills.

"Angel Five's down! Angel Five's down! Six is defending!" Angel Six, a new female hire named Jocelyn, shouted. "Fuckers got PADs!"

So far the Marauders had witnessed few weapons amongst the hoard of crazed rodents, but there had also been little interaction between the horde and the Marauders' flyers. Complacency had led the flyers to believe their enemy wouldn't have Portable Air Defense capabilities. Maya pulled up the flyer's unit frequency, something she rarely did, and listened in.

"Angel Two, take the lead," Maven ordered. "You're going in first, gun the first few ranks, break south, and hit the deck. Six, hook back, beam the valley, time to rejoin Two. Two, Six, you're my decoys so I can make a full pass."

Maya's ground-pounder brain processed the guidance. Maven had directed her wingman to shoot a little and then turn south to draw fire. Angel Six would also fly perpendicular to the valley and give the Avaka another target, but Six would pass over fast enough they wouldn't have time to shoot. Maven planned to use the distraction to strafe the valley.

"Second Squad, forward on jets, reform on me," Maya directed. Two good bounds and they'd be overlooking the valley the horde flowed through.

"Maya, that you moving in?" Maven asked.

"Yeah, give me an ETA, and we'll work on sniping whatever PADs we ID," Maya answered.

"I knew you listened in on all the freqs, you crafty bitch," Maven said. "Appreciate the support. If I don't die, I'm naping the whole damn valley. ETA is two mikes plus fifteen."

"Sounds good, Maven, we'll be there," Maya answered. She held the last jump and watched her clock. Two minutes, fifteen seconds. Jump in one plus forty-five, we'll be there waiting without alerting them too early. "Second Squad, when I move forward, focus all fire on any anti-air you ID."

"Angel's One and Six, and Ghost Two, say posit," Hammer said.

For the love of gods, Marc, shut up and let us do our job.

"Stand by," was all Maven replied.

Sure as hell, Maya thought, she's got Lemieux pacified. He would have immediately reprimanded anyone else for a "stand by."

She just might be my first girl crush since Jessica.

"Second Squad, forward!" Maya shouted. "Target all anti-air. Hammer, Ghost Two, we're in line above the valley covering the run."

"Good copy, Ghost Two," Lemieux replied, his tone diffident.

Yeah, Maven's our girl.

* * *

"Time to bring her in, Maya," Hex stated. "They'll be back, and we need a better plan."

The northern column turned out to be the smallest of the three, and Maven survived several runs until she roasted the last of them. Panzer Platoon, Third Squad, and First Squad chewed up the southern column almost as easily as Second and Command Platoon had. Big Lou's tank took the worst damage, suffering a broken track. When the fighting subsided, Lemieux had repair crews race up to fix the immobilized tank. Further, resupply trucks loaded with ammo, fuel, and jump juice rolled up just as quickly. Of all the bad things Hex might say about Lemieux, their boss was good at logistics.

"Copy, Hex," Maya answered. "Here we go."

Maya and Second Squad regrouped where the hills met the plains, at the back edge from the assault. A few moments passed while Hex organized his thoughts. A larger wave of Avaka would swarm much further than the three columns had, likely faster than the tanks could respond. Hex brought the concern to Lemieux, who told him to leave tactics to the experts.

"Maven," Maya said, "still up?"

"Yeah, just landed," Maven answered. "Wait, what channel is this? I didn't set this! You do this, Maya?"

"Yes, Maven, I set up a private channel with Hex, and we brought you in," Maya explained.

"Oh, you guys set up a line to whisper sweet nothings to each other; that's cute," Maven said. "And now you want a threesome? Things get stale already?"

Hex chuckled to himself. *She works really hard at this image, doesn't she?*

"No, Maven," Hex said. "We want to talk strategy."

"Doesn't our illustrious boss believe that's his realm?" Maven asked sarcastically.

"Yeah," Maya said with heavy snark. "How do you think that's gonna work out for us? We've got a different plan, and we want to ask your advice, and then, hopefully, your help."

"Okay, but let's make it quick," Maven said. "I gotta go talk to Jocelyn about seeing her lead blow up."

"Understood, Maven," Maya said. "First question, what's the difference between you guys flying over those hills and flying over the plains?"

"Well," Maven started, "over the hills we can terrain mask, but we can also crash into the hills. Over the plains, we can stay down low, so by the time they see us, we're already tearing them apart and speeding off again. What are you thinking?"

"My biggest concern is our tanks," Hex said. "Though Lou has given up trying to argue with Marc, it's obvious the Panzers have horrible mobility where Marc's put them. We get a bigger group of Avaka in our faces, and they'll overrun the tanks before we can get them out of there."

"You want to fight on the plains," Maven said, "but Lemieux wants to hold 'key terrain.' Got it, now what can I do? As much as I can blow him off and do what I want, I can't give him any ideas, either."

"Yes, you can," Maya said. "Just do it the way we girls do it. Give him offhand suggestions, lead him to ideas, and make him think they're his."

Maven snickered. "I'm guessing you have ideas on what exactly I can say?"

"Yeah, I've got a few," Hex continued. Hex and Maya alternated speaking until they'd fully spelled the plan out.

"You guys really are too cute, finishing each other's sentences," Maven joked in her flat, sarcastic tone. "Agreeing with each other, supporting each other. It's kind of disgusting."

"Okay, but do you think you can do it?" Maya asked.

"I'm not sure if we'll make it through this otherwise," Hex added.

"Better place to kill rats, anyway. Now let me go talk to my pilots. We gotta discuss what happened, and how it's not gonna happen again. Then I'll get to work on Marc." There was a hint of a smile in Maven's voice.

* * *

With a grunt, Maya loaded a final magazine onto her CASPer. With her jumpjuice refilled and power cells recharged, Maya deemed the CASPer ready. Lemieux sat on the hull of his command tank, where he sipped coffee and chewed on a protein bar. A few minutes prior, she'd wandered over to attempt a casual conversation about how to handle the next assault. Thanks to their success with the first assault, the commander of the Marauders had become more convinced of his strategy.

"Which dead German taught you the importance of logistics?" Maya asked. Success galvanized Lemieux's belief in his mediocre plan. Introducing suggestions through forced compliments was part of the new strategy.

"Well, most German military theory revolves around extensive logistics networks," Lemieux crowed. "Even in these days of small mercenary companies, if a unit survives the first engagement, it's the unit that resupplies the quickest that will win out."

"Oh, I assumed there was some tank commander or something who'd written a book or something," she said casually.

"Um, well, Guderian, a German tank strategist, said 'Logistics is the ball and chain of armored warfare.'" Lemieux even spoke in a cheesy German accent while recalling the statement.

"Guderian," Maya said, and nodded her head thoughtfully. "Yeah, I think I heard about him in school. Anyway, I should go help reload the CASPers. We'll be ready if they come back, sir."

"They'll come on in the same old manner, and we'll meet them in the same old manner," Lemieux said as she walked off. "Wellington said something like that after Waterloo."

She turned her head, smiled, and walked back to her CASPer. Loading complete, she crawled aboard. Her radio crackled as Hex finished briefing Lemieux about the Avaka scaling the cliffs on one prong of their attack, while the other followed a low valley.

"Copy, Ghost One. Interesting theory." Lemieux paused. "All units, Hammer. Saddle up, Marauders. Lucille reports cameras from the city show another wave inbound."

"Hex, Maven, you up?" she called. With the whine of a motor and the whoosh of the canopy closing, she resealed the mech.

"Hex is up," he answered.

"Maven's up, though I'm kinda busy, about to launch for recce," Maven said. "He wants me to confirm his program's report. I think he digs that thing more than me."

"I thought it was just an analysis program, but did it just give him an intel report?" Maya asked.

"I think it collects feeds from all over," Hex replied. "Honestly, I don't know how it works."

"Anyway," Maya continued, "I prepped the battlespace. Maven, all on you now."

"Roger that. I'll work him like a Pushtal with a Human pet," Maven answered.

Is that even a thing? Maya blushed as she pictured the implication.

"Hey, if we can somehow just knock Lemieux off altogether, can we readdress that threesome plan?" Maven laughed across the frequency.

"No!" Hex shouted.

"We'll see," Maya said simultaneously, in jest.

"Wait, what?" Hex mumbled. Maya chuckled.

"Messing with both of you!" Maven laughed. "I'm gonna go check on this new wave."

* * *

Lemieux directed them back to the same positions they'd held in the first assault. As planned, First and Second Squads both picked their way through the terrain, ostensibly to save jumpjuice, but mostly to give Maven time to work on Lemieux. During this time, Lou called to complain that Panzer Platoon's progress had stalled out once more, this time in a pool with deeper mud than expected. Hex listened as Lou received direction to deal with it.

"Angel One, Hammer," Lemieux called. "Got eyes on yet?"

"Yeah, Hammer," Maven said, concern in her voice. "There's a metric crapton more of them this time. I can't even make out individual columns this time."

"Copy, Angel One," Lemieux answered. "Hey, are the Avaka piling up over the terrain, or are they funneling down valleys?"

"Uh, kind of funneling for now," Maven said. "Is this where you come up with some sexy, brilliant strategizing? From their numbers, I think we could use it."

"Well, just digging though my list of dead Germans to consult," Lemieux said.

Hex shook his head. *Now he's stealing lines I fed to Maya to sound clever to Maven. Schmuck.*

"I'm sure you'll think of something impressive," Maven said coquettishly. "Anyway, Hammer, just give us the word, and we'll hit 'em with a closed fist."

There it is, Marc, make the connection.

The frequency fell silent. Hex imagined their boss consulting Lucille, the data analysis program he treated like a Human. Lucille did most of his real thinking for him.

"Huh, Maven," Lemieux in his *inspired* tone. Here it comes! "You just gave me an idea. One of my dead Germans used to say 'Hit them with a closed fist, not with the fingers spread.' Now they're spreading their fingers as they dig through those hills, saving their strength while there's no target. Which means if we back out to the plains, they'll pour out in manageable columns, where we can focus fire on them one at a time. Plus, we'll have the maneuverability of the plains, and you'll have open lanes to strafe, assuming you can steer clear of their anti-air. Thoughts?"

"What about key terrain?" Maven asked.

Just can't help but push it, can she?

"The sign of a good strategist is the ability to throw out the rules when the situation dictates," Lemieux said with swagger. "Keep an eye on them, Angels. All other units, fall back to the plains. Check in with ETAs to the objective markers I'm about to send you."

With one exception, all units checked in with a reasonable estimated time of arrival to their marker. Panzer Platoon, however, checked in with a predicament.

"Say again, Panzer Lead?" Lemieux demanded.

"Like I said, Panzer Two got stuck in a mud flat; you knew that," Big Lou explained. "The damn rats chewed up my treads. We repaired 'em, but they're jury-rigged, and I'm not gonna trust 'em traipsin 'through crap terrain, am I? I had Panzer Two leading, but they got stuck in mud, now I'm trying to drag 'em back out. Wish you'd come up with this damn plan of yours earlier, Hammer; like yesterday woulda been good."

"Copy, Panzer, move the others while you two sort it out," Lemieux said. "Third and Fourth, move back up and try to lead the Avaka away from Panzer. Don't get too close, just let them notice you and pull back and away. First, you stay on with Panzer Lead and Two and support as needed. Second Squad, be prepared to fall back to the city for final protective fire."

First Squad found a good rocky outcropping as a vantage point, where they could see the Avaka approach at a good distance, but keep some concealment. Hex watched the intel feed of the horde's advance and constantly checked on the progress of the stuck Panzers. After a few nervous minutes, Hex ordered half his squad down to render what help they could. On the display, the lead tendrils of the Avaka split away as the other two squads successfully diverted them. The overall flood, however, still moved across the whole area. When, not if, the Avaka discovered their presence, they would surround the six CASPers and two tanks on three sides.

The pucker factor increased when Hex made out dust rising in the distance. At a glance, he checked on the tanks. Lou's Greengold tank tug furiously at the cable attached to Panzer Two. Though the CASPers had found materials to shore up the rear tread of Panzer Two, the two tanks still struggled to rock back and forth in concert. The CASPer leader restrained himself from shouting a word of warning. The tankers knew the urgency of their situation.

The fuzzy little psychopaths became visible over a near ridge. With a rock forward and a perfectly orchestrated thrust backward, Panzer Two leapt from the mud and raced forward onto dry ground. Panzer Lead jerked back but was able to arrest its momentum before they struck another boulder to their aft. The jury-rigged tread snapped apart.

"Panzer Lead's immobile," Lou said in a strange calm. "I'm sending my loader and driver over to Panzer Two."

Hex ordered his squad up, where the six CASPers began bursts of fire along the front of the inbound wave. Panzer Two picked up the two strays, ambled over a hill to get past Panzer Lead, and rolled away as directed. As it cleared, Hex pulled First Squad back.

"Lou, I'm bringing First Squad down," Hex said. "Get yourself out of there, and I'll carry you out."

"Dammit, Hex, I've had a good run," Lou answered. "My family's good and set up, and none of 'em care about the mean old bastard who's never there, anyway. Get on out of here, I'll kill as many as I can to cover you."

"Fuck you, Lou," Hex replied. "I'm staying. First Squad, bound your way back, I'll wait until this stubborn POS rethinks his life choices."

"Well, it's your goddamn funeral, Hex," Lou grumbled. "Maya's gonna be pissed you got yourself killed over an old grumpy asshole like me."

"No, Lou," Hex argued. The low rumble of encroaching Avaka announced their closure. "She'll be pissed if I leave a Marauder to die. Look, they're gonna close in from the sides soon; we gotta move. I know you'd rather die in the pathetic hope Lemieux blames himself and learns some stupid lesson, but don't kill yourself just to prove a point to him. Don't. Come on, climb out of that hatch, grab these handholds on my back, and I'll get you out of there."

"Fine, Hex, I'm coming, just shut up," Lou barked. The hatch popped open again, and the burly, heavily-bearded man plodded over and climbed up. From outside, he heard Lou shout, "You just ruined my blaze of glory, bastard!"

"Ghost One, Ghost Three, hurry, they're closing in on the sides," the Third Squad leader called. Hex had assumed as much and planned to run as much as possible.

"Copy," Hex replied.

"That goes for all of you!" Lemieux announced. "All Panzers, especially Two, move your asses back. Third and Fourth Squad, engage as able, then jump clear. First, cover Panzer Two. If you're getting closed off, grab the crew and jump out!"

"Hammer, Ghost One Two," Private Espinoza called in. "There's seven crew here, only five of us."

"Figure it out, Ghost One Two," Lemieux responded. "Ghost One, catch up and help them out."

"Copy, Hammer," Hex answered. "Hang on, Lou." He ran along the path Panzer Two had taken. With his peripheral vision, Hex saw the wave of Avaka closing on both sides, a couple hundred meters off. He rounded a corner and found Panzer Two high centered on a rock with his squad clustered around, trying to free the tank.

"Panzer Two, everybody out!" he shouted. "First Squad, pick 'em up. Sullivan, McQuitty, take two each. Lou? Crawl around to my front."

With Big Lou gingerly cradled in the arms of his CASPer, Hex fired his jumpjets and bounded low and flat to the Panzer Two tank. He found it somewhat difficult to see around the big tank driver, but he managed. Three members of his squad had already blasted away carrying four of the crew. He freed his left arm, as those shells would eject away from Lou, and fired controlled bursts into the nearest Avaka. The swarm closed in as he verified the other two had jumped away. Hex spun to jump. Three of the giant anteaters leapt onto him as he lifted off. He waved one off his left arm as delicately as he could, but he could only watch in horror as the other two bit hard into his passenger. Lou's skull popped in front of his eyes with a loud crunch. Hex ripped another one off with his left arm. Finally, as the survivor latched onto his right arm and chewed into the armor, Hex shrugged to maneuver the Avaka into range of his free arm and wrenched that one off. Lou's corpse dropped away into the mammalian horde. His jump nearly ended, Hex refocused at the last second to land upright.

"Lou's gone," Hex reported. Over another hill he caught up with the trail end of First Squad, only to find Private Sullivan's CASPer sprawled out, immobile, piled over with psycho rats, and covered in a mess of blood and bone. He'd carried two of Panzer Two's crewmen. Without a thought, Hex bounded again and raked the fallen mech with hand cannons as he passed over. He found it necessary to fire a sustained burst and toss another grenade into the swarm to clear himself a landing spot. One more bound put him clear and into the open plains. He found two tanks, the rest of Panzer platoon, and he leapt over them to relative safety.

The line of Marauders, composed of the remnants of Panzer Platoon and First, Third, and Fourth Squads, began a steady withdrawal toward the city. The Angels buzzed past periodically, so low they almost threatened to suck up the furry invaders through their lift fans. Missiles fired from the mass when the flyers went over, but the formation popped countermeasures as a group and buzzed away as fast as they'd arrived without loss. Without fail, the CASPers targeted the launch sites immediately, and the rate of fire decreased. As the numbers in front of them dwindled, Lemieux ordered the Angels to focus more to the north, where the horde slowly shifted to the far right of Command Platoon, Fifth, and Second Squads. Toward Maya.

* * *

Maya felt more exposed than she had earlier in the day, seeing as Second Squad had become the far northern end of the defensive line. The entire line blasted away at the encroaching horde for over forty minutes. The action lasted so long that Lemieux ordered units to fall back a few at a time to reload. However, ammo and fuel trucks had run dry. There would be no more resupply.

In the meantime, the greatest mass of Avaka slowly crept toward her, and Lemieux's tanks could not slide in that direction quickly enough. The Angels had all Winchester'd out and landed to reload. She and her squad could only delay the inevitable; if the flyers or the tanks couldn't come in quickly enough, the Avaka would overrun her. Nothing would stop them from taking the city four hundred meters behind them on the last stretch of flat land between the city and the hills.

The enemy remained in the lower areas until they reached the plains. The flood appeared easily dealt with at first, but over time the sheer numbers poured into a massive carpet that lengthened to the sides, eventually connecting the columns of the flood together. Though the psycho rats had initially charged straight for the tanks and CASPers, they'd shifted north when it became apparent the Marauders' firepower dominated.

"Branch, head back to the city and warn any civilians we might not stop the horde!" Maya directed. With two clicks of the radio, her trooper bounded back toward the closest buildings. Once again, she considered the strange arrangement in which no roads led out of the city.

"Maya, slow them down at all costs!" Lemieux shouted. He only used first names when the situation became uniquely desperate. "Significant loss in pay if these bastards reach the city!"

At all costs?

Does that mean me or my troopers?

"Branch, just broadcast a warning and get back on the line," Maya clarified.

"Ghost Two, I'm in the city." Branch sounded confused. "There's no one here. Parts of it look kinda… fake."

"What?" Maya exclaimed. "Branch, get back here and on the line. We'll deal with it later."

She checked status feeds on her squad and continued to fire with minimal attention. In a glance, she processed that the squad had spent all its missiles. MAC ammo was down to yellow status, low but not out. .50 cal ammo was red. Jumpjuice appeared nearly dry all around.

"Any more K-bombs, toss 'em now!" Maya shouted. The CASPers flung out one last line of grenades into the wall of death. Explosions rippled down the line. Fur, blood, and bone leapt into the air, only to disappear as more murder rats surged toward the squad.

The Avaka closed within a hundred meters, a few seconds of charge away. Branch rejoined them.

"Second Squad, blades out!" She held her breath, closed her eyes, and pictured Hex for half a second. "Charge!"

The five CASPers lumbered forward into the ranks of razor-toothed freakish anteaters. The mechs clustered together and struggled in a frantic mess of hack and slash. Whenever an Avaka latched onto one of them, their neighbor would slice it off. Bennett, at the far left end, lacked a neighbor to clear off the beasts that piled onto his exposed side. His left arm went red, followed by his left leg, and with a scream over the squad comms, his suit turned red altogether.

The last four CASPers slowly collapsed into a square. Her perception narrowed down to the pile of frenzied rats who assaulted her squad.

Maya hacked through a pair directly in front of her and then paused at a strange sight. Chunks of fur and bone popped out from the Avaka in a line starting from her right and rippling down to her left. Three more similar lines traced their way down the swarm.

Explosions appeared further down the line. Maya and Second Squad still fought desperately for their lives as a group of shadows passed over them, heralding the flyers.

"I appreciate you savin' some for me, Maya!" Maven announced on the private line. Then, on the command freq, she said, "Angels overhead and thinning the ranks, Hammer!"

The Sky Raiders screamed past and poured 20 millimeter rounds into the Avaka. The sheer numbers around Maya decreased significantly, but it was still too much of a snarling tide around them.

"Ghost One, slow it down and stay with Command Platoon!" Lemieux shouted. More slugs cut into the surrounding crowd, this time from her left.

Another CASPer, with a familiar paint job and a big Roman numeral one, landed on a burn of its jumpjets, firing well-aimed, measured rounds into the remaining Avaka. The other members of First Squad arrived shortly after him, and they helped finish off the vicious, razor-toothed anteaters.

The two squads backed away from the pulverized mass and scanned for any sign of survivors. The few Avaka who pushed themselves up from the open burial site immediately took decisive rounds.

"Maya, all good?" Hex asked on the private freq. "I tried calling, but you stopped answering."

"Yeah, I got a little focused, sorry," Maya said. She found herself in a bit of a daze, and she stalked her CASPer over toward the nearest buildings of the city. Once again she noted there were no roads that lead out of the city. There were, however, roads inside the city, the closest of which ended in a short little expanse with well-manicured grass and a few shaped trees. The buildings to either side of the landscaping appeared constructed of a shiny, reflective metal, interspersed with a good deal of large, artistically arranged windows. When she staggered onto the street, she looked around and verified there were absolutely no signs of life.

In her periphery, she heard the whine of a Sky Raider coming in to land somewhere behind her. She also heard the tank turbine engines rolling up.

Maya peered into one window on the building to her right. It contained no furniture, no life, and very little internal structure. The same was true of the building to her left.

"Maya, you can climb out now," Hex shouted as he walked up behind her, dismounted from his CASPer.

Maya sighed and then obliged by hitting the release on her canopy. Her CASPer opened up, and she unstrapped herself.

"What're you looking for?" Hex asked.

"Answers," she replied, and climbed down to see a lost look on his face. He peered into the windows.

"Were these two just built?" Hex asked.

"All of it was," Lemieux said as he strolled up.

"The whole city is fake, isn't it?" Maya said incredulously.

"Yeah, Dream Worlds Consortium model city," Lemieux said with that stupid grin of his. "They use it for marketing, you know, 'Come see what we could build on your planet.'"

"So Lou, Sullivan, Livingston…" Hex started.

"…Andrews, Bennett, all the other crewmen from Panzer Platoon died defending an *empty city*?" Maya finished.

"We fulfilled the contract," Lemieux scolded. "Colony defense. Doesn't matter that the colony was empty. Their yack accounts sure won't be. We thinned out the Avaka so the DWC could move their folks in with a smaller security force. Lucille says we killed at least twelve thousand of them. Good thing they weren't Oogar, huh?"

"Oh fuck off, Little Hammer," Maven said as she approached. "That's pretty damned close to genocide."

"Jesus, Maven, don't call me—"

"I mean it, fuck off," Maven said. "You should have told us the city was empty."

"It didn't matter. Besides, they've already booked us for a recovery mission. Smash and grab on some unnamed planet," Lemieux said. "All we have to do is—"

"No," Hex said. "Immediate thirty-day liberty for the entire company. You're not saying shit about it, either. Our folks need time to get their affairs in order, because nothing is smash and grab anymore."

"Why a month?" Lemieux frowned.

Hex turned to Maya and then back to his commander. "You can personally apologize to the families for this shitshow. The rest of us are on earned leave."

"Why now? We have another mission."

"It can wait." Hex slipped an arm around Maya's shoulders. "If I wanna propose, I gotta ask permission from her parents, Hammer. It's only right."

* * * * *

Kevin Ikenberry Bio

Kevin Ikenberry is a life-long space geek and retired Army officer. As an adult, he managed the U.S. Space Camp program and served as a space operations officer before Space Force was a thing. He's an international bestselling author, award finalist, and a core author in the wildly successful Four Horsemen Universe. His eleven novels include Sleeper Protocol, Vendetta Protocol, Runs In The Family, Peacemaker, Honor The Threat, Stand or Fall, and Deathangel. He's co-written several novels with amazing authors. He is an Active Member of SFWA, International Thriller Writers, and SIGMA—the science fiction think tank.

* * * * *

Casey Moores Bio

Casey Moores was a USAF officer, as well as a rescue and special ops C-130 pilot for over 17 years—airdropping, air refueling, and flying in and out of tiny little blacked-out dirt airstrips in bad places using night vision goggles. He's been to "those" places and done "those" things with "those" people. Now he is looking forward to a somewhat quieter life where he can translate those experiences into fiction. He is a Colorado native and Air Force Academy graduate, but has also become a naturalized Burqueño, planning to live in New Mexico forever.

# # # # #

The Price of Victory by Zane Voss

Sergeant Connor Manning sighed as the diminutive, red-headed Private First Class Lewis strutted his way past the two Lumar and through the blue curtain into the Lyon's Den like he owned the place. He was clearly still feeling cocky about the promotion he'd received after the Rangers completed their most recent contract. In his defense, he'd done well in the assault, and his evident skill as a pilot had earned him a shiny new Mk 6 CASPer, making him the first rookie in the company to get one of the new mechs and the 'CASPer Therapy' that allowed him to take more damage while he operated it.

Only a few of the bigger Human merc outfits like the Horsemen could afford to upgrade many of their units to the new version. The Rangers had been able to afford a dozen of the new suits with the substantial bonus they'd earned from taking their contract's objective completely intact.

Manning's people were the only full squad of Mk 6s in the company, and that made them a little cocky. Too cocky for their sergeant's tastes.

Manning stopped the rest of the squad following along behind him and politely stood aside to let two older gentlemen pass through the curtain and upward toward the exit. Lewis barely paid them any attention, but to Manning, they stood out like a sore thumb. The one in the lead was wearing civvies, which was unusual in the merc-frequented bar. But his short-cropped hair and the way he held himself said he was no stranger to military life. His back was ramrod straight, and his cold eyes flitted over everything, silently judging the condition of the squad's dark blue uniforms as he passed by the younger mercs.

The second man wore a familiar uniform, dark green and black tiger stripes topped with the blue beret of Cartwright's Cavaliers. Manning didn't recognize him, but that wasn't a surprise. The Cavaliers were a big unit, with detachments constantly rotating off planet for a host of different contracts. Like the first man, this one carried himself like a soldier, and he exchanged a courteous nod with Manning as they passed.

Manning's assistant squad leader, Corporal Arthur Chiang, watched the two men head toward the parking lot. "Weird to see a bunch of old geezers here at the Den."

Manning stopped, annoyed, and turned to look at his squad. "Chiang, how many contracts have you completed?"

The young mech pilot blinked at his squad leader's tone, "Ah, seven, Sergeant."

"Alright, I've finished nineteen offworld contracts in the past ten years, and I'm not yet thirty." He paused and twitched his head in the direction the two men had taken. "Those fellas have gotta be at least sixty or seventy, which means they started merc work back in the days of the Mk 1 or Mk 2 CASPer, and the one's still on active duty. Think about how many contracts they've completed and show a bit of respect."

The younger man hung his head in shame. "Sorry, Sergeant, that was dumb. Won't happen again."

Manning nodded and looked back at the rest of his people waiting in the hallway. "Remember why most mercs are young'uns and respect the skills of someone who's spent a long life in this business." The other seven members of the squad nodded solemnly, but Manning wasn't sure it was a lesson that would stick with them.

"Are you guys coming, or what?"

Manning turned around as Lewis held back the curtain and motioned the squad to follow him inside. Most of them had never been to the Den, and it looked like a group their size might have a hard time finding a table today. The place was crowded, with a couple of smaller empty tables scattered around, but nothing that would fit all ten of them. After surveying the possibilities, Manning said, "Let's just hang out at the bar; we'll wait for something to open up."

An eclectic fusion of violin-heavy classical and throbbing techno music played through speakers in the background, but the place wasn't that loud for how many Humans and aliens were loitering around. His eager squad pushed in and claimed a section of the bar, and Manning followed at a more measured pace. He glanced around the room, taking in the typically varied clientele of the Den. There were half a dozen alien species represented, all of them merc races, but the crowd was mostly Human today.

At a large table not too far from the bar, a couple of Human males caught his gaze. They were older men, like the two who had passed them on their way out. Both were in civvies, making Manning wonder if they had all been part of one group, maybe a reunion or something, based on all the empty drink cups and food trays at the table. The two were standing at the edge of the table, chatting quietly. One of them was turned mostly away from Manning, but his dark skin and short black hair contrasted sharply with the cream suit jacket he wore. He was probably average height, but looked short next to his towering companion. The taller man probably topped two meters and was dressed more casually in slacks and a light blue dress shirt.

He laughed at some comment and reached up to run a hand over his gleaming bald scalp.

The two men shook hands, then embraced in a back-slapping hug. Manning couldn't help but smile at the two old comrades saying farewell one more time. The sharply dressed black man turned and headed toward the exit, but the other sat back down, evidently to finish his drink.

Manning turned his attention back to the bar and ordered a beer from the bartender. Some of his squad were ordering exotic drinks with price tags that made him wince, but he had simple tastes. A nice cold beer was his go-to when he got back from a job, and there was no better place than the Lyon's Den to get one.

He smiled as Carrie Thomas, one of his most experienced pilots, began playing out her part in the flanking maneuver that had won their last contract. The talented young pilot had short-cropped blonde hair, and her passion for dancing gave her a figure that drew admiring glances from several patrons in the Den.

Carrie had gone through the feigned retreat and subsequent counterattack with hands waving and punctuated by her own sound effects at least half a dozen times, but the rest of the squad chipped in their own comments just as if it were the first time through. For a while, Manning sipped his drink and lost himself in the hum of the bar and the details of the story.

Chiang's voice knocked him out of his tranquil reverie. "Looks like Lewis is determined to get us a table."

Manning cursed under his breath as he saw the diminutive Lewis strutting over toward the tall, bald man in civvies occupying the table all to himself. He set his drink down and pushed himself away from the bar to hurry after his brash young PFC. He worried the youngest member of his squad was about to create a monumental incident.

Manning had carefully laid out the rules of the Den to everyone, and the last thing he wanted was to draw the ire of the proprietors.

Just as Manning was about to reach out and grab Lewis' shoulder, the PFC addressed the sole occupant of the table, who coolly watched him approach. "Hey, how about you beat it and leave this table to us, huh? This place is supposed to be for mercs, anyway."

The bald man just sipped his drink and gazed back at Lewis, not saying anything. This scrutiny from the still green eyes must have unnerved Lewis, who glanced around, seemingly discomfited by the lack of a response to his demand.

The older sergeant caught up to his wayward PFC and grabbed Lewis' shoulder in an iron grip, steering him back toward the squad intently watching the unfolding drama. "Lewis, get back to the bar. We'll wait our turn for a table."

"But, Sarge, we've got a big victory to celebrate, and this guy's just sitting here alone at this table!"

"Lewis, shut the hell up and go back to the bar," Manning said through gritted teeth.

"Big victory, huh?" the old man drawled out, his southern accent not hiding the rough, gravelly timbre of his voice.

Lewis puffed his chest out and replied, "Fuck, yeah, we smashed a Lumar merc company on Dalfeen 3. Suckered them right out of their positions and hit them with a flanking attack. Took our objective with almost no losses. It was awesome!"

"I bet it wasn't awesome for the ones who did get killed," the bald man said quietly, his eyes narrowed.

Manning winced at the stinging comment, but Lewis remained unrepentant. "Shut the hell up, old man! What do you know about victory, anyway?"

That old man's eyes snapped up, locked on Lewis like the targeting lasers of a missile battery, and held the PFC rooted to the floor.

"I know plenty, boy, plenty." He sat back in his chair, took a deep breath, and visibly relaxed his shoulders. He started to continue, but they were interrupted by one of the Den's waitresses.

"Major Adams, you doing ok?" She looked at Manning and Lewis skeptically. "Are these fellas bothering you?"

"I'm fine, Lisa, thank you," he said without taking his eyes from the now-cowed Lewis. "Actually, these young men and their friends were about to join me."

Manning started to politely decline the offer, but Adams held up a hand to forestall protest. "No, I insist, Sergeant. Please, grab your drinks and come sit down."

Manning glanced around. Lewis' confrontation had drawn attention, and his squad was all watching, waiting to see what was going to happen. As the waitress began clearing the plates and glasses from the table, Manning waved over his people. He turned back to the major sitting at the table. "Sir, I'm Sergeant Manning of the Texas Rangers Mercenary Company. This numbnuts is PFC Lewis."

"Ah, you're Mark Simpson's people, right?" Major Adams said, referring to the Dallas billionaire who'd funded a mercenary company just to name it after Dallas' baseball team, which he also owned. Adams sat back in the chair and sipped his beer again.

"Yes, sir, and this is the rest of my squad."

The major nodded politely to his new guests and motioned them to take the seats around the table. As they all settled in, his gaze moved back to Lewis, who looked like a man about to head to the gallows. From the look on his face, he knew he'd screwed up. It wasn't likely he'd get off without repercussions when Colonel Bush heard about him telling a major from another mercenary company to shut the hell up.

"PFC Lewis, you asked me what I know about victory, yes?"

Lewis nodded stiffly, not meeting the older man's eyes.

"My name is Curtis Adams." He set his glass down on the table and his dark, almost haunted eyes panned across the young mercs assembled at his table. "I'm retired now, but I served in Rawlins' Raiders for nearly forty years."

Manning sucked in a sharp breath at the mention of Rawlins' Raiders. Theirs was a sad tale, too familiar to Human merc units, of a top-notch mercenary unit brought low after one too many contracts went south. They were still around, but bottom feeders these days, who would take any unsavory contract, as long as it paid. And they weren't called Rawlins' Raiders anymore.

Looking back at Lewis, he continued, "Do you want to hear a story? About victory?" Lewis' eyes twitched back up and met those of the older man. He nodded choppily, and Adams picked up his glass again for another sip.

As Manning motioned to the waitress for another round for the table, Adams began.

"Ever heard of a planet called Ksshtah? No? Interesting place, lot of weird shit there, ridiculously humid, too. It's three hyperspace jumps from Earth over to the Centaur region of the Jesc arm. Not much of real value or interest to most in the Union. Neither the planet nor people are well known, outside those interested in xenobiology research.

"The local inhabitants, also called Ksshtah, are a peculiar species with a trilateral symmetry. They're a little bit like a four-foot tall brown mushroom, with three eye stalks, three knobby little legs, and three arms sticking straight out from their trunk. They were notable mainly for what they call Ipt'afh, a kind of spiritual commune they enter into with certain species of fungus native to their home planet. They talk about Ipt'afh as something like a 'discussion' with the fungus, where they convince it to grow in certain ways and produce different varieties of this sap that's kind of like maple syrup. Like I said, weird.

"The strange-looking little aliens had almost nothing of value until about thirty years ago, when they discovered how to process the sap of one of the bajillions of varieties of fungus that grow all over the planet. After it's processed, this fungus has a range of healing and life-extension effects on a bunch of different species. Apparently that made Ksshtah valuable enough to draw some attention.

"It was supposed to be an easy job…a nice, unopposed landing on a conflict-free planet, then just hold the fort until the engineers finished setting up all the automated defenses ordered by the client, and wait out the rest of the contract in peace." Major Adams paused for a second, his eyes staring off into the distance. The silence drew out uncomfortably, some of his audience starting to shift and squirm in their seats. Finally, the old merc snorted a bitter laugh and shook his head ruefully. "Right. Like things ever go according to plan in this business."

* * *

Thirty Years Earlier

Curtis jerked his legs further up under the battered computer console as more debris clattered down from the ceiling of the control room, joining piles of junk already brought down by the heavy missile strikes and stray MAC fire going through the building. He blinked his eyes furiously to clear the dust from them, dirty tears skimming down his face as he worked desperately to save his friends.

"The problem is here somewhere, it has to be, but where the fuck is it?" he snarled as he swiped through the status reports for the state-of-the-art heavy automated defenses scattered in and around the sprawling Ksshtah processing facility.

One of his slates snarled an emergency tone as it received an incoming priority call from a Raiders senior officer. He slapped the acknowledge button to accept the call, and the stock picture and rank insignia of Major Jacob Rawlins popped up on the screen.

"Curtis! Thank God you're alive!"

Curtis let out a shuddering breath, relieved beyond measure that his best friend was still among the living. It was probably a bit unusual for a major to be friends with a lowly tech sergeant, but Human merc units tended to be far less formal than the old professional militaries of Earth. The two young men had become close while they were putting together the Raiders' first CASPer company and had remained that way since.

"I'm still here, Jacob, at least for now. Ready for a SitRep?"

"Go!"

"Something is preventing the fixed defenses from engaging. Still trying to locate the cause. We'll localize and get it fixed ASAP. Our infantry platoon is still holding the building, but has taken heavy losses. Not sure how long they'll be able to hold."

The brutal hammer of Jacob's fifty-caliber M2 machine gun replied to the situation report. Three thunderous bursts ripped out at an unseen enemy. "Curtis, you've got to get this figured out. My CASPers are kicking the shit out of the Zuul, but we can't be everywhere, and there are a lot of them. They're going to pick the company apart if we don't get help from the defenses!"

"We're on it, Jacob, we'll get it done."

"And stay alive, Curtis! We're clearing out Zone 3 right now, and we're going to replenish ammo and power cells at the secondary supply cache here. Then we're headed into the center of the compound, and we'll be there soon. Hang on!" The slate let out a mournful beep as Jacob cut the connection, and Curtis turned back to the scrolling status reports.

He reached over to brush pieces of the ceiling from one of the three slates he had plugged into the guts of the workstation and tried to make sense of what he was seeing.

The console had been the primary control site for the automated defenses until it had shielded Curtis from the debris and fragmentation that scythed down half his tech crew as they raced to bring everything online. That frag had also destroyed the screens and controls on the terminal, leaving Curtis in his current position, half inside the console, frantically trying to activate the fixed defenses to engage the Zuul running wild across the whole compound.

The Zuul had played their transport off as a normal freighter doing a pickup of the refined biologicals from the processing facility. When they were close above the compound, Zuul dropships had erupted from the transport's holds and dropped their mercenaries all over the facility. They were almost entirely infantry with a few soft-skinned vehicles and would normally have been an easy match for the automated MACs, lasers, and missile batteries all in hardened enclosures spread out in concentric rings around the Ksshtah facility's centrally located headquarters building.

But something had gone terribly wrong. None of the defenses were even trying to acquire targets. They just sat in their bays, doing exactly nothing.

Early in the assault, the Zuul dropships had delivered salvos of missiles on several points throughout the city, including the building where the control room was located. Curtis had always thought the lightly built HQ building a poor choice to house the vitally important control room, but the Ksshtah loved symmetry and overruled the Human engineers installing the defenses.

The waves of Zuul missiles had smashed both outer wings of the building and collapsed the rear exit entirely, leaving the surviving techs and infantry with only the main entrance. The Humans were lucky that the massive concussions hadn't brought down the central portion of the building on their heads, but the Zuul seemed determined to take the HQ building intact. Luckily for the Humans, the front entrance of the HQ opened to a wide courtyard, giving them a perfect field of fire to cut apart the Zuul attacks before they could reach the doors.

Curtis coughed roughly, his throat scarred from the acrid smoke of burning electronics. Shaking his head, he pushed aside the lingering disorientation from the missile strikes. "Ok, ok, ok, ok…" he mumbled to himself as one slate finished a self-diagnostic on part of the defense control system. "Sensors and targeting parameters are good, so what's going on here?" He shoved himself back inside the console and unsnapped the diagnostic slate's cable from where it was attached to the terminal. "Maybe the main power system has some issue? Just need to get hooked in there and get a diagnostic running."

Curtis pawed around in the guts of the terminal through the multi-colored bundles of wires and connectors, but the main lighting in the building was down, and he could barely see. Turning to look over his shoulder, he roared, "ASHIZ, LIGHT!" at the terrified apprentice technician huddled under another workstation across from him. The beam from the big flashlight Ashiz held whipped back up into the access panel, giving Curtis a much better view of the console's wiring.

"Better! Now let's see here…" Curtis grabbed the correct data connector with shaking hands on the second try. He clumsily snapped the lead from the slate into the computer terminal controlling the main power distribution for the defense system and started another diagnostic test. As the diagnostic began, he could hear the pulses of the laser rifles fired by the defending infantry platoon as they opened up on the attackers. Seconds later they were joined by the rapid chatter of a pair of crew-served machine guns. The Zuul had rushed the HQ building four times now, and the only thing that had saved the Raiders so far had been the multi-barreled Gatling on the APC they'd grounded near the front entrance.

Curtis heard the high-pitched electric whine of the Gatling in question as it spun up, ready to deliver a hail of penetrators to the Zuul infantry storming across the wide plaza surrounding the HQ building. He tried to tune out the droning roar of the weapon as it engaged the enemy and concentrate on the slates in front of him.

"Tech Sergeant Adams, what seems to be the problem?" Curtis looked up in astonishment at the Ksshtah standing up in the middle of the room right beside him.

"Sir, you really need to get down right now! It's dangerous to be standing up like that!" Curtis looked around at several Ksshtah bodies scattered around the control room, victims of stray weapons fire or debris falling from the roof. The fungoid-descended Ksshtah twisted around, evidently arriving at the same conclusion as Curtis. The Human stared in fascination as the mushroom squatted, lowering itself down to the ground, all three legs and three arms sticking straight out from its torso.

"I see, Tech Sergeant, this area does seem to be somewhat dangerous; perhaps we should evacuate?" came the same mechanical voice again. A pendent hung from one of the three stubby eye stalks protruding from the walking mushroom's cap to translate the whistles and tones the Ksshtah used for speech.

"No, not yet, we need to figure out what's preventing the automated defenses from firing, and fix it, otherwise the Zuul are going to destroy the Raiders, and all of you afterwards." Curtis turned back to his slates, silently urging the diagnostic on. He recognized the alien from his unique color pattern as one of the engineers involved in the defense system project, but couldn't remember his name.

"Hmm…that would be unfortunate," the disturbingly calm Ksshtah mused. "This is a new experience for us Ksshtah, you understand. We have no natural predators on our planet, so the concept of one sentient preying on another is very strange to us."

"I get it, not used to being shot at, sure, sure," Curtis mumbled distractedly. The slate dinged as the diagnostic completed, and he hurriedly sorted through the multitude of error messages thrown out by the program.

"The main reactor is online, so how can every single weapons installation be cut off from main power? This makes no sense!" Curtis slammed a fist into the console beside him, desperately searching for some sort of explanation.

"Probably because the main power relay for the defense system was damaged by missile strikes while the fusion reactor was spinning up to full power," the Ksshtah said. "Based on my quick survey, it appears the inrushing power surge from the reactor combined with some damage caused a short ahead of the main relay switch, which shut down automatically to protect itself."

Curtis turned and stared at the Ksshtah in disbelief. "How could you possibly know that? And that should affect only one of the main power runs, not all of them. The backups would take over and…" Curtis looked around at his surviving tech crew and the bodies of friends who hadn't been as lucky. "How the hell did you get in here, anyway? You weren't part of the control crew!"

"Oh, well, you see, I came in through the passageways in the maintenance sub level from the shelter in Zone 1. I was curious as to how exactly this 'fighting' worked, and I thought I would come see for myself." The short alien crouched as a handful of MAC rounds slammed through the building above them, raining more debris down. "It's very loud here; I didn't anticipate the volume. Interesting, very interesting!" The alien wiggled happily, apparently delighted by his discovery that desperate combat included loud noises.

"And to answer your question, as I came in through the passageways, I observed the damage to the relay. There's only one main power relay and one power run feeding all of the weapons systems you installed, so it was easy to see the damaged component. We reviewed your recommended design of the power system and felt it was inelegant. We revised the design to be much more in keeping with our principles. The main power run starts underground here, in the relay enclosure adjacent to the reactor, and then spirals outward through all nine zones of the complex, supplying power to all required stations. It is a beautiful design! I believe you Humans call this a Fibonacci spiral…Tech Sergeant? Are you well? Why are you striking your cranium against this console?"

Curtis struggled to contain his rage at the naïve alien. Of course they'd revised the power system design! They'd attempted to do the same thing to every other aspect of the automated defenses. It was just that the entire power system was underground and had been installed entirely by the Ksshtah before they arrived, so none of the Humans had even thought to check it.

"Nevermind that, can you lead my people down through those passageways to the damaged relay?" Curtis demanded of the confused Ksshtah.

"Yes, Tech Sergeant, it's quite simple. The entrance is down this corridor in the room used for…"

"Ok, great, one second," Curtis cut off the rambling alien and shouted, "Howard! Can you move the wounded?" The short, barrel-chested Sergeant Howard Smith had organized several of the uninjured techs to try to care for the wounded infantry and support staff.

He leaned out around the corner of a smoking console and shouted back to Curtis.

"We can! There's only a couple of the infantry and Tech Owens left. None of the others made it." Curtis closed his eyes at the grim news. A lot of their people were dead, and all because some Ksshtah had wanted a nice, pretty design for their power cable!

Howard crawled over a pile of debris and dropped down by Curtis, glancing at the seated Ksshtah in surprise. "We got a tourniquet on Owens' arm, and the bleeding has stopped. He should be ok for a little while." He reached up to brush debris out of his high-and-tight, then motioned towards Curtis' collection of slates. "Making any headway?"

They both flinched as several explosions rocked the building and prompted the Ksshtah to comically cover his head with all three hands. The Gatling fell silent as well, and for a few minutes all they heard were the calls of the infantry platoon for aid or ammo. Curtis looked back at the other sergeant and replied, "Yeah, this Ksshtah found out what happened. Listen up, this is what we're going to do. You organize everyone mobile to get the wounded and follow him to the service passageways. He's going to lead you to where the power relay is damaged. Once you get there, send all the wounded over to the Zone 1 shelter so they can try to get some medical attention."

Curtis pulled one of the slates over to him, setting the automated defenses to engage automatically when able, then shoved the slate back inside the console. He slammed the access panel closed and locked it. "If the Zuul get in here before we can get the relay repaired, maybe they won't think to check inside a destroyed console. If they leave it alone, it should automatically engage when power comes back on." Curtis turned back to Howard. "You get a team started working on the damaged relay while I tell the infantry platoon leader what's going on. For some reason I don't have comms with them anymore, so I have to go in person. I'll be down as quickly as I can to help, but you've got to get started at least."

Howard nodded assent. "We'll get on it." He motioned toward the Ksshtah. "Come with me, but stay low so you don't catch a bullet. What's your name, anyway?"

"Very well, I'll guide you to the relay room. And please, call me Mike."

Both Humans stared at the alien, then glanced at each other incredulously.

"Your name is Mike?" Curtis asked, not sure if he'd heard the alien correctly.

"Why, yes, it's a new descriptor I've adopted since meeting you Humans. You have such lovely names! Short, succinct, and full of meaning. In our language, Mike is an almost perfectly symmetrical tone sequence. Quite pleasant!"

The alien did his happy wiggle again, and Curtis shook his head. "What a strange fucking planet. All right, Mike, get going with Howard. I'll find you in a bit. Show Ashiz where the tunnel entrance is and have him wait for me." Curtis slapped his Egyptian apprentice on the shoulder and moved off toward the front entrance of the building.

He got up into a crouch, then darted around Ashiz's console to the half-shattered door leading out of the control room. He peeked through the opening to make sure it was clear and pushed through the portal into the wide, spiraling corridor beyond. The first side corridor he reached was totally collapsed from the missile strikes, and another room further down was rapidly turning into a crackling inferno. He moved down the corridor in a crouch to avoid the choking smoke, his boots crunching through a layer of broken glass from the shattered skylights above. The pale yellow sunlight flooding through the jagged openings illuminated dense streams of smoke lazily drifting up and out of the building.

If we don't get out of here, we're toast anyway.

Outside, he heard the distinct scream of dropships rocketing back and forth over the compound, punctuated by the harsh crash of airstrikes hitting their targets. Weapons fire of all types filled the background, creating a roaring cacophony of sound that made Curtis' guts clench in fear.

He reached the end of the hallway and dropped down to the debris-strewn ground to get a little cover from any incoming fire. Coincidentally it let him catch his breath in the clearer air and let his nerves settle. Steadier now, he eased down the last few meters of corridor and into the antechamber.

The high-ceilinged vestibule had once been a beautiful entrance to the building. Decorative containers with carefully chosen varieties of colorful fungi native to the planet had been scattered around seating configured for the many different species that might visit the facility. Strange art had been hung on the walls with cleverly placed windows to allow the natural sunlight to accentuate different pieces at different times in the long Ksshtah day. Curtis had passed through that beautiful chamber only an hour before, but now that seemed like some soft-edged dream he had only imagined in his sleep. As he entered the entry foyer of the building, he halted and stared open-mouthed at the embodiment of Hell.

The outer wall of the foyer was riddled with holes, to the point that Curtis was shocked the roof hadn't fallen in yet. Thousands of projectiles had gone through the building, and missiles had blown gaping holes in at least four places he could see. One of the holes was conveniently located near ground level, and the soldiers had piled debris all around it to convert it into a firing position for one of the medium machine guns.

Small fires smoldered everywhere as infantrymen and women crawled around checking on wounded comrades and pulling chemical charge packs for laser rifles from dead soldiers. Just outside the front doors of the HQ was the grounded armored personnel carrier, solidly ensconced behind the concrete barriers the Raiders had added for just that purpose.

Curtis crawled over to the closest surviving infantryman, trying not to think about the warm, sticky blood soaking through his uniform coveralls. The young soldier saw Curtis making his way over and crouched down to meet him. "Any news on the defensive turrets, Sergeant?" he asked hopefully. The trooper was almost unrecognizable in the filthy gray battle dress and light combat armor he wore. His face was smudged with dark grime where he'd wiped his face with a dirty glove.

The tech sergeant nodded but had to cough to clear his smoke-scarred throat before replying, "We think we know what the problem is and can get it fixed, but I need to tell your CO. Know where he is?"

The dust-covered private motioned toward the grounded vehicle. "He was over by the APC with Sergeant Tulls a while ago, check there first."

Curtis waved his thanks and moved over toward the platoon commander's position. It seemed like the firing had died away almost completely, so Curtis felt safe to get back up into a crouch and dart over to cover behind the vehicle.

He found Sergeant Tulls and Lieutenant Baker where the young private said they would be, covering behind the bulk of the APC. "Lieutenant, I think we can get the fixed defenses back online! My people are headed down now to start work on repairs."

The lieutenant and his platoon sergeant looked at each other.

"Ok, Adams, we'll just have to hold here while you get it done." Baker took a quick look around the corner of the APC at the buildings across the plaza. "I'm not sure how much longer we'll be able to give you, though. We're down to 22 effectives. Second Platoon isn't responding to radio calls anymore. We have no idea what happened to them. The other infantry company is clear on the far side of the complex, getting hammered by Zuul dropships. The tank company is bogged down in street fighting, and Major Rawlins' CASPer company is running low on ammo and power." He shook his head in resignation. "If you're going to get the defenses online, you have to do it now, or there won't be anything left of the Raiders."

Curtis grimaced at the news. He was particularly worried about the technicians and admin folks in the Raiders' section of the compound. Hopefully they'd been able to hole up and defend the place.

He nodded to Baker. "Got it. I'm on my way!"

Curtis turned and scuttled back through the ruined corridor to the control room, hoping Ashiz had kept it together and waited for him. As he passed through the doors of the control room, he heard the renewed snapping of laser blasts behind him.

He stood up and began to run as he moved through to the corridor on the far side of the control room. As he neared the end, he saw a terrified Ashiz peek his head around the corner. "Friendlies coming through!" he yelled at the pale-faced apprentice. Ashiz lowered the sidearm he'd been holding in a trembling hand. "Back that way, Sergeant, two rooms down." He motioned with his free hand back down the hallway.

Curtis reached out and gently took the pistol from the other man, worried that Ashiz was going to shoot him on accident. "Ok, Ashiz, thanks, you lead the way." The younger tech nodded and started back toward the entrance to the maintenance tunnels. Curtis safed the pistol and slid it into a cargo pocket before following.

The two Raiders passed through what seemed like a utility room of the HQ complex and through a back door Curtis had never noticed before. The shallow, Ksshtah-designed stairs led down in (what else?) a spiral 10 or 12 meters underground. Curtis followed the much shorter Ashiz through the uncomfortably small tunnel, having to duck the whole way because of the low ceilings. They emerged into a wide room with slightly higher ceilings to find Howard and three techs working to clear rubble from one corner.

"How does it look?" Curtis asked the other tech sergeant.

"Not sure yet; it looks like part of the ceiling caved in here and fell onto the enclosure, causing a short to the enclosure itself. For sure, the main power coupling from the reactor needs to be replaced; the insulator is damaged." Howard motioned to the black burns where electricity had arced across the top of the enclosure. "Hopefully the transformer built into the relay is in good shape, but we don't know yet. The breaker tripped, so it's safe to work around now, but we'll see more when we get the panel opened up." The five Humans ducked and looked up fearfully at the weakened ceiling as a massive explosion boomed somewhere above them. Dust and small pieces of debris trickled down onto the floor, making an odd musical counterpoint to the explosion.

"Ok, I'll check out the local control system and get everything reset. You guys get the enclosure open and start working on whatever's damaged."

Howard nodded and sent two of the techs over to pull spare relays and computer cards from the storage rack on the other side of the room.

Curtis cycled through menus on the local workstation, getting ready to reset the breaker to the big relay, and shook his head. Somehow his life always seemed to revolve around power relays, all the way back to when he'd worked for old Tech Sergeant Garrett as an apprentice.

He studied the readout on the panel carefully as Howard began replacing components in the relay enclosure. Since the main relay itself combined all the functions of a high-power switch, transformer, and power conditioner, it had better be in good shape, or they were shit out of luck. "Ok, it seems like the breaker caught it early enough, maybe this'll work."

"That's excellent news, Tech Sergeant Adams." Curtis jerked up in surprise and smacked the top of his head on the low ceiling as the voice spoke to him out of nowhere. "What the hell, Mike!" Curtis yelled at the offending mushroom. "I thought you were going back to the Zone 1 shelter with the wounded?"

"I felt I might be able to assist your team here, Tech Sergeant."

Curtis rubbed his head, still smarting from the ceiling. "Ok, help Ashiz with that replacement power coupling for the relay; it's delicate and needs to be installed with the right insulator." He motioned at the apprentice currently unboxing a spare coupling.

"Of course, Tech Sergeant!" With yet another happy wiggle, the three-legged mushroom trundled off to assist.

Even with his team working as fast as they could, getting all the damaged components replaced took precious minutes. Minutes the Raiders upstairs, fighting for their lives, didn't have to spare.

Curtis watched Howard swap out the last damaged control card in the enclosure and then slam the cover shut. "All right, we need to get this fired up now!"

"We need to at least run some diagnostics to make sure everything is in good shape first!" Howard argued.

"No time, the diagnostics will take at least half an hour! We either get it going now, or everyone upstairs dies." Curtis turned toward the control panel, hoping against hope they'd gotten the repairs finished in time.

He'd barely taken two steps when Ashiz, who'd been standing out of the way near the entrance, let out a gut-wrenching scream as Zuul claws opened his back from shoulder to waist. As bright crimson blood splattered the doorway, more Zuul crowded in behind the first, eager to get at the unprepared Humans. Curtis was just as flat-footed as the rest and paid for his lack of caution when agony erupted from his right shoulder. Amid the pain, he caught the distinct smell of burning pork, and was overwhelmingly hungry for a split second.

The laser round sent him stumbling against the wall, but fortunately for everyone, it got him just close enough to the control terminal for the power relay system.

He lunged for the bright green button on the console and felt his fingers just brush against it before the darkness took him.

* * *

A wracking cough jerked Curtis out of a deep, dreamless sleep. He hunched over in the bed, body convulsed by spasms as his lungs tried to clear themselves.

"Easy there, Tech Sergeant Adams. It'll pass in a few seconds." Curtis felt a hand on his back, helping hold him upright while he hacked.

When the coughing finally eased, Curtis was able to look around the room with dry, bleary eyes. He had to blink several times to make out the figure of one of the Raiders' medics, the lithe, dark-haired Maria Gutierrez, standing at his bedside. The ever-competent Hispanic woman had her hair tied up in a bun and looked exhausted, with dark bags under her eyes and rumpled BDUs, as if she'd been up for days.

"Here, let me raise this up a little." Using controls on the side of the bed, Maria raised it up so Curtis could lean back comfortably.

"Thanks, Maria. Where am I? And what's going on?" Curtis asked of the medic, his voice raspy and throat on fire from the coughing. Looking around the odd room, he saw few of the features that would be in a Human hospital. The walls were a khaki color, but were definitely not square, and seemed to flow into the floor and ceiling. Soft lighting glowed from sconces mounted high on the wall all around the chamber. The room was shaped like a truncated pie shape, with the door on the short end of the pie slice. In fact, the room looked almost as if it had been grown instead of built.

"We're in a Ksshtah building, part of our temporary quarters while everything gets rebuilt. The Zuul did a number on our barracks, so the Ksshtah offered us some free space." The medic clasped his wrist and looked at her watch, taking his pulse. "The colonel asked us to get him as soon as you woke up. You ok here for a minute?"

Curtis nodded his assent and lay back as the medic pulled aside the curtain in the doorway and walked out. Taking stock of himself, he felt pretty much like crap, which was probably not too bad, considering what had happened. Reminded of the laser blast he took when the Zuul stormed into the underground power room, he pulled at the neck of the hospital gown he wore. A few inches in and down from his right shoulder was a pink, mostly healed patch of shiny burn scar. Curtis blinked at the sight of the mostly healed tissue. *How long have I been here?* he wondered.

He heard muffled footsteps out in the hallway and looked up as Major Rawlins pulled the curtain aside and stepped in the room. Like Curtis, Jacob Rawlins was a tall man, but much more heavily muscled, and he exuded confidence. He had joined the Raiders when his father founded the company and had a distinguished career commanding the CASPer company.

When the Raiders had bought their first Mk 1 CASPers seven years ago, Jacob had jumped at the opportunity to master the new weapons system. And for four of those years, Curtis had been Jacob's personal tech. He maintained and upgraded Jacob's CASPer and spent long hours with the other young man talking about how they could make the amazing machines even better.

Curtis struggled to sit up as Jacob pulled a folding chair over to the bedside. "Relax, Curtis; take it easy. You've still got some recovering to do."

The tech sergeant lay back in the bed again, scrubbed his face with one hand, and ran his fingers back through his hair. His long, shaggy brown hair. *What the fuck?*

"What's going on, Jacob?" he demanded of his friend, glancing up from the long fingernails of his right hand.

Jacob sighed deeply and leaned back in the chair. As he did, Curtis' eyes caught the glimmer of silver eagle's wings on the lapel of his BDUs, the insignia of a full colonel, not the gold oak leaf he normally sported.

"I guess I should pick up where you got left out, huh? What's the last thing you remember?" the normally energetic Jacob asked.

Curtis stared at him for a second. He looked exhausted. Dark bags hung below both eyes, and his posture wasn't the ramrod straight military bearing he usually sported. "I remember the Zuul getting into the power relay room. Ashiz…Ashiz getting attacked. Lots of shooting, and I tried to activate the relay and power up the automated defenses. I guess I managed to get the relay online before I passed out?"

"Nope, not quite. Your new best friend Mike says you hit the initiate button, but the software requires an additional confirmation.

You were passed out, so you couldn't finish the startup sequence. But Mike was able to turn on the relay and get power back to the defenses. Good thing, too; if he hadn't been able to do it, there wouldn't have been anything at all left of the Raiders." He let out another sigh and patted Curtis' shoulder gently. "You guys saved everyone, no question about that."

"Mike finished the activation sequence? What happened to everyone else? And what about the Zuul?" Curtis head swirled, and he had to lay back against the bed again.

"Easy, buddy. Here, have some water." Jacob held a straw as Curtis took a few sips out of the cup Gutierrez had left on the table. Jacob continued, "To answer the easy question first, *Mike* happened to the Zuul." Jacob smiled at Curtis' uncomprehending stare. "Our Ksshtah friends may not have any natural predators anymore, but it seems they kept some of the defense mechanisms of their ancestors. It appears when a Ksshtah is terrified, like when a pack of Zuul are about to dissect and eat you, they release some kind of fungal spore to protect themselves. In the case of both Humans and Zuul, this spore doesn't really harm you, but acts as an extremely powerful, very quick-acting sedative. You and the Zuul were all affected. That's actually what caused you to pass out, not the laser wound. When he calmed down a little, Mike finished the activation sequence and turned on the defenses. Unfortunately that spore is really potent; it basically put you in a coma. You've been asleep for over a month now, Curtis."

Curtis was stunned speechless. *A month!*

Jacob shook his head. "You guys did a great job laying out those emplacements. When the defenses activated, the Zuul dropships didn't last more than 10 seconds, and the vehicles they had not much longer. And apparently most of their officers were in the vehicles. A bunch of the infantry got caught in the open and were just torn apart. The big missile batteries blew the crap out of their transport. It ended up crashing off to the south of the compound. Once they took so many casualties and realized they had no way off planet, the rest mostly surrendered."

The Raiders' survival in the face of the massive attack helped, but Jacob's avoidance of his other question told him what was coming next. "And the rest of my team?" Curtis' whisper caused Jacob to lean forward, elbows resting on his knees.

"Of the team you had in the power relay room, it's just you and Mike, Curtis. No one else made it. I'm so sorry, you guys were non-combatants; you shouldn't have been put in that position. The three wounded you sent to the Zone 1 shelter all recovered. If you hadn't done that, they would be dead, too. You saved them." The colonel reached out again and gripped Curtis' shoulder, trying to offer what support he could.

Curtis clenched his eyes, trying to stem the tears. *Nineteen.* Nineteen men and women of his tech team were dead. None of them were trained for combat, or even expected it. They'd just been in the wrong place at the wrong time. He took a shuddering breath, trying to get control over himself. He rubbed his eyes with his hands, wiping away the incipient tears, and looked back up at the insignia on Jacob's lapel.

"Your dad?" he asked softly, almost afraid to voice the question. Jacob's face tightened in response, and he shook his head.

"No, he didn't make it. His command section encountered a Zuul anti-tank team trying to get to Second Platoon, where they were encircled." Jacob gave a sad smile, his eyes echoing Curtis' pain. "He was out front, leading, as always. This time the business caught up with him."

"I'm so sorry, Jacob."

The new commander of the Raiders nodded his head, his jaw clenching and unclenching. He scrubbed his face with his hands and looked down.

"What about the rest of the company?" Curtis asked, breaking the pregnant silence.

It was Jacob's turn to take a deep, shuddering breath. He picked his gaze up from the floor and faced Curtis again. "It's bad; we took a lot of casualties. Across the board, not just the combat troops. The company will probably survive, the Ksshtah are paying us well, at least, but we'll be a long time rebuilding from this. And I need your help, Curtis; we've got a lot of work ahead of us. I need someone experienced I can trust to head the deployable support group. That's you now, if you're up for it."

It took Curtis a second to process what his friend had just said. "Captain Roberts? Lieutenant Acharya? None of them made it?"

Jacob's face tightened again, and Curtis' heart clenched. "Casualties were really bad, Curtis. Really bad. Even without the promotion I'm giving you, you're the senior Raider of the entire non-combat group right now. None of the officers survived. Not one. The Zuul broke into the maintenance compound and killed everyone, Curtis." Jacob's face twisted into a snarl that caused Curtis to flinch away from him. "They cut them down as they tried to run away, support staff with only a handful of sidearms!" The colonel's hazel eyes, and he was The Colonel now, blazed. The fire that had been absent earlier was back, this time focused on the aliens that had devastated his command and killed his friends.

After a few steadying breaths, the colonel calmed down enough to continue, "The combat units are in awful shape, too. There's less than a platoon of infantry left, barely enough to guard the Zuul we took prisoner. We have six functional CASPers, but only five pilots. There are two tanks and a single APC in operational condition to back them up." He looked Curtis square in the eye this time, back in control of himself. "Lieutenant Borland and I are the only officers who survived, and Borland is a dropship pilot. Including you, there are seventy-three Humans left on this planet."

Curtis stared back at Jacob in shock, almost unable to comprehend the staggering casualties. The Raiders had deployed to Ksshtah with a full company each of CASPers, tanks, and APCs backed up by two companies of infantry and the outsized support staff to install the automated defenses. Forty CASPers, twelve tanks, twelve APCs, and a total staff of more than six hundred…reduced to a bare handful of survivors huddling behind the turrets of the fixed defenses.

"The good news is our contract is up in three weeks. And then we're taking our dead and getting the hell out of here." Jacob's steady gaze reassured Curtis a little bit. With good leadership at the helm, the Raiders were going to survive; thrive, even. They would come back from this mess, and Curtis would be a part of it.

"Duty calls, Curtis. We're so short on personnel, I'm part of the ready group in case we get hit again. It's my shift, so I need to head back." The tall man stood up and looked back to Curtis. "We won, Curtis. We'll put this unit back together with the best people we can find when we get home. Pretty soon we'll be giving the Horsemen a run for their money." He gave an encouraging smile and patted Curtis on the shoulder again.

Curtis nodded mutely and watched his friend walk back to the crushing responsibilities that had landed on his shoulders. He laid back in the bed and finally let the hot tears flow down his face. He thought about the friends he'd never see again. The competent, ever-reliable Howard, who had been another of the Raiders' first CASPer techs. The young, eager Ashiz, whose family had immigrated to the US from Egypt just before first contact. Dozens of others, cut down far too early on a planet no one else on Earth had ever even heard of.

Curtis stared down at his hands, sore from clenching his fists, and tried to relax them a little. He closed his eyes and tried to begin thinking about rebuilding the Raiders, and the future they still had in front of them. But he couldn't get one nagging thought out of his head.

This is victory?

* * *

The bar was utterly silent. Someone had turned off the sound system, and it was obvious most of the patrons were straining to hear the story. What was more unusual was his squad was dead quiet, not a word being said among them. They sat and stared at the old man, his gaze still fixed off in the distance.

Manning surveyed his people. There were a couple of pale faces, and all were universally somber, especially Lewis. Maybe this would help rein in that cocky streak.

He reached out and picked up his beer stein. The motion drew the old merc's gaze, and Manning met it levelly. He held his drink up. "To Victory. And to the ones who paid the price."

* * * * *

Zane Voss Bio

Zane Voss holds bachelor's and master's degrees in engineering from the Missouri University of Science & Technology. His day job is working as a partner in an international consulting firm in the steel industry. If you're interested, he will talk your ear off for hours about iron and steelmaking. "The Price of Victory" is his first piece of published fiction. He currently resides in Pittsburgh, Pennsylvania with his wife and son.

# # # # #

The Bitter End by Mark Wandrey

Chapter 1

As soon as the transfer shuttle docked with *Long March*, Teik was moving his people through the connecting lock.

"Go, go, go," he snarled, snapping his sharp teeth at a female with her pups who was struggling to keep them in line. "The commander wants us off this tub in 15 minutes!"

"Watch what you are calling a tub, Aposo," the Maki crewmember yelled at him.

"You don't like it, make me stop," Teik snarled and flexed his hands. The gleam of chromium alloy flashed from his hands, and the Maki's eyes narrowed. Its tail reflexively gripped the nearest hold, freeing the little monkey-alien's hands. Teik felt the blood rush and hoped, oh did he ever hope, the little Kafu would start something. The Maki's whiskers flicked, but it remained silent. Comparing the Maki to one of the useless tree-dwelling rodents from his homeworld was an insult to the Kafu.

"Yeah, I thought so. Hurry up!" he yelled at a technician moving equipment boxes. "The stench of this wreck is making me ill."

Fourteen minutes later the shuttle detached from *Long March*. The constantly spinning *Behemoth*-class transport gave them some free angular momentum, something the shuttle pilot took gratefully. Teik watched through his pinplants, linked to the shuttle's freely accessible monitors, as the gigantic ball of *Long March* receded. Dozens of ships were in the process of docking or undocking with the transport, and would be almost to the last minute before it left the system via a stargate.

"It was a comfortable ship," one of the female creche mothers was saying to a breeder as Teik moved forward.

"So is the grave," Teik snapped. They both bowed their heads. *Ignorant females.*

"Teik, update?" he heard relayed through his pinplants.

"I have all the non-combat staff aboard, and we're away on schedule."

"Well done. We'll see you on the station in two hours, tops. Settle your charges in and take liberty. We'll meet tomorrow."

"So it shall be," Teik replied, and the comms were finished. His commander liked a tight operation, as any merc commander would. Inefficiency cost credits, bleeding credits resulted in losses, and losses led to a failed company. Lashku had been a merc company for 1,012 years. Teik wasn't going to be the last XO of such a long-lived company.

He relaxed in null-G as the shuttle drifted toward the distant space station. He wasn't familiar with the location; his Aposo people didn't have extensive ties in the Tolo arm. In particular, the Cresht region, where they were now, was well known as a backwater area. Few races of any significance called it home. As one of only 37 mercenary races out of untold thousands, his people were among the elite.

Inside the forward cabin, a factor floated nearby and waited to be acknowledged. Teik ignored him for long enough to reinforce his status, then turned his reddish eyes to regard him. As all factors, he was small, with extremely light brown fur. His ears were short, showing he'd been through several companies. The practice of cutting back the ears prior to remarking went far back in his people's history.

"What do you want, Factor?"

"I've been calculating," the factor said.

"That's the reason we feed you."

"Yes, and I'm grateful." He lowered his head below Teik's, offering his ears. "May I proceed?" Teik gave the factor's ear a perfunctory nip of acknowledgment. "Our credit situation is dire. We're scheduled to send the required deposit back to Ap'apal in three weeks. I'm sorry; there aren't enough credits in the general fund to cover the deposit."

"Is Commander Kloot aware?"

"The last time I tried to discuss it with him, he threatened to space me."

Teik's whiskers twitched, and he nodded his understanding. They'd passed up two contracts in the last system before jumping on *Long March* at the last possible minute. It was the typical situation they'd come to face as an Aposo company. In other words, a suicide mission. Entropy-cursed aliens.

Teik looked to the rear of the highborns' area of the shuttle, where the factors worked on their numbers. He despised them occupying the space, but what was to be done? Their caste was highborn, though only because of ancient times, before computers. Because of their tenuous hold on the highborn, they were abused incessantly.

"Send me the data," he said. The factor nodded and did the best thing possible; it left.

Despite the annoying factor's existence, it was correct. Their financial situation was becoming steadily worse. You didn't have to be a factor to know how many credits were in their account. So how was *he* to discuss this with Kloot without ending up sucking vacuum?

* * *

Chapter 2

Jandu Station was favorable for Lashku's business interests for many reasons, not the least of which was that the owners simply didn't care who did business there. From Pushtal and SleSha pirates, to questionable KzSha operations, the Bugitar were equal opportunity capitalists.

"On docking approach," the pilot announced.

"Understood," Teik said. He didn't mind interacting with pilots; at least they belonged with the highborn.

"The fixers say we need maintenance on both shuttles," the pilot said.

"Everyone wants credits," Teik said.

"I agree with the fixers this time."

Teik grunted and floated away from the pilot. The breeders were complaining through the creche mothers that the food was poor quality as well. *Feeders, workers, breeders, all they do is complain.*

He used his pinplants to review some of the figures the fixer had sent to him. They were all carefully ordered, tabulated, and presented with clearly defined bottom lines. In short, Teik could easily tell why Kloot had threatened to space the factor. You never tell a leader the straight truth; they didn't appreciate it.

Having come up as a simple fighter to earn his position as a planner, Teik had made the climb because he understood how leaders thought. They were guided by only one goal, victory through battle, leading to profit and greater status for the Aposo.

The shuttle bumped, and he verified his gear was in place. Jandu Station wasn't the place you wanted to go without a gun, a knife, and maybe an extra gun or three. When the shuttle bumped again, the docking status light lit, and he moved to the rear.

Of course, all the lowborn wanted out of the shuttle. The rear half was packed with breeders, workers, and feeders, all mewling about this or that, taking up space, and eating valuable food. Teik's whiskers twitched at the stench they made. It was one of his jobs as a highborn planner, or XO, to deal with all these lowborns, which made his job disagreeable. The sooner he had them off and into the station, the sooner he could be out of their presence.

The shuttle non-pilot crew, workers, opened the hatch and got out of Teik's way. The station only had a small gravity deck. All docking was at the immobile part of the station in zero-gravity. That suited Teik just fine; unloading would be much faster.

He cleared the hatch and went to the inner lock, then opened it, too. Station security was in the form of a pair of armed Lumar, who were waiting along with a single Bugitar. The simian Bugitar glanced up from the slate it held and examined Teik for a moment before speaking.

"You're Kloot of Lashku?"

"I am Teik, XO of Lashku. Kloot is on the next shuttle."

The alien showed no sign of hearing or understanding him. He simply spoke again. "The two-spacecraft docking fee is 10 GCU per day, per vessel. Fuel at standard rates. Your personnel are charged at 1 GCU each, or a total of 500 GCU for however many occupants of the shuttles for the duration of your stay, whichever is more."

Teik held out his UAAC, or Yack. "Charge 500 GCU."

The Bugitar looked back up, it's big, disconcerting simian eyes registering surprise. Their species had such expressive faces; Teik found it amusing to deal with them. He merely continued to hold the Yack out, finally releasing it to let the card float between them. Finally the Bugitar snatched the card and registered the transaction. The two Lumar looked on stupidly.

"The rules are simple," it explained. "You're responsible for any damage to the station. Any weapons fire that compromises atmospheric or structural integrity will result on your ship being confiscated."

"You're welcome to try," Teik snarled.

"Pay any fees you owe immediately," it continued without seeming to notice Teik's comment. "No credit, no exceptions. Finally, we, the management of Jandu Station, reserve the right to deny you service for any reason, at any time."

"Your station, your rules."

"Yes," the Bugitar said and held out its slate for Teik to approve, which he did.

"Are we done here?"

"Yes," the alien said, and made notes on its slate, glancing along the massive docking hallway for its next job.

Teik used his pinplants to let the pilot know they were good. A second later, the shuttle disgorged the hundreds of lower-caste Aposo he'd been shepherding. The Lumar watched in surprise as they kept coming, while the Bugitar gawked in wide-mouthed shock. Its flattened teeth were as offensive as the simian stink.

He made sure the shuttle was emptied of all the lowborn. If you didn't watch them every moment, they would inevitably get themselves into trouble. He gave the creche mother a chip with the space they'd rented in the station, effectively giving her responsibility for the mid and lowborn, then headed for the central promenade of Jandu Station.

He floated down the connectors away from where their shuttles had docked. All manner of aliens passed going in the opposite direction, while some followed him. None passed him; he was moving too quickly. Aposo were naturally adept in zero gravity.

A few of the races were impossible to mistake, such as the MinSha. The massive insectoids were always trouble. He hated fighting them; they were difficult to kill. A big purple Oogar bowled past him, actually causing Teik to rebound off the connector's wall. He hurled a curse after the retreating form. Then several more Oogar came afterward. He was glad to clear the connector and find a glideway to suck him down to the gravity deck.

"What a dump," he mumbled as the glideway deposited him into what felt like 1/3rd gravity. Every station with a gravity deck tended to cluster its trading and other businesses there. Most called this section of the station a promenade, despite the many varied forms it took. In Jandu Station, it was three small rings situated at one end of the main tube, which was the core. One was habitation for races dependent on gravity, the second was for businesses requiring gravity, and the last was entertainment, where he'd landed.

The first thing he saw was the uncollected trash. *What race runs a station without basic maintenance bots?* The next thing was the homeless aliens basically camping in alcoves. Squatting. His whiskers twitched in disgust, lips skinning back to show his razor-sharp incisors. *Who would tolerate this?*

He used his pinplants to interface with Jandu Station's network and find his destination. He logged in and waited…and waited…and waited. As the network struggled to fulfill his simple request, he upped his opinion from dump to disaster, wondering if he should advise Kloot to pack up and head out.

"Spare some credits?" a reptilian alien asked, its alcove full of eggs and filth.

His pinplants translated the words, so it was a Union race. He snarled and kicked at the hand. The alien hissed and spat back at him as he moved away. A sound made him spin back around, one of his pistols in hand. The alien stopped, a knife in one of its own hands. "You decide, piteous creature."

With an untranslatable curse, it retreated.

He watched it go before replacing the weapons and continuing on his way. The only reason he hadn't killed the petulant being was simple; it wasn't worth a single laser charge.

Teik's pinplants finally informed him of his simple request being fulfilled. The station's public maps were now at his disposal. He realized he was going the wrong direction and was forced to turn around and come back the direction he'd come. As he passed the reptilian's lair, he kept an eye on the occupant, who didn't move as he went by. "The station should get some of these scum to clean it, if they can't afford bots."

* * *

Chapter 3

"The Last Pit," Teik said, reading the name through his translator. The area the merc pit was located in looked a little less filthy. There weren't any of the homeless squatters he'd seen on the other end of the ring where he was accosted.

Teik went to the door, which demanded his Yack. He slid the card across the scanner, and it admitted him, supposedly after verifying he was who the card said he was, and that he had a positive credit balance. He went inside and found, to his dismay, the pit was in the same poor condition as the rest of the station.

Merc pits were the center of his industry, a place you could go to offer a contract, or where a merc would go to accept the contract. Many also used pits as an unofficial club where they could get together to celebrate completed contracts or party with other mercs. He had no interest in doing either. The only celebration he liked was large credit balances, and partying wasn't something he ever did.

Inside, Teik looked for any sign of their contact. It did have one thing in common with every other merc pit he'd ever been in; it was dark and loud. Being so far from any legitimate trading or merc hubs, he wasn't surprised to see a group of seven Pushtal eyeing him suspiciously. He stood and stared back at them for the longest time until they fell into a hissing huddle.

"Yes, you better look away," he said and walked over to the bar. It was robotic, unlike most of the station around it. He used his pinplants to order Peef, an alcoholic, nut-based drink from Ap'apal. He smelled its rich aroma even before the little autochef popped it out. For a second, he was fresh out of the creche and tasting it for the first time. It was a delicious memory.

As he waited for either a sign of his contact or Kloot to show up, he watched the clientele closely. The Pushtal were splitting their interest between a pair of Veetanho drinking in the corner and Teik. He casually wondered if the stupid felinoids wanted to fight. Despite the fact they were easily five times his size, he considered seven of the pathetic pirates less than a match for one Aposo.

He also noted, interestingly, a pair of huge Tortantula taking up a vast amount of space at the far back corner of the pit. They were riderless and seemed to be sitting without doing much of anything. Curious. The other occupants of the pit were largely merc races like himself, with only a tiny handful of others. It confirmed something else Kloot had confided in him; contracts in the Tolo arm were highly contested.

Teik was just considering another Peef when the door opened, and Kloot came in with an entire squad of midborn fighters. This was all to plan, and his commander spotted him immediately. The fighters headed for a table, while Kloot went to meet with Teik.

"Any sign of the contact yet?" his commander asked immediately.

"No, sir."

His nose twitched in agitation. "So much for their vaunted promptness. I'm not thrilled about taking a contract from them in the first place."

"Have you looked around?" Teik asked quietly. His commander glanced around the pit, his little eyes pausing for a moment on the Pushtal, who'd stopped glaring at Teik when another 20 Aposo came in. He also noticed the Tortantula then the Veetanho. Of them all, he spent the most time examining the latter. Veetanho and Aposo were close enough in appearance, many races got them confused. Aposo were proud warriors; they didn't hide behind other races and let them do the fighting.

"What am I missing?" he asked finally.

"Where are the clients? Merc pits often have as many clients as mercs."

Kloot looked around again, this time taking closer note. Teik saw him nod several times. "You're correct, it's unusual. However, we're far from the busy areas of the galaxy. There aren't as many lucrative contracts here."

Which is why we're here. Teik nodded. "Do you want some Peef? The autochef makes a passable version."

They both sat and waited, watching the pit and sipping Peef. The squad stayed in a private cubicle, out of sight. It was unlikely anybody in the pit would remember they were there. He'd been there just over an hour when the door opened and in walked a Zuparti. Teik caught his commander's eye and nodded toward the new arrival.

"Got it," Kloot said, and he raised a hand to get the Zuparti's attention. The alien looked at him, around the room, then slinked toward their table. It's elongated body and short legs produced a comical gate, not like the properly squat body of an Aposo.

"You're Lashku?" the Zuparti asked.

"I'm Kloot, commander of Lashku; this is my executive officer, Teik."

"And I'm F'slan. Thank you for taking this contract."

"We haven't taken the contract yet," Kloot reminded the alien.

"You said you'd take the contract."

"I said we'd review the contract and consider it."

F'slan's strange bluish eyes shifted nervously between the two of them, uncertain. He looked around the merc pit, his gaze stopping at the Pushtal, and then the Veetanho. It was obvious he was uncertain.

"Show us the contract," Teik said, "and we'll decide."

"I was expecting you to just accept it."

"You were expecting us to be fools, then," Kloot said and shook his head. "Go, hire the Pushtal. They'll stab you in the back or steal whatever goods you want to protect." Kloot jabbed a claw at the Pushtal, who looked around as Kloot raised his voice. "Or hire the Veetanho, who'll just as likely sell your secrets to the highest bidder. Come, Teik, this Kafu has wasted our time." They both stood up.

"Don't be so hasty!" F'slan exclaimed, holding up his little hands and looking nervously from side to side. The pit had gone considerably quieter at the disturbance, making the already agitated Zuparti even more so. "I'll show you the contract." He removed a small, securely designed slate from an equipment belt around his narrow waist and slid it across the table to Kloot.

Teik leaned in closer to his commander so he could see the contract as well. Kloot interfaced his pinplants with the slate and instructed it to render the contract into Aposo, which was the extent of what he could do to the contract without F'slan's approval. With the nature of the secure slate, he couldn't copy anything, either. At least not without some cheating.

The contract was a basic dispute in change of ownership of a planet. The bare minimums of the terms were present. No actual locations or possible adversaries. It did state the required duration, distance of travel, and payment, which was 26 million credits. The payment made Kloot's whiskers twitch excitedly. Teik was immediately suspicious.

"More details on the planet," he immediately asked the Zuparti. "Industrial?"

"Agricultural," F'slan replied immediately.

Kloot linked his pinplants with Teik. "This is an easy meal," he said.

"Too easy?"

"Bah, Zuparti has too many credits and not enough brains. We'll take their credits gladly."

"I'm suspicious," Teik said.

"You're always suspicious." Kloot looked at him. Teik remained respectful, but persistent. Kloot sighed audibly before asking what Teik wanted to assuage his paranoia.

Teik wanted to know what race they'd be facing as well as contractual guarantees there wouldn't be unknown forces or additional funds. He also wanted details on the terrain conditions and world environment. He got everything except the race; the Zuparti didn't want to volunteer this without a signed contract. Kloot was even more confident. Teik was not.

In the end, Kloot overrode Teik's concern and signed the contract. Teik did get the Zuparti to agree to a 15% down payment in advance, and to reimburse transportation to and from the target world to Ap'apal, which was a win in any situation.

"You'll have the finished contract in three days," F'slan said.

"My factor will review the final version, and we'll counter sign."

Satisfied, the Zuparti left the pit. Kloot wanted a couple drinks of Peef to unwind. Teik was in no mind to join, but had one to avoid insulting his commander. He couldn't overcome his disquiet over the unrevealed parts of the contract. He was still musing about it when the doors opened and a group of ten Zuul entered. The big canine species, not nearly as massive as the Besquith, immediately noted the seven Pushtal. They all showed teeth and elbowed each other.

Entropy, Teik cursed to himself as he saw what was coming.

"The down payment will cover our costs and the deposit going to Ap'apal."

Teik nodded and looked for a place to stop his commander from talking to make him aware of the developing situation. He went on and on about what they could do with the extra funds as the Pushtal stood up from their table and approached the group of bristling Zuul.

Teik wasn't close enough to pick up the conversation. Truth be told, he didn't need to hear the conversation. Simply based on the hissing and barking, it wasn't cordial. Off to the side, the pair of Veetanho were no longer ignoring the other goings on, they were intently observing the ongoing confrontation. One of the Pushtal drew a blade and gesticulated at the Zuul, who snarled in response. Teik finally decided he needed to bring the situation to Kloot's attention, now. He cleared his throat, and his commander stopped mid-sentence.

"What, you want more Peef?"

"No, I thought you should look at—"

Kloot put a hand to one ear, clearly having trouble hearing what his XO was saying. Annoyed, he looked around behind him, which was exactly what Teik had been trying to get him to do. Unfortunately, instead of becoming aware of the developing situation, the Peef had degraded Kloot's rational faculties, and the results were sadly predictable.

"Will you entropy cursed fools *shut up*?!" Kloot roared at the belligerent group of 17 mercs, all at least twice his size.

"What did you say, Veetanho?" the biggest Pushtal demanded.

"Oh, fuck," Teik said.

With amazing speed, Kloot produced his laser pistol and shot the Pushtal. Unfortunately, his Peef-dulled senses had distorted more than his judgement; it also threw off his aim. The laser burned a hole through the huge feline's left ear. The alien responded much like you'd expect; it screamed and pounced.

Teik, having only had two servings of Peef, had true aim and drilled the attacking Pushtal between the eyes with his own laser pistol. The Pushtal, already in the air, crashed into Kloot and carried the two into the table. Like most merc pits, this one was designed with fights in mind, and the furniture disintegrated from the impact. Pushtal, Aposo, and furniture parts flew in all directions. The surviving Pushtal and the Zuul drew down, and it devolved into a free for all.

"This is *just* what we needed," Teik yelled as he rolled aside. Laser pistol in one hand, he drew a long blade with the other as a pair of laser beams narrowly missed him. A second later, the 20 members of the squad Kloot had brought with him exploded from their table, and the free for all devolved into a full-fledged battle. "Still, this isn't entirely unexpected."

A few minutes later, all three forces were reduced by roughly half their numbers, and it appeared the fighting was beginning to wind down. Kloot had extracted himself from the Pushtal corpse and was urging his surviving squad members to mount an attack.

"Show the stupid cats we aren't Veetanho cowards!" he yelled drunkenly. Then a laser bolt bisected his head.

Teik would never be entirely sure, because you couldn't tell what direction a laser came from. Speed of light, and all that sort of stuff. There didn't seem to be any enemy in the direction of the Pushtal and Zuul. However, he did remember the two Veetanho had been slipping out the door when the shot came. *Probably wasn't the best move, insulting the Veetanho when two were skulking around.*

That's how Teik ended up in command of Lashku and on a contract he'd considered ill-advised from the beginning.

* * *

Chapter 4

"Taluu," Skep, Teik's new XO, said in their shared quarters. "Never heard of it."

"Me neither," Teik said. He'd vowed to treat his XO better than Kloot had treated him. In the last week, he'd largely succeeded.

"We haven't traveled the Tolo arm often."

"Because there isn't much there," Teik agreed. "Do you have the update on the mid and lowborn?"

"We should have left them at Kafu."

"I didn't ask your opinion."

"Sorry, Commander."

Teik grunted and waited for the report.

"One of the breeders got into a supply of Peef and drank herself to death." He held up a hand. "I've restricted all lowborn from Peef for 30 days to encourage them to police each other."

"They're like children still in the creche, all of them."

"I understand, Commander. I have midborn fighters keeping an extra eye on them." Teik nodded for him to continue. "Births are as expected. The creche mother says there will be 52 more stormers ready to fight by the time we land on Taluu."

"That's better than expected. Good." The previous three contracts had cost them a good number of stormers. Luckily they hadn't lost many fighters or shooters. Those couldn't be replaced on contract; it took training. If any of the stormers survived, maybe they'd be fighters or shooters someday. Some could rise to be planners. The rare, lucky, and smart might even become a leader.

"We have plenty of fixers, and they've been working to ensure all our equipment is ready." Skep blinked as he accessed his pinplants.

Teik was lucky enough his new XO had them. Skep was the last planner along with them who had pinplants. If his XO hadn't had them, things would be more difficult.

"Arms and ammo are sufficient, as are supplies after we used some of the advance."

They'd collected 3.9 million credits from the shifty Zuparti as a down payment on the contract Kloot had signed. Most of it went back to the home world, yet enough remained to resupply Lashku and prepare them for the contract.

"Good. We arrive in the Taluu system in a few hours. Have everyone ready."

"Yes, Commander." Skep floated toward the exit, but stopped short. "Commander?"

"Yes?"

"What do you know of this race we'll fight?"

"Simians," Teik said. "We've faced them in the past. They're nothing special. In fact," he looked at his XO and showed his razor-sharp teeth, "they're soft."

* * *

The shuttles landed at the main starport of Taluu. They were met by their employer, F'slan, who appeared excited to see them. He was in a ground car, along with a dozen other obviously nervous Zuparti, who watched the shuttles disgorging Lashku's forces and support.

"Welcome, Commander Kloot," F'slan said.

"Kloot is dead," Teik told him. "I was his XO, Teik; I command now. This is my new XO, Skep."

"I hope you didn't kill Kloot to be in charge," F'slan said, the other Zuparti with him laughing.

The Zuparti's tall, thin body made him taller than Teik. It didn't mean the Zuparti was larger. Teik stared the alien in the eye without comment long enough it looked away.

"I meant no offense, Commander."

"Show us the barracks."

"Yes. Yes, of course."

Later, in the barracks as their forces were moving in, Skep caught up with him. "I'm surprised you didn't kill the weasel."

"It's poor form to kill your employer," he reminded his XO. "There are rules against that in the Mercenary Guild."

"That's unfortunate."

There was an immense amount of work to accomplish in the coming week, and Teik found no time to work with his new XO. Like himself, he'd started as midborn, so he would require training to understand his new status. He felt a lot of responsibility to bring Skep up to acting like a highborn, not how he thought he should act by bad example, such as Kloot was. The longer Teik was in command, the more he realized how poor a commander Kloot had been.

Slowly, as they assumed the planet's defenses, Teik came to understand the nature of their contact, and how they'd ended up here. Taluu was a medium-sized world of a somewhat uncommon type in the galaxy. It had a rich habitat with abundant life, almost none of it native. Certain types of biospheres lent themselves to being easily adapted to other world's lifeforms. Some flora, some fauna, some both. Taluu was the latter.

Sometime thousands of years ago, the world was colonized, only the colonization had failed. The world's ecosphere, while vibrant, had almost no seasonal variability. This was a problem for many races. The life they depended on didn't do well, and failed. Thus the colony failed to thrive and left. No records survived from the Great Galactic War, so nobody knew how many different races had tried to make Taluu home. Somewhere in history, it was further discovered the vast shallow oceans were also full of volcanoes. Eruption led to massive tsunamis. This occurred regularly.

Finally, the planet was relegated to minor mineral operations and some manufacturing. These were located in the mountains some hundred kilometers from the largest area hosting settlements over the years. Huge fertile plains covered the lowlands. Regularly swamped by tsunamis, they were engulfed by sediment. Good for growing, bad for colonizing, terrible for industry.

Some time in the last century, a conglomerate had a brilliant idea. A species of herbivore grazer was perfectly suited for the growing plains, because they were adapted to a marine environment as well. After a few decades of testing, the animals survived and flourished, and a small caretaker operation was installed, as well as harvesting facilities, because the animals being grown were for another race entirely.

"Equiri?" Skep asked when he heard about the end purchaser.

Teik and his XO were in a flyer reviewing ground defense installations. When he'd seen the huge herbivore grazers moving across the grassy plains, he'd wondered who wanted them.

"Yes," Teik said. "The Equiri enjoy fresh meat. Like, living. Most of these creatures will be slaughtered and processed to be shipped to their colonies, though some are eaten alive."

Skep looked over the side at the animals. Averaging four meters at the shoulders, with necks half that long, they moved in large herds with equally long legs propelling them across the marshy plains. "The beasts are huge; why aren't the Equiri a merc race?"

"They don't like to fight."

"Cowards." Skep sneered.

Teik shrugged. He wasn't willing to make such a judgment. He'd met a pair of Equiri Peacemakers years ago, and they were the toughest beings he'd ever seen. Perhaps the Equiri were simply a complicated race? He didn't know.

Finally, they were fully set up, and they officially took over from the Lumar mercs who were leaving. The big, stupid, four-armed aliens slouched onto their shuttles and left without a backward look. Teik considered the Zuparti lucky that nobody had tried to take the colony from them before Lashku came to the world. Which brought them to the whole reason for their presence.

Nobody wanted to take over the food operation. Rather, the colony lease was lapsing. The Cartography Guild controlled lease records of worlds. They held the authority to grant ownership of a world. However, in the Galactic Union, possession was 99% of the law. It wasn't against the meager list of laws in the Union to simply refuse to recognize a change in ownership.

When the lease on Taluu expired, the Zuparti were gambling that nobody would be interested in the world. After all, for thousands of years nobody except them had made a go of it. Who in their right mind would try with such a long precedent of failure? The Zuparti even had an exclusive contract with the Equiri to provide the food animals. There was nothing to be gained by taking Taluu by force. Mercs were expensive. Their gamble hadn't paid off.

Six days after the Lumar left and Lashku officially took responsibility for the planet's defense, an enemy merc ship arrived at the emergence point, and the battle began.

* * *

Chapter 5

"How big a force?" Teik asked, entering the command center. Nothing more than a bunker dug into the mountains east of the main livestock plains, it housed all the various orbital and ground-based defenses, which would make it extremely difficult to land.

"One ship," a midborn fixer reported. "Not a cruiser, probably closer to frigate in size." He examined his screens closely for a moment. "Its readings don't match any design in the GalNet database."

Teik's biggest concern was that the enemy would bring a big transport and land dozens of individual combat shuttles. It would split his forces up badly and force piecemeal engagements. A single small warship meant he might lose his orbitals, but the enemy wouldn't have a swarm of landing vehicles.

"Incoming transmission."

A grunting, yipping voice came over the command center's speakers. It took a second for the computer to translate. "Taluu, this is licensed Mercenary Company Caudill's Army, Colonel Caudill in command. Responsible merc force, please respond."

"This is licensed Mercenary Company Lashku, Commander Teik."

There was a pause. "We were expecting a Lumar unit."

"They've completed their contract; we've taken over."

"Is visual comms allowable?"

Teik nodded to the fixer, and a second later an image of their adversary appeared. They were even uglier than he remembered. Big, round, flat faces with blunt noses, and an equally big, mobile mouth. Two largish eyes with colored irises were high on the face. They were mostly hairless, like a newly born pup, except a patch on top of their heads. This one had some on its jaw as well, which Teik had never seen before. Taken as a whole, the Humans looked weak and soft.

"Ah, Aposo," the alien said.

Was he an idiot? Couldn't his translator have told him that? "Yes, Human. You wanted to see me, now you do. Go ahead with what must be said."

"We are here to take possession of Taluu with a leasehold approved and paid for from the Cartography Guild. Will you yield?"

"We will not," Teik responded immediately. "We are done."

"There's no need for this," Caudill said.

Teik was taken aback. "What do you mean?"

"A new legal leasehold is filed. This world isn't worth your blood. We don't want to kill you. We'll offer you safe transit to the stargate."

"Why would we abandon our contract?"

"To survive."

"You overestimate your chances, Human. We'll see you on the field." He ordered the connection cut. "Prepare for orbital assault."

* * *

They didn't have long to wait. The Human frigate took a fast approach to Taluu, and for a short time Teik thought they were going to come straight in with their ship. It would have been suicide. All the planet's valuable assets were on the plains, between the sea and the mountains. If you landed offshore, you'd have to approach over the ocean, an easy target for direct fire lasers. If you landed in the mountains, the missile batteries were located there, and the ship would be killed before it got below 10 miles, the highest a spaceship could legally fire on a planet.

Teik was preparing to give weapons release when the Human ship altered course and launched smaller craft at a high angle of approach.

"Dropships," a planner announced. "Flight profiles are a perfect match."

"Who uses dropships anymore?" Teik demanded.

"MinSha use them regularly," the planner said. "Also the KzSha."

"Bugs," Skep snorted.

Teik agreed with his XO. Insects had a high G tolerance and wouldn't mind a ballistic approach. The Humans were certainly not insects, yet they were using dropships. The problem was as the dropships hit the atmosphere at high speed, the natural ionization of their interface made them extremely difficult targets. He couldn't use nuclear weapons because of the side effects to his defensive mission.

"See if we can predict their approach and prepare interceptor missiles once they get into the lower atmosphere."

"So it shall be," his XO reported.

They never got the chance; the two dropships only skimmed the upper atmosphere and discharged dozens of smaller objects. They were too small to be weapons and didn't appear to have more than cursory attitude control capabilities. The planners had no idea what they were, and neither did Teik.

"Is the course of the dropships staying within profile?" Teik asked.

"Negative, they appear to be boosting back toward orbit on a circumspect course."

"Expend some missiles on them," he said.

On the far side of the tactical command center his factor's head popped up. Despite the cash infusion, he was just as nervous as he was back on the Jandu Station. If anything, he was worse, because Teik allowed him to voice his opinions more than Kloot had. When he'd reviewed the contract, after their commander was dead, he was upset at the vagueness of many points just as Teik had been.

Exercising his commander position, he speared the factor with a glare, and the factor looked away. He had enough to deal with without adding an annoying factor to the mix.

Missiles left the launchers and raced into the sky. Within a second of launch, each of the targets split into six or more targets. The fixers worked with their instruments trying to resolve which were decoys and which were the real targets. It was impossible to tell. So much so the missiles went crazy and hit absolutely nothing. The targets, whatever they were, plummeted down and disappeared from the screen.

"Where did they land?" Teik demanded.

"Far western plain, near the water. As far as you can get from here without having to land in the mountains or the sea."

"What is it?" Skep asked.

"I don't know," Teik admitted, "my guess is armor." He didn't say but the size was too small for substantial armor, even APCs or flyers. He simply didn't know. "Prepare scout drones."

* * *

Chapter 6

The little recon drones flew at 250 kph, hugging the ground and perfectly moving around any terrain or other obstruction in their path. They were capable of 400 kph, though that was reserved for emergency maneuvers and to escape threats. At 25,000 credits each, you expected quality and versatility. Four of them had been dispatched.

Teik decided if the factor didn't stop twitching every time he committed an asset to the operation, he'd have him taken to the lowborn barracks and tied up. Right then, he was concentrating on the monitors relaying data at high speed from the drones. At the same time he kept an eye on the two dropships rendezvousing with their ship in high orbit, well outside their ground-based defense's range.

"Drones approaching landing area."

The view skimmed over the grass and past a herd of the grazing creatures. It had just seen something and went dead.

"Drone 1 down," a fixer said needlessly. Another went out. "Drone 3 down, too."

"Evade," he ordered, and the main plot showed the two remaining drones turn on wildly different courses. The images from one showed the unmistakable image of a laser, which narrowly missed. "Keep them back and run a circuit so we can plot out the LZ." He looked at the factor, who was grumbling under his breath. "You, shut up."

"S-sorry, Commander."

The map slowly built up as the drones circled the area when the targets dropped below radar. Sensors were picking up metallic signatures and medium to high energy readings, which would make sense if the enemy had brought lasers down with them. In a minute they'd mapped the alien LZ out, but it wasn't enough.

"Can we get a satellite view?" he asked a fixer.

"They were all in power-down mode when the invasion began. Bringing them online will risk them."

"We have four with a view of the area, yes?"

"Yes, Commander."

"Activate one and get as much intel as you can, as fast as you can."

Several fixers reconfigured slates and prepared to recon. They knew their jobs well and coordinated perfectly. When the satellite was woken up, data flowed in. It survived 29 seconds before a laser from the enemy frigate fried it. He didn't have to look at the factor to know they were responsible for the satellites, which were existing infrastructure.

"Show me an image as soon as you can."

"On the main screen." The big wall-sized Tri-V lit up with a 3-D construct of the plain. Dozens of smoldering impacts pockmarked the grasslands, impact points for whatever had been dropped. They were interesting, but nothing compared to the huge metallic shapes moving about the LZ, setting up a static defense.

"What are those?" Skep asked, pointing. "Combat armor? It's so bulky."

"I've never seen anything like it," Teik said. "Get the planners to start going over the GalNet for any matches. For now, muster four squads and APCs for an assault."

"Wouldn't it be better to wait?" Skep asked. Teik gave him a critical look. "Just until we know what those are."

"They're getting ready for another wave," Teik said. "Go, bloody their noses. Destroy them if possible. Quickly."

"So it shall be."

* * *

Skep raced out of the main barracks motor pool with a pair of their hover APCs. The lightly armored transports skimmed at 200 kph. With little to no obstructions on the plains, they made top speed. He'd taken three squads of stormers and a squad of fighters. It was a classic force distribution designed to overwhelm enemy positions in a rapidly moving wave. The stormers would close to hand-to-hand, killing indiscriminately. The fighters came in behind and cleaned up any survivors.

Two more expensive drones rode with the assault force and were released when they were a kilometer out. Seconds later, the APC grounded and disgorged their forces. They deployed in two waves in squad strength, all stormers. The young Aposo had just enough training to use their weapons, but not enough to switch or reload. Most wouldn't live long enough to matter. It was a tactic intended to swarm a static defense, and it had worked perfectly a thousand times in the past.

Only Tortantula used similar tactics, though with considerably less subtlety. Their frontline troopers were released by the hundreds of thousands to slaughter indiscriminately. Anything before them would be killed in an orgy of blood and violence. Aposo stormers were a blunt weapon because they were indiscriminate. That was why shooters and fighters were sent along, to guide them.

Moving in formation, Skep took command of the fighters as they ran, just a hundred meters behind the stormers. The two new drones moved in behind the advancing force to observe the battle. Teik would record everything. They'd learn quite a bit from the slaughter of the Humans. The fixers had confirmed there was nothing like what the simians were using in the databases.

"Won't matter," Teik said. "We'll figure it out from the pieces left after we kill them all."

They had good telemetry from the combination of four drones building a virtual battlespace. Teik could watch in his pinplants, but because only a few of them had the brain implants, the command center's Tri-V was showing the battle.

"They aren't coming out to meet us," a planner said. "Fools."

Teik nodded. He'd expected the Humans to rush out and meet their Aposo attackers head on. Without improved fortifications, letting the enemy into your midst was suicide, especially Aposo, who like to engage hand-to-hand. The lead element of their stormers were about to reach the enemy. *Here we go.*

One of the two drones was with the stormers as they rushed into the enemy LZ, so Teik had a front row seat to the slaughter. Lasers flashed, and heavy weapons cracked. "Those are magnetic accelerator cannons," a planner said in disbelief. The drone only survived a few seconds longer than the 20 stormers, which wasn't long at all. They were, however, treated to the first closeups of the alien's armor.

"It's powered armor," Teik said. He hadn't thought it possible that the Humans had powered armor. Horribly expensive, complicated, and difficult to train your troopers on. He'd been pretty sure the only race who used it was the KzSha. They were an insectoid race who used their powered armor for multiple-environment contacts. He activated his comms link to Skep.

"Withdraw, it's powered armor. Your first squad of skirmishers were wiped out."

"We can flank," Skep said. "Did the enemy take any losses?"

"None," Teik replied. "Withdraw."

"Pulling back, stormers covering our retreat."

Teik could tell even through the pinplants that Skep was mad about retreating. It wasn't the Aposo way. Only you didn't assault a reinforced position, and the amount of fire coming from the Human powered armor was staggering.

The armor was powerful and probably provided impressive protection. It would also be slow and cumbersome. Once Skep fell back, Teik would take four more squads, and they'd attack the Humans from multiple flanks at the same time. It would chew up a lot of stormers, but that's what they were for.

The flanking drones from their positions at maximum range picked up strange bursts of fire. Teik took control, moved one of them in closer, and watched in horror as the hulking combat armor *flew across the sky*! He estimated their flight speed at 150 kph using a parabolic arc a half kilometer long. More of a jump than flying.

Regardless of how it worked, the Human combat armor caught up to and fell in the midst of Skep's retreating forces in seconds. Skep linked his pinplants to the data feed, letting Teik watch everything. The two remaining drones were too far away to get detailed views of the fight. The outcome was brutally fast; Skep's forces were completely wiped out.

The command center was deathly silent. Teik used his pinplants to rerun and correlate data from the drones and his former XO's pinplants. It was a disjointed mess. For the first time Teik had a sense of what it would feel like to be on the other side of an Aposo stormer attack.

He learned a lot of details about the armor, such as height, mass, and mobility. They were shockingly dexterous and responded fairly quickly. Not as fast as his stormers, of course. There were several images of a stormer on the back of an armored Human. The stormer was using his teeth to tear at the exposed joints, power lines, attached equipment, or anything they could find. He could see they were inflicting damage, too.

The problem was, the Humans worked well together. They quickly came to support a besieged trooper using mechanical hands and small chainguns to kill stormers. The armor was impervious to the small arms, which Teik also saw. The only thing that hurt them was lasers, and he couldn't tell how well the handheld lasers did. There simply wasn't enough footage to judge.

The last bit he got was Skep's end. One of the enemy powered armor suits produced a long blade from one arm and ended his XO's life in an efficient manner. *Entropy, this is bad.*

"I want a missile strike," he ordered. For a change, the factor didn't react. He'd watched the slaughter as well and knew what it meant. The fixers programmed the missiles, and they launched seconds later. The batteries were located on the top of the mountain, above where the command bunker was located. Teik could hear the distant echoing of the missiles leaving their tubes; the sound carried through the tunnels leading to the surface.

Once again he only had two drones to watch the results. The Humans used their jumping ability to clear the target area before the missiles arrived. They also used small lasers mounted on one or more of the units to shoot down several of the weapons. From what he could see, none of them scored a hit. *Entropy.*

"Enemy dropships inbound. Another launch is underway."

How many of these suits do they have? This time it was weapons, not powered armor. Small autonomous missiles homed in on the bunker antenna and ground fire systems. In minutes, they were blind.

"Prepare all forces for assault. They'll be coming."

* * *

Chapter 7

With the lowborn moved into the bunker's storage areas, it was crowded. The worse part was the shuttles. There was no way to protect them. Teik left them secured on the runway up on the surface. By the time he had the lowborn out of the surface installation, enemy drones were scouting their perimeter.

He didn't have time to give a new XO any thought. There were only two planners left, and he didn't think either were capable of the job. Lashku was reduced in force by 20% from one engagement. If he didn't play it right, there would be no need to promote anyone. Once they were set, he met with the leaders of each squad.

"The Humans have powered armor. They're formidable. They've taken out our static defenses, and face to face inflicted heavy casualties. Now when they attack the facility, we'll turn it on them. They dealt with a head-on assault; we'll see how they handle an encircling attack."

He set the most experienced fighter in charge of each of the six remaining squads of stormers, and the two planners along with himself to lead the last three squads of fighters. The APCs arrived back just in time to take cover inside the armored hangars before indirect rocket bombardment. Teik didn't care about it. They were targeting the defensive facilities, obviously wanting to spare any useful planetary infrastructure.

While the ship the Humans had arrived in was an unknown design, it was a frigate class, which meant extremely limited space for a ground force. After the initial landing of armor, then the dropship's second run with missiles, Teik sent scouts into the mountains to observe. The Human dropships landed almost directly next to the Aposo shuttles and disembarked more troopers, though not in armor.

"So they have a limited number of their entropy-cursed armor, good."

The scouts counted 11 powered armor suits, which—based on the recording of the earlier fight—meant one was missing. Unarmored fighters were another 40. He had numerical superiority of three to one. It would be more than enough.

His plan was simple; he'd take the three squads of fighters and move around to flank. Once in position, the stormers would rush out to a full-frontal attack. When the enemy was occupied, he'd take the fighters to land, drive into their midst, and defeat them in short order. They only had the three heavy laser rifles, so he issued them to the two planners running squads of fighters and himself. If the stormers hadn't cracked the powered armor, the laser rifles would.

He'd just set out with the fighters when his pinplant comms signaled. He activated it.

"Commander Teik." It was the Zuparti F'slan.

"What do you want, I am busy."

"We've negotiated a settlement. Cease hostilities."

Teik was stunned and didn't immediately respond. "You can't do that," he finally responded.

"It's in the contract," F'slan replied immediately.

Teik called a halt to all forces. Luckily the stormers hadn't yet set out. He used his pinplants to call the factor.

"What's this Zuparti Kafu talking about?"

"I'm checking, Commander," the factor replied. He was on the command channel so he'd heard F'slan's comm at the same time. "Yes, there's a negotiated truce clause at the end of the contract."

"You're serious?"

"I would never be anything but serious with you, Commander."

"You reviewed this contract before Kloot signed it?" Teik knew the factor had, just as he had. Teik had read it as an XO would read it, with the concern about combat requirements, adversaries, time of service, victory conditions, and he'd noted his problems. What he hadn't read was the add-on clauses. Like most Mercenary Guild contracts, there could be thousands of them.

He wanted to have the APC take him back to the base and kill the factor. It would provide some degree of satisfaction, at least. Was it the factor's fault? Yes and no. Would it fix the problem? No, and he'd then be without the factor. Plus, when they got home, he'd have to explain why he'd killed the factor and request a new one.

"There's an exclusion," the factor said.

"I'm listening."

"Sub-clause 5 of clause 33, being the negotiated settlement clause, states no retreat in the face of substantial losses."

"We only lost four squads," Teik reminded the factor.

"Four squads out of thirteen, which is 30.7 percent. The sub-clause states we can't be forced into retreat or surrender if we've sustained more than 30 percent combat losses."

"Is this negotiated peace under such a case?"

"It's not specific, and neither is merc law. Thus, without precedent, as Commander you can proceed based on your judgement."

"Your diligence is noted, factor."

"Thank you, commander."

"F'slan."

"I've been trying to get your confirmation of stand-down!" the Zuparti nearly screamed over the comms.

"As commander of Lashku, I, Commander Teik, exercise subclause 5 of clause 33. We've taken 30.7 percent losses in combat against the enemy. I refuse to stand down."

"You...you..." the Zuparti spluttered, "...you can't do that!"

"I'll contact you after the battle is over." Teik cut the comms and smiled. "Proceed with the attack as planned."

* * *

He knew the stormers had attacked by the boom and clash of fighting. "Take us right up to their perimeter," he told the APC driver. "Use your weapon to support us once we've engaged." Their APCs weren't heavily armed or armored, but he wanted every edge he could get.

Seconds before they would have stopped to unload, a MAC round punched through the APC. It started through the driver, then the weapon operator, and continued through four of Teik's fighters before exiting the rear loading door. Luckily, the hovercraft APC was already slowing as it immediately nosed into the ground, flipped twice, and came to rest on its roof.

"Get out!" Teik yelled at his fighters, unstrapping and smacking heads indiscriminately. Some moved, some didn't. "Get out! Move, you worthless dregs!" Someone reached the controls of the rear door and blew the explosive bolts, letting the armored ramp fall away and allowing Taluu's sunlight to flood in.

Teik did what any good commander did, he kicked every ass he could to force anyone alive out of the APC. They'd been overcrowded; each APC was only designed to hold a squad, and they'd held one and a half apiece. The overcrowding might have saved a few fighters, though it also had probably increased minor injuries, because everyone hadn't been strapped in. Strapping in on a hover APC was highly advisable.

As he was the last to clear the APC, he tallied five dead, three more too severely injured to be combat effective, and another 10 with minor injuries. Clearly the enemy knew they were there.

"Everyone, form up," he yelled. His fighters gathered behind the stricken APC. Not far away the other hover APC had taken fire as well, though it had successfully landed without the results his had suffered. The turret on the craft's upper deck was firing its ballistic chaingun, and fighters poured out of the crew compartment. "Move, squad, prepare to advance!"

In the near distance toward the enemy position an explosion echoed, and he heard alien screams. A smile crossed his face. The stormers were tasting blood. *Good.* "Ready!" He waited another second to be sure. "Go!" They came around the APC in a rush, Teik urging them around until they were all gone, then he fell in behind to push them onward. Just as was passing the front of his wrecked APC, it took another MAC round and turned into a fireball. He was blown high into the air, and then the ground came up to meet him.

* * *

Chapter 8

Teik came back to his senses in their base's small medical center under the mountain. One of the creche mothers was tending to a bandage on his arm. "How did I get back here?" he demanded.

"Highborn," she squeaked and jumped. "I didn't know you were awake!"

"Answer the question." Teik reached up and felt his head; there were thick bandages.

"T-they brought you."

"They who? Make sense, female."

"I had you brought back."

The voice was obviously through a translator. Teik's head tracked the voice and he saw a Human standing behind the creche mother. She retreated away from the towering simian, head lowered in the same sort of submissive gesture she would have reserved for him. The meaning was obvious.

"We lost," Teik said, giving voice to what he knew.

"Yes," the Human said. "Your troops put up quite a fight."

"They're all dead?" Teik asked.

"The crazy ones that came in first, yes. Of the others, about half are dead. We saved as many as we could." The Human came closer and looked down at Teik. It was so incredibly ugly, with its flat, hairless face and big, colored eyes. This Human had greenish eyes.

"Are you Caudill?"

"That's me. Colonel Tim Caudill. I already know you're Teik."

"How many did we kill?"

"Of my people? Eleven."

"The armor?"

The Human's big, expressive eyes narrowed in a meaning Teik didn't understand before answering. "Two."

Over a hundred Aposo dead, and only two of the powered armor suits brought down. "I fought you when I was younger, years ago. You didn't have this armor then. We tore you up easily."

"Humans lost to you aliens more often than not. The original four merc units who survived years ago developed them. We call it a CASPer, which stands for Combat Assault System, Personal. This is the Mk 4; we just got them a month ago. They've really worked out the kinks." His strange face curled, and blunt teeth became visible in what Teik guessed was a smile. "They level the playing field pretty well, wouldn't you say?"

Teik didn't feel like answering the question, so instead asked his own. "What's to happen to me and the remains of my company? Aposo don't pay ransom."

"We're letting you evacuate with your surviving personnel and equipment. That was part of the terms agreed upon with the Zuparti before you…decided to fight."

Teik blinked, whiskers twitching in confusion. "We never accepted the offer. We exercised a clause that allowed us to fight."

"The Zuparti explained this."

"Then why still allow us to leave?"

The Human made a series of yipping barks and *smiled* again. "Because that's how we are. Your people are already loading the shuttles. We unloaded all your weapons, of course. You guys just like to fight a little too much. Farewell, Commander Teik. Maybe we'll meet again someday."

Teik watched him go and hoped he never saw another Human ever again.

* * * * *

Mark Wandrey Bio

Living life as a full-time RV traveler with his wife Joy, Mark Wandrey is a bestselling author who has been creating new worlds since he was old enough to write. A three-time Dragon Award finalist, Mark has written dozens of books and short stories, and is working on more all the time. A prolific world builder, he created the wildly popular Four Horsemen Universe as well as the Earth Song series and Turning Point, a zombie apocalypse series. His favorite medium is military sci-fi, but he is always up to a new challenge.

Sign up on his mailing list and get free stuff and updates! http://www.worldmaker.us/news-flash-sign-up-page/

# # # # #

Roland the Headless Mech Driver by William Alan Webb

Winston Cromwell dove forward a microsecond before a laser cut through the space where his chest had been. Coming out of a roll, he jumped straight up, bringing his legs high as another beam cut the ground beneath him. When he landed, he immediately leapt up again, avoiding a second laser pulse in the same spot. Once down again, he flattened to avoid a beam that came in a foot off the heat-resistant artificial turf. Back on his feet, he ran three steps before a laser beam struck him from above, and the training exoskeleton locked up, sending him crashing to the floor.

"Shit!" he yelled as pain shot through his shoulder. Not from the laser, its intensity wasn't high enough to cause actual damage, but from the force of falling without being able to brace himself. The exoskeleton absorbed most of the impact, though, which meant it only hurt like hell and didn't cause any real damage.

Master Sergeant Rambahadur Limbu, universally known simply as Ramba, bent down to the paralyzed trainee with a concerned look and sympathetic voice. "Does it hurt? Do you need a medic?"

Cromwell clenched his teeth against the fire that had spread from his shoulder to his neck and into the back of his head. "No, Master Sergeant, I'll be fine."

"Are you sure? That was a pretty hard fall."

"I'm sure, Master Sergeant Ramba. I'm fine."

"You're being very brave," Ramba said, "but I don't think you're fine," His voice dropped even lower. "Do you know why I say that?" Ramba moved his mouth within inches of Cromwell's right ear, and screamed so loud his already dark face turned deep red. "Because you're dead!"

Even though they stood on the sidelines, the other five CASPer trainees jumped from the sheer volume of his scream. Cromwell watched them and cursed himself for putting them through all this yet again. Ramba's yell left him so temporarily deafened that he struggled to hear what came next.

"You people are still thinking in two dimensions! How many times have I told you that modern combat takes place on a three-dimensional battlefield? If your objective is to die, then you're doing a great job of learning how, but if you want to *live* to fulfill your contract and get paid, you'd better starting using your head for something besides a place to shove food."

Hands on hips, the diminutive Gurkha studied his cadets as if daring them to argue with him. They had all snapped to attention, though he hadn't told them to. He inspected them through narrowed eyes, and a nod let them know he was satisfied they'd heard him. He pushed a red reset button on his belt, and Cromwell's XTS-4, Exo-Training Skeleton 4, unlocked so Ramba could pull him to his feet. The XTS-4 was Ramba's own design, and he was hoping to sell it to other training schools and Mercenary outfits. Ramba braced the cadet with a hand on each of Cromwell's arms, and they locked eyes.

"You have a real aptitude for merc work," Ramba said to him in a near whisper. "But your mind is holding you back." He then spun and raised his voice so they could all hear him. "Every one of you is too deep in what you believe to be reality, but when dealing with alien species, you'll find their reality isn't the same as yours. To survive, you have to believe in the possibility of the impossible…never take anything for granted, and never be shocked by anything that happens."

Cromwell and the five other cadets all nodded as if that made sense.

* * *

Ramba came into the men's locker room after they'd all showered and put on clean clothes. Cromwell had his leg on a bench, adjusting the thigh holster that held his old-style 9mm pistol. A flechette gun already hung in a shoulder holster, with a US Marine Ka-Bar knife in its sheath hanging from his belt on his left hip.

"Are you expecting to run into a squad of Besquith?" Ramba said, grinning.

Cromwell wasn't sure what to say; Ramba had never joked with them before.

"Can't be too careful, Master Sergeant."

"What about you boys?" Ramba said, turning to the other two cadet privates in the locker room, Shapiro and Vasquez. "You strapped, too?"

"Uh, no, Master Sergeant."

"You're too tough to worry about some punks on the street, right?"

"Something like that."

Ramba shook his head and unzipped his jacket to show a sidearm on his left hip. "Then you're tougher than me. I always carry. So who wants to be first to buy me a beer?"

They all chimed in, with variations on "you bet" and "sure thing."

"Just let me get my handgun," Shapiro said.

"Meet up in the lobby. I'll ask the ladies to come along, too."

* * *

Mad Otto's might have been a dive bar, but it was a merc dive bar. It was in an abandoned industrial area of Houston, not far from the starport, and nearly all of its clientele were mercs or former mercs. Whether retired by choice, medically retired because they were too wounded for even the nanites to fix, too old, too crazy, too rich, or just tired of the lifestyle, Otto's was a place you went to hear stories from mercs who'd been there, done that, and lived to get the t-shirt. There were usually plenty of working mercs, too, but that particular night, every company with offices in the Houston area was deployed to the max. Even the small companies were somewhere out in space, getting rich or getting killed, which left only the former mercs to tell each other stories they'd all heard a hundred times before. The only difference that night was Ramba's six 'wildebeests,' local slang for mercs-in-training, i.e. fresh meat.

Cromwell was first behind Ramba through the sliding steel front door, like a puppy on the heels of its owner. Cromwell expressed relief they'd made it without being accosted, only for Ramba to scoff that most thieves weren't complete idiots.

"Otto's is a merc bar," he said. "If they were really stupid enough to accost a party of mercs, they'd at least wait 'til you're drunk and can't react as fast. Otherwise it'd just be suicide-by-merc."

"Is that a thing?" asked one of the other trainees, a petite redhead named Gloria Jane Numis. "Is that like suicide-by-cop?"

Ramba rolled his eyes. Her application said she was twenty-one, but she looked about fifteen to him. Had he really been that young once? "It's a good thing your reflexes are upper half of the charts, Numis. Otherwise you'd have already washed out."

On the way over, Ramba had cautioned them what to expect. The cadets expected a loud, boisterous bar, filled with once highly-paid men and women who'd survived their last contract and drank to both celebrate still being alive and to salute lost friends. Either was a great reason to drink, after all.

"I called to let Otto know we were coming," Ramba said, "so we'd be sure to get a table, but every merc who can walk is off-planet right now, and he said the place is only half full. That's good for you people, though; old mercs love to tell stories to Wildebeests, and all it costs you is the price of a drink or five."

They were close to Otto's when Ramba spoke again. "One more thing…you might think this is stupid, but don't say that once we're inside. A lot of these mercs believe Otto's is haunted."

"Haunted?" Cromwell asked, laughing. "They really believe that?"

Ramba nodded. "Yeah, they do. Mercs can be very superstitious, and they don't like Wildebeests who haven't gotten hired on yet laughing about it. Understand?"

The cadets all said, "Yes," though four of them did so through a smirk.

* * *

Ramba watched their faces as the six cadets stood in the entrance looking around. Most of the patrons were Humans, spread out in a large, wooden-floored common room with an old style bar to the right. Then the cadets spotted the hulking form of Kaffnar, the bouncer, sitting on his haunches in a dark alcove. All six stopped in their tracks, gaping.

"Hey," Ramba said. "That's rude. Haven't you ever seen a Jivool before?"

"Not in person," Numis answered. The rest of them nodded in agreement.

"Well stop gawking; Kaffnar's a friend of mine, and it's embarrassing. Now I've gotta go apologize."

* * *

Ramba stepped close to the burly, bear-like Jivool and leaned in close so Kaffnar could understand his whisper.

"Is he ready?" Ramba said.

The Jivool spoke English, but his accent was too thick to understand when he whispered, so instead he spoke his native language through the universal translator and turned the volume down.

"Champing at the bit."

* * *

Once Ramba rejoined them, they hadn't moved four feet before Otto's head popped up from behind the bar, and the cadets stopped again with mouths open.

"Greetings, Ramba!" Otto said. Otto didn't need a translator to speak English, although his accent made some of the more guttural words hard to understand. The sounds of 'g,' in particular, had a growling undercurrent. "It's good to see you again."

"Greetings, friend Otto! Please forgive my cadets, it appears they've seen neither a Jivool nor a Cochkala before."

"Then I'm pleased to be their first, and I hope I represent my race well. I have the table you requested ready. I believe you know its location."

"I do. Could you bring four pitchers to start, with eight glasses? Put it on Cromwell here's Yack."

"It's my pleasure," the lanky, badger-like Otto said, holding out a paw for Cromwell's Yack. The cadet had a stunned look, like somebody had clocked him with a hammer, as he handed over the device.

* * *

Cromwell wasn't happy about buying the first round. His credit account was already low from the tuition at Ramba's Mercenary Factory, the training academy they all attended. Nor had he yet bought food for the week. Paying everybody's beer tab nearly emptied his account. So when he rejoined the group, he was determined to drink his share and then some.

The table had eight chairs in the center of the room. Directly over the table hung a square chandelier made from two over-the-shoulder M2 fifty-caliber machine guns off a CASPer Mk 3, and two 10mm auto-cannons from a CASPer Mk 4, arranged in a square pattern, with recessed lighting on all sides. Ramba sat at one end of the table and told the six trainees to sit in the middle chairs, leaving the one at the far end empty. When Otto brought the pitchers of beer, he placed a glass in front of the empty seat.

"Are we expecting somebody?" Shapiro asked.

"I wouldn't be surprised," Ramba answered. "See, it's an Otto's tradition that an empty chair with a glass is an open invitation for somebody to come by and shoot the shit. You six are getting close to graduation, so I thought you might want to hear war stories from somebody other than me."

They had all barely poured themselves a first mug of beer when a lean man with iron gray hair and a scarred face sat down in the empty seat. Pushing away the mug provided for him, he lifted the nearest pitcher and drank from it instead.

"Good stuff," he said, smacking his lips. Some sort of accent flavored his speech. "Thank you, girls and boys."

They all assured him it was no problem, all except Cromwell, who was the only one actually paying anything.

Ramba laughed. "Ladies and gentlemen, allow me to introduce Spokelse, the only Norwegian merc I've ever known. And the best."

Spokelse bowed his head, and Cromwell noticed that it wobbled, as if the man's neck muscles couldn't quite hold it in place. It was only after he tilted back for another draught of the pitcher that they all saw the thick line of scar tissue circling his neck.

"*Takk Gutten*," Spokelse said in reply. Cromwell was surprised that his accent wasn't thicker. "Thank you, lad, but I daresay I'm not the best Norwegian merc to come along. That honor would go to my dear friend Roland Sigurdsson, may he rest forever in a bar where the beer is free and never runs out."

Ramba nodded. "I never met Roland, but I've heard bits and pieces."

"Ya mean ya haven't heard the tale?"

"No. Have any of you?" Ramba said, looking at the cadets, who all shook their heads. "I guess we haven't. Do you have time to tell us?"

"I've got a lot more time than money. If ya want me to, I'll stay as long as there's beer to drink. Is that alright with you folks?" He looked at the cadets when he said it. They all assured him he could drink as much as he wanted. "Well then, ladies and gents, fill your glasses and settle back to hear the story of Roland the Headless Mech Driver. It all started about thirty years ago, when Mk 6s were still front-line mechs, but 7s were the new hot shit…"

* * *

Roland Sigurdsson heard the rumble of thunder even inside the office building and wondered if there was something significant about the weather. He'd studied the mythology of his Viking ancestors, who would have seen the hand of Thor in the thunder snowstorm raking Copenhagen. As much as he considered himself a modern man, some deeply ingrained remnant of his people's collective memory wondered if the weather wasn't an omen of things to come.

"Sigurdsson?" asked a man missing his left ear and leg.

"Here."

Using his index finger, the scarred merc, because what else could he be, motioned for Roland to follow. He rose and matched the man's pace down a long hallway, surprised at his speed using an artificial leg. At a nondescript office door, the merc knocked twice and opened it without waiting for permission.

"Sigurdsson," he said to whoever was inside. Seconds later, he pointed to the single chair positioned in front of a large, old style desk, where a burly, bearded man sat reading a slate. The chair appeared comfortable enough, with burnished red leather upholstery, but when Roland sat down, he found it hard and unyielding.

"I'm Colonel Dieter van Owen," the man behind the desk said, glancing up from his slate. He wasted no time shaking Roland's hand or getting to know him. "My company is called Triple-A Temporary Volunteers. We supply over-stretched merc companies with short-term replacements, who may or may not work themselves into a full-time job. Right now this planet is devoid of mercs because of an unusual surge in contracts, so we have openings. Even better, we have a contract for a simple escort operation, so you'll be getting experience right away. Now, I see here you did your initial training on CASPer Mk 6s; do you still remember how to operate one?"

"Like riding a bike, Colonel," Roland said. He saw no need to mention that, while he'd taken a course on operating Mk 7s, he'd never actually done it.

"Notes from your training instructor say you're the most natural mech driver he's ever come across, that you operate a CASPer by instinct more than sensory input. Is that accurate?"

"I don't know how to answer that, sir. When I'm in a CASPer I just...I just *do* things. It does seem like whenever the suit tells me something, I already know it, and the data is more of a confirmation of actions I've already taken."

"Remarkable," van Owen said. "You're hired."

"Just like that?"

"Is there a reason not to hire you that doesn't appear in your file?"

"Uh...no sir."

"Do you want the job?"

"Yes, very much!"

"Do you understand that our CASPers have all been salvaged, as it says in your sample contract?"

"Uhh...yes. *Sir*!"

"And that in the event of your death during the execution of a contract, our only obligation is to transport your body home, if possible, and to provide 500 credits to your heirs, or to the government body responsible for burying your remains?"

"Roger that, Colonel."

"Then if you already knew all that, you've just wasted thirty seconds of my time! Don't do it again. Sergeant Mistalovich will lead you to the assembly area."

* * *

Spokelse took a long drink from the pitcher and drained half before setting it back down. Beer ran down his chin, which he wiped on the sleeve of his denim jacket.

"I'd known Roland a long time by then, but that's when everybody else first met him, in the cafeteria of this old office building in Denmark that was being used as an assembly area for Triple-A Temps. At the first instant, they all knew there was something different about him. It was this feeling he gave off, like he was more than just another merc. I never talked to anybody who didn't feel that way about him. It was like this aura."

The battered old man, that's how Cromwell thought of him even though he couldn't have been much past sixty, tilted his head way back to drain the last of the pitcher. When he did so, Cromwell saw a ring of thick, dark pink scar tissue around his neck. At some point the man's throat must have been slit. Surviving a wound like that required the immediate use of multiple nanite injections. Whatever had happened, Spokelse was lucky to be alive.

"Triple-A had recruited a platoon, and everybody grew close, real quick like. Ramba here knows what I mean…when you go into training for real, your life depends on everybody else around you. Roland was the youngest, but it weren't long before he got recognized as the best driver in the platoon. Better even than Colonel van Owen or the noncoms."

"How'd the Colonel feel about that?" Cromwell asked.

Spokelse leaned back and waved for another pitcher. The others were on their second beers. "If you're gonna be a merc, ya gotta learn to drink like one." They all took the hint and drained their mugs.

Otto glided over with two more brimming pitchers, using his fluid gait and rock-steady hands not to spill a drop, unlike a Human waiter, who surely would have slopped some of the liquid onto the floor. Using his long tail, Otto refilled the other glasses from one of the other three pitchers, emptying it.

"Shall I bring you another?" he said to Spokelse, despite there being two other half-filled pitchers.

"I'd say so!" the grizzled merc answered before Cromwell could say "No!" then he drained a quarter of his pitcher in one pull.

"Now where were we?"

Cromwell had pulled out a slate and punched in some numbers. At Spokelse's question, he answered quickly. "You mean before emptying my credit account?"

"For a good cause, my lad, for a good cause! Beer is never the wrong choice for spending your last credit."

"You were telling us about the platoon," Ramba said.

"Oh, right. Well let me tell ya, for being such an inexperienced bunch, the platoon learned fast how to do our jobs, and Roland, he learned faster than anybody. It was like he'd been born inside a Mk 6. He was the youngest of the lot, but he got promoted to corporal almost right off. As good as he was with the mech, though, he was even better at reading people. It was him who first had doubts about Colonel van Owen.

"The trouble didn't start right away. The platoon landed on this swampy shit-hole of a planet…I'm not sure anybody ever knew its name. The contract was a simple escort mission. It didn't pay much, but rookie mercs need experience as much or more than money. See, everybody knew that when the merc companies came home, they'd need some new recruits—"

"Because of casualties," Shapiro said, interrupting.

Spokelse squinted and laid the sarcasm on thick. "When your business involves things that blow up, yeah, there's gonna be people who don't make it home. It's kinda part of the job description, ya know? So everybody needed experience and believed van Owen when he said he had contacts with the Horsemen and could get those who performed well an interview once the contract was paid. All rookies are young and stupid, so everybody believed him…nobody was suspicious at all, except for Roland. He had a feeling something weren't right."

"Did he say why he felt that way?" Ramba asked.

"No, not right away, he didn't. It was all right there for anybody to see in the contract with Triple-A, but only he figured out what it meant. And even Roland didn't see it right off." Spokelse raised his right hand in a 'stop' motion. "But let's get to that when it comes up, and get on with our story…"

* * *

Few roads through the swamp allowed for the use of heavy trucks, but they were necessary, because the cargo the platoon escorted was uranium. The mines were in a series of low hills surrounded by sixty miles of deep, tree-lined muck. The truck's shielding only added weight to an already heavy metal, so the trucks frequently got stuck. The road was paved, but narrow, constantly slick with mud or water from the incessant rain, and the road's surface tended to buckle under such a load. Trucks proceeded at a creeping speed, and still slid off the shoulder multiple times per mile, or got stuck in sinkholes. Since the Triple-A mercs only got paid when the convoy arrived safely at the mobile processing plant, and none of the Humans wanted to stay on-planet longer than absolutely necessary, that led to them using their CASPers to push the vehicles back onto the road or pull them out of craters.

The last thing any of them wanted was a uranium spill. Colonel van Owen bitched about any delays though, and constantly urged the drivers to go faster. He finally became so obnoxious that the leader of the drivers told him they weren't part of his contract, they weren't under his command, and he could fuck off. They'd do it the safe way or not at all. Van Owen backed off, but he wasn't happy.

"Hey, Top, what's the hurry?" Roland said over the inter-squad net on the second day of the planned three-day move to the refinery. "I've only been here two days, and I already know the faster we try to move, the slower we go."

First Sergeant Allison Kovak was one of the few veterans along for the mission. Roland couldn't see her inside the CASPer, but if a voice ever sounded like somebody was shaking their head, it was hers.

"Ours not to question why, Corporal Sigurdsson…ours but to do and get paid."

He laughed, but it sounded hollow even to him. "I like that better than the original."

"I doubt Kipling would understand mercs."

Roland tilted his head like a German Shepherd, although inside the mech nobody else could see it.

"Who's Kipling?"

"Never mind," Kovak said.

During their short escort mission, Roland received a number of compliments from his fellow noncoms, to the point the privates all joked that he must be blowing them during downtime, the females included. At least five times a truck cracked the roadbed and started toppling, but Roland reacted so fast, he prevented all of them. Even the taciturn Master Sergeant Henrik grunted he'd never seen a Mk 6 move so fast or so efficiently, and Henrik was a genuine asshole. Getting praise from him was thought to be impossible.

The trek took four days, not three, because the weight of the CASPers, combined with a convoy of trucks filled with the heaviest metal known to humanity, uranium, left the primitive roadway in shambles. Instead of jumpjetting on a battlefield crisscrossed with laser beams and magnetic cannon rounds, the platoon might as well have been digging ditches. Fortunately for them, all it would say on a resume was *escorted a high-value convoy four days through potentially hostile territory without loss.*

But like all military and para-military units throughout history, and regardless of circumstances, the Triple-A rookies complained about everything. The food was bad, the hours were too long, their

CASPer chaffed…on the fourth day, with the mobile processing plant less than five miles away, Top Sergeant Kovak had heard enough.

"Quit'cher bitchin', people! You're getting paid for what's essentially an on-the-job training mission. Nobody's trying to kill you, and based on what I've seen in the last four days, with some of you that wouldn't be too hard."

"Great feats are performed not by strength, but by perseverance," chimed in Private Numis.

"What the fuck does that mean?" Kovak said.

"No idea, Top, I just like the way it sounded."

A fifty-foot-high steel wall surrounded the mobile processing plant, with main gates wide enough for the trucks to pass through. Interspersed with auto-cannon mounted at regular intervals along the perimeter were anti-aircraft laser and missile batteries. Anybody and anything that assaulted the plant was going to pay heavily for doing so.

A landing area stood just outside the walled perimeter, surrounded by hangars large enough to service surface-to-orbit shuttlecraft. One such building was provided to the Triple-A platoon so they could get out of their CASPers and await transport back to Earth, scheduled for the next morning.

The contract paid 300,000 credits, but each person's share was below standard rates, except the two veteran non-coms, Kovak and the surly Master Sergeant Henrik. For the rest, it was the first time being paid for merc work. They all looked forward to seeing the credits appear in their accounts, but Colonel van Owen cautioned them.

"The contract isn't finalized yet," he said when some of them wondered why they hadn't yet been paid. "First, our employers have to randomly sample ore from each truck to make sure nothing got switched out along the way."

"How long will that take?" Roland said. Some instinct raised the hair on the back of his neck. Others backed up his question with cries of agreement.

Van Owen waved away their concerns. "Overnight, no more. We'll get paid before we lift off. What would you spend it on tonight, anyway?"

That's not the point, Roland thought, but didn't say. The colonel hadn't spent much time among the rank and file, but that night he arranged for a hot meal, which was a welcome change from field rations. He even passed around several bottles of Tennessee whiskey, which grew in value the further you went from Earth. It wasn't worth the same as F-11, but it wasn't all that far off, either. The colonel stood by to make sure that every merc got a hit from the whiskey. Even if they didn't usually drink, he was insistent. It was a bonding experience, he said. So with bellies full of food and alcohol, and absolutely nothing else to do, the platoon went to sleep early, and before long, snores filled the vastness of the hangar.

All except for Roland. He ate his fill along with the rest of them, but refused the whiskey bottle when it was passed to him. Instinct warned him not to drink. After the colonel insisted, he tilted the bottle and pretended to swallow while his lips were actually closed. That satisfied Colonel van Owen. When nobody could see him, Roland wiped his lips on his sleeve.

They set no watches, since the colonel assured them they were safer than back on Earth. The hangar nearly abutted the perimeter wall, after all, and the processing plant had some serious firepower. With no known threats and all their eyes drooping, nobody argued. Even Roland lay down to sleep, but he was pretending. Something in the back of his mind kept screaming a warning.

An hour after Colonel van Owen left, Roland slipped out of the sleeping area and climbed into his CASPer. He'd always had premonitions about things happening before they did—he called them instincts—and he'd come to trust them. If anybody asked, he'd just say, since he didn't know when he might get another CASPer, he wanted to spend as much time in the one he had as possible. It sounded lame, but plausible. The truth was different. He sensed imminent danger.

Climbing into the mech felt to Roland like going home, as if the armor was his real skin. Once powered up, he armed weapons and waited. The suit was equipped with an over-the-shoulder 20mm chain gun and snap-out arm blade, along with a holstered laser carbine for backup. It wasn't the heaviest weaponry out there, but nobody expected trouble. As quietly as possible, he moved into a tall doorway that led into the hangar where his buddies were asleep.

He waited for more than two hours and began to feel like a fool. What exactly was he worried about, anyway? Why would anybody want to attack a platoon of rookie mercs, especially after they'd fulfilled their contract? The only thing worth stealing, the uranium, was already safe. After a while Roland himself began to drowse inside his harness.

Thirty minutes later two dozen men entered the hangar, carrying laser rifles and driving a LAV—a Light Armored Vehicle—armed with a Magnetic Accelerator Cannon mounted in an open-topped turret. Darkness hid Roland's CASPer in the doorway as the intruders spread out to surround the huddled forms of the platoon, who slept on cots in the center of the hangar. The MAC-equipped vehicle slipped behind a large metal work station, so without conscious thought, he zeroed the chain-gun on a cluster of three men. It seemed like the right thing to do; if they started something, he'd finish it. But then Colonel van Owen stepped into view.

What the hell? Maybe this was some sort of test, a way to teach the new recruits a hard lesson in the field. Van Owen clearly knew what was going on, as he directed the newcomers where to go. Roland relaxed.

Until they opened fire.

For two and a half seconds, ruby-red laser beams slashed into the helpless mercs, simultaneously cutting through flesh and cauterizing the wounds. The odor of burning flesh filled the hangar as the sleeping Humans thrashed and rolled in panic. Prayers, curses, and screams echoed from the rafters. And then another sound drowned out their voices, the metallic hammer of a chain-gun firing on automatic.

The three intruders closest to Roland disappeared as 20mm rounds ripped into their bodies and exploded a tenth of a second later. At the first laser burst, he'd shut down IR on his suit's external cameras to prevent being blinded, but when he did, the world turned dark. All he could use for targets was the point where the laser beams originated.

"No!" screamed a voice over the platoon network. It was Colonel van Owen. "CASPer driver, stand down! You don't know what's going on here! Stop!"

Roland ignored him. All of his suspicions about van Owen came to the fore. Without a pause, he changed targets and mowed down another cluster of three shooters, before lasers suddenly targeted him from all directions. From that point on, too much happened too fast for him to keep track. He only picked up fleeting images in the darkness around him.

Lasers tracked him as he jumped across the hangar, scraping the ceiling's support beams at the apex of his flight path. Some hit, most missed, and only two yellow lights warned of damage. He landed behind three shooters, two of whom vanished in a mist as the chain gun vaporized them.

The third nearby shooter, however, hit a spot on the suit's left side, under the armpit, where the anti-laser reflective coating had mostly worn off. The shooter had obviously turned the power to full, because it only lasted a brief time, but it was long enough to burn through the armor to Roland's actual flesh, leaving a nasty hole in the muscle under his ribcage. A three-round burst atomized his attacker.

Mercs were on their feet now, charging the shooters or picking up rifles from the dead. The hangar became a chaotic free-for-all, with Roland being more careful when picking targets. Pain shot up his side from the laser wound even as a second laser penetrated near the same spot. That shooter paid when a cannon round took off his legs above the knees.

Then Roland staggered backward as something much heavier than a laser struck his chest. Once, twice, three times…it was like being inside a suit of medieval plate armor and getting hit with a sledge hammer. Red lights warned of multiple imminent systems failures. Roland tried to jump, but something was wrong with the jets, so he leaned sideways just as three more rounds flashed by where his right arm had been, and he saw where they came from: the MAC on the LAV. He'd forgotten all about it. Being a rookie, he'd make a rookie mistake, the one every training program harped on, but every rookie made anyway; namely, never lose track of the enemy's most powerful weapon and deal with it first.

Only two lasers targeted him. Elsewhere, a firefight between the surviving intruders and a few mercs who'd managed to arm themselves sent crisscrossing beams of light over much of the hangar. But the two aiming at him had free rein to shoot, because now Roland *had* to deal with the MAC or go down for good.

Motors whined as he tried to move laterally. He barely avoided more incoming rounds and missed with his own because of the movements. Then a low-ammo light caused him to make a desperate move. Once his chain-gun ran out, he'd be helpless against the LAV, so instead of dodging, he stood and took careful aim at the MAC. It was a crew-served weapon in an open turret, but surrounded by an armored cupola. The first couple of rounds confirmed his fear that they wouldn't penetrate the turret's armor, so he tried the only thing left. He aimed right down the barrel of the cannon itself. If he could damage that, the MAC would be useless.

The lasers had stopped targeting him; maybe the shooters were dead, or maybe just engaged with the other mercs. Regardless, it was now just him against the cannon. Setting the gun to automatic, he leaned forward to offset the recoil, and opened fire. The MAC gunners did likewise, and for what seemed like hours, but in reality was about three seconds, they traded shot for shot. MAC rounds chewed up the armor on both of his legs, his torso, and his chest. In return, his 20mm chain gun rounds splattered against the turret armor and glacis plate. Impact after impact knocked him backward and, combined with the recoil pulling at his shoulder, Roland began to topple backward.

Concentrating against the pain wracking his body and the warning lights flashing all over the control panel, one of his final three shots struck home. Some part of his overwhelmed brain realized that a round must have gone straight down the barrel before detonating. The chain reaction of explosions inside the LAV sent a fireball mushrooming high overhead. Flames licked at the high supports and caught the ceiling on fire. One of the last of his systems to shut down was the platoon comm network, which was why his fading consciousness heard the screaming voice of Colonel van Owen.

"Damn you, damn you, damn you!"

* * *

Spokelse took another long gulp from the second pitcher. Then, glancing up, he met Ramba's eyes for the merest instant, just long enough for the Gurkha merc trainer to give a short nod. Using his right foot, Spokelse felt for the latch near his chair. Once he'd found it, he waited until Ramba had distracted the rookies with some observation of his own and slid the latch aside. To his left, a grizzled old man with half his lower jaw missing pointed to a black sack at his feet. Spokelse winked. Everything was set.

Except he'd drunk more than he should have, and needed to slow down until he'd finished the story. He was already slurring a few words, and it wouldn't do to fall down and mess up the payoff; it wouldn't do at all. But it wouldn't hurt to go ahead and order another pitcher while somebody else was still paying for it, either, even if he had to wait a while to drink it.

"Otto! Another pitcher here!"

* * *

Cool night air blew over his face when Roland finally woke up. He wasn't in his CASPer anymore. In fact, judging from the stars and scudding clouds overhead, he wasn't even inside the hangar. When he tried to sit, pain radiated down his spine, into both hips, and down the back of both legs, but he fought through it until he finally sat upright. Two more of the platoon sat beside him. One was Top Sergeant Kovak, while the other was a private named Umcheki, or something like that. There hadn't been that much time to bond.

"Where's everybody else?" he asked Kovak. Pain twisted his words, so he had to repeat it before Kovak understood. She opened her mouth to respond, but was drowned out by Colonel van Owen.

"They're all dead!" His eyes slowly focused on the man squatting six feet away, too far to grab in one lunge. "Thanks to you, they're all dead!"

Behind the colonel stood six or seven dark figures he didn't recognize, and one he did; Sergeant Henrik.

"What are you talking about?" Roland said.

"I identified an imminent threat within your ranks and hired a second platoon to take out the malefactors. It was to be a surgical strike, over before they knew what hit them. We knew the position of each person in the conspiracy."

"So you arranged a hit squad for our own good?"

"Exactly."

"Bullshit," Kovak said. "Those rookies just wanted experience; they weren't plotting anything. I'd know if they were. You just murdered them. What I don't know is why."

His instincts warned Roland to shut up, but he couldn't help speaking up again. "She's right. I saw the whole thing."

Van Owen sighed, loud enough for them to hear it. His face drooped with sadness, or so Roland thought. It was very dark.

"What about you, Kumcheekwa?"

"It's Umbeckwa, and I trust Top."

"Well, that's too bad. I'm very sorry you all feel that way; I could have used you." He pointed at Roland. "You in particular, Sigurdsson. Talent like yours doesn't come along every day. Now I have to figure out what to do with you. I mean, you three murdered a lot of good people tonight. Are you absolutely positive you saw what you thought you saw?"

Roland couldn't make out his features, but there was no question the remarks were aimed primarily at him. He didn't respond, nor did his fellow prisoners.

"So be it then. You went berserk and wiped out your whole platoon as part of a conspiracy to steal the uranium for yourselves. A lot of good people died trying to stop you. If it hadn't been for the second platoon providing internal security for the processing plant, you would have gotten away with it."

"Do you expect anybody to believe that?" Roland said.

Van Owen laughed. "I don't expect anybody to *care*. But you're a waste, Roland. You're the best natural mech driver I've ever seen, you could have had a long and prosperous career working for me. One last chance to change your mind…"

"Eat shit and die."

The colonel rose and walked behind the line of riflemen. Roland didn't see him give any signal, but he must have, because seconds later seven laser beams cut down Umbeckwa and Kovak. Roland gaped at seeing his comrades sliced into pieces. As the limbs of the dead mercs twitched, Roland looked up at van Owen.

"På forfedres språk legger jeg denne forbannelsen på deg." *In the language of my forefathers, I lay upon you this curse.* "By All-Father Odin, though I be judged worthy of entering his presence, I vow not to enter Valhalla until I have avenged myself upon you and all who walk with you this day."

Van Owen had to wait a micro-second for his translator to render the Norwegian words into English. When it had done so, he smiled and shook his head.

"I like you, Roland. If I ever have a son, I want him to be just like you."

The colonel tapped Sergeant Henrik on the shoulder. The last thing Roland saw was a flash of red light.

* * *

Spokelse massaged his throat and sipped from the pitcher. Alcoholic sparkles danced across his vision, and it was difficult to keep his voice steady. What he really wanted was a glass of water, but that would wreck the illusion.

"Is that the end of the story?" Cromwell said. 'Story' came out as 'sshhtory.'

The six cadets stared at Spokelse like kids listening to a ghost story around a campfire.

"The end? No, lad, that's just the beginning. You see, Henrik didn't just shoot Roland, he burned his head off with the laser. And you know what the colonel did next?"

They all stared at him, some with drooping eyelids. As near as he might be to drunk, he'd nursed the second pitcher while Ramba and his cadets kept drinking with both hands. Fifteen empty pitchers and three partially full ones cluttered the table, not counting his.

"Wha'd he do?" Shapiro said, leaning forward.

"He took it, the head that is, as a warning to others not to fuck with him. Kept it in a clear acrylic box filled with preservative solution on his desk. Used to show it off in bars all over the galaxy, including right here in Otto's."

"So what was van Owen's angle?" Ramba asked after giving his cadets plenty of time to ask it themselves. "What was it all about?"

Spokelse nodded and had to catch himself so he didn't topple to one side.

"That's a great question, lad, and let me tell you, it was a damned complicated business…it took most of a year for van Owen to sort the fallout from the loss of Platoon A, Triple-A Temporary Volunteers. The contract signed by Roland and the rest of 'em called for a small remuneration to the family in case they died during the mission. It was only about one-tenth what a standard contract called for, but the rookies were so desperate to get into the field, they didn't care. And van Owen didn't want to pay even that pittance. So there's a lesson there for you guys." He pointed at each of the six enrapt cadets. "Read your contracts and ask questions if you don't know something. The rookies didn't do it, and it cost them their lives.

"Most of 'em had no family to speak of anyway, which factored into why van Owen had hired them. In fact, he'd only hired and trained them at all because the uranium was a tempting target for pirates, and he needed actual trained mech drivers in case of a surprise attack. After deducting for expenses and split among the platoon, it wasn't what you might call a lucrative contract…if everybody survived, that is.

"After collecting on the contract, he would then use his access to the processing plant to hijack the uranium using his pirates. They'd take the CASPers with them, either to sell or for his new crew to drive. Kovak, Henrik, Umbeckwa, and Roland had all been tagged to survive the massacre, since he wanted them to join his pirate crew. They were the cream of the platoon and could teach his pirates how to use the CASPers, since the pirates were all outlaws who couldn't get merc jobs through legitimate means. Arming them with CASPers would increase their lethal potential by an order of magnitude. Van Owen could then run variations on his scam across the entire galaxy, or at least until the Mercenary Guild kicked him out. Then he could either retire to enjoy his wealth, or become an out and out pirate.

"He told the Mercenary Guild that Kovak had organized and led a mutiny involving everybody in A Platoon except Henrik. He, the colonel, found out and tried to stop it, but failed, with heavy casualties. Kovak, Roland, and the others murdered the crew of the processing plant and all the truck drivers, took the uranium, stole the plant's starship, and disappeared into space. The bastard wound up with the credits from the contract, didn't have to pay any death benefits because the rookies all allegedly broke their contracts, was able to sell the uranium on the black market, and wound up with a platoon of CASPers and a starship. Not bad for one crappy escort contract.

"As for why Roland and the others got surprised, none of them suspected their employer was a cold-blooded murderer. Only Roland had an inkling of something being wrong, but he ignored it because that wasn't how mercs operated. Commanders just didn't betray their own kind, so none of them could imagine such a double-cross. That was their mistake, a fatal one, as you heard. But after killing Umbeckwa, Kovak, and Roland, there's one thing the colonel overlooked…"

He paused for dramatic effect as the cadets blinked and gaped in rapt attention.

"…Roland wanted his head back. He hadn't believed in Roland's *nid*…that's what the Vikings called a verbal curse, a *nid*. But it was a real thing, a very powerful thing."

Cromwell shook his head and blinked, trying to focus. He chugged down another gulp of the lager, as if that would help. "You mean like magic?"

"Yeah, I'm not believin' that," added Shapiro.

Numis' head rested sideways on the top of her hand. "Me neither."

The other three cadets moved their heads in what might have been agreement, or might have been drowsiness. Spokelse shrugged.

"Suit yourselves. You want the resht o' the story or not?"

All the cadets nodded.

* * *

The clues were all there, but van Owen ignored them until it was too late. It started in an out of the way dive bar on a ramshackle station orbiting a backwater planet. To attract customers in such a low-traffic place, the bar had a small merc museum displaying items from various companies that had passed through over the decades. It even had an Earth item, a relic from one of the companies that didn't survive the Alpha Contracts, something so unique it was likely the only one of its kind anywhere in space: an M1921 Thompson Submachine gun with a fully-loaded Type C drum magazine, which held 100 rounds.

News of the uranium theft had made it hard to sell, and van Owen had to be very careful to fence it piecemeal in obscure places where shady business dealings were the norm. One of them turned out to be the bar with the Thompson. The colonel took the opportunity to visit the little museum and instantly fell in love with the old gun. The bar's owner refused all offers to sell it, however, so van Owen left empty-handed. He considered stealing it, but security was surprisingly good, and he finally decided it was too risky.

Two hours after closing, the bar's security system screamed a warning. When the owner showed up to check it out, he found the Thompson gone, along with an extra box of ammunition. Van Owen was the prime suspect, but when it was proven that he was already back in space when the theft occurred, the owner had no options except to swallow his loss. Cameras showed the locked glass case being shattered and the gun lifted out, but no figure was in the video.

News could take months to cross space. Van Owen was back on Earth, sitting in Mad Otto's of all places, when Henrik brought word that all six pirates who had been with him when Roland died had themselves been gunned down in various places across the galaxy. And by 'gunned down,' he meant shot by an old-style automatic weapon firing .45 caliber pistol ammunition.

"The Thompson," van Owen said.

Henrik nodded. "Has to be."

"Did anybody see who did it?"

"Nobody. Just like the cameras at that museum…nothing to see."

Several times during their travels Henrik had mentioned worrying about Roland's curse, but the colonel had scoffed. Now he picked up Henrik's implication that this was tied to Roland.

"Let it go, Sergeant; let it go. There's no such thing as curses, and there's no such thing as ghosts."

Their next stop was in Mombasa, Kenya, and a ramshackle bar called Kukra's, where wannabe mercs from all over Africa came to network and trade terrible advice about how to hire on to a company. In places like that, the Colonel van Owens of the world never had to pay for a drink, but in return they had to listen to scores of elevator speeches from would-be mercs. Van Owen didn't mind; he reveled in the near-adoration.

Henrik wasn't with him that night, but the colonel held court at a corner table. At least two dozen local wannabes crowded around him, sitting, standing, and leaning in to catch every word like he was some sort of prophet. He drank French 75s, a favorite he couldn't get anywhere but Earth because of a lack of sparkling wine or decent gin. Sitting on the table was the acrylic container with Roland's preserved head inside, looking much the worse for wear. Van Owen brought it along as a prop for the highly doctored version of Roland's fight in the hangar, one where Roland was the villain, which he'd now told so many times the words came out in chilling, well-practiced perfection. He'd just begun his story when the crowd parted, and a new figure moved into the gap. Or rather, *materialized*. Witnesses later gave conflicting descriptions of what the figure looked like, but they all agreed on two things: first, it had no head, and second, it used a Thompson submachine gun.

The last thing Colonel Dieter van Owen saw in this life was the muzzle flash from the end of that Thompson submachine gun. He felt the impact of the first two rounds, but not the next thirty.

The crowd scattered as van Owen's riddled body slumped sideways, and then rolled onto the floor. One brave man later reported that he peeked around the corner of an overturned table to see a headless figure pick up the container with the head and vanish.

A week later the body of Sergeant Henrik bumped against a barge moving down a nearby river. It was identified by fingerprints and DNA because the head was missing.

* * *

The cadets gaped at him as if the story wasn't over. Spokelse thought a moment, and then raised his nearly empty pitcher. He motioned for Ramba to make sure everybody had a full mug.

"So now, my friends, let's toast the memory of Roland Sigurdsson, the Headless Mech Driver!"

Cheers rippled through the bar from eavesdropping patrons. Each of the cadets leaned in to clink their mugs against Spokelse's pitcher, and then they tilted their mugs high, draining them. Spokelse only sipped from the pitcher. The man behind him, the one missing part of his jaw, took the opportunity to push the cloth-covered object toward Spokelse, who used his foot to drag it close.

"Is that really a true story?" Cromwell asked. His head wobbled.

"By all the Gods of Norway, I speak nothing but the truth, lad. And I'll tell you one more thing besides..." The pitcher was nearly empty, so he tilted his head far back to drain it. The scar around his neck seemed much darker now than it had earlier. "They say to this day Roland still roams the universe carrying that old submachine gun, and if he thinks you had anything to do with him losing his head...*budda-budda-budda*..." He put his two hands out like he was holding the weapon himself. "He shoots you where you stand. Others say the head keeps falling off his body and getting lost, and Roland yet walks this Earth searching for it. As for me, I think he has his head back right enough, yet I do believe his shade haunts us yet, as a precautionary tale for young would-be mercs like yourselves."

"That's bullshit," Shapiro said, sounding less than convinced and very drunk. "There's no such thing as ghosts."

Spokelse shrugged. "Maybe not, lad, maybe not…maybe I've gone too many rounds with too many aliens…well anyway, thanks for buying an old merc a beer."

They all assured him it was okay and told him not to worry about it, all except Cromwell, who was the only one who'd actually spent any money. Ramba slammed down his own mug, and their eyes met again. By unspoken agreement, it was time.

"Alright cadets, heads up," Ramba said. They all turned to face him, although Cromwell sensed something going on behind him and began to turn back. "Hey, Cadet Cromwell, eyes front!"

Cromwell snapped around to face the sergeant. "When I talk to you, Cadet, you look at me and nowhere else, is that clear?"

"Aye, Sergeant!"

"How 'bout the rest of you?"

"Aye, Sergeant!"

The ex-mercs in the room snickered, watching Ramba put them through their paces.

"It's zero-twelve-twenty hours, drill starts at zero-eight-hundred. We need to leave now, and we'll move as a group for security reasons. Does anybody need to piss before we go?"

The cadets looked around to see if anybody answered 'yes.' It was obvious they all needed to go, but nobody said anything.

"Last chance. Go now, or hold it 'til we get home. No pissing in the street. Nobody? Alright then, thank our guest for the story, and let's get out of here. Oh, I forgot. Spokelse has a challenge coin from each of the Four Horsemen; this might be the only chance you ever get to see them. Ask him to show them to you."

As one they turned, although several were shaky, and Cromwell started to speak. But Spokelse was gone. At least, most of him was. The only thing left was a head sitting on the table and leaking blood.

The mouth opened and spat out four challenge coins bearing the logos of Cartwright's Cavaliers, Asbaran Solutions, the Winged Hussars, and the Golden Horde. Blood covered each of them. Then the mouth formed words, and the voice belonged to Spokelse. "I hope you enjoyed the story," it said.

"That can't be real," Numis said. "It can't be."

"It sure looks real."

"Pick it up, Winston," Shapiro said. "See if it's real."

"I'm not touching that!"

The head spoke again, this time to Numis. "Why don't you give us a kiss goodbye, dearie?"

Shapiro puked, barely missing Numis, who screamed, although nobody knew if it was because of the near miss with Shapiro's vomit or the disembodied head. Cromwell fell over his chair. Within seconds the six drunken cadets had staggered and pushed their way through the crowd and out the front door. Ramba followed at a leisurely pace and threw the room a casual salute on his way out.

In the street outside, everybody in the bar heard him shouting at his cadets, something about the possibility of the impossible. After a couple of gunshots, Ramba yelled again, this time for them to put away their guns before somebody got hurt.

* * *

After the steel door clanged shut, Otto glanced at the camera covering the entrance and watched Ramba lead his six shaken cadets away. Two fell down. The sergeant turned and waved at the camera, but his cadets were running flat out to get away, so he had to catch up.

With his seemingly effortless walk, Otto made his way over to their table and went to the far end, behind Spokelse's chair. Using his heel, he thumped twice on the wooden floor beside the latch Spokelse had opened earlier. A trapdoor slid to one side, and Spokelse climbed out.

Standing on a chair, acting as if the bar was the stage of some grand theater, he spread his arms and took a bow as the other mercs clapped and hooted. He then peeled off the thick strip of pink latex around his neck and pushed the top button of his jacket. In response, the eyes of the head on the table opened, and it spoke in his voice.

"Don't applaud, just throw money."

* * * * *

William Alan Webb Bio

As a West Tennessee native raised in the 60s and 70s, and born into a family with a long tradition of military service, it should be no surprise that the three chief influences on Bill's life have been military history, science fiction and fantasy and the natural world. In 1972, he won the Tennessee State High School Dual Chess Championship, and spent every waking moment playing board games, role-playing games, and naval miniatures. College featured dual concentrations in History and English. Everything after that is anti-climax, except for wife, kids, published books and all that kind of stuff.

Website: www.thelastbrigade.com

Facebook page:
https://www.facebook.com/keepyouupallnightbooks

# # # # #

About the Editors

A Webster Award winner and three-time Dragon Award finalist, Chris Kennedy is a Science Fiction/Fantasy/Young Adult author, speaker, and small-press publisher who has written over 20 books and published more than 100 others. Chris' stories include the "Occupied Seattle" military fiction duology, "The Theogony" and "Codex Regius" science fiction trilogies, stories in the "Four Horsemen" and "In Revolution Born" universes and the "War for Dominance" fantasy trilogy. Get his free book, "Shattered Crucible," at his website, https://chriskennedypublishing.com.

Called "fantastic" and "a great speaker," he has coached hundreds of beginning authors and budding novelists on how to self-publish their stories at a variety of conferences, conventions and writing guild presentations. He is the author of the award-winning #1 bestseller, "Self-Publishing for Profit: How to Get Your Book Out of Your Head and Into the Stores," as well as the leadership training book, "Leadership from the Darkside."

Chris lives in Virginia Beach, Virginia, with his wife, and is the holder of a doctorate in educational leadership and master's degrees in both business and public administration. Follow Chris on Facebook at https://facebook.com/chriskennedypublishing.biz.

Living life as a full-time RV traveler with his wife Joy, Mark Wandrey is a bestselling author who has been creating new worlds since he was old enough to write. A three-time Dragon Award finalist, Mark has written dozens of books and short stories, and is working on more all the time. A prolific world builder, he created the wildly popular Four Horsemen Universe as well as the Earth Song series, and Turning Point, a zombie apocalypse series. His favorite medium is military sci-fi, but he is always up to a new challenge.

Find his books on Amazon at https://www.amazon.com/Mark-Wandrey/e/B00914T11A/

Sign up on his mailing list and get free stuff and updates! http://www.worldmaker.us/news-flash-sign-up-page/

*****

Connect with Chris Kennedy Online

Website: http://chriskennedypublishing.com/

Facebook: https://www.facebook.com/chriskennedypublishing.biz

Twitter: @ChrisKennedy110

* * * * *

Connect with Mark Wandrey Online

Website: http://www.worldmaker.us/

Facebook: https://www.facebook.com/mark.h.wandrey

* * * * *

Do you have what it takes to be a Merc?

Take your VOWs and join the Merc Guild on Facebook!

Meet us at: https://www.facebook.com/groups/536506813392912/

* * * * *

The following is an

Excerpt from Book One of the Salvage Title Trilogy:

Salvage Title

Kevin Steverson

Available Now from Theogony Books

eBook, Paperback, and Audio Book

Excerpt from "Salvage Title:"

The first thing Clip did was get power to the door and the access panel. Two of his power cells did the trick once he had them wired to the container. He then pulled out his slate and connected it. It lit up, and his fingers flew across it. It took him a few minutes to establish a link, then he programmed it to search for the combination to the access panel.

"Is it from a human ship?" Harmon asked, curious.

"I don't think so, but it doesn't matter; ones and zeros are still ones and zeros when it comes to computers. It's universal. I mean, there are some things you have to know to get other races' computers to run right, but it's not that hard," Clip said.

Harmon shook his head. *Riiigghht,* he thought. He knew better. Clip's intelligence test results were completely off the charts. Clip opted to go to work at Rinto's right after secondary school because there was nothing for him to learn at the colleges and universities on either Tretra or Joth. He could have received academic scholarships for advanced degrees on a number of nearby systems. He could have even gone all the way to Earth and attended the University of Georgia if he wanted. The problem was getting there. The schools would have provided free tuition if he could just have paid to get there.

Secondary school had been rough on Clip. He was a small guy that made excellent grades without trying. It would have been worse if Harmon hadn't let everyone know that Clip was his brother. They lived in the same foster center, so it was mostly true. The first day of school, Harmon had laid down the law—if you messed with Clip, you messed up.

At the age of fourteen, he beat three seniors senseless for attempting to put Clip in a trash container. One of them was a Yalteen, a member of a race of large humanoids from two systems over. It wasn't a fair fight—they should have brought more people with them. Harmon hated bullies.

After the suspension ended, the school's Warball coach came to see him. He started that season as a freshman and worked on using it to earn a scholarship to the academy. By the time he graduated, he was six feet two inches with two hundred and twenty pounds of muscle. He got the scholarship and a shot at going into space. It was the longest time he'd ever spent away from his foster brother, but he couldn't turn it down.

Clip stayed on Joth and went to work for Rinto. He figured it was a job that would get him access to all kinds of technical stuff, servos, motors, and maybe even some alien computers. The first week he was there, he tweaked the equipment and increased the plant's recycled steel production by 12 percent. Rinto was eternally grateful, as it put him solidly into the profit column instead of toeing the line between profit and loss. When Harmon came back to the planet after the academy, Rinto hired him on the spot on Clip's recommendation. After he saw Harmon operate the grappler and got to know him, he was glad he did.

A steady beeping brought Harmon back to the present. Clip's program had succeeded in unlocking the container. "Right on!" Clip exclaimed. He was always using expressions hundreds or more years out of style. "Let's see what we have; I hope this one isn't empty, too." Last month they'd come across a smaller vault, but it had been empty.

Harmon stepped up and wedged his hands into the small opening the door had made when it disengaged the locks. There wasn't enough power in the small cells Clip used to open it any further. He put his weight into it, and the door opened enough for them to get inside. Before they went in, Harmon placed a piece of pipe in the doorway so it couldn't close and lock on them, baking them alive before anyone realized they were missing.

Daylight shone in through the doorway, and they both froze in place; the weapons vault was full.

*****

Get "Salvage Title" now at:
https://www.amazon.com/dp/B07H8Q3HBV.

Find out more about Kevin Steverson and "Salvage Title" at:
http://chriskennedypublishing.com/.

*****

The following is an

Excerpt from Devil Calls the Tune:

Devil Calls the Tune

Chris Maddox

Available from Theogony Books

eBook, Paperback, and (Soon) Audio

Excerpt from "Devil Calls the Tune:"

Kenyon shouted, "Flyer! Fast mover!"

Everyone grabbed their packs and started running. When McCarthy didn't, Devlin grabbed him by his uniform shirt and yelled, "Come on!"

The little outcropping they had weathered under was part of a larger set of hills. Devlin and McCarthy made for a sheer cliff face that was tall enough that it would make strafing difficult. They dove behind a few rocks, and Devlin peered over one. The flier had overshot the group and was circling.

McCarthy reached into his pack and pulled out a rail pistol and magazine. He slapped the magazine home into its well and charged the pistol.

"Where the fark did you get that!" Devlin panted. He reached over and took the pistol. McCarthy let him.

"This was the surprise," McCarthy said. "I found the pistol, then searched the wreckage for ammo. I found some and parts to a bunch of rifles. Most were in bad shape, but Pringle figured he might be able to cobble together a couple from the parts. He was going take the lot back to the camp so they would have something to defend the wounded with. He sent me with this for you. Best we could get together at the time. Sorry."

"Don't be sorry. This is pretty good. I won't beat the shit out of you now for the fire."

"The fire?" McCarthy looked blank for a moment, then realization hit. "Oh, you think that the fire attracted—"

"Our flying friend over there. Yeah, I just—get your head down!" He pulled at McCarthy as rounds from the flier dug into the earth. There was something odd about this one.

He took a quick look. This wasn't the same flier that had attacked the camp, this one was…

"Drone!" Devlin yelled. He watched the thing from the rocks, watched it circle around again. He braced the pistol on the rocks, steadied, and waited.

When the drone started its run again, Devlin sighted in, breathed out, and fired.

The drone disintegrated in a fiery cloud as the rail gun round entered its main capacitor bank. He watched it fall and then rose from behind the rocks. McCarthy joined him.

Devlin looked over at the tree line and waved his arm. A moment later, Kenyon appeared, followed by Gartlan and MacBain.

"Devlin!" Decker's voice came out of the tree line. Kenyon and the others started to where Decker's voice had come from. Devlin started to run.

He found the group gathered around Decker. She was holding Moran's head in her lap. Moran's uniform had a red stain in the abdomen that was growing larger by the moment.

"Got hit as I dived into the woods," Moran croaked. Her blond hair was already slick with sweat, her face pale.

"Sorry, Devlin. I…I…" her voice trailed off as her implant fed nanites and nighty-night into her system. A moment later she looked dead, which for all intents and purposes she was.

Devlin rubbed his scalp. He glared over at McCarthy, whose shocked face got even paler as he looked at the body, hibernating though it was, of Lisa Moran. He bowed his head and started to stammer, "I'm sorry, I didn't…"

"Shut up, Tom. Just shut up," Devlin said tiredly. "You didn't know; you had no way of knowing. This wasn't even the same flier that attacked the camp. Just a stupid mistake, but it's one that we have to deal with now. Is anybody else hurt?"

Arnette was sitting on the ground beside Decker with her legs crossed. She held one ankle in her hands. "Well, now that you mention it..." She looked at Devlin with pain-filled eyes. "I think my ankle is broken. I stepped straight into a hole as I came into the woods."

Decker moved her legs out from underneath Moran's head and laid it gently on the ground. She made her way to the other woman. Gartlan bent down as well and said, "Let's get your boot off."

Together, the two started trying to get the girl's boot off. When Arnette hissed once and nearly passed out, they realized they'd have to cut it off. Gartlan produced a tactical knife and used the monomolecular edge to slice down the side of the boot. His cut made, he handed the knife to Decker, who sliced down the foot portion of the boot, careful not to cut too deeply.

"Here you go, Wolf," she said handing the knife back to Gartlan, who folded it and put it back in his pocket. Together, he and Decker were finally able to peel the ruined boot off the injured girl's foot.

Her foot, already purple, immediately started to swell. They propped her leg up on a rock covered with Gartlan's tunic. Gartlan shook his head at Devlin. "She isn't likely to go nighty-night, but she might as well. She ain't going anywhere on that foot for a few days. And she's not going to like this, but we're going to have to set it and splint it so that the nanis don't knit it wrong. Probably still will, but the canker mechanics should be able to fix it without too much problem if we get home."

Sarah Arnette's eyes went wide as Gartlan's words hit home. "Oh Gods!" she moaned. "This is going to *suck!*"

"Do it," Devlin said. "Come on, guys. They don't need an audience, and we've got to get our shit together."

He turned to walk away as Gartlan bent back down, and Decker opened a med kit.

Another drone flier came to halt in front of them, and a voice came over its vocoder, "State your name and passcode."

*****

"Devil Calls the Tune" now at: https://www.amazon.com/dp/B0849QYWMJ.

Find out more about Chris Maddox and "Devil Calls the Tune" at: https://chriskennedypublishing.com/imprints-authors/chris-maddox/.

****

The following is an

Excerpt from Book One of the Earth Song Cycle:

Overture

Mark Wandrey

Now Available from Theogony Books

eBook and Paperback

Excerpt from "Overture:"

Dawn was still an hour away as Mindy Channely opened the roof access and stared in surprise at the crowd already assembled there. "Authorized Personnel Only" was printed in bold red letters on the door through which she and her husband, Jake, slipped onto the wide roof.

A few people standing nearby took notice of their arrival. Most had no reaction, a few nodded, and a couple waved tentatively. Mindy looked over the skyline of Portland and instinctively oriented herself before glancing to the east. The sky had an unnatural glow that had been growing steadily for hours, and as they watched, scintillating streamers of blue, white, and green radiated over the mountains like a strange, concentrated aurora borealis.

"You almost missed it," one man said. She let the door close, but saw someone had left a brick to keep it from closing completely. Mindy turned and saw the man who had spoken wore a security guard uniform. The easy access to the building made more sense.

"Ain't no one missin' this!" a drunk man slurred.

"We figured most people fled to the hills over the past week," Jake replied.

"I guess we were wrong," Mindy said.

"Might as well enjoy the show," the guard said and offered them a huge, hand-rolled cigarette that didn't smell like tobacco. She waved it off, and the two men shrugged before taking a puff.

"Here it comes!" someone yelled. Mindy looked to the east. There was a bright light coming over the Cascade Mountains, so intense it was like looking at a welder's torch. Asteroid LM-245 hit the atmosphere at over 300 miles per second. It seemed to move faster and faster, from east to west, and the people lifted their hands to shield their eyes from the blinding light. It looked like a blazing comet or a science fiction laser blast.

"Maybe it will just pass over," someone said in a voice full of hope.

Mindy shook her head. She'd studied the asteroid's track many times.

In a matter of a few seconds, it shot by and fell toward the western horizon, disappearing below the mountains between Portland and the ocean. Out of view of the city, it slammed into the ocean.

The impact was unimaginable. The air around the hypersonic projectile turned to superheated plasma, creating a shockwave that generated 10 times the energy of the largest nuclear weapon ever detonated as it hit the ocean's surface.

The kinetic energy was more than 1,000 megatons; however, the object didn't slow as it flashed through a half mile of ocean and into the sea bed, then into the mantel, and beyond.

On the surface, the blast effect appeared as a thermal flash brighter than the sun. Everyone on the rooftop watched with wide-eyed terror as the Tualatin Mountains between Portland and the Pacific Ocean were outlined in blinding light. As the light began to dissipate, the outline of the mountains blurred as a dense bank of smoke climbed from the western range.

The flash had incinerated everything on the other side.

The physical blast, travelling much faster than any normal atmospheric shockwave, hit the mountains and tore them from the bedrock, adding them to the rolling wave of destruction traveling east at several thousand miles per hour. The people on the rooftops of Portland only had two seconds before the entire city was wiped away.

Ten seconds later, the asteroid reached the core of the planet, and another dozen seconds after that, the Earth's fate was sealed.

* * * * *

Get "Overture" now at:
https://www.amazon.com/dp/B077YMLRHM/

Find out more about Mark Wandrey and the Earth Song Cycle at:
https://chriskennedypublishing.com/

* * * * *

Made in the USA
Coppell, TX
04 May 2020

23771320R00312